The PICKLE KING

The PICK

LE KING

Rebecca Promitzer

Chicken House

Scholastic Inc. / New York

Text © Rebecca Promitzer 2010

First published in the United Kingdom by Chicken House,
2 Palmer Street, Frome, Somerset BA11 1DS.
www.doublecluck.com

Library of Congress Cataloging-in-Publication Data

Promitzer, Rebecca.
The Pickle King / Rebecca Promitzer. – 1st American ed.
p. cm.
Summary: During an endlessly rainy summer in the town of Elbow, eleven-year-old
Bea and her misfit friends solve an unlikely mystery involving an unidentified dead
man who is missing an eye, an evil surgeon, a ring shaped like an old castle, a bag
full of smelly intestines, and a helpful ghost.

ISBN 978-0-545-17087-1

[1. Mystery and detective stories. 2. Ghosts—Fiction. 3. Supernatural—Fiction.
4. Crime—Fiction. 5. Rain and rainfall—Fiction.] I. Title.

PZ7.P94336Pi 2010
[Fic]—dc22

2008055435

10 9 8 7 6 5 4 3 2 1   10 11 12 13 14

Printed in the U.S.A. 23
First American edition, March 2010

The text type was set in Adobe Garamond.
The display type was set in SignPainter HouseScript.
Book design by Phil Falco

For Piers

The PICKLE KING

CHAPTER 1

In Elbow, the town where I live, it rains all summer. Not the kind of rain that is fun to run through, stomping your feet. Not the kind of rain that is fine and warm and accompanied by a rainbow. No, in Elbow it rains heavy, dark rain. Rain that makes a noisy clashing sound like hundreds of angry fingers. The angry fingers beat down hour after hour onto sidewalks, cars, and umbrellas, and people turn pale because there's no daylight for their damp faces, only darkness and wet. Some people go nuts because of it and run into the streets in their pj's screaming, "Stop it! Stop it! I can't take it anymore!"

Every single summer is the same in Elbow—from May through September there's nothing but rain. It's been like this as far back as I can remember. Normal people leave town before the rain begins, and fly to sunny places like Florida or Fiji or to favorite European destinations like Tuscany or Saint-Tropez. Was I one of the lucky ones? Do I *ever* get to spend the summer on a beach or in the countryside with my parents? Nope. Not a chance. I get to stay in Elbow, in the rain.

We don't have much money. Dad died when I was nine and Mom is in a place called St. Agnes's, where they take care of people who don't know what's real and what's in their heads. Maybe in Mom's head it's warm and sunny—but I doubt it. I think the rain got in and now it won't leave.

I live with Bertha, my mom's best friend. She came to live in our house after Mom went to St. Agnes's. Everyone who knows her calls her Big Bertha—but that's an understatement. She's as big as a house and she's warm and soft like freshly baked bread. She's not home too much because she's a nurse at the hospital and works shifts. She can be pretty tough on me sometimes, but I think she must kind of love me because she makes me pancakes in the mornings and leaves me these little notes saying things like, **Please buy milk and eggs today XXX.**

Anyway, it was summer vacation in Elbow and, of course, it was pouring rain.

I don't know if you've ever been anywhere where it rained for a few days without a break, not even a little one. If you have, you'll know that it makes you feel edgy, kind of jumpy inside. There are shadows, an unnatural kind of light, strange rainy noises, and you start to feel like you can't trust the regular things around you, the things you take for granted. Sometimes it seems like the things you've seen in scary movies or your own nightmares have come alive and are real—and have moved in for good. Other times it's as though you're living underwater and there's no air, and you really start to believe the sun will never *ever* shine again. It's no good for anybody to spend the summer in Elbow, but it's the kids like me who have to hang around; kids with no money or no parents or a bit of both. Some of us have got green growing between our toes from all the rain. It's a kind of mold. Bertha says it's the start of webbed feet.

Every year the school secretary sends a list to all the kids who are stranded here over the summer. It's called the Summer Club List. But it's not a club and in Elbow there's no summer, so it's just a list. Anyway, the school expects us to hang out together, even if we're not friends (which we never are), for the whole summer. It's like detention except it goes on for weeks. We're supposed to report back on what we did together and how much fun we had, even if we were so bored we wanted to kill each other.

By the way, my name's Bea. It's short for Beatrice, but nobody's ever called me that. I'm going to be twelve in November.

That first day of summer vacation, I came downstairs for breakfast and, like always, wrapped myself in a blanket on the couch with a plate of pancakes balanced across my knees. I sprinkled some extra Swiss cheese on top and was about to start eating when I realized I was missing the most important ingredient of all, so I headed back to the refrigerator to get my jar of Herman's Devil Tongue Relish. The best thing to eat in the whole wide world is Swiss cheese pancakes with Devil Tongue Relish.

The town of Elbow is famous for just two things: the summer weather and Herman's Devil Tongue Relish. They make other stuff here, too, like Lola's Cola, Bert's Big Cheesies, and Pinehills Honey, but not everybody's heard of them, whereas *everyone* knows about Devil Tongue Relish. There's a giant pickle factory just outside Elbow where the relish is made, and a lot of people who live in Elbow work there. The factory makes Herman's Jamberry Pickalilly, which is a sweet kind of salsa (some people like to eat it on their hamburgers); Herman's Honey-Chunk Chutney, which is dark brown with little cubes of vegetables in it; Herman's Original Horseradish Mustard; and my favorite, Herman's Devil Tongue Relish (which comes in three strengths: Easy Does It, Turning Up the Heat, and Burning Down the House). On the side of each jar of Herman's pickles and relishes there's a picture of Herman himself, the man who makes them, smiling a big cheerful smile that makes you happy just looking at him. He's got dark sparkly eyes and a big beard like a pirate's.

Most of the year you can smell the smells from Herman's factory — funny kinds of smells like sugar beet, boiling vegetables, and licorice. But in the summer you can't really make out that many odors because the rain suffocates them, kind of like putting a big wet hand over the mouth of everything and holding it there. In the summer the smells of the rain take over, wet smells like mud-water, mold, and the liquid of rotting things.

My dad introduced me to Herman's Devil Tongue Relish when I was about five years old and I've been eating it ever since. Even when everybody was saying Herman's Pickles tasted bad, about three years ago, I still ate them. But that was around the time my dad died and I'd kind of stopped paying attention to a lot of stuff. I have Devil Tongue Relish with everything now: in sandwiches, with scrambled eggs, sometimes even with ice cream. Things just don't taste as good without it.

That morning, the long green angry fingers of the rain were tapping down on the roof and the garbage cans outside. It was so dark, it was like the darkest green of the deepest, blackest lake. Bertha had already left for work, probably wearing her yellow slicker, yellow hat, and green galoshes. I was in my pj's, watching cartoons. Maybe it's the bright colors, the funny sounds, or the happy faces, or all those things put together, but they help me block out the weather. They put me in a rainbow-colored daze that's safe to escape to. If you don't find a way to distract yourself, the rain will start to make you drowsy. That's what happened to Mom.

I'm not supposed to, but when Bertha's out, I turn on all the lights in all the rooms — and that helps, too.

Sometimes, when the black rainy sky pushes against the windows like it wants to swallow me up, the cartoons and the house lights just aren't enough. When that happens, I close my eyes tight and try desperately to imagine sunshine: golden sunshine. Soft, warm, yellow light shining through palm trees.

We drove through Florida once, Mom, Dad, and me, in our bug-shaped car, the warm air blowing my hair around. The light sparkled so, so brightly through the trees that, looking up at the blue sky, I had to keep my eyes tightly shut and let the light in a little at a time until big circles of sunshine, like fat jewels, danced on my eyelashes. I like to remember my parents in the sunshine, all smiling and golden. We were a proper family once. I think we were happy then.

If only I could get out of here. Get out of Elbow, out of the rain and the darkness. If only for a day.

All I could think about all day was what I could sell to get the money for a ticket out of here. I only had two things that were worth any money—to collectors, anyway. My camera and my record player. And there was no way in the whole world I would ever sell my camera.

When Dad died, an old man in a brown room read out his will. He said, "Your father would like you to have his camera." My dad was a photographer and a journalist. A photojournalist. He would take pictures and then write the story that went with them. It's an old camera and it's quite heavy and you have to attach a big square flash if it's dark, but it's a really good one and it takes great shots.

And I love my record player. It's big and old like my camera and it used to belong to my mom. In the evenings my parents would play songs they liked for each other, and I would listen and sometimes dance. I couldn't sell that, either.

What I really needed was a job. Trouble is, nobody gets their newspapers delivered in the summer because they get wet; there's no gardening because . . . you guessed it, there are no gardens (although Mrs. Greenblatt did once ask me to stir the mud in her backyard); Sam already had the job at the arcade; and you have to be fifteen to work in one of the stores. There just aren't many jobs for (almost) twelve-year-olds.

I promised myself that next year, as soon as school started, I would do lots of jobs for people. I'd mow their lawns and wash their cars. I'd work really hard while the weather was good, save up, and get out of Elbow. Just go. Somewhere sunny, somewhere like Florida.

My eyes were still staring at the vivid characters dancing and jumping in front of me on TV, but my brain had stopped taking them in hours ago. When Bertha arrived back from work I was in a kind of happy trance, half-asleep and half-awake.

"You look like one of those zombie creatures!" she said as she pushed her big dripping body through the front door. It was about ten-thirty and she was home from her shift at the hospital. (Bertha's specialty is very old people. "Geriatrics" is what they're called. Bertha says that when people get old they become like children again. They need help eating, walking, getting up, sitting down, and even going to the bathroom.)

Bertha took off her galoshes and rain gear, wrapped her big arms around a stack of brochures, and carried them into the living room. They made a loud thud as they hit the floor next to me, and my heart suddenly leaped with happiness. They were travel brochures. I reached over and lifted one from the top of the pile. The picture on the front had so much sea on it, the whole page was blue. It was so blue, I felt like I was already swimming in that warm, transparent blue ocean with the sun on my face.

"Now don't go getting all excited," Bertha called from the kitchen. Sometimes Bertha seemed to leave her eyes in the room with me. "They're not for us. They're for the patients to cut up and make collages with. It's supposed to make them feel better."

"Can I keep one? Just to look at?" I said, feeling my warm fingertips stick to the glossy cover.

"Now don't you go making me feel bad—you know we can't afford to go no place sunny. I already promised you, if you're good, I'll take a few days off and we'll take the bus out to my dad's place for Thanksgiving."

Bertha stood there for a moment, waiting for me to say "Great" or "I'd like that a lot." And I tried to smile, but it didn't come out right. I needed to get away *now*! But Bertha didn't notice; she'd landed on the sofa and become part of it.

Bertha's feet were up, her TV dinner was on her chest, and she'd switched the channel to her favorite game show, where people win houses and cars and kitchens and holidays to sunny places. I didn't like that show, with the lady with teeth that were too white and the contestants who got sweatier the closer they got to winning, but I liked cuddling up to Bertha, who was big and warm and soft. Sometimes she would put her arm around me during the commercial breaks and give me a kind of quick squeeze.

I lay curled up next to Bertha, looking at my brochure of different oceans and beaches, letting the buzzing and cheering of the game show wash over me. As I drifted in and out of sleep, dreaming of sunshine and seas of a hundred different blues, for the first time in a month I barely even noticed the sound of the rain.

CHAPTER 2

I took the brochures to bed with me that night and woke up with my face stuck to one of the shiny pages. When I opened my eyes, there was a giant shiny palm tree folded over my forehead and the deep blue waves of the ocean were lapping my chin.

I peeled the tropical scene off my face and went downstairs for breakfast, taking my brochure with me.

I sprinkled Swiss cheese on my pancakes and added an extra big spoonful of Herman's Devil Tongue Relish. By the time I'd eaten that first pancake, I'd made my way through Europe, Asia, and South America for the second time. I wasn't really interested in the places, I just wanted to look at beaches. I compared different oceans to find the most sparkling turquoise sea that I could. I imagined my bare, suntanned feet sinking into different types of sand, feeling its dry warmth between my toes. I liked the look of the really, really white sand. Starting my second pancake, I had to open a new jar of Devil Tongue Relish, and that's when I saw the ad. There was Herman's picture as usual and his promise that his relish was homemade using his grandma's recipe, but on this jar, the other half of the label had a picture of an orange sun setting over palm trees and a beach. It said, **Win a Trip to Florida in Our Photography Competition.**

My stomach suddenly went fizzy inside—and it wasn't the relish. My whole body came alive, as though it were suddenly plugged into an electrical circuit, and my heart started beating fast in my chest like someone was inside trying to get out. *This is meant for me!* I thought. It seemed so perfect I even looked around the kitchen to see if somebody was playing a trick on me. I ran my finger over the label and then held it under the lightbulb. It was real, all right. It said they wanted *an original picture on the theme of Family* because *Herman's relishes are based on traditional family recipes*. It said they wanted pictures of *the people of Elbow*.

I had a camera and I was pretty good at taking pictures. The more I thought about it, the more excited I got. It felt like I had firecrackers going off in my stomach.

When I hold my camera, which is pretty heavy, I imagine my dad holding it in his much bigger hands, and I feel like he's still alive. And when I look through the lens, it's like he's looking through it with me. Things look different through the lens of a camera, like they belong to a different world. I used to look through it, then look at the real object, and then look back through the camera to try to figure out what was going on, what it was all about. "The camera transforms things," Dad used to say. "It's like magic." And he was right.

I didn't want to waste any time. I needed to get a good photograph. One good enough to win the competition. It was so dark and so wet outside, there was no chance of just snapping people passing by on the sidewalk. I was going to have to ask some people if I could photograph them.

I was certain I was going to win that competition. I was going to win that competition and get out of Elbow. This summer I was really going to do it. And I was going to Florida—the Sunshine State—the exact place I'd dreamed about going. The place I'd gone to as a little kid with my parents. The warmest, sunniest, dreamiest place in the world. I didn't care about those exotic white beaches and tropical turquoise oceans in the brochure; they weren't real anyway. I was going to Florida. Flo-ri-da. FLORIDA!

CHAPTER 3

I didn't hear the doorbell at first because of the TV and the noise of the rain outside. Then I couldn't ignore it. I glanced over the top of the couch, and through the stained glass of the door I could see a distorted version of Sam wearing his old blue rain hat over one eye.

"Go away!" I shouted from the hallway. "We're not home!"

"Then how come you've got all the lights on?" he yelled back. "Open the door—or I'll start to shrink!"

Sam's dad was always in and out of jail, and his mom only came home when she ran out of money. Sam was the kid everybody's parents referred to as "The Wrong Crowd." His older brother, Jed, was supposed to be taking care of him, but he had other ideas, and being mean to Sam was like a sport for him.

Sometimes Sam was kind of annoying—mainly 'cause he was always coming over and interrupting my cartoon time—but he could be funny, too, and he liked to break the rules, which made things a bit more interesting.

I opened the front door a little. Sam pushed himself in and headed for the living room, leaving a trail of muddy water behind him. He was followed by Jellybean, his dog, who left an even muddier trail before shaking his wet fur all over the carpet and jumping happily onto the couch with his tail still wagging. I could already hear Bertha complaining. I was going to have to clean up before she got home.

Sam sat down on the couch next to me and, wiping a couple of streaks of sandy hair out of his eyes, lifted his smelly wet sneakers up onto the coffee table. Jellybean, who was bigger than Sam, climbed on top of him and started showering his face with warm kisses.

"Get down, boy," Sam said, pushing him onto the floor.

"Did you get the list?" I asked Sam.

"What list?" But he knew what I was talking about.

Mine was stuck to the fridge. The Summer Club List had the names of all the kids in our class who were stranded here. We knew we were going to have to call them sooner or later, but we always tried to avoid it for as long as we could. Last year, Sam and me came up with our own name for that list. Because we're kind of imprisoned here in Elbow, we decided to call ourselves the Raintown Convicts.

Sam switched off the cartoon I was watching. The sounds and colors disappeared into a tiny dot before vanishing completely. We'd had that TV since before I was born, and Sam was one of the few kids who didn't laugh at it.

It seemed like Sam didn't have much of a plan for the day, he just wanted to bother me. That was until he picked up one of Bertha's travel brochures and started flicking through it.

Sam frowned. I could see him wondering if we suddenly had the money to go on vacation after all. I saw him notice my dad's camera sitting on the corner of the Devil Tongue Relish label I'd peeled off. *Win a Trip to Florida!* it announced to Sam. His eyes took in the ad, then he looked over at me and the note I was writing to myself: People to Photograph — Mitzy, Pete, DW. A dark thought traveled across Sam's face and his eyes narrowed slightly.

A moment later, he got jumpy, like he didn't want to hang around, like he suddenly had something urgent to do and if he didn't do it now, he was never going to.

"C'mon! Let's go — I've got something to show you!" Sam said, giving the sleeve of my sweatshirt a tug. "Get your camera!"

"But I've got things to do. You're only going to make me do some weird stuff, like take pictures of Boyd Applebaum's butt."

He threw me a look as if to say, "Do I *look* like I'm in *that* kind of mood?"

"I can't take pictures in the rain," I said.

Sam looked over his shoulder as we stepped out into the darkness. "That's OK, it's not raining much where we're going."

It was a long walk, up and down the steep streets with the lights from stores reflected in bright, shimmering streaks, and it was noisy with the rain beating down on the sidewalk and the parked cars. Trucks and cars with their windshield wipers flicking furiously from side to side sloshed past at full speed, throwing even more water at us. Jellybean didn't seem to mind the rain; he just wagged his tail and stuck his steaming pink tongue out to the side to catch the drops.

"Where are we going?" I shouted.

A truck zoomed past.

"What?" yelled Sam.

It was hard to have a conversation walking along like that, so we didn't talk much.

When we'd walked past the hospital and the mall and almost to the edge of Pinehills Forest, we stopped outside a rickety old house. Sam walked straight in like he owned the place. I wanted to shout, "Hey! What are you doing?" but we were already inside. And that's when it happened. That's when my finger started up.

The pinkie finger on my left hand does this funny thing: It always seems to tingle when something's up, when something's not right. And that's when I *should* think, *This means trouble—I'm out of here.*

It was clear that whoever lived in the house hadn't been taking care of the place. It smelled bad, of rotting food and something sour, like old pee, and the rain was coming in through the roof.

"It's down here!" Sam's voice echoed through the damp building.

I wasn't sure I wanted to know what "it" was. A part of me already felt sick but another part of me—the curious part, the part that always gets me into risky business—wanted to find out.

Sam was standing in what must once have been a nice spacious living room, shining his flashlight through a big hole in the floorboards. At first I couldn't make out very much. There was a lot of stinky water down there, like a dark indoor pool, with household objects floating around. Then I saw a boot, and then a foot that had no boot. The bootless leg was twisted around. I remember thinking how white that foot looked against the black-green water it was sticking out of.

"We shouldn't be here," I said, a little more quietly than I meant to.

"Look at his face! His neck must be twisted!" shouted Sam, and before I could look away, the yellow beam of his flashlight found the side of the man's face.

It seemed like time slowed down at that moment. Even when I'm doing other things now, I can see that face. His mouth was wide open, like he was drinking in the dirty water, like he couldn't get enough of it, and one of his eyes was looking up at me. It was dark but had a kind of milky-blue glaze over it, like a fish eye when it's cooked.

"He's dead!" yelled Sam, breaking through my thoughts.

I was suddenly aware of myself, a small figure in that creepy house I wasn't supposed to be in. I wanted to say something but couldn't speak.

"A real dead body." Sam was acting tough, but I could see the shock on his face, and something else in his eyes, something sad.

Sam aimed the handle of a broom at the man's back.

"What are you doing?" I cried.

But he ignored me and poked down into the bulky shape.

The movement made waves in the deep murky puddle and the body turned and lifted. His gaping mouth left the water and seemed to want to breathe the air again. Then we saw the other eye. It wasn't bluish-white like the other. In fact, it wasn't there at all. There was just a shadowy hole where an eye had once been.

"C'mon, take the picture!" ordered Sam, looking around kind of anxiously, like he expected someone to show up.

And suddenly I felt calm. I had something to do. I thought of my dad taking pictures of the things people didn't want to know about, things they would have preferred to forget, things that were supposed to be kept secret.

I lifted the camera to my face. The man looked different through the viewfinder—somehow less scary, less sad, and less real.

I took a couple of shots from different angles and then a couple close up of the dead man's swollen features.

As I focused in on that pale floating face, with that gaping mouth and a hole for an eye, something really strange happened.

"Did you hear that?" I asked Sam.

"No. What?" he said, looking around. He was checking out an old overturned chest of drawers, spilling damp papers onto the dirty floorboards.

The sound I'd heard was a kind of low, breathy moan, like a deep wind, blowing through the dead man and out of his mouth and missing eye. My skin prickled all over with a sudden iciness and my pinkie finger began buzzing, flicking, and twitching faster than ever before. I pressed down hard on my camera's silver button and took the photo.

The whole room lit up with the brightness of my flash, like silent lightning striking. I heard the shutter open inside, and then a long pause that seemed like time stopping altogether. Finally there came the clap of the shutter closing.

The moment it captured that final shot, my camera shook—just gently—but it shook all the same, and it shook from the inside.

"What is it?" Sam's eyes were glistening in the darkness and I could see the fear in them.

"I don't know," I croaked.

Still holding the camera, I felt the tremor again and my heart began beating so hard in my chest that it scared me. Then came the shouts from outside and a voice that yelled, "What are you kids doing in there?!"

And Jellybean started barking.

Sam was out of there like a bullet, shooting out the back of the house.

"Wait!" I ran after him.

I ran fast, following the furious speed of Sam's figure down the muddy pathway, behind the tall dark trees. I skidded but picked up my feet again, blood pumping through my body like electricity; the dead man's face, as cold and clear as a police mug shot, flashed in and out of my head.

Safe in the bright yellow glow of a convenience store, we saw the lights come on in the house on the hill, and watched the police cars and an ambulance arrive. Sam and I looked at each other. I could see he was as shaken up as I was, but he was trying to act cool.

"D'you want a soda?" asked Sam.

"Sure," I said, as though nothing had happened.

But we knew it had, and I had the evidence in the camera around my neck.

CHAPTER 4

That night, no matter how hard I tried, I just couldn't get to sleep. Every time I closed my eyes, that dead man's pale face rolled and bobbed up out of the dirty pool and stared at me with that fish eye of his. Every time I saw him, his open mouth and empty eye socket got closer and made that strange groan I'd heard just before my camera shuddered. I wanted to erase that image from my mind, but it was too late.

I sat up in bed watching streams of silver raindrops travel down my window and converge into little rivers. When the whole window was flooded, smaller rain tracks began to grow, and the whole cycle started over. The strange, changing map of rain on the window was projected onto my bedroom wall like a shot from a weird movie. The watery scene played across the wall and all the things on it, like my fuzzy red bulletin board, which is covered with photos I've taken. There's a picture I took of Mom and Dad when Dad was alive and Mom wasn't crazy. The shadow of raindrops from the window trickled down their faces and it looked like the photo was crying.

It was tough when part of you was a kid and part of you felt grown-up, I thought to myself. How were you supposed to know what was OK to think and feel and what wasn't? How were you supposed to know when it was OK to be scared and when you had to be tough? I wished I were still a little kid, so that I could snuggle up in bed with Bertha and feel safe.

I lay back and looked up at the skylight with its broken blind. Every time my eyelids tried to droop I made them stay open. I also tried to stop myself from imagining the dead guy's arms creeping up around the bed. I tucked my shoulders, arms, and feet under the quilt so that only my face was showing.

The wind was howling and thick black clouds were hurtling past and the rain was making different shapes on the skylight, circles this time; the circles of rainy fingertips tapping hard and pressing down, one after the other. It was as though they were saying, "Let us in! Let us in! We'll get in sooner or later!"

Sometime in the middle of the night I slipped into sleep. It wasn't a comforting, warm, safe kind of sleep. It was a heavy, dark, sickly sleep and I knew it had to do with being in that house, seeing that dead guy, and taking those photos.

That night I dreamed the rain got in.

It broke through the glass of the skylight. A tidal wave of murky green fingers descended on me and the weight of the water took my breath away. The rainy fingers swarmed over my face and body, licking me like evil tongues.

They began to crisscross over my face, weaving a deadly cloth over my eyes and mouth. I turned, thrashing and clawing, gasping for air, and sank down lower. I saw that I was lying right on top of the dead man. As I struggled, desperate to get away, my fingers pushed through the water-soft flesh of his face and then there was just blackness.

I woke up sweating and breathing so fast it was like I'd just run a race. And I kind of had—a race against the rain, a race against the dead guy who was living in my head.

CHAPTER 5

In the morning my eyes were sore and itchy from not sleeping, and I found it hard to swallow my pancakes because my throat was swollen inside. I put extralarge spoonfuls of Devil Tongue Relish on top to make them juicier, and ate them slowly, tasting the creaminess of the cheese with the spicy tang of the relish on my tongue.

Watching the bright characters of the cartoons, I realized I was trying hard to ignore my camera, which was hanging silently from the chair at Bertha's desk. The more I tried to ignore it, the more it bugged me, that dark shadowy shape looming in the corner of my eye. It even started to make the cartoons seem eerie.

What if a part of the dead guy had gotten into my camera when it shuddered the way it did? What if he were living inside now, sloshing from side to side, drinking in that muddy green water through his mouth and eyehole? I shivered as I thought of it.

Still chewing my pancakes, I picked up the camera and headed down to my dad's darkroom in the cellar. He built the room himself, and I could remember the smell of the chemicals he used for developing film, and his funny face peering through the foggy, scented air. He used to let me watch as he moved a picture carefully around in the liquid until an image emerged as if by magic, before getting darker and darker. In those days I didn't mind the summer rain outside. We were too busy having fun, seeing what pictures would appear under the glow of the ruby light. There were still some of his photos on the wall: a couple of shots of me as a small kid and one of me as a baby in Mom's arms — she's looking up at my dad, all sleepy-eyed and smiling a beautiful, gentle smile.

I put the camera down on the counter, but something inside me didn't want to develop that film, because when I thought about it I felt sick. Maybe I'd just throw it away and forget I ever took those photos, forget I was ever in that house. Anyway, Bertha was coming home early to take me to visit Mom, so the pictures of the dead guy were going to have to wait.

Bertha and I visit Mom once a month, but I hate going. Mom just sits in an armchair staring into space, or drifts around like a ghost. Most days she doesn't get dressed, she just wears her nightgown with all the food stains down the front. She doesn't recognize me anymore, so I don't see what the point is.

"Inside she knows who you are; she just can't show it on the outside," Bertha said, taking off her yellow rain hat and starting the car engine. I wiped the window with my sleeve and noticed my reflection against the black rain outside. "I'm not leaving till you've got your happy face on!"

I watched my eyes roll. Why couldn't she just leave me alone? I flashed a toothy, bright-eyed grin the way the lady with the glowing teeth does on Bertha's favorite TV show.

"That's better. Now, that wasn't difficult, was it?"

She pulled a big brown paper bag from the backseat and dropped it in my lap. "I picked up some things for you to give your mom. There are some snacks, some flowers, some pj's, and a hairbrush. I thought it would be nice for her if you fixed her hair a little." And I remembered how the last time we visited Mom, her hair was all sticking up in the back like she'd been caught in a small tornado.

St. Agnes's is in the old part of town, and set in the center of its own gardens. It must have once been a fancy-looking building. It's still a really pretty place, although it could use a lick of paint. Not that the people who live there would know the difference. Bertha told me it was built about two hundred years ago by a rich family with a weird name: Feverspeare. It made me think people had been going crazy for a long time.

"She's in the dayroom," said the nurse, leading us down a squeaky corridor. I could hear Bertha's shoes on the floor, the sound of her legs rubbing in her waterproof pants, and I could feel my heart beating in my stomach. Every time I came to visit Mom, a part of me thought she might be dead. Dad was already gone—he used to drink a lot and one night he drank way too much and fell asleep in the cold. He left without saying good-bye, so what was to stop the last piece of Mom from drifting off?

I tried not to think of that happening to Mom. Although the mom I knew *had* kind of died, because the lady we were sitting next to now just *looked* like Mom. None of the things that made her my mom were there anymore.

The mom I knew used to take me on midnight sleigh rides through the woods and tuck me into bed. She was the mom who taught me to swim and to ride my bike, the one who would make me weird cakes on my birthday, in the shape of famous people's heads. And she was the mom who chased Brad Adams all the way out of town when he tried to beat up on me the time I wore my dad's overcoat to school. One thing was for sure: My mom, the mom I loved, had left a long time ago.

"Bea said she'd like to brush your hair." Bertha smiled at me and handed me the little red hairbrush. It was a brush for kids and I felt stupid using it on my mom, but I pulled it gently through her hair a few times while she just stared straight ahead like she was far, far away. Bertha had to wipe Mom's mouth with a Kleenex because there was still some orange-colored food in the corner. It looked like tomato soup.

The rain was coming down hard outside, drumming on the roof and tapping at the long cold windows, but most of the people in the room didn't seem to mind. It was like somebody had taken their batteries out. Sam said it's the pills they give them.

When I finished brushing Mom's long brown hair, I smoothed it down with my hands, put it in a loose braid, and gave the brush back to Bertha. I hadn't even thought about taking pictures of Mom for the competition, and for a moment I felt guilty.

"Now, wasn't that nice?" asked Bertha, putting the brush back in her bag, but Mom's brown eyes were empty. I wished she could brush my hair, or even cuddle me, but it was just stupid to wish that because it wasn't going to happen.

When it was time to leave, I stopped for a moment in the doorway and looked back at Mom. She hadn't moved; she was still in the same position, staring into space.

As I turned to go, though, I thought I caught a glimpse, out of the corner of my eye, of her hand reaching slowly for her braid and holding it softly for a second before dropping it again. But perhaps that was just wishful thinking, as Bertha would say.

I followed Bertha down the long corridor and could see other silent, ghostlike people, folded over in armchairs or just standing staring at nothing.

Bertha slowed down at the doorway of a single room where a skinny lady with crazy hair was sitting on the end of her bed nodding to herself. Her furry slippers were way too big for her feet. "Now there's a sad story," Bertha whispered. "That's Lola. She used to own the soft drinks company. You know, Lola's Cola. She had it all. Now look at her."

We walked on, past others in other rooms. They seemed frozen in time, as if under some kind of bad spell, and every month there seemed to be more and more of them. It's got to be the rain; it gets to everyone in the end.

CHAPTER 6

On the way home I watched the windshield wipers *swish* and *click*, *swish* and *click*. They were like the hands on a mean, creepy clock. They told me it was only a matter of time, if I stayed here in the rain, before I ended up just like Mom.

The urgency of needing to win that photo competition suddenly swept through me. It was a real way of getting out of here. It was still only the afternoon, so there was plenty of time.

"I'm going into town to take some pictures."

Bertha kept her bulbous eyes on the road ahead. (*Bulbous* is a word I learned last semester. It means round and sticking out, and when Miss Riley, our English teacher, told me that, I thought of Bertha's eyes right away.)

She scrunched up her face. "But the weather's terrible."

"It's *always* terrible—that's why I'm going to win the photo competition and go to Florida."

Bertha clicked her tongue on the inside of her teeth and made the noise she made when she was annoyed. "There are worse things than a bit of rain, girl. Did you call the kids on the Summer Club List?"

I didn't answer.

"You know you gotta call those kids — it's the rules."

Once I was inside the house, I pulled off my galoshes as fast as I could and I ran down to the darkroom.

That's weird, I thought, *I'm sure I closed the door.* The little wooden door was swinging open with a loud creak and then slamming shut. There had to be a draft coming from outside. I went to check if I'd left the window open. Nope — the window was closed. And, weirdly, the red light was glowing even though I didn't remember switching it on.

I don't know why, but I suddenly felt cold, freezing cold, and I could see my own breath rising in front of me like mist. I felt strange, like I was being watched, and I didn't like it. When my pinkie finger started twitching, I noticed the camera. It wasn't where I'd left it, near the door, but on the table in the middle of the room.

It had been moved.

The back of the camera was open and the roll of film was just sitting there next to it. I knew I hadn't taken it out, because I still hadn't decided whether I wanted to see what was on that roll. And now the film was probably ruined from exposure anyway.

I held the film tight in the palm of my hand. I could either throw it away and forget about it forever, or I could develop those photos. Suddenly I was curious. My pinkie finger was flicking and twitching like crazy, my heart was thumping against my chest, and I could feel something tingly traveling down my arms and legs. Sure, I was scared, but I also wanted to know. To know if what we saw in that house was real.

I turned on the little radio, so it didn't feel so creepy in the darkroom, took a deep breath, and unraveled the film.

It only took me a few minutes to develop a contact sheet, which shows all the pictures on one page. My eyes quickly scanned the tiny squares. The shots looked like little windows, like on a high-rise apartment building, and through every window was the dead guy. It was like he'd moved in and was living in every apartment, his skull-like face with its gaping mouth and eye socket warning people again and again not to enter; his milky foot rising out of inky pools at different angles like deathly signposts repeating over and over: *Stay away, stay away!*

I used the enlarger to make large prints of those shots, turning the dial each time to focus the image on the photographic paper. I put a picture of the milky foot in the developing fluid and it blossomed slowly onto the sheet, becoming as clear and real as it had been in the house, floating in that dark green water.

I lifted it out of the tray with my plastic tongs and let it drip before slipping it into the tray with the fixer solution. Then I hung that sheet up to dry.

The rain came down harder outside, the long angry fingers beating out their rhythm on the garbage cans as I lowered the next blank sheet into the tray. I moved it around gently, making sure the liquid lapped over it evenly. I thought I'd have to wait the usual minute or two, but this time the image appeared instantly, flashing onto the white paper so quickly it made my stomach flip over inside. The dead guy had come to life in that watery tray and was looking up at me with that one cooked fish eye of his.

I'd developed all the pictures and hung them up to dry when the DJ on the radio casually said, "You've only got a couple of weeks to get your photos in. Somebody's going to win a fabulous trip to Florida! Remember, you can take pictures of anybody's family—it doesn't have to be your own. Details can be found on the back of any Herman's pickle or relish jar. Happy snapping!"

I took a new roll of film out of the drawer and went to grab my camera. But as I reached for it, the weirdest thing happened. The camera moved. I could feel the hairs on the back of my neck prickle.

The camera slid away from me along the counter. I reached for it again, and again it moved away. I stood back and it started to spin. It spun around and around and around, going faster and faster. If my camera were a person, I would have said it was angry, really angry. I'd never been so scared. My body turned cold all over, I felt shivery, and suddenly I wanted to cry. I needed my camera to take photos for the competition but I couldn't get to it, I couldn't pick it up. Something didn't want me to take any more photos. I thought about the pictures I desperately wanted to take: I was going to take some of Mitzy, the lady who owns the diner; some of DW, the guy who owns the record store; and some of Pete, who works in the thrift shop. I imagined them doing their "photo" faces for me and could even feel my finger ready on the button. If only I could get to my camera.

That's when the radio crackled and the music stopped. There was a heavy, eerie silence, and my camera started spinning again on the counter, wheeling around and around and around. I'd never seen anything like that in my whole life. My eyes were wide with fear and my mouth hung open, but I couldn't move. When the camera slowly stopped spinning, out of nowhere came the moan. A deep murmuring groan, just like the one I'd heard when I was taking the photos of the dead guy, and I could feel goose bumps dancing all over my skin.

CHAPTER 7

The phone woke me. I'd stayed up as long as I could, reading my dad's old detective books. I thought the books would stop the dead guy from getting into my head and into my dreams, and it seemed to have worked.

"Turn on the TV!" came Sam's urgent voice over the line. "The dead guy's house is on TV!"

He was right. The news program showed pictures of the same house we'd been in. Standing in front of yellow tape, the woman reporter said that the house had been "ransacked," but that "the authorities" were treating the death as suspicious because there was nothing inside to steal. She called it a "shell of a house," because it was going to be demolished so that a sparkly new house could be built on the land by the J&S Property Co.

"I don't get it, how could they demolish a house with a man living in it?" I asked Sam, but he was silent. I could hear his brother Jed shouting at him in the background.

"Meet me at DW's in an hour," Sam said, and then the line went dead.

The whole thing about the dead guy's house just didn't make sense to me. Maybe they didn't know he was still living there. Had he refused to leave? Maybe he left but then changed his mind and came home.

Questions swam around my head like the debris in that deep puddle next to that body. Who was the poor dead man with one eye? Why did he have to die? And why was he in that house, when it was about to be destroyed?

CHAPTER 8

DW owns Washburn's Vinyl, the best record store in town. Sam first took me there the summer before last. His dad used to take him there when he was in a good mood. It's the only place in town you can still buy records.

DW looks like a nice version of Bertha's dad. He has a really kind face and wise brown eyes and used to have dreads when he was young. But now he has short hair and wears a cap.

Sam likes to hang out at the store, not just because DW lets him smoke, but because he loves to listen to music and look at all the pictures on the albums—he says some are so good you could hang them in an art gallery. Sam says if he can't be in a band when he grows up, then he wants to design album covers.

The record store is on the edge of the new part of town, at the bottom of Elbow. I can get there pretty quickly because it's downhill all the way from my house. My orange raincoat was flapping in the wet air behind me as I lifted my legs off the pedals and stretched them out on either side of me. I flew downhill like a rocket, the tires *splooshing* through the puddles that flooded the streets. With the hood covering one of my eyes and the other eye half-shut to keep the raindrops out, I zipped past the arcade where Sam works; past the mall where Bertha makes me go to get my socks and shoes; past the thrift shop and the homeless shelter. I flew through the street with all the beat-up storefronts, run-down houses, and liquor stores, and finally arrived at DW's, with its hand-painted sign (a black record with fat red-and-turquoise lettering) swinging in the wind above the steamed-up window.

The little bell rang as I opened the door. It was so smoky inside I could hardly see, but DW called out, "Over here, Bea!"

Sam and DW were sitting next to each other with their feet on the counter, sharing a damp, squashed-up cigarette. Jellybean was fast asleep, curled up between two stacks of albums. Sam closed his eyes as he took a long drag on the cigarette, then he blew the smoke loudly from his mouth, kind of like he was blowing it at me.

"Get any shots for the competition?" he asked.

"My camera isn't working. Not since the other night, at the house."

"Well, you'll just have to hang out in Elbow like the rest of us, then," he said, with something mean in his voice that I hadn't heard before.

"If you hadn't taken me to that stupid house, my camera would still be working. It's your fault, Sam!"

"Come on! Stop fighting with your friend! There is plenty problem already in this world!" DW tutted and sucked his teeth the way Bertha did when she was annoyed with me.

"I wouldn't have won, anyway." I shrugged. Part of me felt hopeless but another part of me didn't want to give up. Maybe my camera would be OK again, once . . . once the thing inside it went away.

"A few years back, you could get your camera fixed across the street. But everything change. Nobody own nothing no more." DW picked up Sam's cola bottle from the counter. "It say Lola's Cola. But it not owned by Lola no more."

I was suddenly excited as I remembered the lady Bertha showed me, all alone in the little room, wearing the big slippers.

"Yeah, I saw her! I saw Lola in St. Agnes's when I was visiting Mom. She's one of the crazy people."

"She not always be like that. Stress can drive a person over the edge. When you lose your business and you lose your home, it not be very long before you be losing your mind." Holding his thumb over the top, DW showed us the bottom of the bottle. "See here . . . *MHF*?" he said, touching the raised glass letters with his brown fingers like he wanted to scratch them off.

"So?" said Sam, grabbing the bottle back and taking a swig.

"Nothing what it seem to be. You always gotta read them little letters."

"Like J&S," I said. "There was a sign outside the dead guy's house saying the house was sold. But he was still there, floating inside."

"It's true! Them is the little letters on the houses people can't pay for no more." DW took a long drag on the cigarette, waited, and then puffed a great big cloud of smoke into the air. "All them little letters belong in the same alphabet. Y'understan'? And the man who owns the alphabet, he owns the people."

His eyes darkened and his face was suddenly more serious than I'd ever seen it. "Nothing in this town is what it seems to be. This town turn upside down. Inside out."

At that very moment, a jagged shadow crept slowly across the store window and stopped. It was the shadow of a tall man in a wide-brimmed hat, and I suddenly felt like our whole conversation was being listened to. The tall shadow pulled his wide-brimmed hat farther over his face and just waited, covering the window like a black cloud. Then he began to whistle to himself. A slow, eerie tune lifted from his lips like smoke and began to fill the damp air all around us.

DW's eyes kept switching between the dark shape at the window and the door handle, like he was expecting the shadow, the way old people expect Death. Sam and I held our breath. We could hear the rain on the sidewalk, the strange mournful tune from the shadow man, and the record sign creaking in the wind, like it had been forgotten for years and was aching to come inside and be played.

Then the shadow seemed to turn on the sidewalk and move on. Sam looked at me and I looked back at Sam, and both of us knew something creepy had just happened, but we didn't know what.

"What is it, DW?" asked Sam quietly, but DW didn't want to talk about it anymore.

"I almost forget"—DW turned to me —"I save a 45

for you—an original Bob Marley!" He handed his little squashed-up cigarette to Sam and headed into the back room to find the record he was saving for me.

When Mom and Dad used to play each other pieces of music, Mom would sometimes yell at my dad for putting his big fingers all over the record he wanted to play. Mom had a whole special way of doing it. She would carefully take a record out of its cover, balance the middle part on her thumb, and let it drop onto the turntable. Then she'd lift the needle and lower it very carefully onto the black spinning disc. There would always be a few crackles at first, and sometimes there'd be a scratch in the song and Mom would make a face like she'd eaten something bad. Once she played me a record of a singer from a long time ago called Enrico Caruso. Mom said his life was very sad and that he got very ill and coughed up blood while he was singing, but even that didn't stop him. I still have that record, and if Mom ever comes home, we're going to listen to it together in front of the fire, like we used to.

I pulled myself up onto the counter and watched DW walk over to the player and pull the little record from its sleeve.

"In the summertime, this town, Elbow, is like a woman who never stop crying. Must be a whole lot of sadness in her for all those tears. Me like to play her a record, make her stop crying."

"Will it work, DW? Will it really stop the rain?" I asked hopefully.

"Me can try."

I waited for the sounds to come from the record player,

and could hear my breath and the first crackles. Then I got that excited feeling in my stomach, waiting for the music to arrive. DW sat back down.

"No woman, no cry," came the voice. "No woman, no cry . . ."

We listened to the whole song and although I didn't really understand the words, it made me feel all kinds of different things. The man seemed to be telling me not to cry, but the song made me do just that. I don't cry often and I don't like people seeing me cry, because they think you're weak and they try to hug you and ask you what's wrong but they don't really listen.

As the song came to a stop, I watched the heavy raindrops through the steamy store window. I could feel Sam watching me. For a second or two the raindrops seemed fatter and slower as I longed for those rainy fingers to stop.

"You can't stop rain with a record, stupid." Sam pulled his rain hat (which he sometimes wore indoors) over his eyes and took another drag of the cigarette.

I wiped my nose on my sleeve and sniffed the tears away like I had a cold. I don't think Sam noticed I'd been crying, because he was in his own cloud of smoke, but DW did notice, and he kind of nodded his head out of respect because he could see I liked the song. It was a beautiful song. When it was over, he lifted the record from the deck, put it back into its cover, and handed it to me.

"How much do you want for it?" I asked, thinking hard about how I could use a bit of the grocery money Bertha gave me.

"You already pay me—with your appreciation," he said. "I remember your daddy—he was a big reggae fan!"

"Thanks."

"No problem," said DW, winking at me.

Sam, who'd been sitting on the counter swinging his legs, slid to the floor, and Jellybean jumped to his feet, giving his damp fur a quick shake.

"Gotta be at the arcade. See you, D."

As I turned to leave, DW grabbed my arm suddenly and held me there. I was surprised how strong his grip was.

"Stay off the street—it is not safe! Me serious. There are horrible and nasty people out there. Take care of each other, y'understan'?"

As I looked into his deep brown eyes, I saw the same fear I'd seen when the shadow man had appeared at the window. I felt a current of alarm travel quickly through my body, but at the same time it made me want to know about the people and things I was supposed to stay away from.

Sam was standing impatiently at the door. He rolled his eyes at DW and me, like he'd heard it all before, and then the bell rang behind him as he swept up the street, his body hunched against the downpour.

"Wait for me!" I said. "Wait up!"

All I could see was Sam's nose, already red from the wet air, and the little white scar on his top lip, which he said was from trying to open a beer bottle with his teeth but which I knew was from his brother. "What do you think DW was talking about? Sam? What do you think that man wanted? The one at the window?" I was breathless trying to keep up.

"He was probably just trying to stay out of the rain," he said gruffly, using his shoulder to push open the door to the thrift shop.

The thrift shop is a great place to get things cheap, and you can sometimes find really cool stuff in there. It's where Sam got his guitar. Pete, the guy who runs the store, went away to college a while ago but then dropped out, and he's been working there ever since. He's really great because he talks to us like we're real people and not just kids, and he puts things we like aside and saves them for us. Every year he puts on a little more weight and his pants hang down a little lower. He keeps talking about going back to college, but I think he likes it in the thrift shop. The money from the store goes to people in the homeless shelter and St. Agnes's, including Mom, but Pete says he finds it best if he doesn't mention that side too much. He says people generally don't want to give money to crazy people, that it's as if they've brought it on themselves. Pete says they say stuff like, "It's not like cancer—now, those people really need our money," or "Nobody asked them to start listening to the voices in their heads." I like Pete and I like finding stuff in the store, stuff I wouldn't normally think of buying. Like once, Bertha left me some money to buy lunch and instead I bought a pair of brown leather cowboy boots. My stomach rumbled all afternoon but it was worth it.

As we stepped inside, we were welcomed by the smell of old clothes and damp books.

"Hey, Pete!" Sam's eyes tried to find him among the piles of donated items. Pete's head of wild brown curls popped up from the floor.

"Look who the wind blew in! I was just getting some stuff from the basement. Did you want to take a photo of me, Bea?"

"News sure travels fast around here!" said Sam in his grouchy voice.

"Maybe in a few days. I just need to get my camera fixed. . . ."

Sam unzipped his jacket (which Jellybean was licking raindrops off of) and pulled out a plastic bag full of records. He dropped it on the floor. "DW said you could have these 45s."

"Thanks, Sam!" said Pete, coming up the ladder and wiping his hands on his mildewy pants. "Can I get you guys—?"

But Sam was already out the door, heading up the street to the arcade. I chased after him.

"If I help you collect cola bottles, maybe we can play some pinball?" I offered.

"Sure—but I'll beat you. . . ."

I shoved him hard. "You know I always win!"

"Yeah, you're OK for a girl—" Sam broke off suddenly and grabbed Jellybean by the collar. "Wait!" he whispered. We hung back behind a wall, trying to see through the murkiness. "What's going on?" said Sam, squinting through the rain. "Why are they doing that?"

About a block away, some men dressed like sanitation

workers were ripping down posters. They couldn't pull them down fast enough. The posters said: MISSING! HAVE YOU SEEN THIS BOY? There was a photo of a kid, but from where we were standing his face was kind of a blur, apart from his smile and a name . . .

"It says, *Luke Green, Age: 13*," read Sam. "Same age as me." Quickly he took hold of my raincoat and yanked me back behind the corner. "Jelly!" he hissed, pulling him out of sight.

We peered carefully around the brick wall. "Something's up in this town, Bea, and I don't like it one bit," Sam said, shaking his head.

We could just make out the shape of him, the shape of the tall man, the one whose shadow had appeared at DW's window, the one in the wide-brimmed hat. He was waving his hands angrily at the garbagemen and telling them to hurry up with the poster-ripping. One beefy garbageman was practically shaking and his face was all wrinkled up with fear, and we could just about hear his words through the sound of the water coming down all around: "I'm really sorry, it won't happen again. I promise it won't happen again."

Then the shadow man was gone, just as suddenly as before, back into the black spaces between the buildings, but the echo of the tune he whistled to himself lingered on, and the garbagemen, even though they had finished their job, kept looking around in case he suddenly appeared beside them.

CHAPTER 9

With my camera still broken, the idea of winning the photo competition and the trip to Florida, with its palm trees and beaches, started to feel more and more out of reach. I began to resign myself to another rainy summer in Elbow. Only now it wasn't just the rain that was bothering me. There was something else going on. There was something creepy, something shadowy, not just on the outside but on the inside, too. Right inside my house, in fact. The more I thought about it, the more I was sure that some part of that dead guy, the one I'd photographed, had gotten inside my camera and come home with me. I wasn't sure which was worse, the thought of spending time with the shadows out on the streets, or the shadows in my own house.

The best way to deal with all this weird stuff, I decided, was to just keep doing what I'd been doing most of the week already: hanging out with Sam.

When his dad and brother are away, we go to Sam's place, and if they're home, we go to his hideout.

Sam found the tree house last summer. It's high up in a giant old tree that looks like a witch's hand reaching into the sky, about to grab something. The house is made of old pieces of wood and metal and hammered together like a patchwork box. It's got one long horizontal window like a half-open eye watching out from between the branches. You have to climb up a rope ladder to get in, and once you're up you pull the ladder in after you. That way nobody knows you're there—or at least nobody can climb up after you. Sam told me the tree house belongs to the neighbors, who nobody sees anymore because they never go out. They built it for their little girl, but she disappeared. Sam says nobody bothers him up there. It's a couple of houses away from Sam's, but his brother and his dad don't know about it. Last summer when the rain was getting in through the roof, we found some plastic in my dad's garage and used some nails to fix it up. I cleaned out the leaves and put in an old rug and an orange crate for a table. One time me and Sam were playing cards when he said, "I don't mind you coming here sometimes—but it's *my* tree house. I found it." That kind of upset me because I thought of it as *our* tree house, but I guess Sam needs somewhere private he can go.

If I'm looking for Sam, I always go to the tree house first. If the ladder is down, I know he's not there, and if it's gone, it's because he's up there and he's pulled it in after him. If I wait, I can see a cloud of smoke from his cigarette lifting through the window-eye and up into the damp air. Sometimes I feel a bit unsure about calling up to him because I don't know if he wants to be alone or not. Once he told me to go away if he didn't answer immediately, otherwise I'd draw too much attention and his brother or dad might find out about the tree house. It's pretty much hidden among the leaves and branches, kind of like it's grown out of the tree, not like it was built by a person at all. I wished *I* had found the tree house, but it was still good to be able to go there with Sam.

I arrived at Sam's just in time to catch his brother, Jed, pushing him around. He shoved him hard and went to hit his face but didn't — and laughed at Sam's reaction. I hung back, not wanting to complicate things. The one good thing about the rain is that you can be invisible when you want to be; you just cover your face with your rain hat that much more and you're gone — just a blur in the downpour.

Jed got into his truck and drove off to the sound of his radio blasting some cheesy rock music. Sam went back into the house, and I caught up with him as I watched Jed's truck turn the corner.

Jed is so mean to Sam. I think it's because he's jealous because Sam's mom always said Sam was sensitive and talented and would show them all one day. When she'd said that Jed was just a thug like his dad, a big fight had broken out, and Sam had always felt like it was his fault.

Sam's house isn't cozy like mine. It's got wooden floors in most of the rooms — not the homey kind but the kind that have paint spots on them and are usually hidden under rugs. The kind you find in homes where people sell their own carpets for liquor or where they didn't bother putting them down in the first place. But Sam's room is OK, so we either hang out there or in the tree house.

"What did Jed want?" I asked.

"He was pissed because the cops came over last night asking if I'd been up to the old house. I said it wasn't me. Jed said he gets enough trouble from the police as it is and doesn't need me adding to it." Sam took a deep breath and then looked right at me. "They said the body'd been there a couple of weeks . . . and now they're saying it's suspicious."

I swallowed and tried to look calm. I wanted to forget that we were ever there. I wanted to forget about taking those pictures. Those pictures didn't exist. If I could pretend the photos didn't exist, I could pretend the camera hadn't opened on its own. I could pretend I hadn't heard that moaning sound in the darkroom, and pretend I hadn't seen my camera spinning around and around for no reason. Maybe the ghost — no, I wasn't even going to call it that — maybe whatever was going on in my house would stop and go away and let me have my camera again, so I could go back to taking the pictures I wanted to take, the ones I needed to win that competition and get out of this place.

"Did you bring the pictures?"

It was like he could read my mind. I started to fidget and bite my lip.

"I didn't get any. The water got in — it damaged the film. I developed it but there was nothing, just black," I lied.

Sam's face changed.

"All that for nothing?" he said, kicking the toe of his damp sneaker against the floor. He looked disappointed and it made me wonder why he'd taken me to that house in the first place. Maybe it wasn't just his curiosity or his idea of a joke; maybe he did it to get me a twisted kind of competition entry.

"How'd you know he . . . I mean . . . the body was there?" I asked.

"Jed was supposed to be taking me home, but he went to this bar with his buddies instead, and this one guy was joking with the bartender about how he knew of a great place for the bartender's sister to come and stay if she visited, if she didn't mind sharing the place with a dead guy."

"But how did *he* know he was there?" I asked.

Sam just shrugged and said, "You know what this town is like."

"Nope. I don't think I know it at all."

And I think I must have sounded afraid because Sam looked into my eyes and I could see he felt the same way I did.

If this were during the school year, my regular friends would think it was weird that I was friends with Sam. I'm a girl, so my friends are supposed to be girls, too. They'd ask me questions like, "Is he your boyfriend?" and giggle. They wouldn't understand if I told them that he's just a friend. I hang out with Sam over the summer, but everything changes when school starts again.

It's the same with all the Raintown Convicts. We have to get together for the summer, but the minute school starts, we go our separate ways. We all have our own groups of friends and the groups don't mix. We're just expected to hate each other. If we didn't have the others to make fun of, I guess we wouldn't feel so good about our own group. It's just the way things are.

Who knows, maybe this summer'll be different because in the fall we all go to junior high. Sam's a year older because he had to repeat a year—but he's not stupid. I just don't think he was ready to move.

Me and Sam have known each other since I was seven years old. My mom knew Sam's mom before her drinking got really bad, but even then she didn't like me going to his house. She said it was OK for him to come and play here but I wasn't to go there. Now she's away and Bertha's too busy to worry about who my friends are.

I was sitting on the end of Sam's bed. He was lying across a beanbag eating the remains of a bag of popcorn. *Last night's dinner,* I thought.

"So who've we got on the Convicts list?" I asked, shaking my head as Sam offered me popcorn on his sticky palm.

"There's that rich girl, Madison—I heard she didn't go to Europe with her 'rents because she's scared of flying."

I gave him a big fake smile. "She sounds fun!"

"Let's see . . ." said Sam, picking up the yearbook I'd brought and flicking through it.

It was this way every year. Every year we'd talk about who we thought was left behind from our class and who we were going to call. We'd tease each other and say things like, "I always thought you guys were best friends!" We both knew we had to call them all sooner or later and that once the Convicts got together, that was it, we had to put up with them all summer.

I helped myself to a handful of popcorn and fed it to Jellybean, who licked each little ball from my hand and made it all gooey in the process.

Nobody knows what kind of dog Jelly is, but he's pretty big, with really long legs, shaggy gray-brown fur, amber eyes, and the floppiest ears you've ever seen. Sam rescued him from the pound and is trying to keep him a secret from his dad, but his brother keeps threatening to tell. Sam lets Jellybean sleep in the closet on top of his clothes. He always makes sure he's got enough to eat and that his water bowl is full. Sam even designed a special pulley system to get Jellybean up into his tree house with him. He likes to have him up there even though Jellybean hates it and shivers like he's freezing cold. I told Sam it wasn't normal for a dog to be up in a tree, but Sam said, "It's not normal for people to be up in a tree, either. Doesn't mean we don't like it."

Sam's kind of eccentric. That's a word I heard on TV one night when a man was describing an old guy who wore a purple wig and had hundreds of worms in a worm circus. He traveled around with them and you could watch as he made them wriggle through flaming hoops and stuff. I think *eccentric* means doing things that people don't expect you to. For example, Sam has this mannequin in his room he calls the Captain. He found him in a dumpster outside an old-fashioned men's clothing store, and he comes in really useful when Sam needs to pretend he's in bed.

Sam's always talking about the rock band he's going to have when he grows up. I think he'll be pretty good. He bought this guitar and a little amp from the thrift shop with some money he saved from working in the arcade. The guitar's only a basic one, but he says it's good enough for now. He uses it without the amp because he was playing one afternoon and his dad, who was drunk and trying to sleep it off, got really mad and put his foot through it.

We'd forgotten about Madison, the girl from our class we knew was in Elbow over the summer, because we were looking through the yearbook. A couple of days before Sam took me to the dead guy's house, I'd spent hours cutting out kids' and teachers' eyes, noses, chins, and hair, and then gluing them onto other people's faces. Now the yearbook was full of monsters! Sam had told me I was nuts, but he couldn't stop laughing.

"Now her face matches her personality!" Sam said, pointing to a vain girl from our class whose own face had been buried under Mr. Gutch's. Mr. Gutch taught the grade below ours. He was very hairy, had scaly skin, and resembled a startled dinosaur that had just eaten something way too big for its mouth. When I ran my finger over Mr. Gutch's hair, which looked like a wig but was really his own, I got a fit of giggles. "I can't believe that's his actual hair! Some of them look worse than if I'd stuck something on!"

Once we'd gotten to the end of the yearbook for the third time, the fun started to wear off. I realized that there were only so many times you could laugh at the same joke, and thoughts of the evening ahead began to crawl into my mind.

"OK," I said, "I think it's about time to round up the Convicts. How about we start with Madison? Maybe I'll call her in the morning."

Sam rolled his eyes, but he knew we didn't really have a choice in the matter.

"What've we got to lose?" he said at last.

CHAPTER 10

"*Who's* calling?" Madison said snootily.

"It's Bea, Bea Klednik, from school."

"Oh," she said, unimpressed. "What do *you* want?"

I tried again. "I got your number from the list—you know, for Summer Club. We're supposed to get together. You must have heard of the Raintown Convicts?"

"I didn't see that movie," she said.

"It's not a movie, it's our name for Summer Club. Sam Carter and me thought we'd call you."

I expected her to laugh and say, "Why would I want to hang out with you?" But instead she said, "OK. Do I have to pass a test?"

"Only if you want to," I offered.

Listening in with his ear squashed to the receiver, Sam nodded and, smiling like a bad guy from a cartoon, grabbed the phone from me. "Yeah, you've got to do an initiation—or you don't get to be in the gang!"

"Well," she answered, "you'd better come over."

Madison's place was the size of a hotel. We walked past the endless windows and up the steps to the giant polished front door. Sam reached for the big brass knocker just as the neat, pinched-looking housekeeper opened the door. Sam fell forward a little and looked embarrassed. The housekeeper was on the phone but she raised a thin eyebrow distastefully at Sam and me standing there in our faded rain gear.

"We're Madison's friends," Sam announced.

The housekeeper gave us a bored expression and, still on the phone, headed back inside, leaving the door open for us. The hallway was massive. A chandelier twinkled above us, a cluster of giant jewels, as we dripped rainwater onto the expensive-looking rug. "Madison's in her room—third floor, at the end of the hall on the left. Make sure you take off your shoes!" snapped the housekeeper from the kitchen. I lifted my feet out of my galoshes and left them in the hallway.

"Sam—take off your shoes!" I told him, but he'd already sloshed across the perfectly vacuumed carpet and up the stairs.

We climbed the wide staircase with its curling, nut-brown balustrade and found ourselves in a never-ending corridor. Another cleaning lady appeared, a Latina woman, with a basket of cleaning products in the crook of her arm.

"Which one is Madison's room?" I asked.

She smiled and pointed toward a cream-colored door. We walked a little farther down the pale bouncy carpet and then Sam knocked gently—even he looked a bit embarrassed rapping on that pristine door.

"Just a moment," came the reply.

We waited a few seconds—nothing. And then Sam knocked again loudly. "What is she doing—dressing for the occasion?" he muttered.

Madison opened the door for us, then turned and, without saying a word, went back to the full-length mirror she must have been standing in front of. She stood there with a bored expression, one leg bent at the knee, looking at the reflection of the bright blue shoes she was wearing.

"Is she just going to ignore us?" I whispered to Sam.

"I guess so — it's what she does at school, why should it be different now?"

Madison pretended not to hear and, with the same blank expression, slipped out of the blue shoes and into a patent black pair with a buckle on the toe.

Sam gave me a sideways look that said, *What did I tell you?* before dropping onto the floor and stretching his legs out in front of him. His old wet sneakers flicked their dirty shoelaces onto the immaculate pale pink carpet. Madison turned around.

"Didn't you take your shoes off? Now I'm going to get yelled at by Monster Lady."

I realized she meant the housekeeper. Sam shuffled off his sneakers without changing position, and kicked them away. The corners of Madison's mouth turned downward at the sight of those soggy shoes, but Jellybean seized the opportunity, grabbed one in his mouth, and started chewing happily on it.

I wanted to distract Madison's attention from Sam's sneakers, and the holes in his socks that were letting dark green patches of mold peep through.

"Those blue ones are pretty," I volunteered, feeling a little stupid.

"Thanks," she said, flicking her long shiny dark hair behind her shoulders. "It sounds kind of stupid, but me and Paige, we sometimes try on all my shoes and pretend they can take us into another world. You know, like time travel or something."

I liked the sound of that. I got the feeling Madison wanted to leave Elbow as much as I did. Maybe we had something in common after all.

"I have tons of shoes — take a look!"

And with that, she threw open the double doors to her closet and there they all were, row upon row of shoes, all neatly stacked on their own shelves, in every color and style you could imagine. It was like a shoe candy store.

"My stepmom takes me to the mall every Saturday and buys me at least one pair. She's, like, totally obsessed."

She glanced at me with her pretty gray eyes, waiting for the usual reaction of "Wow! You are so lucky!" but I guess I must have looked more shocked or confused or something, because her expression changed. She looked a little bit annoyed and like she'd suddenly woken up at the same time. Then she sort of scanned me all over and the freckles on her little nose got all squashed up as she concentrated for a moment.

"You know, you could look sort of OK if you did something different with your hair," she said matter-of-factly.

I awkwardly pushed my lopsided, toffee-colored bangs out of my eyes. When she remembered, Bertha took me to get my hair cut at the men's barbershop next door to the grocery store and they always cut it unevenly.

"I could fix it for you if you want. You've got nice eyes; they're green, right?" she offered.

"I kind of like my hair the way it is," I lied. "But thanks."

Maybe one day I'd become like all the other girls who worried about how they looked, but I didn't plan on starting just yet. Madison made a face that said, *Have it your way*, then she smoothed her cream silk skirt and folded her cream cashmere cardigan arms.

"I'm ready for my initiation now," she said.

Sam played along. "I don't know what you've heard, but we usually devise a test for new members—it usually involves facing their worst fear. I, for example, had to eat a whole bunch of night crawlers—raw!"

Madison swallowed, as though tasting worms herself, and looked horrified.

"What did you have to do, Bea?"

I threw Sam a look to say, *Come on—give her a break.* "He didn't eat nightcrawlers. There isn't an initiation—we're *supposed* to get together, remember? It's a school requirement!"

"But I *want* to do an initiation!" insisted Madison.

I looked at Sam, who was grinning at the chance of making one of the rich girls do something terrible, something disgusting.

"Well, OK . . . what do you want to do?" I said.

"Don't ask her, Bea, we get to choose what she does!" Sam said, shoving me hard on the shoulder.

I realized he liked Madison—or what he thought she stood for—even less than I did.

"I could walk in some dirt with my best shoes on if you like," she said enthusiastically.

"That sounds terrible—we wouldn't want to put you through something like that," Sam responded sarcastically.

"It's OK—really! We can go outside and do it now if you like," Madison answered, heading into her shoe closet.

So that afternoon, we watched Madison Anderson take almost two hours to stand in a puddle with her best shoes on—and it took her a while to choose those, having close to three hundred pairs. In the end she settled on a pair of sparkly, cotton-candy pink pumps that she had worn at her dad's wedding to her stepmom a year earlier. Standing at one edge of the puddle, she took lots of deep breaths, panting in and out like she was about to jump off a tall building. Then she'd walk a little closer and back away again. Eventually Sam lifted her up and put her in that puddle up to her knees. She started to cry. Suddenly I felt really bad. *Here's a girl*, I thought, *with so much money she can have whatever she wants—sure, her parents got divorced, but both of them are alive—and yet she's a complete mess.*

"I feel good, I really do," she said, her tears mingling with the rain dripping down her face.

I could see Sam was thinking we'd made a big mistake and that we should just ignore the whole Summer Club List, even if we got into trouble once we were back at school. But I unwrapped a piece of foil and handed Madison a damp stick of pumpkin-flavored gum (left over from Halloween) and said in my cheeriest voice, "It's my great pleasure to present you with this honorary piece of gum and to announce that you are now an official Raintown Convict!"

After that, Sam said, "Let's go to Bea's place for hot chocolate and marshmallows!"

"I'd like that," replied Madison, managing a little smile.

I was uneasy about going back to my place because of the feeling that was now living there like an invisible gray fog. I unlocked the door to let in Sam and Madison, but waited on the porch, shaking the rain from my umbrella for a little longer than usual. When I saw that everything seemed OK, I followed.

Sam switched on the TV right away and sat down on the couch, putting his feet up on the coffee table. Madison sat down next to him self-consciously, bringing her knees neatly together so they both faced the same direction—no doubt somebody had told her that that's the way ladies sit.

I headed into the kitchen to make hot chocolate. The trick to great hot chocolate is to add lots of cocoa powder and to mix up a paste before adding the rest of the milk. My mom showed me how to make two things before she went to St. Agnes's: hot chocolate and scrambled eggs. She used to say that a girl could pretty much survive on chocolate and eggs, and I agree (except plus Swiss cheese pancakes and Devil Tongue Relish, of course). I prepared three perfect, steaming mugs of hot chocolate and carried them out on a tray for Sam and Madison.

Sam had gulped down his hot chocolate in no time and was now distracted by the way Madison was sipping delicately at hers. He kept on looking at her in an irritated way, like she made him uncomfortable.

"You don't have to act like a girl around us — you know, worrying how you look and act and stuff. I know your friends at school think they're twenty-five, but we're pretty much just ourselves around here. Right, Bea?"

I nodded. "He just means you can relax."

Madison seemed to take this in. She smoothed the creases on her tights and pulled her legs up under her. "So is it going to be just the three of us?" she asked.

"Let's see who else is on the list," I said, swallowing a gulp of chocolate and putting my mug back on the table. I got up and walked into the kitchen, pulled the sheet off the refrigerator, and brought it back with me. I handed it to Madison, and she held the crumpled paper in front of her and looked at me.

"I tried to throw it in the trash, but Bertha, the lady I live with, fished it back out," I explained.

Madison looked at the paper squeamishly, moving her fingers around so they weren't touching any of the dried garbage that had formed colorful scabs around the kids' names.

"I can't even read this one," Madison huffed. I peeled off a piece of dried egg yolk and Madison went back to reading the names of our classmates.

"What's that noise?" said Madison suddenly. From downstairs, the darkroom door was squeaking open and then slamming shut again.

"It's just the door to the darkroom." But I knew it wasn't just the door. I'd been trying to ignore it. Now that Madison had noticed, I had to think about it, and thinking about it gave me the willies.

"Are you going to, like, shut it?" Madison raised her eyebrows at me to say the noise was annoying her. Sam let out a loud laugh at a cartoon.

"I've seen this one! This one's funny."

I forced myself off the couch and headed down to the darkroom. I held the little wooden door open and walked very slowly inside.

It's OK, it's OK, there's nothing here. It's just Dad's darkroom. I'm not scared. I'm not scared, I kept saying to myself.

As soon as I was inside, the door stopped creaking to and fro and slammed shut behind me. I jumped and held my breath. *It's just a door,* I said to myself to try to stay calm. Looking around the room, I noticed my camera sitting where I'd left it. *See, everything's OK, everything's normal. I'll just bolt the door and go back upstairs. . . .*

But as I turned to go, I came face-to-face with the pictures I'd developed, hanging from the line in front of me. It took me a second to register what was wrong. What I should have seen on those pages was the dead guy's face or his foot poking out of that pool. I'd seen those images; I'd taken the photos and printed them and hung them up. And that was the thing: There was nothing on those sheets. Absolutely nothing at all. They were completely blank.

"Eric Schnitzler's in Elbow! I know he's a total geek and he's supposed to have a pet chameleon, but . . ." Madison burst into the darkroom, making me jump again.

She must have seen how the color had drained from my

face, because she looked at me in a weird way. As she stood in the doorway, her eyes traveled slowly around the dark-room, trying to figure out what was up. Then her eyes fixed on something by the blacked-out window, and she looked at me strangely.

"Who's in there with you?"

"Nobody," I said. But the way she'd said it gave me the creeps.

"I thought I saw something, like a . . . a shadow."

I didn't want to look, but it didn't stop the goose bumps from coming alive all over my body.

"I took some pictures a few nights ago . . . you're going to think I'm crazy .. . . I took some pictures a few nights ago and they've . . . disappeared." I pointed to the blank sheets of photographic paper lit up by the little red light on the oppo-site wall.

Madison looked at me for a long moment and then said, "Pictures of what, exactly?"

CHAPTER 11

It was a new day of dark rain and we were on our way to Eric Schnitzler's house. Like me, he lived in the old part of town, but much higher up, on the outskirts, where all the bigger houses were, including Madison's. Pinehills Forest started to rise up behind those big old houses and the thick blue-green conifers went on for miles and miles. Nobody I knew had walked all the way through Pinehills and survived. There were tales of mountain lions and deadly giant bees living in those woods.

The sky was black with rain and for a second I was seized by panic. Being here was like living in an underwater cave, and every day I stayed I got more desperate to swim back up to the surface. My body and mind ached for sunshine. *As soon as all the Convicts have said hi and maybe spent, like, a day together,* I thought, *I'll see if Bertha will lend me some money to get my camera fixed and then I can take those photos. Maybe I still have a chance. Maybe I can still win that competition and get to Florida.*

"I can't believe you guys—I thought about it all night. I can't believe you found a dead body and you didn't tell anybody!" Madison stopped and stood there in her pale pink rainwear and we were forced to wait. She still looked horrified.

Sam and I nodded. I must have looked nervous, and Sam was acting all excited and kind of showing off, but he couldn't fool me. I knew Sam was a whole lot more complicated than he let on.

"Pretty cool, huh?" he drawled. Then he put on his deep movie trailer voice. "There comes a time in every man's life when he must look mortality in the face!" Jellybean woofed, like Sam's new voice confused him.

"Who was he?" asked Madison, suddenly looking a bit tearful again.

"How are we supposed to know? He wasn't the talkative type," said Sam. "And we weren't gonna hang around and get blamed for his murder!"

Madison's eyes almost popped out of her head.

"Murder?" she screeched.

"We don't know that for sure," I said.

But Sam insisted, "The story was on TV and in the newspaper." Then his expression changed, as if he were realizing for the first time how serious the situation was. "It said his death was suspicious—that means murder."

It was true. Bertha had brought home a copy of *The Elbow Herald* and shown me the article. There was a picture of the dead man's house, the one we'd been in. The article said a bit more than that first TV report—how the man must have surprised some robbers who had broken in to steal stuff. It also said he couldn't be named until after the investigation.

I still didn't want to tell Sam about the photos. About how the dead guy's face had disappeared and how Madison thought somebody was in the darkroom with me. *There must have been something wrong with the film,* I kept telling myself. Maybe the film got wet and the pictures could only appear for a short time. Maybe I got the developing fluids mixed up or something like that. There had to be a reason behind it. I didn't like the idea of ghosts one bit, and I sure didn't want one following me around or living in my house.

Eric Schnitzler's mother beamed as she welcomed us into the hallway of their house. She didn't even seem to mind Jellybean, 'cause he just ran right inside and began sniffing around the place.

"It's so great you guys came over. I was beginning to think Eric was going to spend the whole summer in his bedroom! What can I get you all to drink?"

As she led us toward the kitchen, a pale, grumpy-looking man slipped out of it. Eric's mom stopped him with her cheerful voice. "Oh, I changed your bedsheets today, Mr. Jeeks!"

The skinny man was forced to stop for a moment, and he hovered awkwardly with his back to her. "That's extremely kind of you, Mrs. Schnitzler, I'm forever indebted," he said, kind of nodding his head like he was bowing to an invisible king.

His bones jutted out of his pointy face and he had small, mean-looking, pink-rimmed eyes. *Not what you'd call a people person,* I thought. *Misanthropic.* That's what Miss Riley called people who didn't like other people.

"It's really no bother," said Eric's mom, blushing a little, but Mr. Jeeks had already slipped across the hallway and crept into his room.

With a few words of advice from Eric's mom ("Best leave the dog with me. Careful where you sit, don't touch anything, and watch out for flying objects!"), we headed up to Eric's room, which was in the attic. As we got higher up, more and more random objects littered the higgledy-piggledy stairs: a punctured football, books open and facedown, a traffic cone, a bird's nest, a hubcap from a car, and plates of moldy food. There were signs on Eric's door: **KEEP OUT OR DIE!** and one that his mom must have bought him: **Danger — Genius at Work!**

Sam knocked and we waited. Me and Madison half expected something to fly out and hit us in the face. Instead there came a bored-sounding reply. "It's open."

Through thick blue-gray smoke we could just make out the figure of Eric, small, wiry, and lonely-looking. He was sitting at a high table, wearing a pair of old-fashioned pilot's goggles, and holding something burning between a pair of tweezers. Despite the impressive fog he'd created, he had a gloomy expression on his face. A couple of thick brown curls were glued to his forehead, and behind the goggles his brown eyes looked almost tragic.

Madison started coughing while me and Sam absorbed the large attic room. Shelves lined the walls and were filled with strange things in test tubes and jars. Things floating in cloudy water, things that were green, yellow, gray, and hard to identify. There were other objects hanging from the ceiling on ropes and string—balls of stuff, like clay or plasticine and straw—the kind of raw materials Eric probably used in his "experiments." There were tools of all kinds, and mechanical objects like bicycle wheels and ancient-looking kitchen equipment lying around. There were pictures and drawings—detailed, spidery pen sketches—pinned to the walls and hanging from the large table Eric was sitting at. The drawings were of unusual machines and creatures, all no doubt the wonders of Eric's weird imagination. Although most of them had been crossed out, probably by Eric himself.

On his large desk were containers and more jars filled with liquids, powders, and an impressive collection of meteorites arranged according to size, from tiny to kind of enormous.

"I've told my mom I hate having strangers in the house," said Eric, taking off his goggles. "It's bad enough having that creep living here. I keep telling her there is something highly suspicious about him, but does she ever listen to what I think?"

"We're not strangers, we go to the same school," I said.

"You guys have never spoken more than two words to me."

"We know," said Madison. "And now I know why," she said under her breath. "But necessity calls for extreme measures."

"We came to see if you wanted to hang out with us for the summer—you know, the whole Summer Club thing," I said.

"Except we're Raintown Convicts now," added Madison.

"What's the difference?" asked Eric.

"The difference is we *are* the Convicts, it's our gang, our idea—not some stupid school thing," answered Sam, putting his hands in the back pockets of his jeans and making his tough-guy face.

Eric seemed to be calculating a long and complicated math equation in his head—at least, that's the kind of expression he had on his face.

"Thanks, but I kind of just want to be left alone," he said, returning to the thing he was busy lighting on fire. "I've got things I need to do."

"Like burning a piece of plasticine? Sounds really interesting," said Sam.

"Everything falls apart sooner or later, so I might as well get a head start," Eric said grouchily to himself.

Sam picked up what had once been an Action Man, which now resembled a monster alien with a melted face. "Come on, let's get out of here," he said, losing his patience and heading toward the door. "It's no big deal, Eric, we just came to see if you wanted to have some fun with, you know, some other human beings, instead of playing with deformed dolls or trying to blow yourself up all summer."

"Why me?" asked Eric. "Why would you guys want to hang out with me? I mean, is it because you've heard about my skills as a scientist and inventor? Because if you have, it's all lies. My mom likes to boast about how smart I am, but it's just so she can show off to her friends."

I couldn't see Sam's face, but I knew what he was doing. He was rolling his eyes to himself and thinking, *Here we go—another loser,* and *I'm not* that *desperate for company.*

But he turned around and said, "We think your skills—and *everybody's* got some skills—could be just what we're looking for."

Eric's chest seemed to puff out a little with the pride he felt for being asked to join the Raintown Convicts, and I smiled inside. That's one of the things I love about Sam—he's got everything against him, and yet he can still be big enough to make other people feel good.

CHAPTER 12

While Eric's mom decided which equipment he should take ("just in case") and made us all sit down for meatloaf and lemonade, Eric introduced us to Sigmund. Madison had said, "The girls at school say you've got a chameleon," so Eric went back upstairs to get him. We hadn't noticed him when we were in Eric's room because his cage was covered with books and stuff, and Sigmund was good at camouflage, making himself into a books-and-stuff kind of color.

"The best thing about Sigmund is his eyes. They can move independently in all directions—like two separate eyes," announced Eric, placing his pet on his shoulder. For a minute I wished I could do that—it sounded very useful. Sigmund focused his sleepy-looking outer eye on Madison, and she looked a little uncomfortable at being looked at like that.

"It's like he can read my thoughts."

"That's why Mom called him Sigmund," explained Eric.

"After Sigmund Freud, the psychoanalyst," said Eric's mom, wrapping some meatloaf in tinfoil.

"What's that? Some kind of mind reader?" asked Sam.

"You could say that. He was the guy who discovered

the subconscious—the part of our mind that has a life of its own."

"Mom . . . ," said Eric blackly.

"I know, I know, no teaching at home. Sorry, kids." She winked at us and put the leftover meatloaf in Eric's backpack.

Sigmund slid down Eric's arm and onto the counter.

"I tried feeding him different foods for a while to see if they made him change color, but it didn't make any difference. He only does it when he's scared or when he gets too hot or too cold." Eric patted Sigmund matter-of-factly on the head.

"Eric nearly killed poor Siggy. He gave him a whole bar of chocolate to eat and we had to take him to the vet's to get his stomach cleaned out," said Eric's mom.

"He changed color then—he turned completely white and his eyelids kept drooping shut like this." Eric demonstrated. "He hates it when I make loud noises—that's when he changes color most. I'll show you!"

But Eric's mom said, "Do I have to tell you again, Eric? Sigmund is a living creature. If you keep frightening him, we'll have to find him a new home."

Eric looked fed up and lifted Sigmund back onto his shoulder, where he sat for a moment, looking at us with one sad eye and then the other, before Eric took him back upstairs.

"Dinner's at seven, Eric, don't be late!" Eric's mom called after him, but he'd already raced back downstairs and was bundling us out the door.

We planned to head back to my place and were halfway

down Eric's street when we heard a muffled shout through the rain.

"Can I come?"

We turned around to find that the voice belonged to a little boy. He wasn't wearing a rain hat and his hair was filled with hundreds of silver raindrops. Jelly went over to sniff him, and the little boy smiled and stroked his damp head.

"That's Nelson—don't pay any attention to him," said Eric, "he's only seven."

"I may only be seven but I'm still a boy!" said Nelson.

"Where's your mom?" I asked.

"Working. My sister takes care of me in the summer—she's twelve!"

"He's Butterfly Williams's brother," said Eric reluctantly.

Madison frowned. "Her name wasn't on the list."

"We were going to go and stay with Dad, but then he got too busy," Nelson said helpfully, just as Butterfly came down the steps holding a big purple umbrella.

"Hi," she said shyly, twisting the end of one of her braids around her finger. They curved down either side of her head and stuck out at the back. "Come inside, Nelson, you're gonna catch cold."

"I'm playing with my new friends," he said, giving us the biggest smile I've ever seen.

Butterfly pulled her little brother underneath the umbrella. "How come you guys are here?" she asked.

Sam and I looked at each other. My face was saying, *She could hang out with us, too,* but Sam's face was saying, *No— we've got enough.*

"I love your umbrella!" I said. "Purple is my favorite color."

"Thanks. It was a gift." Butterfly smiled shyly.

"I have a purple bike—I painted it myself!" Sam looked at me strangely and I was suddenly embarrassed by my own enthusiasm.

"Hi, Butterfly!" said Eric, stepping out from behind us.

"Oh, hi, Eric," replied Butterfly, and it was clear to me they weren't exactly best buddies.

"We came over to see if Eric wanted to join our gang," I said.

"*I* had to do an initiation," said Madison proudly.

"What did you have to do?" asked Butterfly.

"Stand in the biggest, dirtiest puddle in my best pair of shoes!"

"Oh," said Butterfly, trying to look understanding, but mostly looking a bit confused. "That must have been hard."

"It was," said Madison. "But I feel like I'm a better person now."

"I want to do an initiation, too," said Eric.

"Me, too! Me, too!" shouted Nelson, jumping up and down in his galoshes underneath his sister's umbrella.

"How about you, Butterfly?" asked Sam, with a dark tone to his voice.

"Sure. I'll just go get my coat."

Nelson followed her inside, shouting, "I want to come, too! I'm coming, too!"

With Nelson leading the way, we walked in pairs up the sidewalk against the tide of rainwater, back toward Eric's house. All that was visible of Nelson was a pair of small red rubber boots under the giant purple umbrella, and those rubber boots were stomping their way happily through as many puddles as they could find.

"So who is that mean-looking Mr. Jeeks guy who lives in your house, Eric?" Sam asked bluntly.

"He rents the spare room, but he's hardly ever home. Mom says he only stays in town when he's got business."

Butterfly turned around. "Isn't it weird having someone you don't know living in your house?"

"Of course. Why do you think I lock my door?"

I scrunched up my nose. "He is kind of creepy."

"He makes my skin crawl," said Eric. "I think he's a vampire or something. Mom says the money helps. If she hadn't made Dad leave, she wouldn't need a tenant."

"What kind of business is he in?" I asked.

Sam said, "Yeah, why's he so pale? He looks like some kind of dead thing." And I looked at him, remembering *our* dead thing, *our* body. But Sam seemed to have forgotten about him.

Eric filled us in. "Mom says he's in the property business, but he goes out a lot at night. Like I said, I'm pretty sure he's a vampire."

"He looks like he doesn't get enough sunlight. I read in a magazine that you can get sick if you don't get enough sunlight," said Madison.

"Like us, you mean. We don't get any sunlight, either. We could get sick, we could get really, really sick." My voice struggled to hide my desperation. There are no days in

Elbow during the summer, just one long black night with the rain beating down hour after hour, day after day, week after week. Sometimes I think it's what hell must be like.

Just then a white station wagon with ELBOW COUNTY HOSPITAL written on the side screeched around the corner and pulled up outside Eric's house. A short bald man wearing pale green overalls got out, holding a heavy-looking yellow nylon bag, and Mr. Jeeks met him at the door. Jeeks cast his beady little eyes nervously about as he talked to the man, before accepting the bag from him. They seemed to be disagreeing about something. We could just make out the words.

". . . why Smytheson couldn't take it out—is this his idea of a joke?" Jeeks shouted angrily.

The bald guy shrugged. "I'm just carrying out orders, Mr. Jeeks . . ."

Mr. Jeeks looked with irritation at the bag and then watched the man in the green overalls get back into his car. For a moment Jeeks stood there, frustrated, like he'd been the victim of a prank. The bald man waved at Jeeks through the rain-streaked window before taking off with a big *slosh* into the sodden gloom.

I nudged Sam. "Did you see that?"

Sam nodded. We both looked over at Eric, who was oblivious. He was busy being interrogated by Madison.

"You *never* let her clean your room? You could have all kinds of microbes growing in there."

"That's the idea," said Eric, his eyes twinkling.

"Your mom seems like a nice person—I wouldn't have expected her to be so . . . normal," Madison continued.

"Well, she's not nice, OK, she just acts that way when people are around," barked Eric.

Standing on the dripping porch of Eric's house, Mr. Jeeks didn't notice the lady in the floral raincoat with the little book (in its own waterproof jacket) making her way down the street. Just as he turned to go inside, clutching his nylon bag, he was surprised to find that very lady holding his arm, smiling her sweet smile right in front of him.

"There's no need to suffer the damnation of this rainy hell—all the Lord asks is that you confess your sins and ask for forgiveness." The Bible lady was very insistent, taking one of Mr. Jeeks's hands and placing it on the little waterproof book, forcing him to reluctantly put his bag down on the front step.

As the lady talked, she smiled and embraced Mr. Jeeks. Mr. Jeeks looked more and more embarrassed to be handled so affectionately by a complete stranger. But I couldn't take my eyes off the nylon bag that sat fatly on the wet stone step. And then it happened. My pinkie finger started tingling. That tingling always spells bad news, but there's no point ignoring it. I just have to go with it. It's like a mosquito bite—you know you shouldn't scratch it but you always do.

Just then, Jellybean leaped forward. He snatched Jeeks's nylon bag between his teeth and ran down the street as fast as dog-lightning.

"Jelly!" yelled Sam.

It would have been kind of funny if it hadn't been for the vicious, hateful look that suddenly filled Mr. Jeeks's face.

"Get ready to run, you guys," I said to the others, who were now watching Sam whistling for Jelly to come back.

"Run!" I shouted, and we all ran, even Nelson, who thought it was a fun game.

Mr. Jeeks shoved the bewildered Bible lady out of the way and flew down the steps after us.

We were halfway up the steep street, with Jelly in the lead, followed by Sam and the rest of us, when I turned to see Jeeks catching up. His face was mean and sharp and his skinny body was cutting quickly through the rain. My finger wasn't tingling anymore, but my throat was dry and my heart was beating fast in my chest.

"Come on!" shouted Sam, grabbing the pole on the back of a passing streetcar. Butterfly lifted Nelson up and we ran faster until one by one we'd hauled ourselves on. The streetcar driver rang the bell and we were lifted quickly up the steep hill. We were taken up and up, farther and farther away from the pale figure of Mr. Jeeks, who stood defeated on the street below, the steam of his warm, angry breath rising in the cold watery air.

"Thanks a bunch, you guys!" said Eric, kicking the inside of the streetcar. "He lives in my house, remember. Now he's probably going to put something gelatinous in my bed."

"What's gelatinous?" asked Nelson.

"It means like Jell-O," Butterfly whispered back.

"Yuck!" said Nelson, obviously eager to join in the conversation.

"Don't worry," said Sam knowingly. "I'd say from the look of him, he's got some other stuff on his mind."

Eventually the streetcar turned and traveled its route back to my neighborhood. My house looked so lonely against the wet black sky, like the ghost of a house. I felt so sad for it, I wanted to put my arms around it and say, *It'll be OK.*

Jellybean, who amazingly was waiting for us on the doorstep, sat up as we arrived. The nylon bag with its tight little knot was sitting there right next to him.

"Good boy, Jelly!" said Sam, patting the dog's side proudly. "He came all the way here! Jelly always knows where to find me! I don't know how, but he does."

The others followed me inside and took off their rubber boots while I switched on all the lights, upstairs and downstairs. Then I turned on the TV.

"Cartoons!" Nelson jumped straight onto the couch.

I put Mr. Jeeks's bag down on the floor next to the couch and Jelly started sniffing at it like it was the yummiest thing he'd ever smelled. His tail was wagging so fast it was hitting Eric in the face.

"You stay away, Jelly! Go sit with Nelson," ordered Sam, throwing my raincoat on top of the smelly bag. Nelson happily welcomed Jelly's enormous body onto the couch next to him and Jelly rested his hairy chin on Nelson's knee.

I went into the kitchen to make everyone hot chocolate. I needed to open a new container of cocoa and it burst open, making a dusty chocolate cloud in the air before covering the kitchen floor. The powder made me sneeze. *I'll clean it up later,* I thought.

We were quietly sipping our chocolate when my pinkie finger started to buzz and twitch again, and I noticed that the yellow bag sitting on the linoleum floor under my rain-coat was starting to leak a thin, pale, pinky-brown juice. I felt a shiver run down my body like a million icy ants crawling all over me and I got that creepy feeling again, like someone was watching me. Sam's eyes seemed momentarily drawn to something in the kitchen, and that made all the hairs on my arms stand on end. I tried to shake off the feeling by rubbing my arms, then I took a big gulp of hot chocolate.

"You can't just steal things that belong to other people!" Madison said suddenly.

"It wasn't me, it was Jelly," said Sam, annoyed.

"Same thing," replied Madison. "If I get into any kind of trouble, I'm telling my parents it was you guys! Besides, that man was *horrible*—he was really scary, and did you see the way he pushed that poor lady?"

"She's right," sighed Butterfly. "We should probably give it back."

"Don't you want to know what's inside?" asked Eric.

"We can always give it back and say that it was an accident. If you give something back, it's not stealing," I said.

"Bea's right—we're not stealing, just borrowing." Sam shrugged. "Anyway, it was Jelly who took the bag—I didn't make him do it!"

Madison and Butterfly were watching Eric, who had a giant cocoa mustache across his top lip. They looked at each other and then back at Eric, and started giggling.

"What's so funny?" said Eric.

"Nothing," said Madison, which made her and Butterfly laugh even more.

"What?!" demanded Eric angrily, and they laughed until Butterfly had tears rolling down her cheeks.

"You have chocolate on your face," said Nelson, glancing over for the briefest moment before returning his attention to the cartoons.

Trying to stop herself from laughing, Butterfly got up to take the empty mugs into the kitchen. Eric wiped his mouth on his sleeve and scowled.

"So when do we get to do our initiations? I can tell Butterfly is dying to do hers."

"Maybe after Bea tells us what she thinks is in Mr. Jeeks's bag," said Sam, looking straight at me, like he wasn't my friend at all. "Come on, Bea, what do you think it is?" he insisted.

Madison and Eric looked at me for what seemed like forever.

"Why are you asking me?" I said.

Nelson was deep in the cheery world of cartoons; I wanted to be there with him.

"You knew there was something off about that bag before Jelly grabbed it. It was your pinkie finger, wasn't it?" Sam asked.

I nodded.

"Bea has this thing with her little finger," he explained to the others. "It's kind of a sign that something's not right. It's like one of those rods people use to find water, except her finger finds things that people don't want found."

"I don't know what's in the bag. But I know it's not going to be nice," I said, glancing over at it.

The others were all looking at the lump under my raincoat, too.

"She's right," said Eric. "I keep telling Mom that that guy is up to no good — maybe now we'll have some proof!"

Just then Butterfly came out of the kitchen, skidded on some of the liquid oozing onto the floor, and almost fell on top of Mr. Jeeks's bag. "Ughh! Well, whatever it is, it's making a puddle here and it stinks!"

Eric seized his chance. "That's your initiation, Butterfly: You've got to open that bag and take out what's inside!"

Nobody said anything.

"Hold on," protested Madison, "you're not an official Convict yet, either, you can't decide the rules!" But neither Sam nor I said anything.

Butterfly looked at us. "Should I?"

Sam and I looked at each other and then at Madison, and very slowly we all began to nod.

Butterfly rolled up her sleeves and, turning her face away because of the smell, carefully lifted off my raincoat to reveal the wet bag. "It smells really bad," she said again, "and it's really heavy."

Me, Sam, and Eric moved closer, and Madison turned away.

"I'm warning you, if it's really gross I'll throw up!" she said.

Butterfly and Eric started giggling because Madison really did look nauseous.

At this point Nelson began to find the cartoons a little less interesting.

"You watch the TV!" his big sister ordered.

Nelson's head turned toward the TV, but then his eyes drifted back to the dripping bag Butterfly was holding.

"I said watch the TV, Nelson, or you can go straight home!" She took the bag into the kitchen and we followed.

In the kitchen, the cocoa dust still covered the floor.

"What a mess," said Madison, joining us against her better judgment.

Butterfly was just about to open the dripping bag when I noticed the trail of footprints. All the way across the linoleum, through the chocolate powder.

I couldn't take my eyes off those footprints, and it was at that moment that I knew it was too late — something terrible had begun. It had started in my camera the night I took those photos, and now, no matter how much I wanted to leave, there was no going back.

The others noticed me staring.

"I was just in here a second ago, and those footprints weren't there," said Butterfly.

"I'll go and get a broom. All kinds of bacteria grow on food if you leave it lying around," said Madison.

And that made me yell. "No! Stop it! Who cares about a messy kitchen? We've got much more serious stuff to think about than bacteria. I knew it. I knew we shouldn't have gone to that old house."

The others all stopped what they were doing and looked at me.

"What house?" said Eric.

"The house with the murdered guy," Madison said slowly.

Butterfly suddenly looked very worried and her big dark

eyes traveled the length of her arms to the heavy, leaking bag in front of her.

"None of us is wearing any shoes. They can't be our footprints," said Madison.

"They're way too big, anyway. They're adult-size," added Sam.

"That's because they belong to an adult," I said. "They belong to the dead guy." I swallowed and looked around to see if he had appeared. As if acknowledging him would summon him. I was looking out for extrasmall things, like a breeze or a sound or the movement of something out of the corner of my eye. All I could see was Nelson, a cozy little figure on the couch, laughing along with the happy colors on the TV.

"What are you talking about, Bea?" asked Sam.

The fear that I had been hiding from Sam and from myself, the fear I'd been holding in since the night in the lonely, broken house, suddenly flooded out of me.

"They belong to *him*. The dead guy. The dead guy we saw in the house. The one I photographed! The man who was murdered!"

Everyone stiffened and seemed to hold their breath. And then I swear I saw something move quickly between us and Nelson. Something like a shadow. Normally I would have tried to persuade myself it was just a dark shape on my eyeball, like when you look at a lightbulb for too long, but I knew it wasn't.

"Did you see that?" asked Butterfly.

I looked at her and she could see that I had.

"I don't believe in ghosts!" Eric said. "There's a rational explanation for everything. Open the bag, Butterfly!"

"For your information, my grandma sees ghosts all the time. She talks to them and they talk back." Butterfly turned her attention back to the bag. She looked more than a little unwilling to open it, but put on a brave face so as not to give Eric the satisfaction. She undid the tight knot at the top with her nails and peeled the sides apart. Inside was another plastic bag and that, too, had a knot to untie. She pulled the wet, sticky nylon apart and the full smell hit her like a dense, invisible cloud. She dropped the bag, which hit the floor with a thick-sounding *splat*, and turned away as if she were going to be sick.

We held our hands over our faces and peered in.

"What is it?" asked Sam.

Butterfly pushed her way back between us and, holding her nose, said, "It looks like sausages. A whole lot of sausages."

"Jelly loves sausages," said Sam. Jellybean looked up at the sound of his name. "No wonder he grabbed the bag!"

Eric moved us out of the way to get a better look. "I know what that is. It's intestines. And they look long enough to be human."

"Human? Are you serious?!" Sam let out a kind of nervous laugh.

"He's making it up—right, Eric?" said Butterfly. She looked a bit pale.

Eric stood there with his hands on his hips. "Nope, I've seen them in Mom's biology book."

"That's . . . horrible!" I said, covering my face with my hand.

"Let Madison take a look!" said Sam, kicking the sloppy remains in her direction.

But Madison just screamed and ran toward the far wall. "I'm going to be sick!" she wailed.

"Cut it out, Sam—that's disgusting!" I said.

"Can I see?" chirped Nelson, who'd wandered into the kitchen.

"There's nothing to see, OK?" said his sister firmly, grabbing his shoulders and guiding him to the door.

"Then why's everybody screaming?" he said quietly.

Thinking nobody was watching, Jellybean crept curiously and silently toward the bag of leaky intestines.

"No! Jelly—go away!" ordered Sam, and Jellybean dropped his head in disappointment and joined Nelson back on the couch.

"I passed the test, right?" asked Butterfly.

"Definitely," I said, and Sam nodded. "I'd like to present you with this very special honorary stick of gum and welcome you to the Raintown Convicts." I peeled off the wrapper and handed Butterfly one of the bright orange pumpkin-flavored sticks.

Butterfly smiled a shy kind of smile and said, "Thanks, I accept."

Madison was still standing against the wall. "I could never have done that. Never ever. Do I get any points for not throwing up?"

CHAPTER 13

Madison volunteered to sweep up the chocolate on the floor, but not until Sam had taken the stinky bag of guts outside. I tried really hard not to think about it sitting there, that soggy bag of slimy gray sausages, on top of the week's garbage.

"What would a guy like that want with a bag of . . . intestines?" Butterfly found it hard to get the word out.

"Maybe he was going to make them into a stew and eat them," said Eric. "It wouldn't surprise me one bit."

"Uggh! Gross!" said Madison, holding her stomach and making a noise like she was being sick.

"That is disgusting," Butterfly said, with her face all scrunched up.

"I've read about these, like, underground societies that are into human sacrifice. It wouldn't surprise me if he was into that kind of stuff." The words tumbled out of Eric's mouth and his eyes were wide with excitement.

"Shut up, Eric, that's just stupid. Maybe people did that thousands of years ago. But people don't have to do that kind of thing anymore because they can see it on TV," said Madison in her superior voice.

"We have to give it back," I said.

"Or," added Madison, "we could tell him that Jellybean ate what was in the bag and that we never even saw what it was."

Butterfly shook her head in slow motion. "There is *no way* I'm touching that bag again."

"If he rips out guts, imagine what he'd do to us," Sam said.

Nelson was laughing at a cartoon where a little guy who looked like a rabbit kept bumping into trees.

"Bea? Those footprints in the cocoa, you said they were made by a ghost?" asked Butterfly.

Eric made his eyes big and starey, and raised his hands to the sides of his face, and wriggled his fingers around like worms. "The ghost of the murdered man . . . whoooooahhhh!"

"Shut up, Eric—it's not a joke!" I said.

"Whoooooahhh!" he moaned again.

"Oh, stop being so lame, Eric," said Madison.

I turned my back on Eric to face Butterfly and Madison. "You know that . . . shadow you saw earlier?" Butterfly nodded slowly. "I think it's . . . he's been in the house since I developed the film. It sounds really stupid, but I think he got here in my camera."

Madison and Butterfly both looked uncomfortable. Madison's eyes flicked around the room and stopped at the rain-beaded windows—blue-black squares of night—that revealed nothing of what was outside, but meant that inside we were lit up for anyone to see.

"I didn't want to tell you about what happened with those photos," I said to Sam.

"You told me there was nothing on that film," he said.

"I know. Because I wished I'd never taken those pictures."

I thought I better walk them through what happened, that way they'd see I wasn't making stuff up. "I'll show you," I said, and they followed me down to the darkroom—even Nelson. Butterfly was worried about leaving him alone.

Just as we got downstairs, Madison's face turned pale. "Remember how yesterday I thought someone was in the darkroom with you?" she asked, and I nodded. I had forgotten she had seen him.

Everybody fell quiet as I slowly pushed open the squeaky door. The others held back.

"Ladies first," Eric said to Madison.

"I thought you didn't believe in ghosts," said Sam.

"I don't," replied Eric.

I switched on the little ruby lamp and the others stepped cautiously into the room. "I left the camera here, see . . . ," I said as I slid the camera along the counter, back to where it had been. "And I didn't touch it, but the next time I came in, it was open, at the back here, where the film goes. But it started before that, when I took the shots in the old house. Something weird happened. I heard a noise and I felt the camera shake."

"Come on, Bea!" said Sam, trying to act tough, but I could tell it was making him nervous.

"Shut up—it's true!" I slammed my hand onto the counter. "Why would I make something like this up?"

"Then what happened?" asked Butterfly.

"The next day I developed the film." I showed them the

trays I had put the prints in: one, two, and three, in the right order. "I saw his face. The dead guy's face. The image was there."

"What's that got to do with a ghost?" said Eric impatiently.

"Well, the image disappeared. When I came back later, his face wasn't there anymore. It was there a couple of days ago, but now the sheets are blank."

Suddenly a loud *bang* came from upstairs. We froze. Jellybean, who was also upstairs, started barking furiously and wouldn't stop.

"What was that?" whispered Madison.

"It doesn't sound good, that's for sure," said Butterfly. Nelson clung to his sister.

"It's not Bertha—she's not due back yet," I whispered.

The *bang* came again, this time louder. Madison jumped. "This just gets worse and worse," she said, quietly but annoyed. "When I think that I could be out shopping instead!"

Jellybean's barking got louder and louder. We listened harder, but could only make out the distant sound of cartoons from the TV.

"Is it the ghost?" asked Butterfly. We waited silently, not daring to breathe in case it made a noise.

Then came footsteps. The slow, deliberate feet were moving around the outside of the house, and they were getting nearer. Nearer to the darkroom window at the back of the house, nearer to us. They stopped just outside the window, but the heavy shutter meant that whoever it was couldn't see inside.

Butterfly looked at Nelson and put her finger to her lips to tell him he had to be very quiet. We waited and the footsteps waited. Then we heard them turn on the gravel path and walk away.

We waited a minute or two more, straining our ears to be sure they were gone, and then burst out of the darkroom in a bundle.

"Where are you all going in such a hurry?" Mr. Jeeks, pale and sweaty and sneering, was looming over us. The footsteps we heard had been his—he must've broken in! "You know, you really shouldn't go taking things that don't belong to you. That can lead to all kinds of problems. Just give it back and I'll leave you kids alone."

Sam's eyes narrowed and he tried to run at Mr. Jeeks, but Jeeks grabbed his arm and twisted it behind his back. Sam's face distorted with the sudden pain.

"What did you do to Jelly?" Sam spat angrily.

"The dog's outside—he wasn't very friendly," sneered Jeeks.

Jellybean whimpered as he scratched on the blacked-out window of the darkroom.

"Jelly!" yelled Sam, and Jeeks twisted his arm harder.

"Let go of him!" I shouted.

"Not until you give me what I came for." Mr. Jeeks spoke in a slow, nasal voice. If a voice could be like slime, that's what his was like.

"Why don't you pick on someone your own size?" said Butterfly, moving in front of Nelson to protect him.

"We didn't do anything! Jellybean took the bag—we were

trying to get it back to you!" I insisted, standing right in front of Jeeks and looking into his pale, pink-rimmed eyes.

Jeeks wrenched Sam's arm farther still, making him groan. "Are you going to give it to me or am I going to have to break the kid's arm?"

"What in the world is going on down here?" came Bertha's no-nonsense voice as the wooden stairs creaked under her weight. With flared nostrils, her eyes flashing, and using her best long black umbrella, she started hitting and poking Mr. Jeeks in the side, on the head, in the stomach. She could move pretty fast when she wanted to. "You get yourself out of my house—you hear? Get out! Call the police, Bea. *Now*, Bea!"

I ran upstairs and grabbed the phone. I'd seen people on TV do it tons of times, but it felt strange to be doing it for real. In my panic, the lady on the phone had to ask me twice for my address. "Four forty-seven Prospect Rise," I said, slowly and clearly like you're supposed to.

Next thing I knew, Bertha was chasing Jeeks through the living room, still poking and hitting him, and just before he fell out of the front door she walloped him really hard on the head just for good measure. The rest of the Convicts were standing behind Bertha, half in shock, half trying not to laugh.

Mr. Jeeks didn't hang around. I'd like to think it was because of Bertha, but it was probably because he knew the police were coming. He ran as fast as he could, and the darkness swallowed him up in seconds. "If I catch you near my house again, I'll snip off the bits that make you a man!" Bertha yelled after him.

When the two policemen did show up, Bertha had to describe what the "intruder" looked like. She said he was, "you know, a nasty-looking type." We all had to tell them about how he broke in and threatened us. But we didn't tell them about the bag Jellybean stole, and we didn't tell them what was in it.

One of the policemen had blond hair and a bored expression, and the other one had red hair, a turned-up nose, and freckles. "We'll get right on it, ma'am," the blond one said. They seemed nice, but Sam didn't trust them, and followed them out when they left.

Sam and I watched from the doorstep, and just before they got into their car, we saw the red-haired one laugh and tear up the paper he'd just written everything down on, everything we'd said about Jeeks. The little white flecks blew around for a second but were quickly caught by the spiky fingers of the rain and pinned to the wet ground. They stuck fast and then drowned in the mud.

We stood together on the porch in silent shock as the police car tunneled away through the dirty rain.

Sam was frowning and looking intensely into the distance. "Either Jeeks is bribing the police or they're all looking out for each other—DW's right, nobody's safe in this town."

"But he broke into my house and beat up on you! And for what, a bag of old guts? *Somebody's* got to arrest him!"

Sam didn't understand any more than I did why those remains were so important to Jeeks, but he'd never trusted the police and now he knew he was right not to.

I needed to believe there were some good people out there

taking care of things, protecting people and the idea of right and wrong; but that idea was starting to dissolve along with the pieces of our report. I shivered, feeling the hollowness in my stomach grow. The rain seemed to taunt us as it hit our tired faces.

When I got back in the house I threw my arms around Bertha to give her a big hug, but she pushed me away, saying, "We need to have a talk, young lady . . . but right now I think everyone should get some rest."

Sam took the hint. "Night, Bertha," he said, like he was the same age as her, not a kid at all, and put on his raincoat before heading home.

"Wait for me!" Madison called after him. "Thank you so much for having me, Mrs. . . . ."

"Er . . . see you later, Bea," said Eric.

"Bye," said Butterfly.

Nelson smiled a wicked smile and, cupping his hands around his mouth, said very loudly, "I won't tell about the smelly bag!"

Bertha frowned and narrowed her eyes, trying to figure out what she had missed, and for a minute I thought that was it—she'd want to know what'd been going on and we'd have to tell her, and then we'd never know why Mr. Jeeks wanted those guts.

"You've been watching way too much TV, Nelson," said Butterfly, nudging him out.

I waited at the door for a moment as the faded colors of their slickers disappeared into the black haze of night rain. Then Bertha's yelling distracted me. "You could have been killed, Bea! How do you think that makes me feel? That is the *last* time I leave you alone in the house!" And she sounded like she really meant it.

Maybe she'll quit her job, I thought. *Maybe we could go to the zoo, Disneyland* (not that I really wanted to go to Disneyland), *the ice-cream parlor, even on vacation—away from the darkness and the rainy fingers.*

But the next morning at seven she set off for work, just like she always did. I could tell she felt bad because she made me an extra pancake and left me five dollars for candy.

CHAPTER 14

Mr. Jeeks had visited my dreams the night before. I kept seeing his sweaty face and pink eyes, and his clawlike hand reaching out to grab me. Sam's face kept appearing, too, all squashed up from the pain of Mr. Jeeks bending back his arm. And when I woke, again and again, I made sure that only my eyes peeped over my quilt in case the dead man's ghost came upstairs. I wanted to tell Bertha about the ghost and about the bag of guts (I couldn't help thinking about them slowly oozing all over the week's garbage), but I knew she wouldn't believe me. She never did. So what was the point? Adults only hear what they want to hear and that's whatever suits them. Sometimes I think that grown-ups are more scared than kids. They invent a world for themselves and if something doesn't fit they just pretend it's not there.

My dad wasn't like that, though—he always went looking for the stuff that was hidden. The stuff below the surface that people didn't know about, or didn't want to know.

Most days he would take pictures at his little run-down studio in town. People would come in for birthdays, weddings, and special occasions. They'd dress their fat, spoiled kids in bow ties and frilly dresses and make them smile so they could hang a pretty photo on their wall or send it to relatives overseas. "Bread and butter" is what Dad called it, taking those photos, but his real passion was telling stories. I could always tell when he'd gotten a story; there was something about his step and the way he held his camera, like there was something precious inside.

Sometimes I got to go with him, even if it was dangerous, which sometimes it was. That's one of the things he and Mom used to fight about. "Honey, she's just a little kid!" Mom would say, and I guess I might have looked little to her, but I've *never* felt little on the inside.

Dad would pull up somewhere mysterious and say, "Stay here, Bea. If anyone comes, duck under the seat." And I'd wait in the car while he crossed the street and knocked on a door.

There was one house in particular I remember seeing, just before my dad died. We were sitting in the bug-shaped car, hidden by Pinehills Forest, watching this gigantic palace. I just remember there were about a million windows catching the light of the moon. I can't be sure it wasn't a dream, because the place was so big and so eerie. Like nothing I'd ever seen before. And there was something different about my dad while he was watching that place. He said it reminded him of a house he'd seen in a movie—*Sunset Boulevard*, I think he said it was called. In it a crazy old lady, who used to be a famous movie star, has a funeral for her pet monkey, and later on she kills a writer who's supposed to be writing a story for her. Dad said it was like a horror story but that it was also real, and that one day I'd understand that sometimes real-life things can be worse than your worst nightmare. Sitting in the dark forest watching that house was the first and only time I ever saw my dad scared. Not just scared—quietly terrified.

And I thought my dad was the bravest, best dad in the world.

CHAPTER 15

Sigmund swiveled his bulbous eye away and blinked, as if he was bored by my company.

"I don't think Siggy likes me, Eric," I said.

"He *does* like you. But he's not a person, he's a reptile, and they're pretty simple. Just feed him a cricket and he'll be your best friend," said Eric.

I pulled a dead cricket from a box Eric kept on a shelf above Siggy's cage and dangled it in front of him. There was a pause and then his tongue flicked out to catch it. I squeaked, and Madison gave me a funny look. It was usually her, not me, who did the squeaking, but Siggy had caught me off guard.

Then Siggy and Jellybean checked each other out. They stared at each other for a whole ten minutes, but I don't think they spoke the same kind of language. Siggy must have gotten scared, because he turned orange, and Jellybean must not have liked orange things very much because he did a funny kind of sniff like something had gone up his nose, and then walked away with his tail tucked between his legs.

"Siggy turned orange!" I called to Eric, who spun around to have a look.

"Cool! He's never turned that color before! How did you do it?"

"It wasn't me, it was Jellybean," I said.

"Poor Siggy," cooed Madison, suddenly on the reptile's side.

Jellybean curled up in the corner with his head resting on his front paws, let out a bored sigh, and looked up at us with heavy eyes like his life wasn't worth living. Sam patted his head, and the next minute he rolled over for a tummy tickle. Sam bent down to give Jellybean's belly a quick, distracted rub, but he was more interested in the fat book on Eric's desk, the one Eric was leafing eagerly through. It was one of the books Eric's mom used in her classes. Eric's mom, who had asked us all to call her June, is a high school biology teacher.

We watched as Eric traced the squiggly shape of the intestine with his finger and read out loud from the book. *"The human small intestine is six meters or twenty feet long and four centimeters or one-point-five inches in diameter, and the large intestine is one-point-five meters or five feet long and six centimeters or two-point-five inches in diameter."* He looked up. "The ones we saw looked just like this picture. So they *were* human, just like I said."

"They sure didn't smell like anybody I've ever met!" said Butterfly, remembering her initiation.

Sam leaned on Eric's shoulder to get a closer look, and Madison leaned on Sam. Her face wrinkled up at the sight of the diagram. "I don't have those inside *me*, do I?"

I wasn't too sure I liked the idea, either, and noticed my

hand making its way to my stomach, as though it might be able to feel the lumpy snakelike organ within.

Eric laughed. "We've all got them! That's how we digest stuff."

"That is so horrible," Madison said, shaking her head. Then another thought crept across her face, one that was far worse. "We actually had somebody's . . . intestines in that bag. You guys, we, like, held them. They belonged to a real person . . . and that person must be dead."

The room fell quiet as we absorbed what Madison had just said.

"If we find out what Eric's creepy tenant was doing with them, maybe we'll figure out who they belong . . . I mean, *belonged* to," said Butterfly.

"He's not *my* tenant, he's my mom's. I told her she needs to check his references and stuff again, but she told me I was overreacting. If I'd told her about the intestines, she'd want to know why we've got them," said Eric.

"So, Eric, when are you going to do your initiation?" asked Butterfly, pulling a plate of rotting food out from underneath Eric's bed and pushing it right back again. Too late—Jelly's taste buds had been alerted. He followed the plate back under the bed, and although only his tail was visible, we all knew what he was doing by the licking and slurping noises.

"Well, I . . . uh . . . Sam and I were just discussing that earlier . . . weren't we, Sam?"

Sam looked confused for a minute and then quickly added, "Oh, sure we were. Eric said he's going to make something, like invent something for us, for the Raintown Convicts."

Eric looked like he'd been put on the spot. "But I don't know how to make anything," he said. "I mainly know how to burn stuff or blow stuff up. My dad keeps expecting me to discover something or invent something amazing, but I'm just not as smart as he is. Anyway, I don't see the point in making stuff. Things always fall apart sooner or later. I like to break things before they break on me. That way I'm in charge. I do know how to make some stuff, I guess, weird things, but I've never made anything that works."

"You don't have to make it right this minute," I offered.

"You can do it, Eric, you've just got to apply yourself," said Madison, and Eric looked a little more confident, but not much.

"What if I can't make anything useful?" asked Eric.

"Then you can't be a Convict," said Sam.

"But it could take me a long time," Eric said.

"We've got weeks," said Sam.

"But I had to do mine right away," protested Butterfly.

"You didn't *have* to do it!" I said.

"I had to do something really gross and Eric gets to invent something, which is fun!" Butterfly said sulkily.

"I've never made anything that works in my life, so my task is a lot harder." There was a pause, then Eric added, "But I still get to hang out with you guys in the meantime, right?"

We all looked at each other. Butterfly didn't look too happy, but the rest of us said, "Sure."

"But just to make it fair," said Sam, "you can't *call* yourself a Raintown Convict yet."

"And you don't get your honorary stick of gum," said Madison. This seemed to please Butterfly.

"OK," said Eric, and with that he accepted the challenge.

"Where's Nelson today? It's cute how he looks up to you," Madison said wistfully to Butterfly.

"Mom took him to get a haircut. I'm glad to get a day without him. Sometimes it's a real drag having a kid brother."

"It's a drag having an older one!" said Sam, and I knew that was an understatement. Sometimes Sam slept in the tree house because he didn't want to go home and see his brother. Sam was always having to keep quiet about things his brother did—once his brother even made Sam keep watch while he and his gang held up a gas station.

"Hey, Eric, you said Jeeks was out, right?" asked Madison.

"Yeah, so?" said Eric.

"We should really look around his room," said Madison sweetly.

"She's right. There's a whole lot of guts sitting in Bea's garbage can—maybe we'll find out why that Jeeks guy had them," Sam said with a shrug.

"So what are we waiting for?" Madison demanded, folding her arms.

She stood there a moment and then walked toward the door, unbolted it, and marched down the stairs.

"Wait! You can't go in there. Girls are so much trouble!" said Eric, looking at Butterfly briefly before running down the stairs after Madison. We all followed, down two floors, making a sound on the stairs like bombs dropping, and piled up on the landing outside Mr. Jeeks's room. Madison was standing there, waiting, her arms folded across her chest. The door was already open.

The heavy curtains were drawn, so the room was dark. It smelled damp and musty.

"What if he comes back and finds us in here?" I whispered. "One of us should listen for the front door."

"I'll do it," said Eric reluctantly. "But don't touch anything, OK?" He went back to stand on the landing, but he kept peering in. "And don't move any of his stuff—or he'll know we were here!"

The room was L-shaped, and Madison was standing around the corner in the long part of the L. The room was very neat, but it had Mr. Jeeks's odor all over it. It was a kind of bitter, man-type smell. There was a hint of aftershave, but mostly it just smelled like a horrible man's smell. Horrible because *he* was horrible. Mom used to say you could tell a lot about somebody by how they smell—she said their smell never lies. You can pretend to be nice, but if you're not, your smell gives you away. She said you should always trust your nose.

Trying to stop Jellybean from sniffing excitedly around the room and knocking the furniture over with his enthusiastic tail-wagging, Sam accidentally kicked a pair of Jeeks's shoes, shiny brown oxfords, which had been placed carefully next to each other by his desk. He quickly moved them back to where they'd been.

"Hey, you guys, take a look at this!" Sam picked up a black-and-white photograph in a silver frame, and me,

Madison, and Butterfly squashed up next to him to take a look.

The photo showed Mr. Jeeks, looking a little younger and a little less mean. He was standing next to an older man who looked a lot like him, and next to him was another, even older man with a white beard.

"They're all dressed like old-fashioned . . . butlers or something," Madison observed.

The photo showed them standing in front of a very large, historic-looking doorway.

"That house looks so familiar—it's like I've been there," I said, trying to place it.

"I think that's his dad and grandpa," said Sam.

"They don't look very friendly. Look how he's turning away from his dad—like he's scared of him," added Madison.

"I'd be scared, too—they all look like vampires!" And Butterfly shuddered at the thought of those three deathly-white men in black suits, three generations of Jeeks, who could quite easily be drinkers of human blood.

Apart from some shirts hanging in the closet, a couple of other pairs of shoes, and a bottle of aftershave, the room was empty. There was an ashtray on Jeeks's desk, but it was clean, which showed he didn't smoke. Inside the ashtray was a box of matches that said **GRAND HOTEL** on it, and a laminated card with a passport-type photo of Jeeks on it that said **Mount Abora, Staff Pass**. I picked them up and showed them to Sam.

Sam shrugged. "The Grand Hotel is that fancy place in town—you have to be a member to go there."

"Yeah, I know; my dad took me there once on my birthday."

The memory flashed into my mind. I remembered a room full of leather armchairs and snooty waiters wearing black suits and bow ties. I remembered my dad showing me a big hall where people came for weddings and parties. He said people danced there all night long. It was my eighth birthday when my dad took me there for afternoon tea. It was the year before he died. I didn't like the way the waiters looked at us, but Dad didn't seem to mind. He said to me, "Always remember, Bea, you're as good as anybody else—don't let anyone make you feel any other way." Then he checked that the waiter wasn't looking and poured some whiskey from his silver hip flask into his tea.

I put the box of matches back into Jeeks's ashtray and felt the smooth plastic of the staff pass and its cold metal clip between my fingers. "What about this?"

"Mount Abora? Never heard of it. Must be the place he works," said Sam.

"But Mom said he works in real estate," said Eric from the doorway, wearing a confused expression. "Are you guys going to be much longer?"

I put the pass back into the ashtray, trying to remember exactly which way it had been facing.

Madison was standing around the corner beside Mr. Jeeks's carefully made bed. I imagined Eric's mom saying, "Such a nice man . . . and he always makes his bed."

"Take a look at this," said Madison, holding a book that had been on Jeeks's bedside table. She read the title out loud. *"Aztec Sacrifice and Other Death Rituals."*

A shudder traveled down my spine.

"Not what I'd consider bedtime reading," said Madison in a voice that made me think that was probably how her dad spoke.

"What is it?" asked Eric excitedly, coming into the room and reading over Madison's shoulder. "What did I tell you? He's in some weird human sacrifice cult. It's just like I said!"

"That guy scares me. I don't want him coming after us again," said Butterfly.

"Shhhhh!" spat Sam suddenly, his eyes catching the rain-light as he pointed at the window. He signaled for Eric to switch off the light, and then we heard it: through the sounds of the watery fingers on the window and the trash cans below, a haunting song, slowly being whistled. It was coming from the alleyway between the houses. Sam and I looked at each other.

"I know that tune," whispered Butterfly. "It's a hymn we used to sing. It's called . . . 'Leaning on the Everlasting Arms.'"

"It's really creepy," whined Madison.

"Shhhhh!" hissed Sam angrily.

Then the tune stopped and the shadow of the man in the wide-brimmed hat loomed across the foggy window. For a second nobody moved.

"Jeeks? Psssst! Jeeks!" came the shadow man's voice. "It's me, Smytheson . . . Jeeks! Come on, surely you know my sense of humor by now. There's no need to move back to Abora."

Stepping back from the window, Sam knocked into the picture frame and it crashed to the floor. My heart jumped and my breathing started to sound too loud. I backed toward the wall.

"Jeeks? Are you in there?" The man waited a moment, and then his shadow vanished, just like it had from DW's window.

Something was digging into my head. I reached up and felt the sharp corner of another picture frame, and, as I turned around, came face-to-face with a large picture of a skull with turquoise-and-black jewels for eyes.

"Great!" puffed Eric. "As though one creep wasn't enough—now we've got two of them snooping around!"

Butterfly looked at me and then at Sam. "So what else are you guys not telling us?" she asked, her hands on her hips.

"What are you talking about?" answered Sam, suddenly defensive.

"You guys know who that was!" said Butterfly.

"No, we don't!" I insisted.

"Like you didn't know there was a dead body in that old house? Like you didn't know you had some kind of spirit living in your camera?" Madison's voice was mocking and her eyes were mean.

"We're all in this together now, right?" asked Butterfly.

Sam picked up the frame he'd knocked over and put it back on the shelf.

"We didn't know his name until just now, but we have seen him a couple of times. Outside DW's and then on the street. He was telling some guys to take down posters."

"What kind of posters?" asked Eric.

"For a missing kid."

"His name was . . . Luke Green," I said, picturing the dripping poster in my mind.

"When Jeeks was given the bag of guts, I think I heard him say the name Smytheson—do you remember?" I asked.

Sam thought for a moment. "Yeah, I think you're right. Does that mean the guy with the hat's got something to do with the bag?" We looked at each other, and I think we were both thinking the same thing—that this was starting to get even more weird.

"Somebody's coming!" shouted Eric suddenly, and we pushed each other out of the room as fast as we could. We jumped the steps up to Eric's room and waited on the landing. We could hear each other breathing for a moment, and then the key turning in the front door, followed by footsteps heading inside. There was a pause and then Mr. Jeeks's door creaked open.

"We didn't shut the door!" I whispered.

"Madison? Exactly how did you get into his room again?" asked Eric as quietly as he could.

Madison raised an eyebrow. "I picked the lock."

We all looked at her and she looked back as if to say, *What's the big deal?*

Then the footsteps came back into the hall and we froze.

"Eric, how many times have I told you to stay out of Mr. Jeeks's room?" came June's annoyed voice.

"Sorry, Mom," called Eric, as we all let out a sigh of relief.

CHAPTER 16

"You said the book was about Aztec sacrifice, right? Those intestines were an offering to the gods!" said Eric enthusiastically as we trudged up one of the steepest hills in Elbow on our way to the library. The rest of us weren't so excited by the idea of human sacrifice. What if Jeeks and his cult decided they needed a nice juicy heart or an arm or a leg—what would stop him from taking one of ours? It was too awful to think about.

"How could he do that—take somebody's insides out, just to say, *Gee, thanks, Mr. Aztec God, I had a nice day!* or *Can I have a new car for Christmas?* or something?" Butterfly was really upset by this idea, and kind of angry. She didn't want anybody taking parts of her without a very good reason, and neither did I.

There was a big mat in the entrance of the library and we all stood there for a while to let it absorb the rain dripping off us. "No dogs allowed!" said a crabby-looking librarian. So Sam had to take Jellybean back outside. I wanted to look up what the Aztecs used to do, but offered to stay outside with Sam and Jelly.

I watched through the heavy open door as the others went up the big wide steps to the next floor and disappeared, Eric leading the way.

Sam was soaked through. His rain gear wasn't that good—it was really old and he needed an upgrade. He crouched down to hug Jellybean, who was still dripping and panting warm air into the cold.

"I'm sorry I took you to that house, to see the dead guy," he said, looking up at me, embarrassed.

"What do you mean?"

"Well, you haven't taken any pictures since then. Sorry about your camera. I know you wanted to enter that competition."

"It *is* kind of hard taking pictures when there's something . . . living inside it."

"I guess I just didn't want you to leave," said Sam, looking down at his wet sneakers.

I wanted to say, "thanks" and "that's OK," but I didn't. I felt kind of shy. Sam and me were good friends, but we didn't tell each other stuff like that. I knew he liked me, but I'd never heard him say it, even in a roundabout way.

I looked up to the second floor of the library and caught a glimpse of Eric pointing out a page and Madison shrinking back with her hand over her mouth. But just then a car drove past, distracting me.

As the car *sloosh*ed by the library, its headlights shone on the metal plaque right by where we were standing. I'd never really noticed, but the library was called the Feverspeare

Library. It was written on the sign in big curly letters, and then in smaller letters below it was: *In honor of Agnes Celeste Feverspeare.*

"Hey!" I said to Sam, pointing at the sign. "Feverspeare is the name of the family who owned St. Agnes's."

"So?" said Sam.

"Well, it's like they owned the whole town or something. I mean when you see their name like that. Weird name."

"Sounds British," said Sam.

"Maybe St. Agnes's is named after the same lady?" I wondered.

The others came out to meet us. "Aztecs offered all kinds of body parts to their gods and even did something disgusting called bloodletting, where they made themselves bleed. The more important you were, the more blood you had to offer," said Madison.

Butterfly shook her head in disbelief. "And the richer and more powerful you were, the more you got to kill people, to ask God to keep you alive longer."

"Jeeks *did* have a book about it, so there's no doubt that's what the guts were for," said Eric.

"That doesn't *prove* anything," said Madison smugly.

"I just noticed this sign," I said, pointing to the plaque on the wall. "Feverspeare is the same family that owned St. Agnes's before it was a hospital."

The others didn't look too interested, now that their minds were racing with human sacrifice, bloodletting, and cannibalism, but Butterfly said as we set off, "Agnes Feverspeare was a famous writer. They named the library after her. Mom told me. I have to hang out here a lot because Mom is studying to be a lawyer."

We didn't talk much on the way to Mitzy's Diner, mainly because of the noise of the rain hitting the sidewalk, and having to keep our heads down to stop the raindrops from getting into our eyes and mouths. Some days it came down so hard, it felt like it was cutting right into your skin. But we were also quiet because there seemed to be so much going on. I think we were all trying to figure it all out—except for Eric, who was trying to figure out what kind of thing he was going to invent. He had a little notebook he kept drawing things in, and when he wasn't drawing, he was imagining. When Eric was "imagining," he focused on something in the distance, his eyes kind of glazed over, and all these little wrinkles formed on his brow. Sometimes I could have sworn I could almost see smoke coming out of his ears from all the effort.

With each squelchy step I took, the more I felt the cold rainwater creep into my boots, and the more I wished Sam had never taken me to that house. All I wanted to do was get a great picture of a happy family so that I could at least try to win that competition. But here I was, still under the spell of the angry fingers in the sodden gloom of Elbow.

I imagined myself getting on the plane, getting one of those special airplane meals on its own little tray, and looking out the window at that sunlit landscape of frothy white clouds. I'd never been on a plane, but I imagined myself on one then, heading to Florida along a soft, fluffy road of gold-and-silver-tipped clouds, taking me all the way to the land of sunshine, while a kind airline attendant smiled and offered me drinks in little cans.

But questions started to creep across that cozy image in my head like bugs. And the more they crawled, the more I began to itch to get those questions answered. There was the question of the dead guy. Why was he dead and how did he get inside my camera? Why was his ghost in my house? What did he want? Then there was that nasty, shadowy man who was as sinister as a ghost, except that he was very much alive. What did he say his name was—Smytheson? And what was the deal with him and Mr. Jeeks and those intestines? Could he really belong to some strange cult that made human sacrifices? It all seemed so crazy.

CHAPTER 17

Mitzy's is the place me and Sam go for burgers, ice cream, and sodas. It's in the middle of the new part of town, not far from the mall. It's almost halfway between Sam's house and mine. We usually sit in one of the little red booths. That way we can have a private conversation without any grown-ups overhearing.

Mitzy is the lady who owns the place. She must be seventy years old, but she still dyes her hair blond and wears frosted eye shadow and draws a wiggly black line on her eyelids. She wears turquoise glasses with diamonds all around the edges, and a little pink scarf around her neck. She looks a little unusual, but you can just tell she's a nice person by how she smiles and winks at you, like you're sharing a secret. I often go to the diner by myself, and Mitzy keeps an eye out for me. She knows how much I like Devil Tongue Relish, because if I'm having a cheeseburger she puts a jar down next to me and I don't even have to ask.

One of the customers frowned and another man muttered something angry as Jellybean led us inside, all of us drenched from the rain. "There are no dogs allowed in here!" said the pinched-faced man at the counter.

"This is my burger joint, Norman, and this dog happens to be a good friend of mine!" Mitzy winked at us. She liked Jellybean and always let him sit under the table in our booth. Sometimes she'd give him a leftover burger or steak. "I'll be over in just a minute, Miss Klednik!"

We emptied all our change onto the pale blue plastic table, but it wasn't much. Then we all looked at Madison because we knew her family was rich, but she just said, "Sorry. My parents are really strict about money." We only had a couple of dollars between us and we were hungry. That's another thing about the rain. It makes you really, really hungry.

I looked at the plastic menu and thought about splitting a cheeseburger five ways—six if you counted Jelly.

Mitzy was waiting with her pad. "What'll it be, kids?" I noticed her short-sleeved lilac shirtdress with her name stitched on the collar in script writing. Mitzy's dress seemed to change color every time I saw her.

"Don't you have a pink dress just like that?" I asked, and Madison and Eric looked at me, embarrassed.

"Sure do, and a red one, orange, yellow, green, light blue, dark blue, and this one. One for every day of the week. Saves me washing all the time."

Then Mitzy noticed the coins on the table and looked back at our faces. There was a pause, and she smiled and scraped each nickel and dime off the table and said, "I'm guessing five cheeseburgers, fries, and shakes?" And we all nodded hard.

"Thanks, Mitzy!" I said.

"Thanks, Mitzy!" the others said.

"And don't forget . . . ," I called after her.

"I know, Devil Tongue Relish!" she called back. "Do I ever forget the Devil Tongue Relish?"

"All we need to do is find out where they hold the meetings," said Eric enthusiastically.

"Who?" said Butterfly.

"Mr. Jeeks and the other people in the club. The human sacrifice club," he said cheerfully. I turned around to see if anybody had heard, and a man in the booth behind us looked away.

"Shhh!" hissed Madison, leaning in. "Do you want everyone to know?"

Eric was not always aware of how loud he was. "One of us could try and join," he whispered loudly.

"How would we do that, stupid, we're only kids!" said Butterfly.

"I could wear a disguise, like a mustache or something," offered Eric.

"Then you'd be a kid with a mustache."

Eric looked upset. "I'm only trying to help. I don't hear you having any ideas."

Butterfly just stared at him with her big eyes and flared her nostrils a bit. I was starting to realize that she did that sometimes when she was annoyed with someone.

"And why do we want to go to that meeting, exactly?" Madison asked.

There was a moment of silence. "Don't you want to know why Jeeks wanted a bunch of guts so bad he came after us to get them back?" said Sam.

"Not really," said Butterfly. "He nearly ripped your arm off."

"There must be something special about those guts," said Sam slowly, his eyes twinkling.

"I think so, too—I think they belonged to somebody important," I said.

"So that's settled, we'll go to Jeeks's club so we can try and find out who they belonged to." Eric smiled a satisfied smile. What was it with boys and disgusting stuff?

As Mitzy walked toward us with our food on a tray, she was stopped by a lady even older than Mitzy herself, sitting with her back to us in one of the booths. Wispy bits of her silver hair had come loose from her bun, giving her a kind of halo under the bright lights of the diner. She put her frail, brown-speckled hand on Mitzy's, and Mitzy leaned in so the lady could whisper a question in her ear. Something told me the question was about us, because as the silver-haired lady whispered, Mitzy nodded and then looked up at me, the way people can't help doing when the other person is talking about you.

I was trying to figure out if I knew the old lady when she turned around and looked right at me. She looked at me the way somebody does when they've heard things about you. I tried to think whether I'd upset her or bumped into her or something, but I couldn't remember anything like that. She had sparkly, fierce green eyes that seemed surprisingly awake for an old person, and she quickly took in the details of my face before turning away again.

"Do you know her?" asked Sam, and I shook my head.

"Get down!" hissed Sam suddenly. "Get under the table! It's him—it's Jeeks!"

Jellybean let out a whimper as we crashed down onto the floor next to him.

We saw Mitzy's feet, no doubt with our tray of burgers carried above them, travel in our direction and stop.

"Where?" whispered Eric.

"Shhhhh—he's here!" mouthed Sam.

I imagined Jeeks's pointed face and darting eyes searching for us, first through the window and now around the inside of the diner.

"Anything I can help you with, mister?" we heard Mitzy say.

"Seen any kids?" came Jeeks's sneering voice.

"Nope. It's summer vacation, remember?" she replied matter-of-factly, walking our burgers back behind the counter.

We waited, not making a sound, all squashed up together under that Formica table, and then we saw Jeeks's feet walk past and stop for what seemed like the longest time ever, before walking away and out of the diner.

"Creepy man!" tutted Mitzy. "It's OK, kids, he's gone now," she announced, sounding relieved, as she threw a concerned look over at the lady with the silver hair.

We climbed slowly back up onto the seats and Mitzy arrived at our table, delivering five cheeseburgers, five orders of fries, and five milk shakes. "You kids aren't in any trouble now, are you?" she said, looking at us over her glasses.

"Course not." Sam smiled.

"Well, I don't want to know about it, OK?" she said, winking at us and then heading back to the customers sitting at the bar.

"That was pretty close," said Butterfly, letting out a deep sigh of relief. We nodded, and I noticed how everybody slouched low in the booth after that, just in case he came back.

Nobody said anything for a few minutes because our mouths were full of delicious, juicy hot food. Except Sam did say, after I'd scooped so much Devil Tongue Relish onto my burger that there was more relish than burger, "I don't know how you can eat that stuff."

But I didn't care. It just tasted better than ever, all tangy and tingly on my tongue, and I liked the way it made my eyes water and my nose run.

We'd almost finished eating and I'd given Jellybean half my burger and a tomato (which he was eating off my rubber boot) when Madison said, "My dad is in a secret club. He's away till Labor Day, but when he's home he goes to meetings at the Grand Hotel. He's got this funny little briefcase he takes with him; I know where he hides it." Then she took another bite of cheeseburger before putting it on her plate and covering it with her napkin, even though there was still half a cheeseburger left.

"Well, why didn't you say so before?" said Eric, amazed.

"Are you serious?" asked Sam, doing one of his half smiles.

"Yeah," said Madison. "And that's how I know all that human sacrifice stuff is just stupid, just made-up lies."

"But how do you know for sure? Maybe your dad is one of them and you don't even know," said Eric.

Madison narrowed her eyes at him. "How would you know *anything* about my dad? You've never even *seen* yours!"

Eric looked upset by this, even though he was trying hard not to show it.

Madison composed herself with an angelic smile like the ones you see on holiday postcards. "If you all come over to my house, I promise to show you where my dad hides his secret briefcase."

The food had hit my stomach. It was warming me up and slowing me down from the inside, and I could tell it was the same for the others, because their cheeks were all rosy and suddenly nobody was in any hurry to get going. I put my hand around the Devil Tongue Relish jar and started fiddling with the label, picking at the curling edges. There was the ad for the photo competition, with its orange sunset.

"Why don't you enter that competition, Bea?" said Butterfly, all excited, and Sam looked at me to see how I'd react. I shrugged my shoulders and smiled.

"I wanted to, but it's too late now."

That thought sank down heavily in my stomach and sat there like a stone, next to my cheeseburger. Now I had no chance of getting out of here for the summer. Maybe not ever. I looked over at Mitzy, and as much as I liked her, I thought of myself growing old in Elbow and was filled with horror. For a second I couldn't breathe — it was like all those rainy fingers had come at me at once and tightly gripped every cell of my body.

"Let's see," said Butterfly, picking up the jar. "You still have two weeks!"

"But I can't take pictures. Every time I go near my camera it moves. It's the dead guy—he thinks it's where he lives now."

Eric laughed and some food flew out of his mouth. I stared at him, hard, and he stopped.

A thought traveled across Butterfly's face. "What if . . . ? No, that's stupid."

"What?" I asked.

"Yes, do tell," said Madison in a sort of snooty tone.

"It's nothing," said Butterfly, shaking her head.

"Just tell us already," said Sam.

"I was thinking that if we found out why the ghost is in your camera, we could send him away and then you could use your camera again."

Butterfly put the jar of relish back on the table. I thought for a moment, picked it up, and began turning the picture of the beach and its setting sun around and around on the table. I hoped that way the others wouldn't notice what I was thinking—about how I wished I wasn't there with them, but in Florida.

Then I noticed something. I'd never really looked at a Herman's pickle jar from underneath before, but there was a date saying *Best before* . . . and then some initials, *MHF Inc.*

The initials were raised on the glass and I ran my fingers over them.

"What's up?" asked Sam.

"Do you remember DW saying something about letters on stuff? Like on your cola bottle, remember?"

"Kind of," said Sam.

At that moment my pinkie finger started tingling and buzzing and I knew it had to be about something important. The others stared as my finger moved all on its own, twitching and pointing.

"That's totally weird!" said Madison.

"What is it, Bea?" asked Sam again.

"I don't know, but it's something about those letters, *MHF Inc.* Like DW was saying, why would a Herman's pickle jar have those letters? Herman's pickles are Herman's pickles, right?"

The others looked at me like I was nuts.

Sam took a final gulp of his milk shake, tipping it up to suck out every last drop through his straw. "Look!" said Butterfly, pointing to the bottom of Sam's raised glass. On its base were the very same initials, *MHF,* only this time it said ***MHF Glassware Inc.***

Sam reached behind him into the neighboring booth and picked up the milk carton on the table. "Same thing," he said, showing us the bottom of the carton. Even though it said ***Joe's Dairy***, the hidden initials said ***MHF Dairies Inc.***

Butterfly got up and picked up a Pinehills Honey jar from the counter and showed us the very same initials again: ***MHF Foodstuffs Inc.***

"So what?" said Madison. "It's obvious all those products are owned by the same company. What's so interesting about that?"

"But what about *Joe* from Joe's Dairy and *Herman* from Herman's Pickles?" I asked.

"People like to buy things from regular people, people they can relate to," Sam explained.

"They're probably just pretend names." Madison shrugged.

"But Herman's Pickles are real, and Herman is real! It even says on the jar that Herman mixes his own relishes, the way his grandma taught him. I used to think about Herman's grandma teaching little Herman which ingredients to use, and then letting him stir it all up with a big wooden spoon."

"Maybe he did that at first, but now another company does it instead. It would be kind of hard to make so much relish in such a small kitchen," said Butterfly.

But I wasn't listening. "Anyway, Lola's real—I saw her! When I went to visit my mom. Maybe all those people went crazy or something else happened to them. Herman, Lola, Bert from Bert's Big Cheesies, the Pinehills Honey guy—"

And that's when it happened. The jar of Devil Tongue Relish, the one I'd just put down on the table, moved. It moved right across the Formica table. The exact same way my camera moved across the counter in the darkroom. The pickle jar moved smoothly and quickly right in front of our eyes. Then it started spinning, slowly at first, then faster and faster until it fell over, making a loud hollow ringing sound. Slowly it rotated to a stop.

The other people in the diner gave us a mean look.

We all just stared at the jar, our mouths hanging open and, in Eric's case, with half a French fry dangling from his lower lip.

"I didn't touch it! You all saw. Now do you believe me?"

We were relieved when Mitzy came to clear our plates. She eyed the sideways relish jar, but all she asked was, "How were the cheeseburgers?" Nobody spoke. Madison looked like she was going to burst into tears, Eric's teeth were chattering, even Sam looked pale. As Mitzy turned to walk away with a tray full of our dirty dishes, she said over her shoulder, "You kids look like you've seen a ghost."

CHAPTER 18

We were standing outside the diner under Butterfly's purple umbrella.

"How exactly do we make friends with a ghost so we can ask him to leave your camera?" said Madison, opening her eyes wide and smiling a fake smile.

"My grandma sees people's dead relatives all the time," said Butterfly.

Madison looked at Butterfly and said, "Does she wear gold hoops in her ears and dress like a Gypsy?" Butterfly narrowed her eyes at Madison, but she also looked hurt.

Just then the bell on the diner door rang as the silver-haired lady who had stared at me stepped out. "You take care, Mom!" Mitzy yelled after her, and the lady threw her a look like a thunderbolt.

"I've managed this long—I think I can manage a little longer!" she shot back.

Then the silver-haired lady walked up to me and, pressing something into my hand, said, "Are you Bea? Bea Klednik?" I nodded. She was wearing one of those clear plastic raincoats that made her look like an astronaut or a boil-in-the-bag dinner, but there was something about her that scared me.

Something powerful, something witchy. Her green eyes sparkled. "I didn't want to interrupt your meal, and besides, you never know who's listening. Make sure you stay out of that man's way, all right? There are some people you don't want to get on the wrong side of." Suddenly, real fear appeared on her face, and she looked around suspiciously, quickly searching the shadows before continuing. "I knew your father. He was a very brave man. If you ever want to talk, you can call me." And with that she turned and was gone.

"That was strange," said Madison.

I unfolded my hand to find a little rectangular card there. It said: *Elenor Bailey, Journalist.* I put it in the back pocket of my jeans and watched her translucent raincoat light up under each streetlamp as she walked into the misty distance.

Then a thought came into my mind: *Journalists know things, all kinds of things.*

"Wait! Stop!" I called after her. I was about to call again when she turned slowly and waited for me to catch up. The others dragged reluctantly after me.

"My dad left me his camera. I've taken lots of photos with it before, but recently something happened to it. This might sound strange, but . . . I think it's haunted. And weird things have been happening, like things moving on their own, and footprints . . ."

Elenor Bailey didn't look the least bit surprised. "My dear, this whole place is a ghost town, why shouldn't you have one in your camera?"

"Well, here's the thing: I'd really rather not have him there," I replied, "because I need my camera to take pictures for a competition."

She looked not just at me, but inside me, the way only certain people can. Then she said, very slowly and deliberately, "Everything's got to start somewhere. This is a very old town, full of old stories. Go back to the beginning, where it all started, to the origin of things. And see what follows from there. If you're interested in ghosts, try the old railroad station." And with that she pulled her hood farther over her face, disappearing into it like a tortoise. "Don't forget to get in touch if you want to talk about your dad," she said, with only her nose visible (and a droplet on its end that any second now was going to need a Kleenex). She strode off through the heavy rain.

"What did she say?" said Sam, all tense. Sometimes Sam gets this hunted look, like people were plotting against him or something. I guess if you have a family like his it makes sense.

"She said we should go to the old railroad station. Though I don't see what an old railroad's got to do with the ghost in my camera. I didn't even know there *was* a railroad."

Butterfly was suddenly excited. "I know where it is—my grandpa used to take me there, before he died." She twisted one of her braids around her finger. "He told me the railroad station was built in the 1800s, when all the people who came looking for gold had opened shops and saloons and wanted to move their families here. It's really weird because you can buy streetcar tickets inside, but no train tickets. It's a strange kind of place—only people who are passing through town go there, by accident, usually."

"If I'd known I was going to get a history lesson today, I would have brought my pen," said Madison with a roll of her eyes.

Eric stepped forward. "Do you have a problem with Butterfly?"

"No, just with long, boring lectures."

"We know how hard it is for you to be a nice person, so maybe you could just try keeping your mouth shut." Eric stood there, and then nervously pushed his glasses up his nose.

"Like, when did she hire you to be her bodyguard?"

"Cut it out, you guys!" I yelled. "Butterfly, tell me about the railroad station."

Butterfly began again. "There are a whole lot of pigeons inside. They hang around way up high by the pretty windows. It looks like the inside of a church, almost."

"Wow, that is *so* interesting!" said Madison.

"Shut up, Madison—what have you got, smart-aleck disease?" said Sam.

Ignoring the two squabbling Convicts, Butterfly took a deep breath. "There's this old train. It's a couple of miles from the station. Grandpa told me it was heading into Elbow, but it never got here, and it's been stranded out there ever since."

"That sounds awesome. I want to see it!" said Eric, and Butterfly smiled shyly.

"Why don't we just go back to my house? I'll get Maria to make us some gourmet hot chocolate and I can show you my dad's secret suitcase." Madison smiled smugly.

"Hands up for the abandoned train?" said Sam, and I raised my hand. So did Eric and Butterfly and, finally, Sam.

"Fine, be like that. See if I care," said Madison sulkily.

CHAPTER 19

The next day had arrived, but it was still as dark as night. We walked along the old wooden railroad track in a line, the gravel crunching under our rubber boots in a strange out-of-sync rhythm. The rain beat down hard on the ground and on the trees in the forest on either side of us, enclosing us in a dark tunnel. We'd already trekked way out of town, farther than any of us had ever been on our own, and the rusty iron rails led the way into the misty blackness ahead.

Luckily Eric, who always packed supplies, had his big flashlight with him and was shining it so we could make out the track a couple of feet in front of us. In the yellow beam, we could see just how many raindrops there were and how fast they were coming down, like a million tiny silver daggers flying at the light. We held our faces down under our rain hoods so as not to get splashed in our eyes.

Every so often, Eric would get bored of holding the flashlight straight in front and would wave it in big circles like he was a lighthouse or a searchlight looking for prisoners. Then, aiming it low and behind us, the shaft of light from the flashlight found a whole army of snails traveling along one of the tracks, followed by Sam's sneaker coming down and squishing them one by one. "Another one bites the dust! . . . That was a good one! . . ." Sam was shouting like a sports commentator.

"Sam loves to step on snails. He likes the noise it makes," I explained.

"I can understand that," said Eric.

Madison squirmed. "That's horrible!" she gurgled, so I continued.

"It's true, isn't it?" I asked.

Sam nodded, quietly proud.

"He likes nothing better than finding a really big snail to pop under his shoe," I continued. "The louder the crunch and bigger the splat, the better!"

"Uggghhh! Shut up!" said Madison, holding her hands over her ears.

The rain didn't seem to bother Sam or Jellybean. Both of them would get wetter and wetter over the day and they'd just absorb it like it was their natural state. The rest of us seemed to be at war with the rain most of the time, struggling against it, trying to keep it off our bodies and out of our minds.

Jellybean had been following the snail action and was sniffing curiously at the squashed bits of slime and shell Sam was creating along the metal rail, but when he stuck his tongue out to taste one, Sam pushed him away, saying, "Jellybean, no! That's gross."

Sam stopped popping snails for the day, just to stop Jellybean from eating them.

"This is a really long way to go for a piece of scrap metal," whined Madison, flapping her arms by her sides to show how fed up she was.

"Nobody asked you to come," said Butterfly. It was a long way from the station and it was getting darker and darker. I had no idea how long we'd been walking or how long it would take us to get back.

"If it was easy to find, everybody would want to go there," said Eric, holding the flashlight under his chin so he looked like a character from a horror movie.

"It shouldn't be too much farther," Butterfly said, hoping we didn't want to give up and go home. Just then something flashed past the beam of Eric's light on the track in front of us.

Madison screamed. "What was that?!"

"It was probably just a fox or a small coyote," Eric said.

"They don't attack people, do they?" said Madison with a tremble in her voice.

"Only if they talk too much," said Butterfly. "Keep quiet, or you might disturb other animals."

We trudged on along the abandoned railroad track. Although none of us said anything, our breathing got a little bit shallower and we all felt a little bit more jittery. Madison jumped at any unfamiliar noise that stood out from the muffling sound of the rain, which made us all twitchy. Not being able to hear very well meant we had to concentrate, and when you're looking or listening for trouble, you usually find it.

"There it is!" said Butterfly at last, and Eric shone his flashlight at the carcass of the abandoned train. The cars were pretty rusty and the red, blue, and gold paint was peeling. It looked like a rare animal that had wandered out of the forest and died a long time ago. It was just a skeleton now and the colorful skin that had kept it intact was also finally starting to shed. There was graffiti on one of the cars. One of the words read **LOONATIK** in big bright letters that were all round and squeezed together.

"This is the coolest place," Eric declared.

Jellybean barked suddenly. "What's up, boy?" asked Sam. We thought we heard something. There was a rustling noise and then the sound of something—or someone—running. Bare feet running on the wet ground. Then a kind of whistling cry swept around us, moving the furious raindrops with it.

"Did you hear that?" asked Madison with a quiver in her voice.

"It was just the wind," I said hopefully, as the pinkie finger on my left hand began tingling.

Madison was looking around anxiously, searching the darkness. "It sounded like a woman crying," she said.

"Don't worry," said Butterfly. "Nobody would be crazy enough to hang around out here in the rain."

I shivered, not knowing if it was the noise or the train making my finger buzz. "What's inside?" I asked.

"Let's take a look," said Butterfly, grabbing Eric's flashlight as we climbed up the metal steps. It felt just like we were getting on the train to go on a trip.

Once we were inside, Eric sat down and started to unpack his stuff. He lit a candle and dripped wax on a table so he could stand the candle up, and then did the same with another.

Butterfly aimed the flashlight around the car. Inside it was as though time had stood still. There were proper seats and luggage racks and tables. Sam sat down and put his feet up on the opposite seat. Jellybean jumped up. Sitting next to Sam, his big, shaggy, dirty white body looked almost like that of a very hairy fellow passenger.

"What did you bring to eat?" Sam asked as Eric began laying out the food his mother had prepared for him.

"And why do you always take food everywhere?" Madison added, sitting down next to Eric.

"Mom packs me something even if I just go to the store. I think she feels guilty for ruining my life," he said, taking off his glasses and wiping the rain from his face.

Butterfly rummaged in Eric's backpack, pulled out a half-empty jar of Devil Tongue Relish, and put it down on the tabletop. "I brought this from the diner. I thought it might help us get in touch with the ghost again."

"Remind me *why* we'd want to do that," Madison said.

"So we can tell it to go away, so that Bea can have her camera back, remember?"

"Good thinking," said Sam, winking at Butterfly before picking up one of Eric's limp sandwiches.

"Surely you're not going to eat that? It's soaking wet!" said Madison. Sam smiled and stuffed the sandwich into his mouth, followed by a handful of Big Cheesies.

"Baloney-and-banana sandwiches?" Sam attempted to say,

trying to guess the contents of his mouth, but it came out more like, "Balunneynbabanasnadiches?"

Eric filled his mouth with Big Cheesies and then forced a damp sandwich in, too. He and Sam smiled at each other, their cheeks swollen with pink and yellow and brown mush as they chewed in the most obvious way they could while Madison said "Ugghh!" and "Gross!" Then Sam opened his mouth and stuck out his tongue to show Madison what a wet baloney-and-banana sandwich looked like from the inside.

While the boys were eating, Butterfly led the way, and I followed her along the train from one car to the next. "This must be where all the rich people sat," I said as I slid the glass door to one side. There were even purple velvety curtains on the sliding doors and windows, and little lamps with green lampshades. I closed the door and lay down on one of the benches. Butterfly put the flashlight on the floor so it lit up the domed ceiling of the carriage, and lay down on the other bench so we were both looking up at the ceiling.

"It's quite homey in here," I said, happy to be out of the rain. "I wonder who was the last person to sit in here and where they went." I watched the rain make silver streams down the outside of the long rectangular window. "If the trains were still running, it would be much easier to get out of this place. I wonder why this one stopped right here."

"Grandpa used to say it was a mystery," said Butterfly, her dark eyes sparkling.

Suddenly we heard a loud thud on the side of the train and Madison screamed a few cars away. Me and Butterfly ran through the train to find the others all agitated, trying to see out of the windows into the darkness.

"What was that?" I whispered, my heart thumping in my chest. We were stuck out in the middle of nowhere in an abandoned train and it would probably take us the rest of the night to get back.

Jellybean pricked up his ears and barked loudly. Sam tried to stop him. "Quiet!" he said, gently holding his muzzle.

There was another thud on the side of the train.

"I really want to go home now," Madison said, starting to cry. We all just stood there and waited. "What if Mr. Jeeks followed us out here?"

"Nobody followed us," said Sam. "We would have heard them."

But Eric liked to point out facts even if they made people uncomfortable. "The rain can stop you from hearing things. You know how hard it is to have a conversation outside, even if you're standing right next to someone."

He discovered a light switch, and the little lamps on the walls crackled and came to life. "They must run on a battery," he said. Having the lights on made us feel a little better, even though it meant we were more visible to whatever was outside, and they were less visible to us.

Another thud on the side of the car made it shake. Jellybean started barking again and wouldn't stop. We all just waited. Madison was sitting on the floor, holding her knees to her chest, rocking back and forth, and sobbing silently to herself.

"I'm going outside," Sam said at last. "Come on, Jelly." Sam looked at Eric for a second, but Eric avoided his eyes.

"I would come, too, but somebody needs to look after the girls — right?"

Eric wanted us to agree with him, but we didn't say anything.

We watched Sam and Jellybean walk down the length of the train car, and heard Sam twist the metal latch to open the squeaky door. For a second we heard the roar of the rain as they stepped down onto the track. The door slammed behind them and the rain was quieter again. There was silence inside for a few minutes. Butterfly, Eric, and me looked at each other and Madison sobbed, "We're going to die. I just know it. We're going to die."

Then came the loudest thud yet and the train car jerked and rattled. We could hear Jellybean barking outside.

Suddenly a face appeared at the window and we all screamed. A man squashed his face against the window, made a nasty expression, and yelled like a crazed animal. His eyes were crossed and his tongue was out. Me, Eric, and Butterfly grabbed each other and held on tight. Madison was still on the floor, her eyes closed. *He's some madman who escaped from St. Agnes's,* was the first thought that flashed into my mind. *There's no telling what he'll do. There are no rules with crazy people.* I tried to push that voice out of my head, but it persisted. *He'll slit your throats and think it's the funniest thing he's ever seen!*

Just then something snapped in Eric and he lost it. Filled with rage, he suddenly let out a roar and ran at the window, whooping and growling like a lunatic warrior, pressing his face and body against the window at the man. I got the feeling Eric had been angry for a while, and now he was getting a chance to let it out. For a second me and Butterfly felt like we didn't know what was the worse deal, being trapped in an abandoned train car with Eric—who must have been nuts all along—or having the madman waiting for us outside in the pouring rain. But then the expression on the face of the guy outside changed. First he looked a little taken aback, even a little afraid, but then he looked really furious, and raised his fist and thumped the window where Eric's face was. That made Eric roar even louder. He flashed his eyes and showed his teeth like a dog with rabies.

"Stop it, Eric!" said Madison. "What are you trying to do? You're making him mad!" But suddenly the man was gone.

I was waiting for the crazy man to burst into the car and kill us all when we heard laughing outside. It was cruel, mocking laughter. There were men's voices, and then another big thud against the car. Then I recognized one of the laughs. I heard Jellybean let out a little yelp and Sam say, "Just leave us alone!" before Sam, followed by his brother, Jed, and two of his crew, tumbled into the car.

"Well, isn't this cozy?" sneered Jed.

"What do you want?" I demanded, trying to sound tough.

"I like a girl who gets right to the point," he said in a creepy way, and his friends laughed. "Don't worry, we're not going to hurt you—much. We just want the ring back."

"What ring? What are you talking about?" asked Sam, shaking his head.

"You know better than to play dumb, right, bro?"

"I don't know what you're talking about," insisted Sam.

I was finding it hard to breathe, and could taste something bitter in my mouth. "He's right. We don't have a ring," I said, trying to stay calm.

For a minute I thought Jed was going to leave us alone, because his face changed and he even looked like a nice guy for a second or two. He smiled at Sam and nodded slowly as he walked toward him, and for some reason I thought he was going to give him a hug. "Why do you always have to make things so difficult for yourself?" Jed said, and then hit Sam hard across the back of the head. Jellybean snarled at him, baring his teeth. "What ya gonna do, mutt?" Jed said as he kicked Jellybean. The dog squealed.

Sam's body reacted before he could think, and his voice changed. If there's anyone Sam cares about more than anything in the world, more than himself, even, it's Jellybean.

"Don't touch him!" shouted Sam as he clenched his hand into a tight fist and, raising it fast through the air, punched his brother, who was more than twice his size, hard in the stomach.

The guy who'd been at the window grabbed Sam and kneed him in the chest. Sam buckled over and made a sound like being sick. He must have hit his nose as he fell, because a streak of bright red blood was trickling down into his mouth. I don't know what came over me, but I ran at that man and started whaling on him. I threw my fists and elbows at his stomach, sides, and chest, and when he tried to grab my wrists I bit hard into the taut, veiny skin of his arms. I could taste sweat and then the sharpness of blood.

"Arrrggh!" he roared angrily, pulling his arm back as though he'd been burned. Seeing the bite, he shoved me hard and I fell against the ice-cold window of the car before his friend grabbed me.

Jellybean was barking and barking. Suddenly Butterfly launched herself onto the man who had grabbed me, and was hitting his head, scratching his face, and pulling his ears. He was holding me with one tattooed arm and waving the other in the air, trying to get Butterfly off him. But she held on tight. As he spun around, the man let me go and I hit the ground. He slammed Butterfly back against the wall while Sam's brother grabbed her legs and pulled her off. The other guy — the one who'd been at the window, the one who I'd bitten — looked at Eric, who was hiding behind one of the high-backed benches.

"Hey, four-eyes, don't be shy. You gonna let the girls fight for you?"

Eric was sweating and his glasses had steamed up. Jed and his two goons edged forward. "Not so tough now, are you?" said the guy Eric had roared at. Eric took off his glasses and squinted. He could probably only see three blurry shapes in front of him. From his face it seemed like he wanted to cry — not just like he was scared but as if a part of him felt sad, and lost, like there was nobody in the world who understood him. He was trying very hard to stay calm, but I could see the tears building up behind his eyes. He was shaking as he dug his hand deep into his pocket and pulled out something that he grasped tightly in his fist. Then he narrowed his eyes to focus on the blur nearest to him and hurled the meteorite through the air. The stone made a faint whistling sound as it flew swiftly through the car. It made a loud, hollow *thuck* as it hit the crazy guy right in the eye.

"What the—?" said the man, momentarily confused, before screaming and yowling with pain.

Jed and the other guy left him there, both of his hands grabbing his eye as he screamed and howled. With a dead look on their faces, they edged slowly toward me, Eric, Butterfly, and Madison.

Sam was still hunched over in the corner where he had landed. He looked dazed, but he'd gotten into a sitting position, using the wall to push himself up. Jellybean was whining and licking the side of his face. Wiping his bloody nose on the back of his hand, Sam tried to focus his gaze.

As Jed and the guy with the tattoos came toward us, I felt my stomach sink. I felt sick and my skin felt hot and cold, hot and cold. The guy with the tattoos pulled out a knife and it caught the light, making a silver streak shimmer on the ceiling of the train car.

"We asked you nicely," Jed said.

Just then I noticed the jar of relish on the table farther down the car, where we'd been sitting. I watched as it began to move all on its own, just the way it did in the diner, the same way my camera moved in the darkroom. It slid toward us and then flipped right over, rolled off the top of the table, and smashed into pieces on the floor, spilling the remaining relish in a gooey *splat*. The noise distracted the guy with the knife for a moment, and I watched the blade's reflection flicker across the train car as he turned to look. But he didn't see anything. Some people never notice things. They don't notice things that are like giant flashing neon signs, let alone the small, unusual things that you can only see out of the corner of your eye.

Butterfly and I looked at each other when we saw the muddy footsteps appear, one after the other, right along the length of the train car, coming toward us. This time Jed turned around, but he only saw his brother slumped in the corner. He didn't notice Jellybean sniffing the air, or his fur standing up all over, the same way people get goose bumps. The lights on the walls buzzed and flickered off and on under their little lampshades.

But Jed and his friend did take notice, finally, when the knife Jed's friend was holding lifted out of his hand and flew all the way through the car and out through a window at the other end, to the sound of tinkling glass. The two of them were frozen to the spot when the luggage rack was pulled from the wall with a sound of ripping metal. As the first half wrenched itself off and then the second, they just stared. When it had freed itself, it soared at Jed's friend and whacked him across the head, throwing him to the other side of the train. He groaned once and, raising his head, slowly realized it was too heavy and dropped it again.

Jed's eyes were wide with fear and his face was so pale it was almost blue. It looked like he didn't know whether to run or to cry or to curl up into a ball and hide, 'cause all he did was kind of twitch in an odd sort of way like a drunk trying to remember how to get home.

But it only took the sound of the first screws coming loose on another luggage rack to snap him out of it and send him running for his life. He leaped through the train and out into the night. He started running as soon as he hit the gravel and I bet he didn't stop running till he was home. (We found out later from Sam that he'd gone straight to St. Agnes's and begged to be admitted. He stayed that night and the whole of the next day, before they decided there were patients more in need of help and told him they wanted his room.)

Madison had a strange expression on her face as she looked out the window. She seemed to be in a kind of trance; she looked half frightened and half sad. Then we realized she wasn't looking *out* the window but *at* the window, and on the steamed-up surface was the dead guy's face. He looked just the way he had floating in that pool in the decaying house. He had one eye missing and his skin was pale, but his other eye was open and it just looked so sad.

We all saw him. Me, Butterfly, Eric, and, through the gaps in the benches, even Sam. It was one of those special moments when we were united by something unique, an experience only we shared. We'd all been aware of his ghost in one way or another, but had been too scared to agree he was real. Now, here he really was, and we weren't afraid because we were all seeing him at the same time.

His damaged face was pale and hazy on the train car window, but somehow he didn't look scary, either, not like the way I'd seen him in my dreams and in the photos I'd taken. I realized then that he hadn't been trying to scare us at all. We'd just been frightened by the idea of him, by the idea of a dead person haunting us. But in a way he wasn't really dead at all. He was very much alive and he had protected us tonight, maybe even saved our lives.

Jed's crazy friend with the bleeding eye helped the one with the tattoos off the train. They didn't look like they were too psyched about hanging around once they had seen what our ghost was capable of, or maybe it was just that once Jed wasn't there for them to impress, there was no point, anyway. Sam told me later that the crazy friend nearly lost his eye and had to wear a patch for six weeks. He also said all three were too embarrassed to see each other, because if they did they'd have to admit they were beaten up by a bunch of twelve-year-old kids and a kindhearted ghost.

CHAPTER 20

In the morning, we met at Madison's place. Eric was the last to arrive, and when I looked out the window to see if he was coming, he was just slooshing the water on the sidewalk with his rubber boots, like he was trying to hurry it on its way.

"Do you think he's OK?" asked Madison. "He's not going to freak out again and throw stuff, is he?"

"He's OK. Mom said his parents broke up a couple of months ago," said Butterfly, "except they didn't even tell him. His dad works away from home on oil rigs—he's an engineer, I think. Anyway, he was away a lot, but one day Eric's mom stopped letting him come home at all. She just changed the locks and took in a tenant—Mr. Jeeks. So you can kind of see why Eric's a bit mad."

"What's up, guys?" said Eric, smiling an awkward half smile as he wandered through the door. I think it was the first time I'd seen him smile, and I realized then that he liked hanging out with us, even if we had gotten into a sticky situation at the old railroad.

"Did you give your brother his ring back?" I asked Sam, who threw me a mean-eyed look.

"I never took his ring. I didn't know what ring he was talking about." None of us said anything and Sam looked hurt. "Why does nobody trust me?" He punched his fist against the wall, making his knuckles crunch. The sound made my stomach feel like it'd been pierced by something sharp. And I felt terrible that I'd asked him, like I'd let him down by thinking he must have taken it.

"Why did he come after us, then?" asked Madison.

"How am I supposed to know? Just 'cause he's my brother? He must have gotten the wrong idea about something."

"We believe you—let's go up to my room now, OK?" said Madison.

The Latina maid was vacuuming the hallway. She waved at us and shouted "Hi!" above the roar of the dust-sucking machine.

While Butterfly took in the scale of the place, with its hallways and rooms disappearing off into the distance, Eric was more interested in the vacuum cleaner. He sat down next to it and did a quick sketch in his notebook. Madison's maid didn't look too pleased at first, but agreed to let Eric dissect the machine if he finished vacuuming the hall. He said, "Thanks, uh . . ."

"Maria-Elena," offered the maid.

"Thanks, Maria-Elena," said Eric.

Meanwhile, Maria-Elena found something else to beautify: Jellybean. She took the bedraggled Jelly, who was now a dripping dark gray with a gasoline-matted underside, by the collar. For a minute Jelly looked pleadingly at Sam, whose expression seemed to say, *Go ahead.* Maria-Elena smiled, like she was going to get to do something she enjoyed for a change, and led Jelly up the stairs to the master bedroom, where the biggest bathtub was.

We sat in Madison's room for a while, because Maria-Elena was in her parents' bedroom, which is where Madison said we needed to go to get her dad's secret briefcase. Sam put on the radio and lay down on Madison's bed with his arms behind his head and let out a kind of an *Aaahhhhh* sound, like he'd never felt such a soft bed. Madison didn't seem to mind that his jeans were covered in mud and that he was pretty much soaked through everywhere else.

"If you're wet you can borrow some of my dad's clothes, if you want; he's got lots," offered Madison.

"OK," said Sam.

"You've got such a pretty house. I like your room a lot," said Butterfly.

"Thanks," said Madison, sounding kind of bored as she moved her hand lightly over the dainty objects on her dressing table. She picked up a handheld mirror with an ornate handle and held it up, but she didn't look at her own face — she held it to one side. I saw her watching Sam as he lay on her bed. Then she saw my reflection watching her and moved the mirror away. She flopped backward in her chair, throwing her head back dramatically, and stared at the reflections her cut-glass perfume bottles, jewelry boxes, and mirrors were making on the ceiling.

Sam had his eyes closed like he was taking a nap, but Butterfly looked at me with an expression of mild horror and, shaking her head, whispered, "She is such a drama queen."

"I know," I agreed.

I could tell Butterfly didn't like Madison too much. Madison did things just to get attention, whereas it always seemed to me that Butterfly worked hard at school, trained hard in her gymnastics club, and no doubt was helpful at home. But I bet it was all just taken for granted. I wondered if she ever wished she were more of a show-off, but I guess she just wasn't wired that way.

We could hear Maria-Elena talking to Jellybean in Spanish, trying to give him a bubble bath in Madison's parents' bathtub. *"Muy bonito,"* we heard her say, just as Eric came back in, looking pleased with himself. He'd finished the vacuuming and drawn a few ideas in his notebook. I guess he liked having a goal, even if he wasn't entirely sure what that goal was. I think it made him feel like he mattered.

"Let's see what you drew?" asked Sam.

"No, it's just rough ideas," said Eric.

"Got to be good if it was worth doing the vacuuming!"

"What's in this box?" asked Butterfly, pulling a battered black metal trunk from under Madison's bed.

"Don't touch that! It's private!" screeched Madison, jumping up and pushing the box back under the bed.

"Sorry!" said Butterfly.

"Some things are just private!" said Madison again.

"I said I was sorry," offered Butterfly.

We could hear the sound of a hair dryer whirring to a stop. A few seconds later Jellybean burst through the door looking like a different dog—he was fluffy and white and had a pink bow keeping the hair out of his eyes. Maria-Elena smiled shyly, petted him, and skipped off down the corridor, humming a tune to herself.

"Jelly, you look gorgeous!" cooed Madison.

"What did she do to you, buddy?" said Sam, looking like he'd eaten something that tasted bad. But Jelly looked happy enough, wagging his tail, his pink tongue hanging out of one side of his mouth like it did when he was having fun. He lay down on Madison's pristine sheepskin rug and fell asleep.

"We can get my dad's briefcase now," said Madison, getting up and looking at Sam. "And I can get you those dry clothes."

I suddenly had a feeling of panic, a kind of restless feeling like we were wasting time, like there were really important things to find out, and here we were playing dress-up in Madison's fancy house. "I don't know about this secret society stuff, you guys. I think we should find out who the dead guy is and what he's trying to tell us! I think we're wasting time. It just feels kind of urgent. I feel sorry for the dead guy—he seems so lonely and lost. It's like he needs our help to understand what happened to him."

Just then the song on the radio blurred to a loud crackle and wouldn't stop buzzing. "See what I mean?" I said.

"Maybe the reception's just weak for that station," said Eric, turning the dial to another one. But I knew he was wrong. A song sang out for a couple of seconds and then that loud buzz of electrical interference took over again.

I talked right in the direction of the radio then—I didn't care. "I know you're trying to tell us something. I don't know what it is but I promise we're going to find out!" As soon as

I'd said it, the crackling stopped and the song came back on. The others just looked at me like I was scary or crazy or both.

Me, Eric, and Butterfly sat on Madison's parents' bed while she decided which of her dad's sweaters went best with Sam's eyes. I saw something different in Sam then, something I hadn't ever seen before. He looked sort of shy and gooey and pleased with himself. *Barf!* I thought. *I think I'm going to throw up. Why is Sam acting like this?*

Madison decided that a turquoise sweater looked best on Sam because of his coloring, which she remembered from a particularly good magazine article was "cool and bright," which meant that "jewel" colors suited him best and showed off his bright blue eyes. They decided against putting Sam in a pair of her dad's pants because they were way too big and made him look really funny. Me and Butterfly and Eric laughed a lot longer than we needed to at those clownlike trousers on Sam, because of how he and Madison were making us wait.

"I know he keeps the briefcase up here," said Madison, standing on a chair with gold legs and reaching up to open two little doors above the closet.

"Do you want me to help?" asked Sam, and I rolled my eyes. What had gotten into him?

Madison moved some ski equipment out of the way, took down the little brown leather case, and put it on the bed. We all huddled around it. The small briefcase had a gold symbol on the lid—it looked like one of those metal things we used in school for drawing circles, a compass, with its two sides pulled apart—and inside were the initials *HA*.

"Ha! Ha!" said Eric, smiling at his own joke.

"Those are my dad's initials: Howard Anderson," said Madison.

Underneath the symbol with the initials were the words **Grand Lodge, Grand Hotel, Elbow.**

"He goes once a month. To the Grand Hotel. Nobody knows what he does there. He's not even supposed to tell my stepmom. No women are allowed," explained Madison.

She clicked open the case and we all watched as Madison lifted out a little book with dates written in it of all the past meetings, a pair of strange-looking red gauntlet gloves with a bright blue trim, and a long, silky red cloak with the same blue trim. The book, the gloves, and the cloak all had stitched in heavy gold thread the symbol of an eye inside a triangle, with beams coming from the eye like rays of sunshine.

"This stuff is like the clothes a priest or somebody would wear," said Butterfly.

"We have to get into one of those meetings. We have to see if they make a sacrifice, and then we have to stop them!" said Eric.

"I don't want to mess with anyone who takes out people's body parts," said Sam.

"I told you, they don't do that kind of stuff—that's just rumors," protested Madison.

"But how do you know?" insisted Eric. "How well do you *really* know Daddy?" he said with a spiteful tone to his voice.

Madison was silent while the weight of the question hit her, and as it did, she looked as though the air were squeezing out of her lungs. Perhaps Eric was right—maybe Madison didn't know her dad at all. For that matter, maybe she didn't know her mom or her stepmom, either. The way the color drained from Madison's face made me think her dad could have all kinds of secrets, including what he did during his visits to the Grand Hotel.

"When is the next meeting?" asked Butterfly.

"My stepmom writes it on the calendar in the kitchen," replied Madison quietly as she arranged all the contents of the briefcase back the way they'd been and tucked the case back in the cupboard above the closet, behind the ski equipment.

We stood in the kitchen while Madison ran her fingers across the squares that made up the month of July on the calendar. They had a picture by a French painter above them. Sam opened the double-wide fridge and looked in awe at all the fresh food. "Here's the next one," said Madison, pointing to her stepmother's writing, which said *Boys' Night — Howard.* "It's crossed out. They must have forgotten they were going away."

I couldn't figure it out—Madison and her stepmom knew about these secret meetings, but they didn't seem to want to know what they were about.

"It's not till the end of next week," I said.

"That's OK," said Eric. "It gives us time to figure out how to get in there."

As we left Madison's mansion, she waved to us from the porch. She was this tiny little figure leaning on a white pillar, the kind you see in pictures of Greek temples. Her porch had its own roof and was probably half the size of most people's houses. I thought about camping on that porch. If anything happened to our house or Bertha left, that would be an option. But then I thought about Madison and her family going in and out past my campsite every day, and I changed my mind.

Madison was still watching Sam, all gooey-eyed, and he turned and waved at her twice after we'd all said good-bye. Butterfly and Eric had curfews and had to get back, so they walked together toward their street, which wasn't too far from Madison's place, and me and Sam continued on downhill.

"We could hang out and watch cartoons at your place?" Sam asked as we got nearer to my street. I pretended not to hear him, which was easy with the rain coming down all around. "Should we head over to your house?" he said again.

"I've got some stuff I want to do," I said.

"Oh, OK," he said. "See ya." He kind of balanced on his heels as he turned back to face me to wave. I could just see Madison's dad's sweater peeking out from under the collar of his coat. And Madison was right—it did show off the color of his eyes. I hadn't really noticed them before. They were the color of the ocean in my travel brochures, where the sea was shallow and the sun shone through it. Almost turquoise.

CHAPTER 21

When I got home, Bertha was there, doing the laundry. I just love the smell of clean laundry. I think it's one of the best smells in the whole world. It's the smell version of sunshine.

I took off all my wet clothes and added them to the pile in the kitchen and put my pj's on. "Bea, will you put the dinner in the oven while I finish up?" said Bertha. "There's lasagna in the freezer."

I watched Bertha's big arms move piles of clothes from the washing machine to the dryer, and then add more clothes to the washing machine. "OK," I mumbled. I opened the freezer and felt the icy air lift up and into my pajamas. It made me shiver. I checked the cooking instructions on the back of the lasagna box and turned on the oven. While I waited for the oven to heat up, I sat down and watched the washing going round and round. As the dirt from the clothes mixed with the soap, the water turned gray, green-gray. I put the lasagna in the oven and watched the dirty water slosh around as the machine, heavy with wet clothes, slowly whirred and moaned, *"Not again, not more washing . . ."*

"My show's on, will you get the food when it's done?" said Bertha, flopping on the sofa with a sigh.

"OK," I said, but I was watching that green water slish-slosh from side to side in the machine. *The rain even gets inside the washing machine*, I thought. Suddenly, framed by the glass circle of the washing machine, was the dead guy's face, floating in that gray water. I felt the hairs on the back of my neck stand up, and turned around to check if he was there, his ghost, standing behind me, but all I could see was the back of Bertha's head poking out over the top of the sofa. I looked back at the machine, but all I saw was soapy water.

Then, I don't know why, but I thought Bertha might be able to help. If I asked her while she was watching TV, she wouldn't get suspicious.

"Bertha?"

"Hmmm?" she answered, distracted by the orange lady with the luminous teeth announcing which prizes could be won this evening. (It seems like everybody, even grown-ups, have got their own version of cartoons. Stuff that helps them forget the rain or other things in their lives.)

"You know that dead guy they found, the one in the newspapers . . . ?"

I didn't need to say any more.

"Oh, that poor man." Bertha clicked her tongue against her teeth the way she did when she was annoyed or upset. "For some reason they dragged him up from the morgue and X-rayed him. They never do that with dead people, but the top guy, the head surgeon, wanted him X-rayed, and whatever he says goes, because everybody's scared of him. Now, what was that poor dead man's name? I remember him because they said he only had one eye. Mr. . . . what was it?"

I was suddenly all jumpy inside. He was actually there: Our dead guy had been at the hospital.

I waited to hear his name. I wanted to hear it so I could say it out loud and know that he wasn't just a pale face suspended forever in that gloomy water with one eye staring blankly into the darkness and loneliness of his broken house.

I felt sick when I thought of him, helpless like that, drifting in that liquid, letting that filthy water lap into his mouth. And now, because I'd taken his picture with my dad's camera, a part of him — his ghost or soul or his spirit, it was hard to know exactly what — had somehow gotten into my house. My dad had told me about the magic of photography. Maybe that's what he was talking about. Maybe he'd captured ghosts with that camera before.

If the ghost man had a name, I could ask him what he wanted, what he wanted me to know. Then I could ask him to leave, just like Butterfly had said. And not just that — if he had a name, he could be a person, and then maybe I could put that picture to sleep.

". . . Mr. Henderson!" As soon the name left Bertha's lips, the lightbulbs in the living room crackled and flickered. "That's it: Mr. Henderson." Bertha released a large breath, pleased with herself for remembering.

And then the ceiling light exploded.

"Oh, those old electrical circuits!" moaned Bertha, adding another household chore to her to-do list. "When you go to the store tomorrow, Bea, make sure you get some more bulbs — they're the ones in the brown-and-yellow box. Mr. Shapirello knows the ones."

But I knew that the bulbs blowing had nothing to do with living in an old house. It was him. The ghost. The ghost I'd carried in my camera, the ghost who'd moved the pickle jar at the diner and protected us from Jed and his gang in the abandoned train car, and he was saying, "That's me! You got it on the first try! Mr. Henderson—that's my name!"

We ate our lasagna in front of the TV. Mine was still a bit cold in the middle, but I didn't mind. All I could think about was getting to the hospital. Calling the other Convicts and then getting to the hospital. He'd been there—Bertha had said so herself—and they kept records at hospitals. I knew that from watching TV but also because (even though they weren't supposed to) Bertha and her friends sometimes read people's files and talked about them while they played cards. "I read on his file that he . . . That explains why he . . . Oh, no, honey, that's the one who . . . I saw it in her file," they would say, and then lean in and whisper the rest so that I wouldn't hear.

Mr. Henderson. Mr. Henderson. I kept saying it in my head. I knew his name and I knew where I could find out more. Maybe his file would tell us who he was, what kind of a person he was. Maybe it would tell us who killed him. It was sure to lead us somewhere. I couldn't wait to call Sam and the others.

I looked over at the phone sitting on its cradle in the kitchen. I'd wait till Bertha had finished her dinner. She always got sleepy after dinner, and sometimes she'd drop off on the sofa. Then I'd call the others on the upstairs phone.

Bertha was watching a woman screaming on the TV

because she'd won the first round on the game show. She was jumping up and down and hugging the orange lady with the too-white teeth. "She's going to win the cruise, I just know it!" Bertha was making a sucking noise with her lips and shaking her head. I suddenly felt bad for Bertha because she didn't know about all the things we'd found out, all the thoughts I had racing around my head. She didn't have a clue about all the feelings I felt in my gut and in my heart. I felt sad because I wished I could tell her, I wished she'd ask sometimes, I hoped she might at least try to understand. But she just thought I was a kid, and kids are pretty straightforward from a grown-up's point of view. As long as you feed them, keep them warm, put a roof over their heads, and send them to school, that's what matters. I watched her calm, happy face, lit up by the TV, still oblivious to what I'd been thinking—and thought about how I'd steal her keys while she was sleeping.

Sure enough, Bertha did drop off in front of the TV. I lifted myself slowly off the couch so as not to make the springs creak, and tiptoed upstairs to use the phone. I called Sam, who called Madison, who called Butterfly, who called Eric. Sam said he would tell them to come over to my place at midnight. I chose midnight because I was sure Bertha would be fast asleep by then. I told Sam to tell Madison and the others that it was urgent. We had a lead now; a lead that could help us solve the mystery of Mr. Henderson's death.

CHAPTER 22

Bertha was snoring loudly. Her big chest was rising and falling happily as she pulled air in and out through her open mouth. For a minute I envied her; I wished I could sleep that well. In the summer I have to kind of trick myself to get even a few hours' sleep. A part of me pretends to be asleep but another part of my mind is on guard, watching out for the rainy fingers, for the damp, for the dark, making sure it doesn't come too close, making sure it doesn't get in while I'm asleep. But it's hard to pretend to sleep, to pretend to relax, and it shows on my face. Even though I'm only eleven (almost twelve), I have dark gray patches under my eyes. Bertha sometimes asks me, "You sure you're not a vampire, out sucking people's blood all night? Because you sure as day is pale as one!" And I laugh. It might be fun to be a vampire for a night—you get to see in the dark and you are kind of invincible, like a superhero; even scary people are terrified of vampires. But I'd hate to have to drink blood. Maybe I could be a vegetarian vampire. . . .

Sam pushed me hard on the arm, reminding me what we were here for. I looked over to Butterfly and Madison, who were waiting at the bedroom door. Butterfly nodded and her face said, *Hurry*. Bertha kept her hospital keys and other valuable things in the top drawer of her dressing table in a broken music box. I once asked her why the things in the box were special, and she told me in a very matter-of-fact way while sorting the dirty laundry into piles.

The more important something was to Bertha, the more ordinary she made it sound, but I knew they were the things that she clutched in her big brown hands when she was lonely or sad, things she cried over and then put away till the next time. These things included a little gold locket that opened up to reveal a picture of her mother and another of her father, facing each other like you'd just interrupted a serious conversation. There was also a brassy ring with a tiny blue stone that a man had given her once (a man she loved but who didn't love her back), and a gold necklace that had been her mother's, with one little clean white pearl on the end, which Bertha always wore on special occasions.

I looked over at Bertha again and then gently pulled on the smooth wooden knob of the drawer, trying to open it without making a noise. I breathed slowly and silently, hoping the drawer would do the same. Then I let the heavy drawer rest where it was and lifted the music box out. Sam was getting impatient. He snatched the box out of my hands and opened the lid. *"Some day my prince will come,"* the music box sang out with its cheerful mechanical voice. Bertha stopped snoring. I slammed the box shut. Bertha adjusted her body in bed, making the old mattress springs groan. There was a pause, and then the snoring started again. I gently closed her bedroom door and we all tiptoed downstairs into the living room.

"I thought you said it was broken!" said Sam.

"It is—look," I said as I opened the now-silent music box and even pushed the little ballerina in her dirty pink net tutu to show them. "Maybe it was how you shook it!" I said, glaring at Sam. He always had to do everything in such a hurry. Jellybean seemed to take after him sometimes, and I was glad that Sam had left him at home tonight; breaking into a hospital would be a whole lot easier without the world's friendliest, most curious dog tagging along.

"Oh, this is so pretty . . . is this Bertha's mom and dad?" Madison's delicate fingers found the locket in the music box.

"Yes," I said. But I wanted to say, "It's not yours to hold—put it back." I didn't like the way Madison put her little pink hands with their shiny manicured nails into Bertha's box—her only private thing, with her few precious objects. It wasn't Madison's to touch, and it reminded me that I shouldn't be touching it, either.

"Here they are," I said, lifting out the bunch of hospital keys with their red LOVE heart key ring. There was one key for the main building, one for Bertha's ward, and one for the medication cabinet. I was relieved to be holding the keys, but I wanted to put the music box back and get out of the house.

In my rush, I didn't check whether Madison had put the pretty locket back into the box. What I certainly didn't know at that point was just how much Madison liked "things." Especially things that were treasured by other people. I also didn't know that she had a whole box of them under her bed, full of things people had loved and that they probably believed were lost forever.

"What are we waiting for? We've got the keys—let's get to the hospital!" Sam headed toward the door.

I reached for my wristwatch, turning the big leather strap of my dad's watch around to read its face. It was already half past midnight.

"If my mom catches me, I'll be grounded for a week." Butterfly looked worried.

"Monster Lady will call my parents, and I won't be able to go shopping for, like, a month!" added Madison.

Eric smiled. "Well, I'm going. I don't care if I make my mom mad."

"We have to go tonight," said Sam, and I knew he was right.

"There's no way we can get in during the day without being seen—there are more people there during the day and the patients are all watching. Besides, Bertha is going to need the keys in the morning."

"OK, who wants to break some rules?" said Sam.

"I don't mind sneaking out, it's just that I need to get some sleep!" moaned Madison. "Everyone knows that if you don't get at least eight hours of sleep, you . . ."

". . . end up looking like me," I finished for her, and Madison looked away, embarrassed.

Eric's face lit up. "We could pick up a cheeseburger on the way." We laughed, and Sam gave Eric a kind of friendly shove—we were starting to realize that Eric wanted to combine everything with some kind of food.

It took us about half an hour to get into town. Even though it was July, it was freezing. Our breath steamed in the cold air and stray raindrops trickled down our backs. We were at the old memorial, right in the heart of Elbow and not far from Mitzy's Diner, when Butterfly seemed to turn and notice something out of the corner of her eye. Then she said, "Hold on," in an irritated voice, and turned and walked back down the hill we'd just come up.

"Where's she going?" asked Eric.

"Maybe she forgot something." Sam shrugged.

Me, Sam, Eric, and Madison were all sitting on the mossy stone wall surrounding the memorial fountain, under Madison's pink umbrella. For most of the year the fountain was empty and dry, but now it was overflowing with inky rainwater. Above us towered the statue of a big man holding a globe in one hand and what looked like a giant ice-cream cone in the other. He had a serious, self-important expression on his face and, when it wasn't raining, a lot of pigeon poop all over his head, which always made me and Sam laugh. The writing on the side said, *In honor of John Ezekiel Elbow, founder of the town of Elbow.* I'd often sat here and looked at those words but never really thought about them, except that I imagined he might have invented ice cream because of the cone in his hand. Whenever I saw that statue, I knew I was getting near Mitzy's, because his cone was like an ad for her diner. Sitting under it now in the dark rain, the statue was like a solid shadow that could turn its head at any moment, blink, and come alive.

Butterfly's purple umbrella reappeared, heading jerkily up the steep hill. Holding her hand was Nelson. "Oh, no, she's got her baby brother," said Eric. Nelson was smiling the way he always did, like he was about to go on a carnival ride. I wondered for a minute if I was ever like that, that happy, when I was a little kid, but I doubted it.

"When I grow up, I might be a doctor or the man who puts the sprinkles on the ice cream," said Nelson proudly, and Butterfly pulled him roughly toward her.

"He followed me all the way to your house, Bea, and then all the way here." She turned to her brother. "Nelson, I said you could come if you kept quiet and didn't cause any trouble—do you think you can do that?" Nelson looked upset. Butterfly looked at us again. "I'm really sorry, guys."

"We better skip the cheeseburgers," I said. "Time's running out, and although she's pretty cool, Mitzy's still going to think something's up if we're all out here at one-thirty in the morning." The others agreed, apart from Eric.

"But I'm starving!" he moaned. "Listen—hear that?—it's my stomach. If I don't get food regularly, the acid builds up and starts to eat away at the lining. Don't blame me if I die."

"Well, you'll be in the right place," said Madison. "We're going to the hospital, remember?"

Nelson walked with quick little steps to keep up with us, and his red boots seemed to squeak with the excitement of a nighttime adventure. "Can I do my initiation when we get to the hospital?"

Me and Butterfly and Sam looked at each other and then at Eric, who was shaking his head, and Madison, who was smiling because she thought whatever Nelson said was cute.

"Listen very carefully," I said, lowering myself to face Nelson. "*This* is your initiation. You've got to be completely quiet and do whatever we say. OK?"

"OK!" Nelson nodded, trying to mask his smile. Then he pulled two fingers slowly across his mouth like he was closing up a zipper, and took my hand. His little hand was hot to the touch and a little damp. But as we walked he seemed to have accepted the initiation, because he didn't speak and even made his steps a little quieter on the sidewalk, not sloshing or stomping at all.

At the hospital, a few windows were lit up in the distance: random fluorescent squares glowing against the wet black sky like one of those foldout Christmas calendars come to life. But the lights were off in the wards because the patients were asleep. Even though I'd been here a dozen times to meet Bertha, it wasn't somewhere I wanted to be at night, and I didn't like breaking into places as much as Sam or even Madison.

As we got closer to the entrance, we could see nurses and doctors huddled over a counter, a few of them sipping from steaming mugs. We stepped into the long wet grass, heading around the side of the hospital, and I switched off the flashlight that had been guiding us through the murky, dripping air.

"Hey!" shouted Madison, grabbing my raincoat. "What are you doing? I can't see anything!"

"Shhhh!" spat Butterfly. "Do you want them all to hear you?"

"If I keep the flashlight on, they can see us coming,"

I explained. That's the thing about the rain. Because it's so dark, lights show up so much more brightly, and the last thing we wanted was a bunch of doctors and nurses asking us what we were doing out here and where our parents were. Also, I've noticed from watching TV that doctors and nurses seem to have a lot of buddies in the police department.

"Can we play pirates now?" Nelson pleaded.

"What did we tell you, Nelson? You just failed your initiation," snapped Butterfly. "It's no good," she said to us. "He doesn't get it. He's just a little kid!"

"I may be little but I'm still a boy!" said Nelson.

"You're not in our gang, you failed. That's it." Eric seemed pleased.

"Shut up, Eric!" replied Butterfly, sticking up for her brother. "Ain't nobody seen your invention!" And she stuck her head out as if to say, *So there!*

I bent down and whispered in Nelson's ear. "We *are* playing pirates. The hospital is an enemy ship, and when we're inside we have to be very, very quiet, or else the bad pirates will cut off our heads and feed them to the crocodiles."

Nelson liked this idea a lot. His eyes grew large with excitement and he zipped up his lips up again. People obviously told Nelson to be quiet a lot.

"Hey, wait for us!" called Eric, but Sam took no notice. He'd already taken off at high speed past the ground floor with all the bright lights and the doctors and nurses.

Butterfly let her arms drop to her sides. "What do we do now?" Nobody said anything. I knew we had to wait for Sam—breaking into places was his territory; it's one of the things he does. So we waited while our breath made fog in the damp air.

"Psssst!" Sam called. "Over here! . . . Pssssssst!" he called again. He was just a fuzzy shadow standing in the distance, and I had to squint my eyes really hard to see him.

"We have to get past the bad pirates now, Nelson, without them seeing us, OK?" I said. Nelson nodded with a very serious expression.

Sam had found a room on the ground floor with no lights on and had opened the window. Me, Nelson, Butterfly, Eric, and Madison crouched down and started to walk quickly and quietly to the side of the building where Sam was standing. We hid behind parked cars, zigzagging in and out of them and then behind an ambulance, where two drivers were standing and talking at the front. When they turned their heads we ran across the squelching grass toward Sam.

"We did it! We did it!" shouted Nelson, jumping up and down with excitement. Just then the light came on in the room, and we all ducked. Butterfly held her hand over Nelson's mouth to stop him from making any more noise. We heard heavy footsteps inside. The footsteps stopped for a few seconds and then carried on. The light was switched off and the door was closed.

"Let's go,'" whispered Sam, pulling me in through the open window. Eric helped Nelson next, then Butterfly and Madison before he followed.

We zipped along a corridor, trying not to let our wet feet squeak on the linoleum floor. At the end of the corridor Sam pressed down on a big metal door handle and made the door swing open. Luckily, the room was empty. We pushed ourselves inside, bumping into each other.

"Why are we going in here?" I asked, falling into the room, sandwiched between Madison and Sam. "Bertha's ward is upstairs. It's on the seventh floor, we need to take the elevator."

"Don't you know anything, Bea? We're doing what soldiers do—it's called flanking—we have to take it gradually, that way we have less chance of getting caught," said Butterfly as she switched on a little metal table light. I caught Eric's expression, and I could tell he was impressed with what Butterfly had said because his eyes twinkled a little bit more than usual.

The white room was eerily quiet. The floor was a shiny gray and in the middle of the room was a long machine like an electronic coffin.

"Cool—an MRI machine! They used one of these on my dad once." Eric rushed over to it and touched it like it was a new car or something. "It's like a 3-D X-ray machine—it takes pictures of all your organs and bones and everything and then sends pictures to that computer over there," he said, pointing to a computer in the corner.

Eric didn't get excited all that often—mostly he was gloomy-looking and angry about stuff—but when he was excited, his enthusiasm was infectious. And because Nelson was never one to need much persuading, anyway, Nelson decided to climb inside the special machine, imagining it to be a spaceship designed just for him. The only thing was, at the time, none of us noticed.

Butterfly left the room first, checking that there was nobody in the corridor and then pressing the button for the elevator. She ran back to us and we waited, peering through the gap in the door. When the elevator arrived and nobody got out, we ran on tiptoes halfway down the corridor toward it. We were almost there when we saw a doctor inside. He had fallen asleep with his head resting on the wall. He woke up suddenly, remembered where he was, and walked out of the elevator right in front of us. Luckily he was too sleepy to notice. He wiped his face with his hands and walked off in the other direction. We piled into the elevator.

We watched the numbers rise on the inside of the elevator. *One, two, three . . .* "What if there's someone waiting to get on when the doors open for us to get out?" asked Madison. Nobody said anything and I noticed a bead of sweat on Eric's top lip. It was hot in there and we'd been running around a lot, which meant we were followed around by a smelly cocktail of wet feet and damp clothes that were slowly starting to warm up.

Four, five, six . . . There was a bell to announce our floor: seven. The doors pulled apart. We held our breath. Nobody there. I led the way to Bertha's ward, feeling the smooth metal of the keys between my fingers in my pocket. "Here it is," I said, looking through the windows of the double doors. I put the key in the lock and turned.

We walked as quietly as we could through a ward filled with old people. Some were snoring, some were curled up like babies, and some looked like they were already dead. I turned to my left and there was an old man sitting up in bed, wide awake, staring straight at us. I sort of smiled and raised a hand to say hi, but he didn't wave back. At the end of the corridor was a nurse, moving around in a little room with her back to us.

"What are we looking for again?" whispered Butterfly.

"We need to find Mr. Henderson's file—it might tell us why he was killed," I said.

"But they never keep patients' files in the same place as the patients," she said.

"Why didn't you say that before?" said Sam angrily.

"I don't know, I thought . . ." Butterfly looked embarrassed.

I felt so stupid. *I* should have known that. Bertha often talked about the hospital's administration policies. "Rosie and Shania from Admin." Those were the friends from the department who she sometimes invited over for cards. I signaled to the others: *We need to get back downstairs.* We tiptoed back past the sleeping people, and I thought how strange it was that they were all in one big room, like brothers and sisters in a fairy tale who had all grown old together.

Back into the elevator. Butterfly stopped suddenly. "Where's Nelson?" We all looked around. Butterfly's brow wrinkled with worry. "He could be anywhere. We have to find him."

"He wasn't in the ward with us," said Sam. "We must have lost him earlier. You, Madison, and Eric go look for him, and me and Bea will get the file."

As soon as the elevator door opened, we checked for grown-ups and then parted ways. Me and Sam hid in a wide doorway as a doctor and a nurse walked past, both checking a chart the doctor was holding. I held in my stomach to make myself even less visible. We waited. When they turned the corner, we ran toward the Admin department. I used another one of Bertha's keys, the long one, and the door opened.

Inside were rows and rows of gray metal filing cabinets lit up by the light of the full moon flooding in from the large windows. All the drawers had letters on them. *A, B, C, D* . . . My eyes tried to find the letter *H* as quickly as they could.

"Over here!" Sam pulled open a large drawer and I began sorting through the tightly packed, thick brown paper files. "Haas . . . Habano . . . Hadley . . . Hatfield . . . Heilbron . . . Hekmeyer . . . Heliz . . . Henderson!" There were two Henderson files and I pulled out both. They said *Henderson, Marla,* and *Henderson, Herman.* I put "Marla" back and started to take out what was inside the other file.

What we couldn't have known was, at that same moment, in the MRI room downstairs, Nelson had grown bored of lying in the darkness of his "spaceship," climbed back out, and pressed the very large button on the outside of the machine. He had seen the red letters saying, **Authorized Personnel Only** and he knew red letters usually meant *Keep Off!* or *Danger!*, but no doubt thought they were for other people, not for astronauts like himself. Then he had followed the instructions on the diagram, which showed the patient lying down on the board. To his great delight, a beeping sound had begun, and some lights had come on as he started to move into the spaceship along the little "runway" he was now lying on.

Upstairs, I began to read the Henderson file. The first page had a little photo stuck on it and I laughed because I recognized the picture right away. "Sam, look! Somebody stuck on Herman's photo as a joke." There he was, Herman of Herman's Pickles, smiling just the same smile he always smiled from the side of his pickle jars, except now he was smiling up from a hospital file.

"It's no joke," said Sam slowly. "It *is* Herman."

"You mean . . . ?"

Sam nodded solemnly. "Herman *is* Mr. Henderson. Mr. Henderson *is* Herman—they're the same person."

The lights in the room crackled and fizzed just like they had before, in the living room with Bertha. One bulb came on altogether and stayed on. "He's here," I said to Sam, scanning the ceiling and then the room to try and see him.

I expected Sam to say, "Don't be stupid," or "You're just being crazy, Bea," but he didn't. He was watching the hairs on his arm and they were standing straight up in the air. Then out of nowhere came a gust of wind, and all the pages of the file blew across the room.

Sam's eyes were wide with fear. "What the heck was that?" he whispered. Sam always pretended he wasn't scared, but I could always tell when he was, and I didn't like it. He was the fearless one—it was like nothing fazed him, except things he couldn't explain.

"Maybe we shouldn't be doing this," I said, just as the X-rays slid out of the file and onto the floor. They were like pictures turned inside out. Negatives. There were dark parts where there were normally light parts, and light parts where there were normally dark parts. And they showed the inside of a body instead of the outside. For a minute I wondered what it would be like if all photos came out like that: people smiling at a party but with all their bones showing; school yearbooks filled with skeletons.

Sam lifted up a large X-ray of Herman's whole body and held it up against the bright moonlight. It was so strange seeing his body lit up like that, just like a map or a puzzle made up of bones. It was like he'd been dead for centuries and we'd found his remains in a cave and put them all back together again. And I realized then that, in a way, that's what we *were* doing. We were putting his story together, one picture, one bone, one name at a time, and our first bone was this X-ray.

It reminded me of the story Miss Riley at school had told us about the Egyptian goddess Isis and her brother Osiris. Their nasty brother Seth chops up Osiris and scatters his body parts all over the place. But Isis, Osiris's sister, goes looking for them and puts him back together again so she can bring him back to life.

It made sense to me then: What we needed to do was put Herman back together. We needed to find all the pieces of his story so that he could come alive again. The truth would make him whole again, and then he could be at peace.

With that thought, a cold breeze blew right through my body. It was the strangest feeling I've ever had. For a second or two I couldn't breathe, and I felt like I wanted to laugh and be sick at the same time. Then it passed, and I understood what it was. It was Herman's spirit, and he'd traveled right through my body.

I wasn't scared. If anything, I wanted to cry. It was as if . . . as if Herman was saying, *Thank you.* But at the same time I could feel his loneliness and his helplessness. There were things he wanted to say and do, things that were unfinished in his life and his death, but he no longer had the ability to carry them out, because he no longer had a body.

But he has us, I thought. *And we're going to put things right for Herman.*

It was at that moment I knew there'd been a reason for me to stay in Elbow for the summer. I needed to stay, at least until we'd solved the mystery of Herman's death.

Things were not right here, and were definitely not as they seemed; there were things that were being covered up, just like DW had said. Maybe it had always been that way, but now the corruption had seeped into Elbow like the rain, and if Elbow was not careful, the town itself would drown in it.

"Hold these!" Sam shoved the X-ray of Herman's skeleton into my hands along with a scan of his intestines — but I didn't have time to look at that.

Waaaaah! Waaaaah! Waaaah! an alarm blared suddenly from downstairs.

My heart thumped faster in my rib cage. "We've got to get the others."

Sam shoveled the rest of the papers back into the brown file, put it back in the drawer, and then pushed it shut. I tucked the two X-rays into my jeans and under my sweatshirt and felt them stick to my damp stomach. I locked the door to the Admin office and put the set of keys back in my pocket. My rubber boots squeaked against the linoleum as we ran, and then I could barely feel my feet as we flew down the stairs, two, three steps at a time.

There was a crowd of doctors, nurses, and security men spilling out from the room with the MRI scanner. Butterfly, Madison, and Eric were standing together, surrounded by hospital personnel, and a nurse was holding Nelson's hand. Butterfly was apologizing to a doctor. "We'll make sure it never happens again."

Apparently, Nelson had been inside the MRI "spaceship" for a few minutes, unaware that his body was being scanned, and Eric, Madison, and Butterfly had burst into the room, having realized where he was. When Eric had switched on the computer to see the printout of Nelson's body, Butterfly had gotten really mad and shouted at Eric. Eric shouted back. Nelson didn't like the noise that people made when they were fighting—it reminded him too much of his mom and dad—so he pressed the big red EMERGENCY button, setting off the loudest siren he'd ever heard.

"Anything could have happened . . . Hospitals are very dangerous places . . . Do you understand, young man?" A tall doctor was talking to Nelson, who was nodding and wiping his nose. This particular doctor was wearing a green mask around his neck, which he had pulled down from his nose and mouth. He was wearing a green cap, too, which made me think he was a surgeon, because I've seen lots of TV shows with all kinds of doctors trying to save people's lives against all odds, and the surgeons are always the ones with the masks and the caps; they're the ones who do the operations.

When he'd finished speaking to Nelson, he looked at me and then came right over. He towered above me and demanded, "And what's your name, young lady?"

And I answered, "Bea, Bea Klednik," the way I do to substitute teachers.

"That's an unusual name," he said, looking at me with his unblinking eyes. He had pale skin and very big, very dark eyes, eyes that were so black they swallowed all the light in the room. But it wasn't so much his eyes as his expression that bothered me, and the way my finger started up as soon as he came over. My pinkie finger buzzed and twitched.

He stared at me for just a second before walking away, but that second felt like forever; it made my skin sort of itchy all over, and I wanted to shrink into the floor and disappear.

At the end of the corridor, he turned and just stood there watching us from a distance. I gave Sam a nudge. "See that man?" I said as we peered between two nurses.

"Yeah. Doesn't look too friendly."

"It's not just that. I feel like I've seen him somewhere—or that I'm going to see him again," I said, watching him slip out of sight at last in a kind of effortless way, like he wasn't a human being at all. Suddenly it hit me. I grabbed Sam's coat and whispered, "That guy—imagine him in a big black hat and a long black coat, whistling a slow eerie tune . . ."

"You're right," he said, his eyes twinkling as he smiled. "Mr. Smytheson—Jeeks's buddy—is a surgeon!"

"Here, you can keep this," said the other, kind-looking doctor, pulling a printout of Nelson's body scan from a big printer near the machine. Nelson's face was transformed into a big smile, and then he looked embarrassed again, knowing he'd caused so much trouble.

Nelson and Butterfly's mom arrived, pushing her way through the crowd. She looked like she was about to bend down to give Nelson a hug, but he beat her to it, throwing his arms around his mother's legs. She squeezed him tight for a second or two, and then, gently but firmly, she pushed him off and, grabbing Butterfly by the hand, dragged them both away, saying that that was that, they were grounded indefinitely. I think me, Madison, Eric, and Sam all hoped she wouldn't notice us, but at that very moment she turned and announced, "I'm driving you all home and I'll be calling your parents to discuss this in the morning!"

The main thing was that we had what we had come for, and Nelson, with his spaceship adventure, had created just the diversion we needed. Nelson never did get his honorary stick of gum, but I'm sure the printout of his body made him a whole lot happier, anyway.

CHAPTER 23

Butterfly's mother dropped us all home in her station wagon. I waved good-bye to Butterfly and Nelson, who looked tired, and saw that Mrs. Williams was watching me in her rearview mirror, like she didn't trust me or something. She waited until I'd unlocked the front door and then drove off.

I shut the door, climbed upstairs to the comforting sound of Bertha's snores, and went to bed with the X-rays still tucked into my pants, close to my stomach. It was a strange feeling knowing that Herman's skeleton was going to be mirroring my own as I slept, but I felt safer that way. I listened to the wind howling and whistling outside, and the *tap-tapping* of the rainy fingers all around the house, but the sounds grew fainter and then disappeared, and suddenly I was asleep, really asleep, for the first time in weeks.

I woke up to the smell of eggs frying and knew it was Bertha's day off. Her days off fell on weekdays sometimes because she worked shifts. Then I remembered the X-rays. I felt around my stomach but there was just skin—no X-rays. I panicked—someone had been in my room while I was sleeping and stolen them from under my sweater! No, it was OK, they'd just moved around to my back. I pulled them out, lifted up my mattress, put the pictures underneath, and headed downstairs for breakfast.

As soon as I sat down, Bertha frowned at me and stood there with her hands on her hips. "Butterfly Williams's mother called me this morning." *Oh, no,* I thought, and my stomach felt hollow. *Why can't grown-ups just let us deal with things sometimes? We're not as stupid as they think we are. Half the time we have to do things by ourselves, anyway, like make our own breakfast, brush our own teeth, get to school and back, buy our own lunch, decide who to be friends with, decide what kinds of things are important to us. That doesn't sound too different from being an adult to me.*

Then it occurred to me: Telling us what to do, and telling us off, made grown-ups feel better about being grown-ups—it made them feel less like kids.

"Are you listening to me?" yelled Bertha.

I nodded.

"Then what did I say?" She waited.

"You're mad because I stayed out late . . . ," I offered.

"And?" She took one hand off her hip and raised an eyebrow.

"I went to the hospital and I'm not supposed to go there on my own?" And I quickly added, "But we only went to the hospital to find Nelson—he ran off and that's where we found him."

"That's an awfully long way for a seven-year-old boy to go by himself. At two o'clock in the morning!" She narrowed her eyes at me, waiting to see if I was going to crack, and then I remembered: I hadn't put the keys back in her box.

"Why would I want to go to the hospital in the middle of the night?" I said, actually meaning it. Who could have imagined that me and a bunch of kids I hardly knew would break into a hospital after midnight to find out about a dead man, whose house we had broken into a few days earlier, whose body I had photographed, and whose ghost was randomly appearing? I couldn't even believe it myself.

I was trying to think up an excuse to run up to Bertha's bedroom and put the keys back in the box when she said, "Maybe it had something to do with the X-rays you stole."

I froze.

"I came to wake you up this morning after Mrs. Williams called, and there you were, sleeping like a baby, your sweater squashed up under your chin, with two X-rays sticking out of your jeans. I had to rub my eyes because it looked like I was seeing right through you!"

Think fast, think fast, I thought. "Yeah, the thing is, we thought Nelson was in enough trouble, what with switching on the MRI and all that. We didn't want to mention that he opened a few drawers he wasn't supposed to. . . ."

But Bertha wasn't buying it. "I suppose you're going to tell me Nelson stole my keys and my locket also?" She raised both her eyebrows and just stared.

"I don't know anything about your locket!" I looked down at my fried eggs and hash browns and bacon, wishing none of this had started. Then my eyes found Bertha's eyes, and she was still waiting for me to confess. "Nelson may only be seven, but he's very intelligent for his age."

"Bea Klednik, I am ashamed of you! Blaming that sweet

little boy. You need to start taking responsibility for your actions, young lady, and you need to find some new friends!" She held out her hand and I placed the hospital keys across the deep lines of her pink-brown palm.

"I want my locket back, and if I catch you stealing or breaking into anywhere again, I swear I *will* disown you. The last thing I need in my life is a juvenile delinquent."

I rolled my eyes and, taking my breakfast plate, turned to go upstairs.

"Excuse me, young lady, I think you're forgetting something."

I knew she meant the X-rays, but I needed to take another look at them.

"I put the X-rays in the darkroom this morning; I just thought they'd be cool to show at school." *That'll buy me a few minutes,* I thought. I put my plate of food back on the table.

"Bea, those are confidential documents. I could lose my job if anybody finds out they're missing. I'll try and get them back without anybody noticing."

I gave her a hug. "Thanks, Bertha. I'm really sorry." Then I rushed upstairs to my room, lifted the mattress, and grabbed the X-rays. I tiptoed back down the stairs, trying not to make a sound—I didn't want Bertha to snatch them from me before I had a chance to look at them.

I had just gotten in the darkroom, bolted the door, and switched on the ruby light when there was a knock on the little window at the back. I jumped. It was Sam and Madison. I opened the window.

"You can't come in—Bertha knows we stole the keys and the X-rays, plus she thinks I stole her locket." Madison coughed and looked away, and Sam looked deflated. I think he thought we'd gotten away with it.

I knew Sam wouldn't be grounded, because nobody really cared about him. If he missed school, the school didn't even bother sending letters home anymore. I had thought Madison's parents would definitely have grounded her, making a call to the housekeeper from their hotel in Europe, but they didn't, and it made me realize that parents didn't need to be poor or drunks to be selfish and neglect their kids.

"There's got to be some kind of clue in the X-ray," I said, knowing I only had a couple of minutes. "Bertha said they X-rayed him when he was already dead."

"Why would they do that?" asked Madison. Sam and Madison waited while I held the transparency of Herman's skeleton up to the light.

"It's really hard to see with this light," I said.

"Bea?" came Bertha's voice from upstairs.

"Coming!" I shouted back.

"Use this," said Sam, handing me Eric's flashlight through the window. I held the picture up and shone the flashlight through it, following the bones, like I was drawing them back on with the light.

"There's nothing, just bones," I said, hearing Bertha's feet on the stairs.

"Bea, I need to get them back to the hospital this morning!"

"Check the other picture!" said Madison. I held the

second picture up to the light and this time I traced the squiggly shape of Herman's intestines.

Nestling in a bend inside Herman's guts was a strange-looking shape. A shape you wouldn't normally expect to find inside a person. My flashlight hovered over that dark object.

"What is it?" asked Sam.

"What have you found?" asked Madison.

"I think it's a ring. It looks heavy. It's a ring that looks like . . . like a castle." It was pretty big and here it was, clear as day inside poor Herman's guts.

"I wonder if that's the ring Jed was looking for," Sam said.

"Herman must have swallowed it!" said Madison.

Bangbangbang! came Bertha's fist on the door. I signaled to Sam and Madison to get down and shut the window.

"What you doing in there, girl?" Bertha boomed.

"Nothing, just getting the pictures." I switched off the flashlight and undid the catch on the door. Bertha looked suspiciously around the room. My eyes darted to the window to check that Sam and Madison had gone.

"Here you go," I said, handing her the X-rays.

She snatched them from me, took a quick look around the darkroom, and said, "You're a very strange girl, Bea Klednik."

I followed her upstairs and stood in the doorway, listening to her slosh through the rain and mud to her old car. As she made her way across the dirt track we currently had instead of a road, her rubber boots sank deeper into the sludge with each step and were sucked back out again with a loud *squelch.*

I saw the tires struggle with the thick brown mud for a few moments, and then Bertha's car made more noise, lifted up and out of the mud, and she set off for the hospital. Once she'd gone, I called out to Sam and Madison and, along with Jelly, we watched from the porch as the distant lights of Bertha's car tunneled their way through the foggy rain.

Stepping into the house, Madison said, "What kind of a person swallows a ring?"

"A scared person, that's what kind," said Sam.

"Herman must have known somebody was after that ring. That's why he swallowed it. To keep it safe," I said.

"Maybe that's why they killed him." Madison was catching on. And then my pinkie finger started acting up. Madison and Sam even looked down to watch the crazy little digit moving of its own accord. Madison's lip curled and her nose wrinkled up between her brows. "What is the deal with your finger again?"

"Sorry," I said, "there's nothing I can do about it. Do you think I'm a freak?"

"You bet!" said Sam.

My finger was pointing in the direction of the garbage cans, and right at that moment the garbage truck pulled up the street, its lights almost blinding us. The truck heaved noisily up the hill, churning the thick mud under its giant tires. The doors opened and two beefy guys got out and hiked up toward the house in their big boots and yellow raincoats.

"What if the intestines we took from Mr. Jeeks belonged to Herman? That would explain why Jeeks chased after us to get them back. That ring must be valuable."

We knew it was true the minute Madison said it. Why hadn't we thought of it sooner? It was so obvious.

"STOP!" we all yelled and waved at the garbagemen. "Stop the truck!" But the garbagemen had already tipped the big metal can into the back of the truck and driven halfway down the slope toward town. I knew where they were heading, and if they got there, I knew we'd never find the nylon bag containing Herman's guts.

I was suddenly filled with urgency. "We've got to follow that dump truck—that ring is in there somewhere—and we've got to get that ring!"

CHAPTER 24

We were on the road into town, running as fast as we could, and I could hardly see because of the rain. Sometimes the heavy rain goes in your eyes and up your nose and it's like being underwater. "C'mon!" yelled Sam, waving at me and Madison running behind him. Sam was one of the fastest runners in the school, even though he smoked his dad's cigarettes, but he never wanted to join the track team because he said it was full of idiots. I think he only liked to run when there was a point to the running.

"Look!" I said, pointing at Sam. He was way ahead of us, right behind the dump truck. He took off in a final sprint and jumped onto the back of the truck, grabbing hold of it with both hands. He turned, and although we couldn't see his face clearly, we saw a flash of white in the gloom—I guess he was smiling. We watched the garbage truck disappear into the muddy rain, with Sam hanging on to the back and Jellybean running behind it, his tail wagging furiously.

Me and Madison slowed to a walking pace, and she looked down to see her pink Wellingtons covered in thick green-brown mud. "I can't do this!" she wailed between breaths, as streaks of rainwater divided the dirt splashes on her cheeks. "We're never going to catch up with him now."

My face felt hot from running and I could feel my T-shirt sticking to my back under my raincoat. "Wait here!" I said, before running back up to the house. Madison looked as though she'd had enough, and we hadn't even gotten to the dump yet. I didn't want to hang around and hear her complain. I just knew I needed to get those guts back and find that weird-looking ring. Maybe it wasn't a ring at all, but something else. But if it *was* a ring, it was no ordinary ring —that was for sure. I wished I had known what that stinky bunch of sausages was when it was in my kitchen. But I guess then we wouldn't have known they belonged to Mr. Henderson, and that Mr. Henderson was Herman of Herman's Pickles. Why did Mr. Jeeks want Herman's ring? Why was that ring so important? As I ran back to the house, the questions circled around and around my head.

Madison looked surprised when I came back down the slippery path on my purple bike. Then she opened her eyes really wide, the way Jellybean sometimes does. "If you've got a bike, what am *I* supposed to do?" she whined.

"You sit on the seat," I said, "and I'll pedal."

She stood for a moment and stared at the saddle.

"Just get on the bike or we'll never make it!" I yelled.

She lifted her raincoat and perched on the seat while I leaned forward, holding the handlebars. We were unsteady at first, wobbling from side to side, Madison gripping my waist like she was about to die or something. When the tire caught in a deep track, I tried to steer out of it, but it was too wet and we skidded and fell.

"Owwwww!" screamed Madison as she landed in the mud, with me and the bike on top of her.

"Sorry," I said, pushing myself up and lifting the bike off Madison. I waited for her to get up. "Come on!" I shouted.

"I don't want to go," she said, starting to cry. "Just leave me here." She turned around and lay back down in the mud. She was covered in it now. The only bit of pink rain gear visible was a tiny triangle on her hat, and that was floating next to her in a thick brown puddle.

I lowered the bike to the ground and sat down next to Madison, who was sobbing into her hands. "We need your help, Madison—we're the Convicts now, remember, the Raintown Convicts. If we don't help each other, nobody will." I was thinking about how far away that garbage truck was by now. "Don't you want to find the ring?" I asked. "Don't you want to know what Mr. Jeeks wanted it for?"

But still Madison lay there sobbing. I began to lose my patience. "You can stay here all day if you want, but the mud will suck you up sooner or later and you'll die. You'll be all alone and you'll die a dark and muddy death!" About to give up, I let out a big sigh. "If I don't go, something will happen to Sam. Somebody's got to watch out for him." I grabbed the handlebars of my bike and yanked it up, ready to head off on my own. I was about to pedal away when Madison lifted herself quickly out of the mud and got back onto the bike.

"You're right, Sam could get himself into trouble." That

was all she said all the way to the dump, because she knew she had given something away, about liking Sam as a little bit more than a friend. But I'd already noticed, the day she lent him her dad's sweater.

It was tough cycling with Madison on the back, through that Elbow rain. We had to walk up the steep hills because I couldn't cycle up those on my own, let alone with a passenger. But wanting to find out more about Herman and that ring kept me going. I don't know about you, but when I really want something, I barely notice stuff like whether my legs hurt or my eyes sting; well, it was like that—I just wanted to get to the dump and find that yellow nylon bag.

"We're lost!" Madison said finally. We were way out of town and there were no more truck tracks left to follow. I was pushing the bike now and Madison was walking on the other side of me. I looked around but there was nothing but a few scraggy trees on the horizon and a massive hill rising up to meet the black, rain-filled sky. I gave the bike to Madison to hold, and walked around to try and see where we had gotten to. Behind us were the lights of Elbow, like watery neon jewels speckling the surrounding darkness. Elbow almost looked nice from here. The lights made it welcoming, like an underwater Christmas scene, and it made me want to go back, like somebody was waiting for me with warm cookies and a blanket by the fire. Then I remembered again the cakes Mom used to bake and how we used to listen to records in front of the fireplace.

Just at that moment I felt something hard under my right foot, which made the sole of my shoe slip to the side. Under a watery coating of mud, I could just make out a flat piece of metal. I dug my fingers under an edge and lifted the square out of the dirt, then wiped away the grime to reveal the bright yellow of a street sign that said MP. I wiped a bit more, starting at the left, and uncovered a D, and then finally the U and an arrow pointing to the left. "It's here—this must be the place!" I said.

But Madison raised an eyebrow and said in her grown-up voice—the one that sounded as though she knew everything, which of course she didn't—"OK, it says *dump*—but which way is the arrow supposed to point?"

There was only one way to find out. I threw the sign back down into the mud, dug my boots into the dirt, and pulled the unwilling wheels of my bike up the steep hill. I didn't wait to see if Madison was following me.

The hill got steeper and steeper and the rain was so sharp on my face I thought it was going to pierce my eyeballs. I was walking through mud up to my knees and my bike refused to go any farther, so I left it there and went on without it. Madison appeared beside me and said, "Wait for me." And we held hands to steady ourselves and to give ourselves leverage as we lifted one buried foot at a time.

Then I started to panic. What if the mud got deeper and deeper and we got sucked under, exactly the way I had teased Madison an hour earlier? Nobody knew where we were, all I could see and feel was darkness, mud, and rain, and I didn't even know which way was up anymore. There was mud in the air, pouring down on me from all around, and I was wading through a dirty, dark sea. I didn't know if my arms were my legs or if my legs were my arms; I didn't know if my left arm was my right leg or the other way around; if my head was my feet and my feet my head. Everything began to swirl inside me, twisting and wheeling around, there was darkness everywhere, I was losing control. I felt sick. Then black. Then nothing.

"Heeeeelpppp me!" I screamed out. "Heeeelllllpppp!" The arms of my mind flailed around me, trying to reach out to somebody, but I didn't even know if it was my voice or if anybody would hear. I was gone. I didn't know where I was. I had disappeared. I didn't have a body. My mind had struggled with the mud like my feet had struggled, to get up and out, not to be sucked in, but the mud had won, the rain had won, at last.

CHAPTER 25

The first thing I felt was the cold wet ground on the side of my face, and it felt good, so cool and fresh. And I could smell dirt—real, thick, earthy dirt—and it smelled good. I remember reading in Bertha's newspaper once about a woman who liked to eat dirt. Bertha said it had something to do with her not eating enough spinach, and at the time I'd thought, *Yeah, right, she's just trying to trick me into eating spinach,* but now I could understand why that woman wanted to eat dirt; it just smelled so real, so alive. Then I was aware of the rain hitting my face, and the thick, sticky mud around me, and I was back.

"You fainted." Madison was kneeling over me, her face filled with worry.

"She does it sometimes," said Sam. "When she's stressed. Did her eyeballs go all white, like in a horror movie? Did she moan and groan, like this: OOOAAAAhhhhh?"

"It's not funny!" said Madison. "Did you eat enough for breakfast?" And I thought back to my breakfast of hash browns and fried eggs and bacon still waiting, stone cold now, on the table at home.

Madison helped me to slowly sit up, and suddenly my legs

disappeared underneath me, swinging into a pit as wide and deep as a canyon. "Watch out!" shouted Sam, grabbing my arm. I felt a sharp electric tingle travel through my feet and right up into my stomach as my body realized it could fall into the giant black cavity beneath us.

"Watch out or the Swamp People will get you," said Sam.

"You don't actually believe that story, do you?" Madison tried to sound casual, but her eyes glistened with fear.

"Sure I do. They're the people who live on the stuff we throw away. They sleep during the day, but at night they find the best things and sell them. If you look real close you can sometimes see them moving across the mountains of garbage." Sam spoke in a way that made it hard to tell if it was real or just a story that kids told each other in the school yard.

In the half-light of the dense rain we could just make out three or four yellow garbage trucks parked across the other side of the dirt canyon, and the shadowy figures of garbage-men removing big black trash bags and tossing them over the edge into the canyon below.

"What happened to our garbage?" I asked, still a little dazed from having passed out.

Sam shrugged. "It's gone. The guy was holding the bag over the edge. I tried to grab it, but he said, 'Come and get it, tough guy,' and pushed me here, like this." Sam hit himself in the chest. "He said if I wanted it, I had to fight him for it."

Sam was never one to avoid a fight if someone challenged him. It was about not showing weakness or something. Sam once said he thought it would be a lot easier being a girl (and I had to swear afterward not to tell anybody he'd said that), but I told him that it wasn't at all easy being a girl, not one bit.

People expected you to be like Madison (even though Madison wasn't really like Madison, she just thought she should be) . . . quiet, pretty, and not too smart or opinionated. They didn't want you to ask too many questions or try to get your own way. All that stuff was OK for boys, but not OK for girls. But *I* tried to think of myself as Bea. Not as a girl or a boy, just Bea.

Jellybean, who was so drenched in mud he was almost completely camouflaged against the filthy wet ridge we were all sitting on, came toward Sam and licked his face. Sam tried to push him away, but we'd already seen a puffy, blue-black right eye hiding under the dirt splatters on Sam's face.

The three of us sat there for a few minutes, not saying anything, our legs dangling toward the black, wet stench of the mud-covered garbage hole below. It was like a glistening black soup that witches from all over were making to cast the nastiest spell in the history of spells, and floating in that dirty giant stew were all kinds of things: burned-out cars, refrigerators with their doors missing, bicycles, ovens, mattresses, TVs . . .

Then there were all the garbage bags, spilling out their contents of rotten, liquified food: baloney sandwiches (probably from Eric's house); maggot-infested meat; milk cartons half filled with rancid lumpy milk; green-black cheese and acid-yellow cheese; paper cups squashed against banana peels, squelching into hairy fruit that had lost all its color but gained a new smell; soiled tissues; babies' diapers; clothes; shoes; and dolls with eyes and limbs missing. And it was all covered with the stinking, slippery, disgusting, oozing mess of that strange man-made garbage soup. And in among that soup, somewhere, was our little, pale yellow nylon bag with Herman's insides in it.

Madison could tell what I was thinking, because she started shaking her head. "No way. There is *no way* I'm going in there. Not for a million dollars!" She made a face like she was about to be sick—and who could blame her? It was the most disgusting place I'd ever seen or, more important, smelled. The stink wafted up in great stench-filled clouds to where we were sitting. It was enough to turn the stomach of even the toughest garbageman. They all wore masks when they got to the dump, and they only went as close as they had to.

Sam's eyes twinkled; he liked a challenge more than anything. "Who's going first?"

Suddenly the idea didn't seem too bad at all. The bag containing Herman's intestines was in there somewhere, and so was the ring, and that ring could be the key to his murder. It was right here somewhere beneath us; we just had to locate it.

"You can't just leave me here!" whined Madison.

"Then you'll have to come with us," I said. "Come on, Jelly! Come on, boy!" I called, and Jellybean took off into the air and down the slippery slope into the garbage canyon, whipping the watery wind with his excited tail. Me and Sam followed, walking at first, our feet sinking into the squelching, belching mire until the sodden ground gave way beneath us and we slid down on our behinds, gaining more and more momentum until we landed in the black stew itself.

"Wait!" shouted Madison, tumbling down the slope after us, holding a tissue across her nose and mouth.

She got to where we were and then the ground caught her right foot in a gummy grip, and, trying to free it, she lost her balance and fell face-first into the filthy slop. For someone who hated getting dirty, she was doing a pretty good job of it. I thought back to her initiation, the way she had to force herself to stand up to her knees in a small puddle. She had come a long way since then.

Me and Sam tried not to laugh, but the more we tried not to, the more we had to. We laughed until our stomachs hurt and I made a snorting noise through my nose. Madison got angry and tried to get up, but she skidded over again, backward, her feet lifting up in the air, before landing on her backside in a deep puddle of slimy rotting food. It was so awful that even Madison started laughing then, because it was the only thing she could do. Me and Sam grabbed her under the arms and pulled her out.

"Try to find hard things—things with a wide surface area," instructed Sam. "Lie across them if you can. This is like quicksand."

I found what looked like the lid of a freezer trunk and stepped onto that, then lay across it and pulled myself along like I was on a surfboard. I tried hard not to breathe in the stink of decomposing food and feces (that's what Mrs. Tooley, the biology teacher at school, said was the proper word for poop). I paddled through the reek of rusty metals, oil, and chemicals, and the smoke of burning plastic and wood from islands of fire that lit our way through the rotting sea. I concentrated on not breathing through my nose, and kept my eyes peeled for any garbage bag that resembled the one we were looking for.

Sam was stepping from an upside-down chair onto the roof of a burned-out car, and Madison was following him, gripping his jacket. Jellybean was happily jumping from one floating thing to the next, and sniffing in one bobbing garbage sack before rooting around in another. I tried not to watch him too closely because every so often I could hear him chewing on something juicy before swallowing it with a loud gulp.

"Over here, Bea!" shouted Sam, climbing a small mountain of garbage bags. He was over on the other side of the dump.

As I pulled myself nearer on the freezer lid, I could see that they must have been the newer sacks because they were only just beginning to spill open and were still piled on top of each other, more or less the way the garbagemen had thrown them. I stepped onto the same burned-out car and tried to follow the route Sam and Madison had taken. As I lifted myself onto a washing machine, my right hand slipped and landed in an open garbage bag. My palm squished down into something soft. *Ugggghhh,* I thought, but quickly stopped myself from looking.

I had just turned back to wipe my hand on a heap of old clothes behind me when a grimy hand reached up from underneath and grabbed my wrist. I screamed as I tried to force the hand loose one finger at a time, but the grip was too tight. I wedged my feet against the car and pulled away with all my strength, but it was the rain and muddy slime on my wrist that allowed me to gradually twist myself free. There were some moments when being soaking wet actually helped.

It wasn't until I'd gotten away and was slithering through the soupy chaos of the dump, falling into the fetid stew up to my chin and dragging myself back out, that the horror of that hand sank in. I was still squirming inside when I made it to the other side, where Sam and Madison were waiting. Sam was smiling through all the dirt on his face, and holding up the nylon bag with Herman's guts in it.

"Somebody or something just grabbed my hand—from underneath. We've got to get out of here!" I shouted.

Madison started breathing fast and her eyes filled with terror, darting around to see who or what it was that grabbed me. She didn't seem to notice that the stinking blackness was starting, very slowly, to move.

"I think it's too late for that," said Sam. "We woke the Swamp People. They don't like people taking stuff—this is their place."

I have never seen Madison look so shocked. "You mean they really live here?" she asked, barely able to get the words out.

We stared as doors of burned-out cars creaked and shuddered open, and filthy men, women, and children pulled themselves out to see what was going on. They were so coated in dirt and brown slime that they were completely camouflaged against the garbage stew. All we could see was their dark silhouettes, lit up by the floating fires as they moved like grouchy reptiles from island to island of waste, the whites of their eyes glinting as they tried to see what it was that had disturbed their sleep. Their teeth were green-brown, which made me think that what they ate was certainly that color, too. Did they really eat garbage?

Canopies of blackened and mud-drenched corrugated iron, furniture, and carpet were slowly lifted and more Swamp People pulled themselves out.

"I'm going to count to three and then we're going to run up that slope," said Sam with urgent authority.

I thought about my bike, the bike I'd bought with my own money, saving up a bit at a time. I got it secondhand from a girl who had grown too big to ride it. It was rusty, but I'd cleaned it up and spray-painted it purple. It's how I got to school and to Sam's house. It was like an old friend.

"But my bike's on the other side!" I said.

"Forget it!" said Sam. "Ready? One . . ."

The Swamp People had seen us and were pointing angrily in our direction. They were shouting and talking furiously and one man was punching the air. They started coming toward us. It was as though the whole filthy stew had come alive and was about to wash over us in a tidal wave of blackened, stinking slop.

"Two . . . ," said Sam calmly, tightening his hold on the nylon bag we'd come for.

"Three!" called Sam, and we clambered up the slope using our hands and our feet, grabbing hold of great chunks of wet, squelching earth. We could hear the sound of the Swamp

People, an angry roar behind us. They seemed to be farther away, but we didn't stop to check.

And in the rain, none of us heard the man, younger and in better shape than the rest, run up the slope behind us. He grabbed me by one ankle and then the other and pulled me back down the slope. My hands tried to dig into the slimy earth but instead they caught on cans and other debris and I could feel sharp blood on my hand, burning and mingling with the dirt.

"Sam!" I shouted. "Sam!" But by then he was back at the top, pulling Madison up over the final ledge. *"Sam!"* I screamed.

But I was pulled down by those hands on my ankles, dragged back into the garbage soup, toward all the Swamp People and their angry, bloodshot eyes, slimy skin, and rotting teeth, waiting for me below. There were angry noises, grunts, and groans coming from beneath me as I was carried over the heads of the crowd. It felt like I was lying on the ground and it was trying to erupt. There were arms and elbows and hands pushing and poking me from underneath. I was so scared I went numb and couldn't breathe.

CHAPTER 26

I must have fainted again, because the next thing I knew, I was propped up, wrapped in a blanket in a strange kind of room with walls made of pieces of old cars, and I could hear the echo of rain, but it sounded far, far away. There was an orange light, glowing like a small setting sun at the far end of the room, and there were patterned rugs on the beaten walls and a fire crackling in the corner, which made the metal glint and shimmer. The room felt so cozy that I fell into a warm, welcoming sleep.

When I woke again and my eyes began to focus, I could see the dirty faces and fierce eyes of Swamp People huddled around, all looking at me.

"Get out of here, you're scaring her," said a man's deep voice. "Come on, let's go . . . move it!" he said, pushing the group of dirty, hungry-looking people out of the room. The men and women looked disappointed, but they turned slowly and left.

The deep voice belonged to a heavyset guy who was wearing tattered, blackened clothes. "It's good to have you back with us!" he said. "We were starting to worry about you."

"Here. I'm sorry I grabbed you." A tall boy handed me a cup of hot coffee. "We gotta be careful—people come snooping sometimes." I watched him as he spoke. My tin coffee cup shook in my hands as I realized he was the one who'd come up the slope after me.

He pulled up a thick piece of wood, sat down next to me, and looked into the fire. I watched the steam rising from my dirty coffee cup. I didn't want to drink it, but I liked the warmth in my hands. The boy had light brown eyes that stood out against the dried dirt on his face, and an earring that shone in the firelight. I thought he must be about fourteen. Older than Sam, anyway. He was long and lean, with taut muscles on his bare arms and a red-and-green snake tattoo that wound itself around his right arm from the shoulder all the way down to the wrist. He was wearing denim and leather, stitched together in places and covered in dried mud that made it look like he was wearing a strange kind of armor.

"What about my friends?" I asked. I wanted to know if Sam and Madison were OK.

"They left. We saw them cross the top ridge," he said.

I tried not to cry, but my cheeks got hot and my eyes started to sting and then filled with tears. I tucked my chin under and lowered my face as far as I could so the boy wouldn't notice. I felt so scared and so alone. I didn't know what to do. I wanted Bertha to come and get me, take me home, and tuck me into bed. I thought about her sitting on the end of the bed, making the whole mattress pull down to one side, while she told me how naughty I'd been or how strange I was, the way she often did. But most of all I wanted my mom and my dad.

The older guy came back in. He saw me crying, then crouched down in front of me and tousled my hair. "Hey, don't cry, we're not gonna hurt you. Sorry about your hand," he said, indicating the dirty bandage on my palm where I'd cut myself as I'd been pulled down the slope. He smiled, showing me that most of his top teeth were missing. "It was just the way you ran—made us think you took something. Made us think you shouldn't have been here. Isn't that right, Leo?"

"Right, Dad," said the boy with the snake tattoo.

"You don't work for anybody, do you?" The big guy was suddenly suspicious.

"No. I'm just a kid. I go to school. I'm twelve. Well, almost twelve."

He narrowed his eyes and looked at me for a few more seconds just to be sure. "It's just that a lot of people come and go—a lot of *us* come and go. We try to live here as best we can, and then more come and we have to get used to them. They're always, you know"—he made a face where his eyes crossed and his mouth went crooked and his finger circled around and around at his temple—"crazy in the head. But the ones that *leave*, they're always OK."

"My mom's crazy. She's in St. Agnes's, in town," I said, trying to make conversation.

"That's the place. That's where a lot of them come from. They stay there for a while and then they find out they've got no home left when they come out again. Can't go to work and pay for a house when you're crazy, so they wind up here. This is the last place to come. This is where you come when the world wants to forget about you. The End of the World," he said, his eyes fixed on the floor.

"I'm not crazy, and I've got a home, and a very nice lady who takes care of me, and I've got friends who I'm sure are going to come back for me." I realized as I was saying it that I might have sounded a little nuts after all.

"You hungry?" grunted the older man, stirring something hot and runny in a pot over the fire. He splashed what looked like some kind of bean stew onto a plastic plate and waved it at me. I shook my head. The thought of being so close to all that garbage made me feel ill.

"Are we underneath all that garbage?" I asked tentatively.

"Used to be a lot closer, but the garbage just kept growing. We never thought there'd be so much. We started building tunnels underground and into the hillside. We had to put in new ventilation shafts," explained the man.

"Gunk still gets inside sometimes," added the boy. "But we take care of it."

They started eating, taking big spoonfuls of the bean stew and shoveling it into their mouths.

"What's your name?" asked the man, spitting some stew at me as he spoke.

"Bea," I said quietly.

"Like the insect?" He put his plate on his lap for a moment, flapped his hands like little wings, and made a buzzing noise. This made me smile. He looked funny, such a big guy making himself look like a bee.

"It's short for Beatrice," I explained. Then there was this long pause. "My dad told me once that I'm named after the girlfriend of a famous Italian poet," I added, to keep the conversation going.

"I'm Jack. Nice to meet you, Bea," said the big guy, wiping his hand on his dirty pants before giving it to me to shake. It was strong and big and warm and reminded me of my dad's hand. "And this is Leo, my son."

There was a banging noise on the metal where the door was. Leo got up and opened it, letting in a young wiry man with a red scarf tied around his head. They said something to each other that I couldn't hear and then the man with the scarf wheeled my bike inside.

"We cleaned it up a little," said the man proudly.

"That's Nathan," said Jack, and Nathan smiled shyly and nodded.

"Thanks," I said, kind of laughing and wanting to cry at the same time. My purple bike, which I'd thought I'd lost for good, was back, and it was sparkling so much it looked like new. I wanted to hug the man for finding and cleaning it, but I hugged my bike instead. Nathan let out a satisfied breath, smiled gently, and left the room.

"The stuff we find, we clean up and we sell it. That's how we buy food. I bet you thought we ate garbage, didn't you?" said Leo.

"No," I said, but I had thought exactly that. "I just wasn't hungry before. I could eat something now. If there's any left."

Jack put a ladleful of stew on a plate and gave it to me.

They both watched as I lifted the spoon to my mouth and tasted. I could see it was somehow important to them that I accepted their food. Like I was one of them.

"It's good!" I said, smiling, and continued eating. But it tasted horrible, like tin and rubber. It had bits of sand in it and smelled faintly of the garbage stew outside. I pretended very hard to like it and that must have worked, because as I was eating I could see Leo's face change; it was like his eyes were smiling.

"We'll wait till the last trucks have left, then it'll be safe for you to leave. There are people watching this place all the time, seeing who comes and goes. It's not safe," said Jack.

"Who's watching?" I asked, but he didn't answer. Then I thought if I told him why we'd come, he might tell me something about what he meant and why they stayed here, living among the refuse. "We were trying to find something that we put in the garbage by mistake. It was something important; it belonged to somebody who died. And we thought it might help us find out why he died."

Jack looked at me suspiciously again. "Hold on . . . ," he said, squinting even harder at me before heading out of the metal room. He burst back in a couple of minutes later. "Do you recognize this picture?"

He held out a crumpled little photo. There were creases and cracks across it, but I could still see the figure on it. It was a picture of a little girl about four years old, wearing red tights and a purple-and-orange smock, with light brown hair and a goofy smile. She was sitting on a tricycle and holding a little plush rabbit in her left hand. She seemed so familiar.

It was the bunny that did it. The bunny was called Emily. I knew that because I'd named her. It was my bunny and the little girl was me.

I couldn't speak for a minute. "How did you get that photo? That's me in the photo," I said, confused.

"Your father gave it to me. I mean, he left it here." I still didn't understand. How could he have known my father? "Your father was a good man," Jack continued. "He was very brave. A good friend. He came here to write a story about us. How we live. He wanted to understand. He took photos. I told him to stay away—that it was dangerous—but he came back after the first story and kept on asking questions." Then Jack's face changed and he looked frightened. His eyes darted around the room for a moment, even though there were only the three of us there. He scared me, looking like that, like something was about to happen. Something terrible.

"Your father showed me this picture," Jack started to explain. "I didn't want to talk to him at first, about my life, about how I'd lost my daughter and my wife, but he told me about you, and he showed me your photo. He wanted me to understand that he had a daughter, too. He loved you very much."

I went to hand the photo back to Jack, but he smiled and said, "You keep it. It's the least I can do." Then he turned to Leo. "Got to get to work," he said, and left the room.

I put the crumpled photo in my pocket and thought about how my dad had kept it all that time, enough time for it to get crumpled. "Thanks for the picture," I called after Jack, but he'd already gone.

I don't know why, but I suddenly felt embarrassed being in the room on my own with Leo. "I 'spect you want to know why I've got this snake down my arm?" he said, lifting his right arm up and bending it forward for me to see.

I shrugged, but I *did* want to know. People didn't get other people to tattoo things onto their skin forever without there being a reason. But I didn't have to ask, because Leo wanted to tell me. "Snakes shed their skin. They become new again. One day *I'll* become new. Get out of this place. I'll be rich. You wait and see! I'm only staying for Dad. When he . . . when he got depressed, I took care of him. We do OK." He looked across the room. "Do you want to see something?"

I nodded.

He climbed over his bed, which was tucked under a sloping metal roof, and opened a drawer. He took out a book, all its pages curling and fat with damp. He handed it to me and said excitedly, "Pick a page—any page!" So I flicked through the book and pointed to a place on that page. Leo started to read, very carefully and very slowly, like the words were a spell he had to get just right.

"I beheld the wretch, the mis-er-able mon-ster whom I had cre-ated. He held up the c-c-curtain of the bed; and his eyes, if eyes they may be called, were fixed on me. His jaws opened, and he mut-tered some in-ar-ti-cu-late sounds, while a grin wrin-kled his cheeks. He might have spoken, but I did not hear; one hand was s-str-etched out, se-eemin-gly to detain me, but I escaped and rushed down-stairs."

Leo didn't seem to care what the words meant; he was more interested in reading them in the right way, taking his time with the harder words, remembering how they felt in his mouth. Then he closed the book before I could see what it was, and put it back in his drawer. "I'm teaching myself to read. So when I get out of here I can get a good job."

"I'm sure you'll get a *great* job. You're a really good reader," I said to him.

"You think?" he asked, and I nodded.

Just then there was a *bang* on the door. Jack lifted and pushed the metal sheet and announced with a wonky smile, "Got some people here asking after Bea."

He moved out of the way to let Sam, Eric, and Butterfly through. They were covered in mud but looked so happy to see me. It was then that I realized we weren't just hanging out with each other because we had to—we actually liked each other and cared about each other. We'd actually become real friends.

"We were so worried, Bea!" said Butterfly, hugging me tight.

"It's good to see you," Sam said shyly. He noticed my bike leaning against the wall and touched the shiny chrome handlebars. "You got your bike back!"

"Leo and Jack found it," I said, smiling at Leo.

"Nathan cleaned it up—we just got it out of the dirt."

"We thought you were dead," said Eric, in a voice that seemed partly relieved and partly disappointed. Then Jellybean bounced through the door, jumped up, and licked my face.

I looked around to see Leo looking a little awkward. "This is Leo . . . my friend." When I said the word *friend,* Leo looked a little embarrassed.

"Hi," he said quietly.

"Leo helped fix my bike and has a cool snake tattoo — show them!" I signaled for him to show them, but he just stood there looking shy, so I took his arm for a second to bring him closer, and he finally rolled up his sleeve and showed them the colorful twisting snake.

"Did it hurt?" asked Eric.

"Not really . . . I mean, yeah, you bet," said Leo.

When Jack said it was safe to go, I hugged him tight, burying the side of my face against his solid belly. It felt like earth warmed by the sun. Jack seemed a little surprised for a moment, and then lowered one of his hands slowly and ruffled my hair the way my dad sometimes used to do. For a minute I didn't want to let him go. He was the closest I'd gotten to my dad for a long time.

"You take care of yourself now," he said. "No more hanging around places like this." Then he took my shoulders in his hands, smiled his wonky smile, and gently pushed me away.

Leo showed us the way out. I went ahead with him and the others followed. We walked along a corridor of metal and compacted dirt lit up by oil lamps in old tins. I could see other corridors leading off in different directions and I wondered where they all went. There were little rooms off to the sides with people in them. In a few there were children, who waved as we walked past. How could children live down here? I felt so sad at the thought of it that my heart seemed to swell up as though it wanted to burst out of my chest. Some of the people looked angry or frightened or both. Often it was hard to make out who was in those rooms because it was so dark. I could see why my dad wanted to tell their story. Why he wanted people to know about them. *Did his death have something to do with them?* I thought. Maybe my dad didn't die from drinking too much and falling asleep in the cold, like Mom and Bertha told me, after all.

Suddenly Butterfly screamed. She was behind all of us in the tunnel when a woman leaped out of one of the burrows and pounced on her. The woman was angry and panting, like a wild animal, and what she said didn't make any sense. Her hands were gripping Butterfly's neck and she pinned her to the floor. "You took him . . . where is he? Give him back! You bring him back to me or I'll kill you!" she hissed.

Butterfly was terrified and couldn't breathe. Leo tried to pull her fingers away from Butterfly's throat. "It's OK, Mary, it's OK . . . OK . . ." He spoke more and more calmly while he held her wrists and gradually moved her away from Butterfly.

Eric put his arm protectively around Butterfly while she held her neck and started to cry. "I didn't do anything," she whispered.

Leo took the woman back into the small cavelike room and kept speaking to her until she just kind of whimpered softly to herself. After a couple of minutes Leo came back out. "I'm really sorry. She lost her son not too long ago. She thinks the garbagemen took him. She gets upset sometimes. Are you OK?" he said to Butterfly, and she nodded.

"What was her son's name?" Sam's voice was slow and deliberate.

"Luke. Luke Green." Leo said the name like he was reading it off a list, but Sam and I looked at each other and the realization began to take shape in our minds.

At the top of the tunnel was a corrugated iron ramp, which made a loud, hollow kind of rattle as we all walked up it toward the little metal submarine-style door. I never thought I'd be relieved to hear the rain, but I was. I was relieved in the same way I was relieved to see Sam and Eric, Butterfly and Jellybean.

Leo said good-bye and I gave him a hug. I felt sad to be leaving him behind in that strange under-garbage world. I wanted to take him home with me. Maybe I could ask Bertha if he could stay with us? But then I thought about Jack and how he would miss him.

"Say thanks to your dad," I said.

"For what?" he asked.

"For the bean stew and for my bike," I replied, taking the bike from Sam, who had wheeled it all the way through the tunnel for me.

Sam gave me a funny look as he passed me the bike. He looked at Leo and then back at me. I don't know what he was thinking, but for some reason I don't think he liked Leo very much. Maybe it was the tattoo. Sam had been talking about getting one since last summer when Roxanne, one of the old Convicts, got hers.

Once we'd climbed out of the camouflaged door and out onto our side of the ridge, I looked back over the garbage soup we'd just traveled across underground. I saw the suspended refrigerators, cars, and mattresses floating like bits of sodden toast, and thought about Leo and Jack and the lady who had attacked Butterfly. I thought about those families living underneath it all, under all that junk. And it made me want to photograph them, the way my dad had, to show other people, to show them how they live, so that maybe things could change. I thought how photos of them, especially Leo and Jack, maybe wouldn't have been great for that photo competition—even though it was too late for that now—but how they would be good to take anyway, to show them to people—and because I liked Jack and Leo. I liked them because they were interesting, because they'd been kind to me when they didn't have to be, and most of all because they were full of courage.

We helped each other over the ridge and started the long walk home through the rain and the mud. "What did you do with Herman's guts?" I asked Sam.

"I threw them out," he said coolly.

"What do you mean, you threw them out?" I couldn't believe it, after all that!

"I threw them out . . . *after* I got the ring out of them."

I breathed a sigh of relief. And then felt sick thinking of him poking through human intestines.

"It was a bit of a mess"—Sam shuddered—"but the ring is inside the Captain now—for safekeeping."

"Who's the Captain?" asked Butterfly.

"Just this kind of . . . mannequin I have," said Sam.

"I really need to see the ring," I said, turning to the others. "You guys should know, there's something terrible going on around here—and it's not just about who killed Herman.

There's something bigger, much bigger and much worse, and it's got something to do with the people who live under the garbage."

I'll never forget their expressions—Sam's, Butterfly's, and Eric's. Their faces were pale and gaunt in the low light, the rain streaking across them like they were half drowned. Fear had started to gnaw away at the parts of them that were still innocent, and those childlike parts had begun to crumble into the inevitable murkiness around us.

"Maybe we should leave the whole thing alone—it's not really our business," said Eric.

"I think Eric's right," said Butterfly. "It's not worth risking our lives just to find out about a guy who died, a guy we didn't even know."

"He didn't die, he was *murdered*, remember, and we *do* know him—kind of—it's Herman the Pickle King. You see him every time you eat relish. You can't say you don't know him. We can't just forget about him. If we let them get away with this, they could kill anybody they wanted and get away with it," I said. "I don't care if you guys want to help or not—I'm going to find out who killed Herman and I'm going to find out what it's got to do with those poor people who live under there." I pointed to the dark pit behind us. "It's the crazy people who end up there. Jack said so—my *mom* could end up there. It could happen to any of us. It could happen to you, too, one day."

"I'm with you, Bea," said Sam. "You know you can count on me."

I was so grateful to him, and so overwhelmed with

thoughts and feelings and what I had just been through, thinking that I was going to die in that pit, that I threw my arms around him and started crying.

"Thank you," I sobbed quietly.

Sam didn't know what to do; he just said, "Take it easy. The others are going to help, too—right?"

And Eric said, "I guess so—but I don't see why I can't just concentrate on my invention."

But Butterfly said, "Of course—we're all in this together. We're the Raintown Convicts, right?"

I smiled and nodded.

"Her housekeeper was really annoyed that Madison was covered in mud and made her stay home and get cleaned up, but she's in, too," said Sam, patting me on the back the way guys sometimes do when they're embarrassed by people's emotions. Sam wasn't too good at showing his feelings, but I knew from what he'd just said how much he cared about me. He could tell how important it was to me to find out what was going on. Maybe it was because he was the one who'd taken me to the body. He was the reason this had all started. Sam wasn't going to let me down now, and he was going to make sure nobody else did, either.

"We need to get out of here." Sam's tone of voice changed suddenly. I turned around to see a group of men on the same side of the canyon as us, about halfway across. They were dressed like garbagemen and were shining a large flashlight through the darkness, into the pit. As they turned, they were lit up by a truck and I could see the unmistakably nasty face of Mr. Jeeks, also dressed as a garbageman.

"It's him," I said. "It's Jeeks!" We started walking away as fast as we could, but it was hard in that thick mud.

When the beam of Jeeks's flashlight swung around in our direction I hissed, "Lie down!" and we threw ourselves into the mud and lay as flat as we could, breathing in the wet earth.

"Do you think they saw us?" whispered Butterfly.

"I don't know," I said.

We waited until the men turned off the flashlights and got back into the truck. The truck roared to life and drove off, mashing its way through the dirty rain. We waited a few more minutes before pulling ourselves up out of the cold mud and heading homeward.

"I think they saw us," I said, and the horrible feeling I'd had ever since Jeeks had come after us and into my house returned. My whole body shivered for a second, not in the way it did when Herman's ghost was around, but in a disgusting, creepy way that only happened when you saw giant spiders or discovered a cockroach in your bed; and as I looked at the faces of the others, I could see they felt the same way, too.

CHAPTER 27

It had felt like the longest day in my life, climbing up to the dump and then being taken inside. The rain made you forget time anyway, but being underground like that, underneath all that garbage, made you forget what country you were in, what planet you were on. I knew I should've probably headed home for some rest, but I wanted to see the ring, so we went to Sam's place. Madison managed to escape the housekeeper and met us there.

"How did Jed know about the ring? That's what I want to know," asked Butterfly.

"He must have known that Herman owned it and that it was really valuable," said Eric.

"I doubt Jed could see inside a dead man's guts, unless he's Superman or something," said Madison.

"And how did he know *we* had it? I mean, *we* didn't even know we had it," wondered Butterfly, frowning.

Sam looked uncomfortable and watched his sneakers slop along the sidewalk, but didn't say anything until we got to the bottom of his street. "You guys wait here," he mumbled.

I guess he was checking who was home. There weren't many houses on Sam's street, and the ones that were there had broken windows and burned-out cars on what should have been front lawns. Some houses had trailers parked next to them where people had moved out of their house and into the new trailer. We saw Sam's signal and walked toward his house.

The smell of stale air, alcohol, and cigarettes hit us as we tiptoed inside, past Sam's drunken, snoring father, who was sprawled out on the couch. The place was unfurnished apart from the old couch and a collection of vodka bottles, beer cans, and ashtrays. I don't think Madison had ever been to a house like Sam's, and she wasn't doing a good job of disguising it.

"Don't worry, he's out cold," said Sam, leading the way upstairs.

It was hard for us to fit into his room all at once, but we weren't planning to stay long. Sam threw back the sheets on his bed to reveal the Captain, who smiled at us in his silly way, one of his eyebrows permanently raised. Sam pulled off his head, took some stuffing out, and grabbed the ring. There it was—not just a picture on an X-ray, but the real thing. Sam held it up for a second and I reached out to touch it, but Sam didn't give me a chance. He tucked it in his pocket, put the Captain back under his bedcovers, and said, "Let's go to my hideout."

Eric and Sam climbed up the rope ladder to the tree house first and then let the pulley down for Jellybean, who seemed to be getting used to the ordeal by now. He just stood there with a startled look on his face, his legs evenly spaced, while me and Butterfly put the canvas under his belly and attached it on both sides.

"OK!" I shouted, and Eric and Sam pulled him up. He looked so funny dangling there. For a minute I looked up and saw him hanging in the air, like a strange kind of flying dog, as the moody gray clouds moved above him, quickly changing from one menacing shape into another. As he swung a little from side to side in that inky, rain-filled sky, the rope creaked with his weight and I was suddenly worried he'd be seen, that he'd draw attention to all of us. Once Jelly was inside, me and Madison and Butterfly climbed up and pulled the ladder in after us.

Sam wrapped his flashlight in an old Lola's Cola T-shirt and switched it on. "I've got food!" announced Eric, shaking the contents of his bag on the floor. There was something to be said for hanging out with somebody whose mom fussed over him, even if Eric thought she was doing it for the wrong reasons. "I've got Bert's Big Cheesies, bananas, and peanut butter and jelly sandwiches."

"Why didn't you say so before?" said Sam, pulling open the bag of cheese puffs and stuffing a handful in his mouth. As he reached for a second handful, Sam noticed something. He turned the big bag of cheese balls over and held it nearer to the flashlight so he could read it. "There's those letters again—*MHF Foodstuffs Inc.* That guy must really own the whole world," he said, letting Jellybean lick a few of the cheese puffs from his palm. "And I just know those letters have got something to do with Herman's murder."

I nibbled on a peanut butter and jelly sandwich. It tasted so good after that strange bean stew I'd eaten with Leo and

Jack—and right away I felt bad for thinking that. I bet they never got to eat peanut butter and jelly sandwiches.

"Let me see the ring now!" I said through a mouthful of sandwich, barely able to contain my excitement. Sam wiped his cheese-dust hands on his wet jeans, pulled the ring from his pocket, and handed it to me.

It was a heavy, brassy ring in the shape of a big palace or castle, a bit like the kind you read about in fairy tales when you're a kid, but wider and less frilly and fancy. "Such a strange type of ring," I said, turning it over between my fingers.

"It must have been hard to swallow. Let me try!" said Eric, grabbing it and pretending to gulp it down.

"Don't!" I shouted. "Give it back!"

I ran my finger over the rooftops and little turrets of the castle ring and imagined standing at the doorway and being asked inside. There was something so familiar about that doorway. . . .

"It's really well made. It looks old," said Butterfly.

"Where did Herman get it?" I wondered.

"Maybe he stole it and they came after him. They knew he had it, that's for sure," said Sam.

"Maybe," I said. "It does look expensive, and kind of important."

"Maybe it's got something to do with that club, the one where they make the human sacrifices," added Eric. Madison frowned. I looked at the remains of my peanut butter and jelly sandwich and suddenly didn't feel so good about eating the rest of it.

As I turned the ring over in the beam of the flashlight, I noticed something on the inside rim. "Look! There's something written on it."

"Where?" asked Butterfly.

I tried to follow the curly, old-fashioned writing. *"For my . . . darling . . . Agnes . . . all my love . . . John, 1831."*

"It was a gift," said Madison.

"We've got to find out why Herman had it." I was thinking to myself as I spoke. "And why Jeeks wanted it."

Our faces had a reddish glow from the color of the T-shirt covering the flashlight. We sat huddled together, high up in the tree house, clutched in that witch's hand reaching up into the eerie sky. For a minute or two nobody said a word. There was just the sound of the wind moaning and the rainy fingers tapping on the roof and on the leaves of the tree. Every so often the tree house creaked with the movement of the branches.

"By the way, my mom's mad at me because Jeeks moved out. She thinks it was my fault, 'cause I made too much noise or something," said Eric. "She didn't even ask me if he could stay in the first place, and now she's blaming me for him leaving."

"He's gone?" I asked.

"Yes. His room was completely empty except for this . . . ," he said, pulling a pile of paper from his backpack. "I found them under a couple of loose floorboards."

Sam snatched the papers out of Eric's hand. "They're official documents about . . . the Jeeks and Smytheson Property Company."

"Let's see," said Butterfly, and Sam handed them over to us.

"Jeeks and Smytheson were in business together?" I said.

"Mom said he worked in real estate—they're letters about buying houses. It's probably nothing, I just thought I'd bring them." Eric took another bite of his sandwich.

"J&S—that's the company that bought Herman's house. It's the company that buys all the houses that people can't afford anymore. DW told us," I said. "And Jeeks and Smytheson own it!"

"It's right here. Herman Henderson's house: two forty-nine Pinehills Drive," Madison read the address out loud.

"We should keep it—we might need it as evidence," said Butterfly, organizing all the sheets of paper and putting them back into Eric's backpack. "Good work, Eric," she said, doing up the zipper. Eric smiled an embarrassed smile and one of his top teeth stuck out over his bottom lip.

"What I want to know is why a surgeon needs a property company. That's what Smytheson is—a surgeon. That day at the hospital, he was there."

"Are you serious?" asked Butterfly, and Sam and I nodded. "I didn't realize it at first because of how he was dressed, but it was definitely him."

"Jeeks being friends with a surgeon would sort of explain how he got hold of Herman's intestines!" added Butterfly.

"Right," I said, feeling something fall into place. "He's the one who made them take the X-ray of Herman's body. Bertha said he's the top guy at the hospital."

Eric's brow furrowed in thought. "Here's another

question—why does a surgeon need to pull down posters of missing people?"

Everybody looked at me, expecting me to have the answer.

"Oh, no . . ." Sam was suddenly on edge as we heard the wheels of a car skid through the mud and come to a stop. "Jed's back." The engine switched off and the door slammed shut as he got out. We heard the sound of another car arrive, *sloosh*ing through the dirt and rain at high speed. Sam stood up and looked through the rectangular eye of the tree house.

"What's going on?" I asked.

"I don't know, but it looks like somebody followed him," said Sam. I got up and pushed Sam over a little to see, and then Butterfly and Eric and Madison did the same. We were all squashed up together, looking out of that little window.

Then Jellybean started barking. "Quiet, boy!" Sam whispered, bending down to him. "You gotta be quiet, Jelly, shhhhh!" He petted him on the head and got up again to watch with us.

The car door opened and one boot *sploosh*ed onto the wet ground, followed by the other. A figure in dark rain gear got out and put his hood up; we couldn't see his face. Jed was heading toward the front door when he turned around suddenly. The other man must have spoken to him.

"Who is it?" Butterfly's voice was breathy with excitement.

"I don't know, doesn't look like any of his gang—they don't drive fancy cars like that," answered Sam.

On the rickety old porch of Sam's house, the figure stood

close to Jed, towering over him. Jed sort of froze, and fear crept across his face.

"I've never seen that before," whispered Sam. "He's scared. My brother's actually scared of somebody."

Then, as the figure turned to go, the wind blew his hood back and there he was again, his sharp, nasty features, red-rimmed eyes, and pasty skin lit up by the headlights of his car. Sam's face took on a kind of haunted expression. What was his brother doing talking to Mr. Jeeks?

"How does your brother know Jeeks?" I asked, but Sam didn't answer.

As Jeeks was about to get back into his car, the two started arguing, and we could hear snatches of what they said through the rain.

". . . couldn't do *one* simple thing! What do I pay you for? All you had to do was get the ring, but you wind up kill-ing him instead—and did you get the ring back? No, you didn't!" Jeeks yelled at Jed.

Madison took a sharp intake of breath, and the rest of us seemed to stop breathing altogether.

The two men continued talking and we strained to hear through the rain. Then Jeeks shouted, "And if you don't take care of those freakin' kids, I will!" He got back into his car, slamming the door after him, revved his engine till the tires caught in the dirt, and screeched off into the night.

Jed stood on the porch for a moment, his arms hanging heavily by his sides, looking defeated. Then he slammed his palm onto the front door, went inside, and switched on the lights. Almost right away we could hear the drunken shouts of Sam's dad.

We tried not to show it for Sam's sake, but we were horror-struck, and you could feel it in the damp darkness of the tree house and hear it in the wind that shrieked through the creaking branches holding us up. It was Jed who had killed Herman; we'd heard Jeeks say so. Jed who lived with Sam, Jed who came after us in the abandoned train. I don't think any of us thought Herman's murderer would end up being so close to home.

"What is it with that nasty man? Why does he keep creeping around—can't he just leave us alone?" Butterfly was suddenly angry.

Sam turned away from the little window, spread out his sleeping bag, smoothed over the bumps, and sat down on it. Then he reached up for a crumpled pack of his dad's Spanish cigarettes, which he kept under the eaves. I knew then he'd be camping out tonight.

Sam put a squashed cigarette in his mouth and let it kind of hang on his lower lip, then he lit a match that didn't take because of the damp, so he tried another. We all sat down and watched until his cigarette glowed and Sam blew a large smoke ring into the air and watched it slowly dissolve. (Sam likes to watch circles of smoke travel and then disappear. I think it calms him down. When it's just the two of us hanging out, I like to wave my hand across the rings like I'm erasing them in midair, and Sam'll say, "Leave them!" like he's made something special and I'm spoiling it.)

Madison looked at Sam with her mournful gray eyes. It was totally obvious to the rest of us that she thought Sam was the cutest guy she'd ever met. And the more he proved he was the kind of bad boy her dad would forbid her to see, the dreamier he probably became.

Butterfly and Eric looked uncomfortable. They weren't used to Sam's smoking like I was. *Normally they'd never be hanging out with somebody like this,* I thought as I caught the awkwardness on their faces. Sam was a loner at school and sat all by himself during recess, out in the yard or in the teachers' parking lot. He didn't really mix with anybody, and the other kids avoided him because they were scared of him. But I knew Sam wasn't really scary; he just wanted to be left in peace.

"Want one?" He aimed the cigarette pack at Butterfly.

"No, thanks," she said, a little embarrassed.

"You?" He waved the squished-up pack in Eric's direction.

"OK," said Eric, pulling one out. He lit the cigarette himself and held it tight between the tips of his thumb and index finger, which looked kind of funny, but, then again, I guess he was kind of an odd kid. As he took a drag, he looked like an old guy smoking a pipe or something, with this hang-dog expression on his face. Then Butterfly took the cigarette from him, staring at Eric as if to say, *Don't you say anything.* She took a quick puff, almost spitting the smoke into the air before handing it back to him.

"That's disgusting!" she complained, making a sour face.

"I know," said Eric, quietly pleased with himself.

"Smoking stunts your growth," Madison informed us

smugly, though I suspected she secretly wanted a drag of Sam's cigarette.

"Good. My mom would be really pissed if she had to have a midget son!"

Butterfly looked at Eric as though she could pick up how sad he really was under all the anger. "Your mom seems nice—I don't know why you're so mad at her. Sometimes grown-ups try their best and things just don't work out for them. I'm sure she didn't mean to hurt you."

Rage flashed across Eric's face, and for a moment we were sure he was about to come back with a typical gruff reply, but gradually his expression changed and a shadow seemed to lift off him. It was as though what Butterfly had said had opened a little door inside him and he was able to let that new thought in.

Sam, though, was somewhere else entirely. As he puffed his smoke rings into the air, he looked lost, so lost that nobody would ever be able to find him and bring him back. "There's something I should tell you," he said slowly. "About Herman's body."

We all waited for him to continue. Eric stopped smoking and stared at Sam, letting the ash build up on the end of the cigarette until it dropped into his lap.

"Do you guys want to know how I knew there was a body in that house?" said Sam.

I'd asked him the night he took me to the body, but I hadn't thought to ask again. After all, Sam was always getting us into strange situations and places we shouldn't be. He had a knack for it.

"My brother made me keep watch," he continued. "He told me they were just going to rob the place." His cigarette shook in his trembling fingers. Tears filled his eyes, and he rubbed his hand across them to stop them from coming, stretching the thin skin roughly, like he was trying to rub them out. This made his eyes even more red.

"Did you know your brother killed Herman?" asked Butterfly, getting straight to the point.

"I don't know. Maybe he didn't mean to, maybe Herman just got in the way, maybe Herman threatened him . . ." Then Sam let his head drop, like he was ashamed and didn't want us to see him like this. "I just waited outside. I let him die." Now Sam's brow was all knitted and more tears appeared in his eyes.

"It's not your fault," I said, touching Sam's shoulder. Butterfly reached out and did the same. "But we've got to stay out of sight—Jeeks, Smytheson the surgeon, *and* your brother are all after us now. The important thing is, we know Jeeks and the Smytheson guy were involved with Herman's death—probably because of this ring. So we just need to stay out of sight long enough to find out how all these things fit together. Herman, the ring, and the people who live in Garbage City," I said, hoping that the others weren't going to try and back down again.

"*And* the secret club—you know, with the sacrifices— they meet in just a few days. . . . I've thought about it, and all we need is to find a grown-up to help us get inside," Eric stated firmly. I was interested in checking out everything and anything that would provide answers, but I couldn't help noticing that Eric seemed mighty keen on that secret club in particular.

"If Jeeks and his friend are involved, we should probably go to that meeting," Butterfly admitted.

"And I need to see if my dad kept files of any of his old stories. Jack, the guy in the dump, told me my dad was writing an article about them. He gave me this." I showed them the wrinkled photo.

Sam snatched the picture out of my hands and started to laugh. "Is that you?"

"What's so funny?" I asked.

"Nothing," he said, handing the photo back. "You were a cute kid."

I was suddenly embarrassed. I let the other three have a look and then I put the photo back in my pocket.

We agreed that Sam should keep the ring for the time being, up in the tree house. It was the safest place for it, we decided, until we needed it.

CHAPTER 28

As I drifted in and out of sleep, wrapped in my warm feather quilt, I thought of Sam sleeping next to Jellybean in the drafty, moaning tree house. At least he had Jelly for company.

When I woke the next morning, instead of switching on the cartoons, I put a record on my player and wedged the door open with one of my shoes so I could hear the music all around the house. I thought that if I played my dad's records it would somehow make it easier to find his old papers and photos and stuff. I was sure there would be something at the back of a drawer somewhere, something about Jack and Leo and the people who lived in Garbage City.

I was spinning around the living room to the sound of "Hungarian Rhapsody" and eating a cheese-and-relish pancake at the same time. "Hungarian Rhapsody" is a piece of music that starts off slow and gets faster and faster and*fasterandfaster*! I spun and spun and spun until my feet were a blur.

When the record stopped I fell into an armchair, out of breath and feeling kind of sick. Once I'd caught my breath and wasn't feeling so queasy, I checked all the drawers in the kitchen, and even Bertha's private desk, which she sits at to pay her bills. The record player was making a whirring drone upstairs. It meant the song had finished but the needle was still going round and round at the center of the record. I went upstairs and put on my new record, the one DW had given me. I pulled it out of its sleeve and read the little words at the center—*Bob Marley and The Wailers, No Woman No Cry*—before lowering it onto the turntable. I lifted the needle arm up with one finger and placed it down gently on the spinning disc. The song played while I opened the heavy drawers of Bertha's desk and rifled through her papers.

All I found in Bertha's desk were boring pieces of paper, bills for the gas and electricity. There were lots of catalogs, too, for jewelry and clothes that you paid for a few dollars at a time. Bertha had marked the things she liked with little stars, but she never bought any of them.

My dad's articles were nowhere to be seen. But as I sat there staring into space, it happened. The pinkie finger on my left hand started tingling a little, just gently at first, and then the buzzing and twitching began. *OK,* I thought, *there's got to be something around here.* I got up and walked toward the TV and the feeling in my finger disappeared, so I walked back toward the desk and it started up again. I moved my hand around the desk, holding it right near the little drawers at the back, the ones that usually just have paper clips and staples in them. I opened each one and moved the stuff around to see if there was anything important there. Then I found something. It was a small metal key with a blue tag on it that said ATTIC. *That's weird*, I thought, *we don't have an attic*. Could we have an attic that I'd never seen?

Attics are at the top of houses, so I headed up the stairs. Once I got to the top landing I looked around, and bent my neck back so much to search the ceiling that it made my head feel funny, like it had been chopped off or something but was still there, hanging on by a flap of skin.

I was looking for a little square or a window, or any shape that might have once been an entrance to an attic. But there was nothing. Then I got fed up. Why did things always have to be so complicated? Why couldn't things ever be simple?

I sat on the landing with my legs crossed and my head in my hands. My record player was whirring again, because the Bob Marley song had stopped. Then I had a crazy idea.

"Herman? Are you there? If you're listening, can you show me where the attic is?"

I felt a bit stupid talking out loud, hearing the sound of my own voice echo around the empty house. *But*, I thought, *what've I got to lose, it's worth a shot*. I was facing the door to Bertha's room, which was shut tight, but just then the handle turned and with a slow squeak the door opened. I looked around, more than a little spooked. I hadn't expected him to answer!

"Thanks, Herman!" I called out, getting up and going into Bertha's room.

Our house is an old house. I don't know how old, exactly, but it's definitely more than a hundred, and that means it's got all kinds of strange nooks and crannies. I knew about the cellar, which my dad partly turned into the darkroom, but I never knew we had an attic. Bertha probably didn't know it was there, either. *Why hadn't my parents told me?* I wondered, suddenly really annoyed, thinking of all the times I could have played in the attic. Attics were exciting places that you read about and saw in movies, places where you discovered things, hidden things, things you weren't supposed to see. Mom once told me a story about a man who never grew old, but had a picture of himself in the attic that got older and older instead. The picture in the attic had wrinkles and white hair but the real man never looked a day older. How weird is that?

At the far end of Bertha's room, next to her bed, on the left side, was what looked like the outline of a very small closet. I had to move her nightstand out of the way to get to it, and then I saw the tiny keyhole.

I turned the key and the door opened easily. I lowered my head to get inside. The darkness appeared suddenly, like something solid, and I waved my hand in front of my face to keep it away. That's how I found the light switch on the wall, which made the dusty lightbulb glow from the ceiling. As I walked farther inside, the room expanded, sprawling in different directions. Coming through that tiny door, I never would have expected it to be so big. It was the biggest room in the house. It smelled of damp and dust, which filled my nostrils and made me want to sneeze; and the sound of the angry fingers rapping on the roof was as loud as ever. There was a streak of bright green slime down one wall where the rain was making its way in. One by one, silver droplets of rain were traveling quickly down the moldy green hairs. It looked like a giant lizard's tongue, snaking its way down the wall, thirstily searching for flies.

There were lots of old suitcases piled one on top of the other, and in the corner was the baby carriage I must have had as a baby, with dust and cobwebs all over it. There were stacks of books and boxes of old clothes; there was broken furniture and camping equipment; pots and pans and plastic cups and plates. Here was all the stuff my parents had used when they lived here together, when we were a family.

I didn't know where to start looking for my dad's old stories, so I just began opening a suitcase here and there, lifting a few things off the tops of boxes. I found all kinds of stuff, like my mom's school reports — even a piece of her auburn hair in an envelope, a thick braid she'd kept when she cut her hair short after dad died. There were photos of both my parents when they were kids, even younger than me, and some photos of their wedding in New York City, where the wind is blowing their hair and clothes all over the place. They don't seem to mind; they're just looking into each other's eyes and smiling like nothing else exists.

I was starting to get tired and was feeling strange from seeing all the old photos and clothes and stuff. I felt a bit like I was a ghost, visiting my parents. It was as though they were still together, having dinner downstairs, while I was trapped upstairs with the things that belonged in a different story, a different version of my family.

Then I clicked open a big trunk that was under a table and lifted the lid. On top were some of my dad's clothes and a camera he had when he was a boy, which he'd shown me once. There was a photo of Babi and Deda, my dad's parents, who I'd only met a couple of times and didn't really remember. They were from the Czech Republic, which is in Europe, and *babi* and *deda* mean *grandma* and *grandpa* over there. They came over at Christmas when I was small and brought me strange things to eat, like a giant salami on a rope, beets in a jar, and candies I wasn't used to. Deda had some fingers missing because he was a carpenter and had chopped some off by accident. They were just smooth stumps. I remember that, and how he put me on his knee and rubbed the scratchy bristles of his beard on my cheek.

Underneath my dad's clothes, camera, and photos were folders, lots of folders. Inside the folders, finally, were what I was looking for: his stories.

I didn't realize how many stories he had written and photographed. There were hundreds. Hundreds of delicate leaves of newspapers and magazines, some laid neatly, like they'd been ironed, some folded over, some yellowing and torn at the edges, and they were from all over the world. Russia, England, India, France, Spain, Africa. My dad had been to all those places! How come I had never known about that? Why didn't he take me with him? *Maybe that was all before I was born,* I thought. But then I saw some of the dates and I could see he was visiting those places while he lived here with me and Mom. Maybe that's why they argued so much, because he was away from home so much, or because he was putting himself in danger.

The story titles all went something like this: "Government

Cover-Up Puts Children's Lives in Jeopardy" or "CIA Blunder Costs Nation Millions of Lives" or "President's Secret Legacy."

I was suddenly scared for my dad. I could feel my heart thumping in my chest, and a tingle that traveled down my legs and into my feet. Even though I knew he was dead, I was scared for my dad then, while he was finding out about and writing those articles. *Maybe that's why we moved here,* I thought. Elbow is the one place where nothing ever happens. Hardly anybody knows it exists. It's where people wind up by accident. Maybe Dad thought nobody would come looking for him here. Maybe Mom thought he'd have no choice but to stay out of trouble. Dad had been writing dangerous stories for years, stories about governments in different countries. He'd been exposing the secrets they didn't want exposed. (If it wasn't in the title itself, the word *exposed* came up in most of the articles, and I imagined it meant something like *undressing* because one time Boyd Applebaum had been sent to the principal's office for "exposing" himself at school. He was always doing that, showing the other kids his butt, even though it was the last thing they wanted to see.)

Suddenly a postcard fluttered down from the top of a dresser, like a sycamore seed. It must have been Herman's work, making it fly like that. It landed next to me and I picked it up. It just said, *Keep up the good work!* and was signed *E. Bailey.* So Elenor really *was* a friend of my dad's. There were postcards and notes from other people, too, from all over the world. My dad had lots of friends when he was alive; he didn't just interview everyone for stories, he also just liked talking to people for the fun of it. He used to make friends with everyone; he didn't care who they were or where they came from.

Then I found something else. It wasn't the story Jack had told me about, about the people who live in Garbage City, the story I was hoping to find. It was the story of Herman. My dad had met Herman! My dad had known Herman! In the photo, Herman was smiling his twinkly, piratical smile and standing in front of his house. In the photo, it looked much nicer than the house Sam and I had been in, the night we found his body. He was holding a jar of his Devil Tongue Relish, the one I like best, and the headline said *Pickle King Robbed of His Crown, by Josef Klednik.* It was funny seeing my dad's name spelled out like that, and I read it to myself a couple of times. Then my eyes became too hungry for information and skipped quickly across the little printed letters.

Herman Henderson, better known as the Pickle King, was a self-made man. In the space of a few years, he went from handyman to millionaire relish maker.

He started out simply, by finding the best pickles and putting them in jars. Then he pickled chili peppers and any other vegetable he could get his hands on. His passion grew and he created relishes, based on his grandma's recipes, cooking up the ingredients on a small stove in his own house, and giving the jars to friends and selling them at summer fairs. But it didn't take long for Herman's Pickles® to become a culinary staple and for him to become a household name. His pickles, relishes, and other condiments are well known to the taste buds of any burger-eating citizen of Elbow and beyond. The success of his relishes made Henderson a rich man, although for him that was just a bonus. It was the cooking he loved. "I just really liked try-ing out new recipes, adding different herbs and spices, seeing what new flavors I could discover."

It might come as a surprise to readers to dis-cover that today, Herman of Herman's Pickles hasn't got a penny to his name. All he has are the clothes on his back. He lost his home (in this photograph Henderson is standing in front of his former home) and lived at the homeless shelter before becoming depressed and spending time in St. Agnes's. Since leaving St. Agnes's he has been living in a place he refers to as "The End of the World."

Where did it all go wrong?

Four years ago, Herman's Pickles weren't doing so well—sales were falling, his popular-ity was waning. The pickles just didn't taste so good. That's when Herman was approached by a company called MHF Inc. They told him his company wasn't worth that much, that really it was just a load of old pots making pickles, and Henderson believed them. After Henderson had sold his company, sales of the relishes suddenly took off again, their popularity exploded, and the company's profits quadrupled in a year.

Understandably, Henderson feels ripped off, cheated, conned. And he suspects somebody was tampering with his recipes to depress his sales in order to persuade him to sell in the first place. Doing my research, I discovered very similar circumstances with other well-known food brands based in Elbow: Lola's Cola, Pinehills Honey, Joe's Dairy, and Bert's Big Cheesies, all of which were bought in the last ten years by the people at MHF Inc. Somebody is getting very rich by gobbling up our favorite food companies and throwing out the people who started them, the people we know and love; throwing them out with the trash!

I folded the article twice, making it into a square, and put it in my back pocket. I thought back to the night at Mitzy's when we'd seen those funny little raised letters on the bottoms of the milk-shake glass and the milk carton. *MHF Inc. MHF Corp. MHF Corpse,* I thought to myself (even though I knew it meant corporation). What did those initials, *MHF,* mean? I needed to show the story to the others.

I put my dad's trunk back the way it was, with the clothes, photo, and camera on top. I locked the attic and moved Bertha's nightstand back to where it had been. I walked slowly down the stairs, kind of pretending nothing was up, like I hadn't been looking at all those articles, like I hadn't just found something important that concerned not just Herman's death but maybe everybody in the entire town of Elbow. This was big. I felt on edge, and for once it wasn't because of the rain. It was as though somebody was watching or about to come into the house, and they'd know what I'd found. My dad must have felt like that all the time. Nervous. Jumpy. Maybe that's why he drank. He always had that bitter smell of alcohol on his breath. He tried to cover it up by taking large bites of any candy bar I was eating. But I could tell, I could always smell it, and it made me sad.

I looked at the clock. It was two. The others were supposed to come over at two thirty. I still had half an hour to wait. Half an hour till I could show them the story. I switched on the TV for the cartoons, but I still felt itchy inside. I paced around the living room, tapping my feet, hoping the others would get here early.

When Sam banged on the glass of the front door, it made me jump. He couldn't get inside fast enough. He was shivering and his lips were blue. "Can I stay here tonight? I can't sleep in the tree house another night—I froze my butt off!"

Jellybean followed him in and seemed as happy as ever, his pink tongue hanging out, his steamy breath filling the cold air around him. "Hello, Jelly!" I bent down and gave him a hug, even though he was hot and steamy and dripping wet.

"Can I, Bea? Can I stay here? I can't stay home with Jeeks and Smytheson prowling around."

"I don't know. Bertha wouldn't like it," I said.

"She doesn't have to know. I could hide under your bed till she goes to sleep." He waited, looking at me with eyes like a puppy dog begging for scraps. His lips *were* bright blue and he *was* shivering. He could die up in that tree house. Get hypodermia or whatever it was called.

"Hey, I know what! You can sleep in the attic," I said, pleased with the idea.

"You don't *have* an attic." Sam looked confused.

"We do now. The only thing is, it's right near Bertha's room, so you've gotta be really quiet."

"OK," agreed Sam. "Thanks, Bea."

"Take a look at this." I unfolded the newspaper article and handed it to him. Sam didn't read too fast. I had to wait for him to take in the whole story.

While he was reading, the others arrived. Madison tapped on the window with her painted fingernails and smiled through the stained glass, not realizing the shapes on the glass made her look a lot like a cartoon. Eric, Butterfly, and Nelson followed just after, up the muddy walkway under Butterfly's giant purple umbrella.

Butterfly, Nelson, Eric, and Madison took off their rain gear, drip-dried a bit, and settled down on the couch. Sam was still reading the article when he caught Madison's eye. "I still have your dad's sweater. It got ripped when I climbed out of the tree house. Sorry." He lifted his arm to show the tear in the wool.

"That's OK," said Madison with a pretty smile. "He has plenty of others. I'm sure he won't even notice."

Sam took his eyes back to the article, but he looked a little uncomfortable, knowing that he was being monitored by Madison. "OK, so somebody got a good deal on Herman's company. Still doesn't explain why they'd want to kill him."

"Let's see!" said Butterfly, taking the piece of newspaper from Sam. Her eyes took it in quickly. "Actually, it kind of could, because, you see, he was speaking out about it. Maybe the company didn't want him pointing the finger at them and they got their revenge," she said in a kind of lawyerlike manner she'd obviously learned from her mom.

Madison and Eric were squashed together, reading the article over Butterfly's shoulder. "This is getting weirder and weirder," said Madison, raising her eyebrows and making a face like it was all just making her crazy.

"By the way," I said, "Herman helped me find the article. I just asked him where the attic was and then the door to Bertha's room opened. He's such a cool ghost!"

Madison looked around the room and hugged her shoulders, like she'd suddenly felt a draft. "Why can't we, just for one day, do something, like, fun?" she said in this kind of snippy voice that came right through her nose and reminded me of all the horrible girls she hangs out with in our class: Candace, Brooke, Meredith, Paige, and Whitney. Their biggest dream, as soon as they get to high school, is to become cheerleaders for the football team and jump up and down in tight tops and short skirts. They already know about things like what's the best way to get a tan, how to stop your hair from frizzing, and how to get really white teeth by bleaching them overnight. Most of them already had breasts, and if they didn't, they had mastered the art of making tissue paper and socks look just like them. But I figured the longer I could go without having to buy a bra, the better. Other than that, it wasn't something I really thought too much about.

"I keep saying we should go to my grandma's; she speaks to ghosts all the time. Herman could tell her who killed him right away," offered Butterfly. Sam and Eric exchanged looks, as if each were trying to see what the other thought. Eric shrugged.

"I'm coming, too. You can't make me go home!" said Nelson, jumping up and down.

"Mom doesn't like us hanging around with Grandma; they don't really get along. She says she's a 'bad influence,'" said Butterfly. After the hospital incident, Nelson and Butterfly's mom said she was going to ground them both, but then she changed her mind because she had a whole lot of studying to do and was relying on Butterfly for her usual round-the-clock babysitting service.

"Oh, I almost forgot. I found this." Butterfly took an old leather-bound book out of her backpack. "It's called *The Lonely Demon* and it's written by James Drake. I was at the library with Mom this morning and I wanted to see if I could find something out about the ring, but I couldn't. And then I wondered about the inscription, you know, the words on the inside— *For my darling Agnes, all my love, John, 1831.* And you know how I said before that the library is named after Agnes Feverspeare? Well, she was writing books kind of around that time. So I asked the librarian if she could show me some of her books, but she couldn't find any. But then, on our way out, I asked my mom and she said that I couldn't find any books by Agnes Feverspeare because in those days women weren't allowed to write books. She wrote secretly at night and published the books under a man's name. And she used the name . . ."

"James Drake," said Eric, taking the book out of Butterfly's hands and flicking through the yellowing pages.

"There's a passage underlined . . . somewhere in the middle. The page is folded over," said Butterfly.

Eric found the page and read aloud in a woman's voice, which made Sam laugh.

"*He could be charming and carefree one instant, and wild and willful, as if possessed, the next. Elizabeth could never tell which side of her brother he was going to reveal, and the not knowing created a state of nervous tension within her. Put quite simply, her brother frightened her.*'"

"Look. Here," said Butterfly, pointing to a pencil note in the margin. "*A description of Max?*'" Butterfly asked the question as if she knew why she was asking it.

"Who's Max?" Sam asked impatiently.

"I have no idea," said Butterfly, letting out a sigh.

"And who wrote that note?" Madison said.

"One thing leads to another and then another. Somehow this all fits together, we just don't know how yet," I said in a kind of daze. Something my dad used to say to me was at the edge of my memory, too, but I couldn't quite remember it. Sometimes my mind would reach out to remember things he said, or his face, or his voice, and come back with just a word or a sound or a look in his eyes. Sometimes the harder I tried, the less I remembered.

My eyes were fixed on nothing in particular, just sort of staring into nothingness, like in a daydream. It was nice and I didn't really want it to stop. Maybe the rainy fingers drumming their rhythm on the roof had hypnotized me for a moment. Only this time it was kind of soothing. I felt sleepy. When I blinked and looked back at the others, they were staring at me like I'd said something strange.

"What?" I said.

"You just did your weird starey-eye thing," said Sam.

"Sorry." I shook my head, trying to clear out the drowsiness, but the feeling stayed. "I think I really need to get out of this place. Get out of Elbow, just for a day. I want to help Herman, I want to know about the ring and the people in Garbage City and everything, but it's starting to get to me. It's like the rain's calling for me. If I don't get out of here, even just for a day, I'm going to wind up like Mom." The others looked at me with worried expressions. It was as though I'd said the thing they were afraid to say. I realized then that we all felt it. That creeping feeling inside our minds. We all feared it, we feared what would happen if we gave in to it.

Madison looked sympathetic. "You can use my tanning bed if you like. It's not real sunshine, but it's close."

"Thanks," I said. "I'd like that."

Eric was reading my dad's article again. "What's 'The End of the World'?" he asked, looking more serious.

For a minute I couldn't think. Everybody else's faces were blank. And then I remembered. "Oh my gosh — that's what Jack called Garbage City! That means Herman was there. We need to go back and talk to Jack and Leo. Maybe they can tell us something."

Nelson was in the kitchen playing with Jellybean. The two of them seemed to be getting along just fine until Nelson decided it would be funny to pull Jelly's tail. First he did it gently, getting Jelly to chase his own tail. But then he started pulling on it, making Jelly skitter backward, his large wet paws leaving streaks on the linoleum. This made Nelson laugh, but Jelly started barking angrily, making him cry.

"That's what you get for teasing the dog!" said Butterfly, sounding like Nelson's mom.

"I didn't tease him," whimpered Nelson through his tears, his nose filling with snot.

It was all quiet for a moment. Then Nelson said, quite matter-of-factly, "Who is that man at the window? He looks like a pirate." And Jelly started barking really loudly.

"Where? Where was he, Nelson?" I asked. Sam and Eric rushed into the kitchen to see, but Madison stayed behind. She was in no hurry to see the ghost again, even if it was only the ghost of a pirate-faced Pickle King.

Nelson pointed at the window. "He was right there. But he's gone now."

"It was Herman," I said. "I think it's because of that article.

We're on the right track. We've got to go back to Garbage City right away."

"What's that about the city?" Bertha pushed her way through the front door in her old-fashioned rubbery yellow rain slicker. It suddenly struck me how much like a fisherman she looked. "I see we got company again?" she said, raising her eyebrows and tutting as she piled some groceries onto the kitchen counter. "Don't you kids have homes to go to?"

I looked at Sam, who looked away, embarrassed. Some of us kind of didn't. Bertha didn't know Sam and Jelly were going to be sleeping next door to her tonight. "Get that animal outta my kitchen!" said Bertha, sneezing and holding a tissue to her face so as not to breathe in any more dog hairs. Bertha's allergic to pets. Otherwise I would probably have a dog or a cat by now, or even a chameleon like Eric. Maybe Bertha would let me have a goldfish. I wondered. Surely she couldn't be allergic to fish?

"And don't think I've forgotten about my locket, Bea."

Oh, no, I thought to myself. Bertha had been so busy with work that we had barely seen each other since her locket went missing.

"Well, where is it, Bea?" Bertha had her hands on her hips. The others all looked at me, all except for Madison, who had an innocent expression on her face but was looking in the other direction and fiddling with the hem of her skirt. I suddenly remembered her delicate pink fingers playing with the locket and chain, and I knew that she was the last one to have it. Our eyes met for a second before she quickly turned her head away again, but I'd already caught the look in her eyes.

I turned back to Bertha and took a deep breath. "I'm really sorry, Bertha," I said, looking at her socks, with their wet toes. "I did take your locket, but I lost it," I lied.

Madison flashed me another look and visibly shrank into her clothes.

"Do you have any idea how important that locket was to me? You have no respect for other people's things, Bea." She took a long breath in and out and then said, "Well, you can just pay me back out of your pocket money."

What pocket money? I thought. I got two dollars a month for doing my chores. I had to sneak some extra from the money she gave me to buy groceries as it was.

"You won't be getting your pocket money until it adds up to one hundred dollars, which is how much the locket cost—and that doesn't include the personal value," she concluded.

Great, I thought. *What's that—like, four years without pocket money?*

It was the expression on Madison's face that made me know for sure that she was the one who'd taken it. She looked really touched, like I'd done her a big favor, and I guess I had. I suppose Madison wasn't used to people doing nice things for her like that. She was used to being *bought* things, sure, but I guess she wasn't used to people defending her, taking her side, when they didn't have to.

Although Madison could easily afford the two dollars a month, it was more about protecting her from Bertha. Bertha would probably forgive me, but she wouldn't forgive Madison. It was just easier this way. But I wasn't happy about it. Not one bit. It was bad enough that Sam acted weird around Madison and she looked at him all gooey-eyed and lent him her dad's sweaters. Maybe I'd call Madison's dad and tell him his daughter was lending his wardrobe to boys he didn't know. Boys who left marks from dirty wet sneakers on his daughter's bedroom carpet.

CHAPTER 29

I had pretended to let Sam out with the others when they left, but he crept back upstairs and waited with me and Jelly in my room until we were sure that Bertha was asleep.

"Hey, who said you could touch my things?" I said, coming back into my room with the sleeping bag. Sam was messing around with some stuff on top of my chest of drawers and had picked up the little card that Elenor Bailey had given me outside the diner.

"Why don't we call this lady?" said Sam, folding the card between his fingers. "She said she knew your dad, right?"

"She *did* know my dad. I found a postcard from her in the attic — Herman helped me find it."

"Well, if she knew your dad, she might know what's going on at the dump. He probably talked to her about the stories he was working on. Let's call her," he persisted.

"OK," I said quietly. I thought it was a good idea to call Elenor. It's just that she kind of scared me and I didn't want to tell Sam. It made me feel weird the way she seemed to be able to look right inside me.

"Shhh! Don't wake Bertha," I whispered as we tiptoed downstairs. Bertha had fallen asleep in front of the TV as usual and was snoring deep snores (not the snorty grunts that were like her nose chuckling, but the deep, loud snores that made her sound like a giant dragon guarding treasure in a cave). I thought we were probably safe.

Sam picked up the receiver and dialed, then we put our heads close together so we could both hear. The phone rang a couple of times and then came a crackly voice: "Ye-es?"

"Is this Elenor Bailey?" asked Sam in his politest voice.

"Who's speaking?" she said sharply. I motioned for Sam to let me hold the receiver.

"Um . . . hello . . . this is Bea, Bea Klednik," I mumbled.

"I can't talk on the phone. Come to my house. The address is on the card. I'm glad you called."

I slowly put the receiver back on its hook.

"What did she say?" asked Sam.

"She wants us to go over to her house."

"Where is it?" Sam rested his head on my shoulder, peering over to read the address. "Market Street. It's in the old part of town. We'll take your bike."

Sam pedaled standing up and I sat on the seat, holding my legs out so they didn't get in the way. Jellybean ran alongside us all the way, his tail wagging, his tongue trying to catch as many raindrops as it could. The worst thing about biking in the wet weather is that you can't see where you're going. But I trusted Sam. I put my arms around his waist and held on tight.

We came to a gray house at the end of Market Street. The yellow streetlights cast shadows of eerie trees across it, and the wind made the shadows dance to a low howl.

Sam lifted my bike onto the porch and leaned it against the wall. I couldn't find a bell or a knocker, so I tapped on the glass, hoping that I had the right place. I saw a small fuzzy shape with silvery white hair come toward us, and Elenor Bailey opened the door. She hurried us inside, looking up and down the street like she was expecting someone to follow us.

"Come in, come in . . . quickly," she said, closing the door and walking straight back down the hallway. Jellybean pit-patted eagerly inside, leaving muddy footprints on the rug and swinging his tail so it beat against the wall.

There were lots of crooked photos hanging in the entrance hall, photos of Elenor when she was younger, standing next to important-looking people, sometimes with their arms around her. She seemed to be smaller than everybody she was photographed with, but it was clear from meeting her that her reduced height bore no resemblance to the force of her personality.

"In here!" she called from her parlor. Sam and I stood awkwardly in the little doorway. "Come in, sit down. Did anybody see you arrive?" she croaked, flashing us a look with her beady green eyes before lowering herself carefully into her armchair.

"No," I said. "I don't think so."

She bent forward and scooped something out of an old can straight onto the carpet for Jellybean, which he gobbled up. It smelled like cat food.

Elenor Bailey was lit up by a big lamp, which she sheltered under as though it were a big umbrella. The light made her hair glow like burning magnesium around her head (just like a science experiment I saw on TV), and it seemed even whiter than when I'd seen her at the diner. Although most of her hair was tucked into a kind of roll that went all the way around the bottom of her skull, little wisps had freed themselves and were reaching up toward the light as if drawn by static electricity. Her face was brown against the halo of white and she smiled at us, showing a neat set of very small teeth.

"I hoped you would come," she said, rubbing her hands together to warm them. "Did you find your ghost?"

"How did you know? He wants us to help him find out how he died," I said. "We're trying to find out how his death is connected to the people who live in the garbage dump."

Elenor wasn't listening; she was watching Sam, who was looking around the room the way he always did, seeing if there was anything that interested him.

"He doesn't say much, your friend, does he?" Elenor said. I smiled awkwardly. Sam didn't really care what people thought of him, but I was a bit embarrassed by the way he acted sometimes. He didn't care that he was in somebody else's home; he was going to look at stuff no matter who was there watching him.

Elenor's parlor was filled with books and photos and dusty awards that said things like *Journalist of the Year*, and there were travel books from all around the world spilling off the bookshelves and forming messy piles on the floor.

"My dad wrote a story before he died, about Herman Henderson, the pickle guy . . . did he mention it to you?" I asked. "Did Herman tell my dad why he was scared, or did he say anything about a special ring with an inscription inside it—we think it's to Agnes Feverspeare?"

Her pale emerald eyes sparkled. They were part wise, part pretty, and part scary—like they could hypnotize you if you looked at them for too long. "You *are* like your father. So curious. You know, they sometimes say it's better not to ask questions, better not to know."

"I want to know," I said.

"Knowledge can be a dangerous thing." Her nostrils flared slightly as she spoke. Then her lips tightened and her eyes narrowed and she looked like a bird of prey or a baby dragon, and I thought she must be thinking very intensely about the questions I'd asked, but instead she farted. It was a surprisingly loud fart for a small lady. Sam laughed out loud. "That's better. Can't think with a windy gut. Now where was I?"

I tried not to look at Sam because I knew I would laugh, too, so I focused on my knees until the feeling of wanting to laugh went away.

Elenor Bailey took a deep breath in and out and began in a different tone of voice, a bit like the voice Mom used to use when she read me bedtime stories when I was little.

"People have a history of disappearing in Elbow," she said mysteriously. I thought about the crazy woman who had jumped at Butterfly in Garbage City, the woman whose son, Luke, had gone missing. I was about to ask if that's what she meant, when Elenor spoke again. "Things haven't been as they should be for many, many years. I'm going to tell you a story. It's a love story, but not the nice kind, the kind with a happy ending. This story doesn't have an ending, the way that all stories should.

"A long time ago, a very bright young man from England came to Elbow to start a new life. He was invited by a friend of his father's, a man named John Ezekiel Elbow, who said he could use the boy's talents to help him design and build a new town. This young man took up the offer right away, for he hated his father, who was cold and mean and showed him no love. But he adored his sister, Agnes, who was only sixteen at the time, and he took her with him."

At that moment a flash of far-off lightning lit up the distant gloom. Elenor counted under her breath — "One, two, three, four, five" — and a crack of thunder broke through the sound of the rain, shaking part of the house. Jellybean winced and ran for cover under Sam's legs. Elenor's cat, who had been asleep on the windowsill, arched her back suddenly and started hissing at Jelly. "Quiet!" Elenor scolded her cat, and then continued with the story.

"John Elbow and the young man became friends and designed and built a whole town together, the town of Elbow. But the young man's ambition grew and he became wealthy and powerful, even more powerful than John. He continued to experiment with science, which was always his passion, and it became clear that his restless imagination knew no bounds. As the years passed, John became fond of Agnes, even though he was much older than she was, but her brother was possessive of her and against the match."

I remembered the inscription. "*To my darling Agnes, all my love, John, 1831.* That's what it says on the ring we found."

"That's, like, history or something—what's it got to do with Herman?" asked Sam bluntly.

"Sam!" I said, glaring at him so that he would know he sounded rude.

"You asked about the ring—and that story is about Agnes and John. And you mentioned a ghost. What makes you think the ring has anything to do with Herman?" she asked, then continued without waiting for an answer. "After interviewing Herman, your father became interested in a new story: He wanted to investigate the disappearance of homeless people. That's all I can tell you about Herman." And then she shook her head.

The lightning flashed again, this time bursting at the window and turning the whole room white. The thunder boomed and crackled outside, and Jellybean shook. I wrapped my arms around myself for comfort.

"It's only lightning, Bea," Sam said.

"Shut up, Sam—I hate lightning, OK? So, what happened in 1831?" I asked Elenor.

"Something terrible," Elenor answered. "That was the year Agnes and John were going to get married."

Another flash of lightning and a roar of thunder made Jellybean howl and bark with terror. Elenor's cat hissed at him, and the more she hissed, the more Jelly barked. Elenor put her hands over her ears and looked frustrated. "I can hardly hear myself think," she said. "Maybe you could come back another time, when the weather's not so bad."

"But I want to know what happened in 1831!" I insisted, but Sam was dragging Jelly out by his collar to stop him from barking, and Elenor hurried us to the door, bundling us out into the pouring rain.

As we set off on the bike once more, wobbling unsteadily, Elenor called after us from her porch. "It's not the ghosts you need to fear, but the living!" And suddenly she seemed like a scared little old lady, and I was pretty sure it wasn't just the storm that was stopping her from talking.

I saw her small figure grow even smaller, her silver hair aglow under the light of her porch, as Sam cycled away. An electric white fork jabbed through the stormy sky overhead and I screamed, grabbing Sam tightly. "Hurry!"

"I'm going as fast as I can!" he yelled back.

CHAPTER 30

Me and Sam tiptoed back into the house, trying to not make a sound. Luckily, Bertha had taken herself off to bed.

"That woman was a little bit nuts!" said Sam. "Why would Herman have anything to do with the story of Agnes and John?"

"I know, but I thought the story was cool," I said. "And it must mean something, but it was like she was talking in riddles."

I slowly opened the door to Bertha's room and held Jelly's collar to stop him from walking across to Bertha's snoring body and licking her face. As quietly and carefully as we could, we moved the nightstand and unlocked the door to the attic.

When we were inside, I handed Sam a bowl of water for Jelly and the sleeping bag I'd set aside earlier, the one that Bertha kept with the bed linens in the big chest in my parents' old room. Jelly was already curled up in the corner, resting his head on his paws.

As quietly as I could, I moved some boxes to clear a space for Sam on the floor, and when I stood up again he said, "Thanks, Bea. I don't know what I'd do without you." He held the sleeping bag in his arms and just sort of stood there looking at me for a while. I started to feel awkward. I wanted to say, "What's up?" because he was looking right into my eyes. Then the strangest thing happened. Sam kissed me. Just very gently, but on my mouth. His lips were soft and warm and a little wet, and it felt kind of nice. The inside of my stomach wheeled and spun and tickled suddenly, the way it did on the roller coaster. Then he dropped onto the sleeping bag, wriggled inside it, and closed his eyes. I left him there, turning off the light and closing the door on my way out.

As I tried to sleep, I kept thinking of that kiss, and each time I did, my stomach turned in spirals, like my insides were leapfrogging over each other. Weren't we just friends? But friends didn't kiss each other on the lips. And anyway, didn't he like Madison?

I knew Bertha's nose had detected Jellybean in the room next door when her snores became sneezes and she got up to blow her nose. *Please don't go in the attic!* I thought. *Please don't bark, Jelly!* Then I fell asleep, and in the morning, Bertha was at work like normal, and Sam and Jelly had gotten through the night without being discovered.

Me, Sam, and Jelly ate half-frozen Pop-Tarts while we watched TV. Sam was watching a nature program about frogs, and Jelly seemed very interested until they started hopping around. Each time a frog jumped, Jelly woofed. I was relieved Jelly was there because there was something weird going on between Sam and me. Something had changed. The kiss had changed us. *Why did you have to go and kiss me?* I thought. I wanted things to be back the way they were, before that stupid kiss. Now I didn't know what was going on. I didn't ask to be kissed, and he'd gone and ruined everything and made me different around him, not like myself anymore.

After breakfast, I carefully peeled the label off a brand-new Devil Tongue Relish jar.

"What are you doing?" asked Sam.

"I want to show this picture of Herman to Jack and Leo. I was thinking about taking my camera—I'd like to get a picture of them and some of the other people." Jack had told me my dad had started taking pictures of the people who lived among the garbage, and suddenly I wanted to do the same. I wanted to carry on where he left off, if my camera let me.

"Are you sure you want to go back to that place? It's not safe there, you know," said Sam, speaking in his new strange voice.

"Of course I want to go. Don't you?"

"Sure. I'm not scared. I was thinking about you." Then he reached into his pocket and took out the palace ring. "I didn't want to leave this in the tree house. I wasn't sure last night if we should show it to Elenor or not. You better keep it for now."

I took the ring, turned the smooth metal shape around between my fingers once, and then put it in the pocket of my jeans.

Sam wandered into the kitchen and poured himself a glass of water from the faucet. As he gulped the water down he looked out the window, past his reflection, at the raindrops hitting the roof of Bertha's car. "Bertha didn't take her car."

"Some days she gets a ride with her friend," I explained. "C'mon, let's go. We'll pick up the others on the way—I already made the calls." Sam grabbed his raincoat and pulled it over his head. "Wait, I need my camera," I said, heading off to the darkroom.

My camera had been in the darkroom ever since I'd developed those ghostly photos. The blank white sheets of photographic paper were still hanging there, but I wasn't scared of Herman anymore, not since I'd found out he was Herman. Herman just wanted to be heard. He wanted somebody to figure out what had happened to him, to tell his story. It was Mr. Jeeks I was scared of. Mr. Jeeks; Sam's brother, Jed; and the surgeon. I knew they were after us, I knew they didn't care that we were kids, and I didn't want to imagine what they were capable of.

I picked up my camera, packed it in its special case with the big flash, put a couple of boxes of film in the front pocket, and slung it across my body. When I got back upstairs, the door was open and Sam was sitting in Bertha's car, with the engine running. A million silver raindrops were lit up in the headlights and the yellow beam was aimed at the house, seeming to yell at it with its brightness. When I said we'd pick up the others, I meant in the usual way, but clearly Sam had other ideas.

I pulled on my Wellingtons, shut the door, and ran to get Sam out of the car. I sat in the passenger seat next to him to get out of the rain, and Jelly, who was sitting on the backseat like a large child, licked my ear from behind.

"What the heck are you doing?" I was trying not to yell.

"It's OK, I know how to drive. I taught myself in Jed's car last summer every night while he was sleeping."

Sometimes I wanted to strangle Sam. This was one of those times. "You can't just take Bertha's car!"

But he was already backing down the driveway and out onto the road. "Why not? We'll get it back before she gets back from work." Another car roared past us and Sam slammed on the brakes.

"Are you *sure* you can drive?" My voice came out squeaky.

"This is a little different from Jed's truck. I just need to get used to it." Sam struggled with the gearshift as I sat back in the leather seat and gripped the sides. We swerved sharply around the corner and I jumped at the blast of a truck's horn. "If we get caught . . ."

"We won't get caught. Anyway, I'll take the blame. What have I got to lose?" said Sam casually, one hand on the steering wheel, the other trying to get the windshield wipers to go at the right speed.

Madison's face was a mixture of shock and awe as we pulled up outside her mansion. I noticed the severe-looking housekeeper squint through the steamed-up downstairs window to see who was picking her up. Madison lifted her long pink raincoat to get in, like it was a ball gown. "I didn't know you could drive," she said, impressed, a flirty gleam in her eye as she looked at Sam in the rearview mirror. Sam acted like he hadn't heard her and put his foot on the gas. We turned a bit too wide onto another street and a car screeched to get out of our way. Right away, Madison buckled up her seat belt and sat as far back as she could, her body pressed tightly to the seat, as if she could protect herself from being hurt if anything happened.

Eric, Butterfly, and Nelson were standing huddled together under Butterfly's giant purple umbrella. When Sam slammed on the brakes, we jerked forward and the seat belt cut sharply across my body. Sam stopped the engine and wound his window down. "Your carriage awaits!" he said, leaning out the window. Eric smiled a big wide smile, mirroring the excitement on Nelson's face. The three of them squashed into the backseat next to Madison and Jelly. The windows had misted up completely. I wiped the front windshield with my sleeve so we could see out.

Sam was about to start the engine again. "What is he doing, Bea?" said Butterfly, shaking her head. "You're not supposed to drive till you're sixteen!"

"Only three years off!" said Sam cheerfully.

"He just took Bertha's car—I tried to stop him," I said, sounding kind of lame. I could have stopped him, but the truth was I remembered the last journey to the dump, getting lost in all that mud, and fainting, and that was before we'd even gotten inside the place and gone down into the garbage soup.

"Whoever wants to walk can get out now. It'll take forever to get there if we walk." Sam told it how it was.

"I'm not complaining," said Madison. "I hate the rain."

Butterfly still looked worried. "We can't take Nelson to the dump. He's too little to go there. It's too dangerous."

"But I like dangerous stuff!" insisted Nelson.

Butterfly stroked her brother's cheek with her hand. "Maybe on TV, Nelson, but this is for real." She looked up at Sam's reflection in the rearview mirror. "We can drop him off at Grandma's. We said we were going to go there, right? She'll be able to speak to Herman. Maybe then we won't need to go to the dump again."

I wanted to go to the dump right away and ask Jack and Leo about Herman. What had happened to Herman there? I wondered. I also wanted to see Leo again, and talk to some of the other people, and take some pictures. The kind of pictures my dad must have taken but that I couldn't find, or were missing from among his things.

"OK, but then we're going straight to Garbage City," I said.

"You mean 'The End of the World'!" Eric boomed dramatically. He had some kind of dark soot all over his face. I also noticed that some of his hair was burned at the front — obviously from something he'd been experimenting with.

Sam noticed, too, his bright blue eyes flicking back into the rearview mirror to confirm what he'd seen. "What ya blown up today, Eric?"

"Nothing. It's just something I've been working on. It's my invention. It's secret. It didn't blow up, I just put my face in the wrong place."

"He wouldn't let me in his room, but he did let me hold Sigmund and he showed me his collection of meteorites," said Butterfly.

"Sigmund thinks Butterfly's OK," said Eric.

And I thought, *What he really means is Eric thinks Butterfly's OK.* I smiled inside because I remembered how they didn't even want to look at each other at the beginning of summer vacation.

"Eric said I could borrow Sigmund for show-and-tell when school starts," said Nelson proudly. "You promised, didn't you, Eric?"

Eric nodded.

"We want San Pedro Boulevard," Butterfly directed. "It's the big apartment building at the end of the street. My grandma lives in a really small apartment, but she has about thirty cats. She rescues cats that people don't want. She's got this one cat that's all bony. He's got lots of fur, but he's just a skeleton underneath. When she found him she kept saying, 'He's just a bag of bones,' so that's what she named him: Bones. She says he's really old so he deserves a lot of respect. She says, 'You gotta think of all the fights he's gotten through and all the trucks he's dodged—he's a survivor!'"

Butterfly and Nelson's grandma's apartment was in the new part of town, near the arcade where Sam sometimes works. Not far from the mall, the thrift store, and the homeless shelter. Around this part of town there were lots and lots of stores advertising liquor in neon lights. Bertha always told me to stay out of this area, unless I was going to the mall. I wondered if this was where my dad used to come. Did he stand around with those other people in doorways like that, in the rain?

"It's OK, Jelly-boy, we'll be back soon. You guard the car!" Sam said to Jelly through the gap in the window.

"He'd frighten all the cats," explained Butterfly again apologetically.

As we walked along the corridor with all the numbered doors, we could hear other people's TVs, couples shouting, and children crying. Butterfly rang the doorbell and we waited. Butterfly could tell her grandma was looking through the peephole because she said, "It's just me, Grandma." Eventually the door whined open and Butterfly's grandma peered out.

"Does your mother know you're here?" she asked pointedly, and Butterfly started nodding but quickly changed to a shake of her head because she knew better than to lie to her grandma.

Her face was pale brown and covered in deep lines going in all different directions, like a map of a magical country, and she had really big pale blue eyes that made her look like she was from another world.

"Grandma, you have to look after me, because I'm not allowed to go where it's dangerous," said Nelson in such a fed-up kind of voice that it almost made me change my mind and take him with us.

"You come right in, you can always stay with Grandma." She held the back of Nelson's head very gently with her palm and waved him inside. "Tell your friends to come in. I have some homemade lemonade in the refrigerator."

We followed her inside, down the narrow hallway and into her living room, stepping over the different colors and shapes of cats that had come to see who we were. We sat down on the sofa while she and Nelson disappeared into the kitchen.

"There he is," said Butterfly as a gray ball of fuzz slowly headed in my direction and wound itself around my calves. "That's Bones, the one I was telling you about. Grandma says he's ancient." I stroked his body with both hands, and as I did, my fingers sank through the soft fur and onto the hard ridges of his ribs. It made me think of Herman's X-ray. How weird that we were made of bones, like this, holding us all together. Sometimes it seemed like bodies were detached from their owners. It was like they were somehow separate from who we really were. It was as if, as you got older, your body and your spirit began to head off in two different directions. Bones was just happy to be petted, and purred so loudly that his whole skeleton seemed to vibrate.

The living room was cozy and filled with embroidered cushions and flowery curtains. There was a small TV in the corner with a stack of magazines underneath, and above it a gold-framed black-and-white photo of a woman. Parts of the photo had been colored in with pale red (the woman's lips) and turquoise and pale green and yellow (the bouquet she was holding).

"That's my grandma when she was young. It was taken on her wedding day," said Butterfly.

"She was so pretty!" cooed Madison, and then added in a breathy sigh, "I can't wait till I'm a bride!"

Me and Butterfly looked at each other and rolled our eyes.

"Plenty of time for that. Try to enjoy being a child first. There's no going back once you're old." Butterfly's grandma had reappeared with Nelson and the lemonade. We sipped the cold, sweet drink out of glasses that smelled of damp and cats, or damp cats, while Butterfly and Nelson's grandma looked at us, each one in turn, with her big, liquid blue eyes.

"You want to ask me something." She spoke slowly and with complete confidence, and then looked right at me.

"About the ring in your pocket." I felt uncomfortable. I didn't know whether to get up and hand her the ring or wait until she asked for it. "Come with me. Not you, Nelson—you watch the TV." Nelson let out a little groan and hung his head like it was too heavy for his body. He was always being told to watch the TV or go to his room or read a book, and he was always being told to do it when something interesting was about to happen.

Butterfly's grandma got up and headed back down the corridor, followed by eight or nine cats that thought it was dinnertime. She shooshed them out of the way as she walked, waving her hand from side to side. "Shoo! Scat now!"

All of us, except for Nelson, followed her into a sweet- and smoky-smelling room at the back of the apartment. There were all kinds of things in that room. There were shelves filled with big fat jars containing multicolored powders, herbs, liquids, and beautiful, luminous stones. There were other things hanging up, like wands with sheeny feathers, gold bells, and pretty pieces of silver cloth. Framed on the wall were a deep blue and a deep red but-terfly, and their wings glinted in the half-light. There were creepy-looking things, too—a small reptile floating in foggy water, one jar filled with fish eyes and another with bird beaks. A thin curl of smoke lifted and twisted around the room from a glowing stick on the table, making a delicious smell.

Butterfly's grandma sat down at a table with her back to all those shelves and gestured for me to sit down opposite her.

On her table, she had a big crystal ball that reflected all the objects and people in the room, and a set of cards with colorful symbols on them. The rain was coming down hard outside, creating silver rivers on the small window, illuminated by the little fairy lights decorating the frame. The lights made the right side of Butterfly's grandma's face glow, and one of her eyes looked darker than the other, like they were two different colors. Then she lit a candle and the flame fizzed a little before growing and swaying, a pale yellow blossom of light.

"Don't be afraid. Let me see the ring," she said, with her small lined palm outstretched.

"It's OK," said Butterfly, reassuring me with her eyes and then doing the same to Sam, Eric, and Madison, who were standing near the door. Sam cautiously fingered a wand with white feathers and a purple gem at the tip that was hanging near him.

"Don't touch!" barked Butterfly's grandma suddenly, making my heart rise up into my throat.

I took the ring out of my pocket and put it in her palm. But she put the ring down on the table and grabbed hold of my right hand. She squeezed it tightly and looked deep into my eyes, a bit like Elenor Bailey had. I wanted to pull my hand away, but she gripped it so hard her nails dug into my skin.

"You are what is called a Sensitive. You have the gift. But it frightens you. Sometimes it leads us where we do not want to go, but we must follow." And that's when my pinkie finger began buzzing and twitching furiously. She loosened the grip on my hand and watched my finger flick around. She smiled. "That is how it began for me."

I felt annoyed. I didn't want a "gift," as she put it. I just wanted to be a regular kid. It was hard enough being a regular kid.

"You have no choice. It is who you are. It will make your life harder but richer. You will see," said Butterfly's grandma, as if she had read my thoughts. Then she frowned and tilted her head, like she was listening to somebody very quiet standing next to her. "The spirit world has been calling you." She opened her eyes very wide and looked very serious. "You must keep your feet on the ground. Your own spirit has been trying to leave. This is not good. You have a job to do in this life."

Butterfly interrupted her. "She faints sometimes. Is that what you mean?"

Sam joined in. "She does it when she's stressed."

I felt like they were ganging up on me. "No, I don't. Just sometimes." I was starting to get embarrassed with all this attention just on me.

"You were very close to your father. He loved you very much." Suddenly my eyes started to burn and I was aware again of the others watching me. I tried not to cry. I frowned hard to stop the tears from coming, and bit my lower lip. "Yes, you must stay focused. A vacation would be good—somewhere with sunshine, like Florida."

Yes, I know! I was yelling inside. I needed the sunshine like I needed air, but there was no way of getting any sunshine in Elbow. It was like living in a tank of slimy water. Maybe that's why I'd been thinking about getting a goldfish. . . .

Before she picked up the ring again, Butterfly's grandma aimed her turquoise gaze right at Madison and seemed to be listening to that very quiet voice again, which none of us except her could hear. She even opened her mouth as if she were about to speak, but changed her mind when Madison looked down at the floor, as if it were something she wasn't ready to hear.

Then Butterfly's grandma turned her attention to the ring. She didn't look at it; she just held it in her hand and then wrapped her fingers tightly around it, encasing it in a tomb of jutting knuckles.

"Grandma, the spirit of a man named Herman has been trying to tell us something," said Butterfly, trying to speed things along.

Her grandma darted her a look and practically spat the words at her. "What have I told you about messing in things you don't know about?"

Butterfly looked upset. "But, Grandma?"

It was no good; she'd closed her eyes and was moving her head around like an antenna, trying to pick something up. "I sense a very angry spirit whose life was taken from him." Her voice became a low drone, like she was plugged into a different channel from the rest of us.

"It's Herman!" said Madison, as if she were in class and had the right answer.

"Not Herman," said Butterfly's grandma. "John. Elbow. John Ezekiel Elbow."

Me and Butterfly looked at each other. "That's who gave the ring to Agnes," I said. "*All my love, John.* It's written on the ring." Then I looked at Butterfly's grandma to see if she hadn't just read the inscription. But the ring only said John, not John Ezekiel Elbow.

"Founder of the town of Elbow," came Butterfly's grandma's voice again, like it was her voice mixed with another voice, maybe the voice of John Elbow. Then she closed her eyes, her face contorted, and her body jerked in pain. When she opened her eyes, they had changed color. The watery blue spheres were now a dark, dark brown, the color of wet earth.

"Oh my God!" whimpered Madison. "I don't like this. Tell her to stop."

I didn't like it, either; none of us did. It must have been Madison's whining that made it stop, because we watched as the dark color drained from Butterfly's grandma's eyes as quickly as it had arrived. "That must have been John Elbow, he must have had brown eyes," said Butterfly, who'd obviously seen this kind of thing before.

Butterfly's grandma became herself again, but her face filled with sadness, all the lines coming together to make a mask of pain, and she spoke to us all carefully and firmly, with a note of warning in her voice. "There is much suffering associated with this ring. I see the death of a young woman," she said, looking right at me, making a bolt of electric fear shoot straight into my stomach. Then my face felt hot and for a second or two I thought I was going to be sick.

Just then the cats that were in the room arched their backs, their fur stood on end, and they showed their fanglike teeth and hissed. "Oh, shoosh now!" said Butterfly's grandma, trying to calm them down.

And then we heard it. A woman's voice, wailing in pain, and it screeched around the room like she was circling us. The sound wheeled around, and with it came a gust of wind that made our hair blow back like we were on a roller-coaster ride. We all turned pale and were suddenly so cold that our breath showed up in the air the same way it does on an icy winter's day. The fairy lights around the window popped and died as little streaks of black smoke wisped and twisted up into the air.

After a few seconds the horrible sound died down, but I don't think it'll ever leave our minds. It was such a bloodcurdling noise, like nothing any of us had ever heard before or would probably hear again.

"You see what I mean?" said Butterfly's grandma. "If I were you, I'd take this ring right back where you found it." At that moment we all looked at each other. We knew we couldn't take the ring back because the place we found it was Herman's guts, and who knew where they were now?

We passed Nelson in the living room on our way out. "Bye, Nelson!" I said, but he just stared at me with a bored expression. The kind of expression that came from a feeling I knew well.

Butterfly's grandma showed us to the door, her collection of strays trailing behind her, back to their old selves, letting out the occasional indifferent *meow*. I felt the shape of the ring through my jeans pocket. I was very aware of it sitting there, like it could burn through to my skin or turn into something else, something that would hurt me.

"Be careful now," she said as we readied ourselves to step back into the wet world of angry rain-fingers. Those fingers always seemed happy to have us back in their grasp, tapping out their nasty sounds on our rain hoods and on the shimmering streets around us. Standing in the hallway outside of Butterfly's grandma's apartment, I took a deep breath, as though I needed one before diving back under that murky sea-sky that would soon be pouring its blackness onto us again one drop at a time. Death by rain, that's what it felt like.

When we were heading down the corridor toward the stairs, Butterfly's grandma opened her door again and shouted for me. I walked back to her. "Take this. Wear it over your heart. It will protect you." She handed me a dark pink ribbon, and on it was a large piece of shell or bone carved in the shape of a heart, with copper wire bound around it and little feathers held in place by the wire.

"Thanks," I said, wanting to hug her.

Standing outside her apartment in the dim light, she was a little figure in the doorway. She looked like a kind lady, somebody's grandma, and not at all like the powerful, all-seeing woman she'd been inside. I tied the ribbon around my neck, let it fall under my T-shirt, and felt the soft feathers, hard wire, and cold bone travel down and settle in the hollow at the center of my chest.

CHAPTER 31

We made sure we were well out of sight of Butterfly's grandma before we got back into Bertha's car; then we quickly grabbed the cold metal door handles, pulled open the doors, and jumped in. Jellybean started wagging his tail and jumping from seat to seat. I rode in the front with Sam, and Butterfly, Eric, Madison, and Jellybean sat in the back.

Madison held on to the two front seats, leaned forward, and whispered, "What was that thing that . . . howled like that?"

"I think it was Agnes. Agnes Feverspeare's spirit," said Butterfly. "It's her ring."

Madison's eyes went soft and focused on something in the distance. "I wonder how she died."

"It would have been a violent, nasty death, that's for sure. Ghosts always die in nasty ways," said Eric matter-of-factly.

Madison narrowed her eyes and snapped at him, "But you don't believe in ghosts!"

Eric looked uncomfortable. "I'm allowed to change my mind. I've seen some pretty weird stuff since I started hanging out with you guys. Anyway, I've been reading about them." Butterfly smiled, and Eric continued. "Ghosts always have a reason for being ghosts. Sometimes it's the shock of how they died that keeps them here, like they didn't have time to prepare for death, and sometimes it's because they have a score to settle."

"That's like Herman. Herman's definitely got a score to settle," I said. "But what about Agnes? We hardly know anything about her."

"There is *another* reason why ghosts come back," said Madison.

"OK, what is it, then?" said Eric sharply. He hated other people knowing things he didn't.

"When people don't want them to be dead," said Madison. "They're so sad that they're gone that it stops them from going all the way to heaven."

There was quiet in the car for a moment and I watched Sam look at Madison in the rearview mirror. It might have been the light, or my imagination, but I could have sworn Madison had tears in her eyes.

"OK, so what *do* we know about Agnes?" insisted Butterfly. "We know that she was a novelist. And that she was the sister of an English guy who came over here to help John Elbow build this town. John gave Agnes this ring and they were supposed to get married . . . and we know that something went wrong, that something happened to them both. Something killed them—maybe even *because* of the ring," she said, making it sound simple. "I heard a woman crying when we went to find the old train. Maybe that was Agnes. Maybe Agnes's ghost was the ghost Elenor thought we were looking for."

"That would explain why Elenor told us the story of Agnes and John," said Eric.

"What I want to know is how the heck Agnes's ring got inside Herman! And why Mr. Jeeks and his creepy surgeon friend, Smytheson, want it so badly!" I announced, frustrated. "It just doesn't make sense!"

Then Sam spoke. Sam doesn't say a lot usually, he mostly listens; but when he does speak, it often makes you stop and think. It's like he saves words up, and by saving them up they became more valuable. "What if Herman wanted somebody to find the ring? It's like a message from him, like the ring leads us to what he wants people to know." Then there was silence in the car and all we could hear were the tires *swoosh*ing through the rain and the drag and *click* of the windshield wipers.

We'd turned off the main road a while back, but it was when the tires started to struggle with the thick mud that we knew we were getting closer to the dump.

"I hope I don't see that crazy woman again," Butterfly said with a worried look on her face, and the others didn't say anything. I could feel they were frightened. Their bodies grew stiff when they were scared and it changed the way the air felt. The air inside the car got thicker for a moment, like the mud outside. I think I was the only one who wanted to go back to Garbage City, and that was because I knew Jack and Leo; and I knew they weren't scary, they just looked it; and they looked that way because they were the ones who were scared.

It was black outside, the windows were covered in a thick mist, and the tires refused to go any farther. Sam kept on pressing the gas with his foot, but the tires were determined to slip: "*Nnnnnaaooooo,*" they kept saying. Sam let the car roll back a little until he felt the ground was more solid, and pulled over.

"We'll have to walk from here," said Sam, turning off the engine and getting out.

We climbed slowly up the muddy slope while Jellybean ran ahead, a blur of gray fur in the dirty rain. I tucked my camera deeper inside my raincoat to make sure it wasn't getting wet. Even though it was in a big leather case that stuck out and made a funny bulge under my coat, I knew how the rain could creep in.

I couldn't see the faces of the others. Sam's hood was pulled right over his face, the brim of Madison's pink hat was folded down, and Butterfly and Eric were buried underneath her umbrella. I was wearing one of Bertha's yellow rain hats with a strap that went under my chin, so I guess the others couldn't see my face, either.

When Jellybean got to the top of the ridge, he started barking. Sam grabbed his face with both his hands to tell him he had done good. We stood there peering over the edge, into the filthy soup of Garbage City. The dark shapes of car carcasses and shopping carts, skeletal sofas and limbless chairs, were illuminated by the floating fires.

"It was somewhere around here, right?" asked Butterfly, using the point of her umbrella to find the metal entrance.

"I think so," I said optimistically.

"It's got to be!" Sam was getting impatient as he stomped the squelchy ground with his feet.

We edged our way higher up the side of the muddy slope looking for that well-camouflaged porthole.

"We'll just have to wait for them to find us," I said. I knew Garbage City was underneath the lake of floating trash, I just couldn't remember where the entrance was, and I didn't want to fall into the wrong part. Who knew what creatures might live in that rotting sea?

Just then the powerful watery wind began to push at us like a giant hand, and Butterfly's umbrella was pulled from her hands. It flew up in the air and over the canyon before spiraling quickly downward, landing in the dark liquid and floating upside down like a magical purple water lily. Madison almost fell over the edge, one heel slipping off, making her lose her balance. Sam caught hold of her arm just in time and she smiled coyly, looking up at him from under her long damp lashes. For a tiny part of a second I wanted to push her into the slop below.

A little farther along the ridge, two shafts of orange light appeared, followed by a 4x4. "That looks like Jed's car—Jeeks must have sent him." Sam sounded worried.

"What are we going to do now?" asked Madison.

Butterfly looked back at her umbrella floating way down in the dump. "That was a birthday gift from my dad," said Butterfly, pulling her hood over her head and wiping the rain from her face. "He doesn't usually remember my birthday."

The five of us looked over at Jed's truck slowing to a stop, and then back at Butterfly's umbrella as it traveled along for a second or two before being pulled right under.

"Did you see that?" I said, not believing my eyes.

"That's how we get in," said Sam. "Let's go!"

We heard the door of Jed's truck slam and saw one of his heavy, mean-looking buddies get out, planting one big boot and then the other into the mud before looking around. Jed slammed his door and joined him on the ridge. When Jed pointed in our direction, Sam yelled at us. "What are you waiting for?" Then he sat down, used his heels to give himself a good start, and slipped quickly down the canyon wall. Jellybean ran alongside him, sliding part of the way when his paws skidded in the liquid dirt. Eric followed, a mischievous smile on his face, and Butterfly went next, her face all scrunched up, trying hard not to notice where she was heading. Madison sat down stiffly but didn't move.

I heard Jed shout, "They're over here!" and saw him and his friend begin to run toward us. Even in the rain you could tell their bodies were made for hurting people. They pushed themselves violently through the viscous atmosphere and their angry faces started to come into focus.

"Come on, Madison! Let's go! Now!" I yelled, turning back to check how many seconds it would take before Jed could reach out and grab us.

"I can't!" moaned Madison.

"You can! Just imagine the mud is snow and we're going on a sleigh ride!" I said, and gave her the biggest shove I could manage. Then I held on to her raincoat and let the weight of her pull me down the slope with her. I could feel the breeze of Jed's hand swing past the back of my neck as he missed us. Me and Madison screamed as we traveled toward the garbage soup at full speed. We scraped against a few stray pieces of junk on the way down but we held our arms and feet in, becoming as ball-like as we could. The rain was coming down so fast it made the mud extraslippery. At that moment I was grateful for the rain. For those few seconds it almost became a friend.

Me and Madison crashed into the soggy mattress that the others had climbed onto. We were floating in the trashy liquid like it was the ocean, and holding on to the side of the mattress like it was a boat. I noticed a peacock-blue oil streak twist and glide across the surface of the water and for a second I thought how pretty it looked, with pinks and greens curling and waving within it, lit up by the glow of a small floating fire nearby. Jed and his friend were still near the top of the ridge, trying to climb down one step at a time. Every so often one of their boots gave way underneath them and they slipped and fell clumsily into the wet filth.

Sam started laughing. "Look how stupid they look!" I laughed, too, even though I was up to my neck in the stinking swamp myself, and Butterfly and Eric joined in.

"They look like two old ladies or something," chuckled Eric.

Madison had a solemn expression on her face and her chin was stained with brown mud, as if she had a beard. "Can you *please* help me out of here!" She threw her words at us like knives.

Sam, Eric, and Butterfly pulled Madison onto the mattress and she lay there for a second, covered from head to foot in the tarlike mess, before starting to sweep it off with her delicate hands. I pulled myself up onto the floating bed with the help of the others, just in time to watch Jed and his friend climb back up the slope and shove each other angrily before disappearing over the ridge.

"We're not afraid of some garbage!" shouted Sam. "Loser!"

We guessed that they'd given up as we watched the orange headlights of the truck fade quickly into the distance and disappear. The sound of licking and slurping told me that Jellybean had found something tasty to eat. "Don't eat stuff in here, Jelly — it's not good!"

It was Madison who screamed first, and then Butterfly. I put my hand down onto something, something that squirmed, and I screamed, too.

"What's going on?" said Sam, and then his face changed and I could tell it was bad news. His eyes nearly popped out of his head, and his mouth drooped like he'd tasted the most disgusting thing in the whole world. I looked down and saw what I'd put my hand on a second earlier. The entire mattress was a mass of maggots, the longest, fattest maggots you've ever seen. Their swollen, writhing bodies were swarming all over the sodden mattress, blindly nudging and prodding with their pointy black noses.

"Agghgghhh!" screamed Madison, and jumped right back into the black soup she'd just climbed out of. Butterfly tried to push the maggots away with her feet, while Sam was picking them up in the middle, using both hands, and throwing them out to sea. Every so often, a firecracker sound burst through the downpour as a hissing maggot popped and sizzled in one of the floating fires.

"They are incredible!" said Eric, and you could tell from his face that he was wondering how he could get one home to dissect. "Sigmund would think it was Thanksgiving!"

"What was that?" Butterfly pointed as we tried to focus on a shadow that seemed to be flying from one island of trash to another. As it got closer we could see it was eating the maggots that Sam was throwing out like bait. It flicked its face toward us, and seeing its sharp white fangs and narrow eyes lit up like dark jewels, we thought it was a cat. When it turned, and its long, glistening pink tail whipped the air, we knew it was a rat.

"That is the biggest rat I have ever seen!" exclaimed Eric. "I didn't even know you could get rats that big!" Butterfly and Madison were in shock and looked like they'd forgotten to breathe.

"I think it's coming to say hello," Sam said, trying not to move.

"It wouldn't bite us, would it?" whispered Butterfly.

"Probably. Rats eat anything," said Eric.

"Thanks, Eric!" I said.

The creature hopped onto a floating upturned shopping cart, making it move and dip in the tarry soup. Its tail curled and twisted, dancing slowly in the rainy air. It looked like it was about to pounce, when Jellybean stood on the edge of the mattress and barked furiously, showing his own sharp teeth. His nose and lips wrinkled tightly as he snarled. He became a different dog.

"You go, Jelly!" cheered Madison.

"Good boy! Good Jelly," I sang.

Jelly wouldn't stop; he just barked and barked, and the rat seemed not to like it very much. Just when we thought the rat was retreating, it let out a horrible piercing howl, and a second later shadowy shapes came jumping through the misty darkness of the swamp, from one trash island to another. It took only a couple of minutes before we were surrounded by the giant rat's family and friends. Their moist, muscular bodies and sleek black fur shone in the firelight and they all cried the same horrible high-pitched cry as their tails whirled and clipped the air with excitement. Jellybean's barking wasn't doing any good. If anything, he was making things worse.

Suddenly the maggot-infested mattress seemed to break up and melt away like wet bread beneath us, and we collapsed back into the filthy water.

One rat, showing its fangs, jumped into the garbage soup with a splash, followed by another and another and another. It seemed rats could swim. Not only could they swim, they were really good swimmers. And they were swimming toward us.

"It's been really nice getting to know you," I said to the others, only their heads visible. I didn't think I'd be saying that to Madison Anderson or Eric Schnitzler at the start of the summer vacation, when they weren't even my friends, but then again I didn't think at the start of the vacation that I'd be eaten alive by giant rats, either. I thought it was bad enough being stuck in Elbow in the endless rain, but things could always get worse—a lot worse. *I must always remember that,* I thought, as the face of a black rat appeared in front of me, its bulbous blue-black eyes shining and its long, wiry whiskers scratching my face. I touched my chest where my special necklace was, tucked under my clothes, and thought, *It'll be OK. This necklace will protect me. It'll be OK. That's what Butterfly's grandma said.*

At that moment something pulled me under, and I just held my breath and shut my eyes tight. I could feel what must have been rats bumping past me and against me, maybe about to fight over my flesh, and then a current pulling me down farther.

Suddenly we were sucked strongly in the same direction, one by one. We slipped down a wide, slimy chute like dirt down a vacuum cleaner. I could hear Butterfly scream, "Whaahhhhh!" and Sam shout, "What the . . . ?" and a roar of air as we traveled fast down the dark tube.

We landed on top of each other with a heavy *splat*, in a large kind of wire cage with a muddy concrete wall to one side. "Ow, that really hurt," moaned Butterfly. Some of the soup dripped through the cage from the enclosed tunnel and onto our heads as we sat there shaking and covered in black-brown filth, while Jelly whimpered and his ear dripped fresh red blood.

Noisy footsteps on corrugated iron came closer, followed by the sound of heavy metal twisting and squeaking as a circle of the concrete wall was pulled away beside us.

"Lucky we kept that old ventilation shaft," Nathan said, smiling and patting Jack on the shoulder as they stepped through the circle in the wall.

"If it wasn't for your dog barking, those rats would have

made a meal of you by now," said Jack as I threw my arms around him. "I told you to stay away from this place," he added quietly but firmly, resting one of his big hands on my head.

"Did any of you get bitten? Tell me now if you did—we need to give you a shot," said Nathan urgently. Eric raised a trembling hand but he couldn't speak. There was a chunk of skin missing on his cheek and blood was pouring out of it, making the mud turn red.

CHAPTER 32

The mud had hardened and was tightening and cracking on
our faces as we sat around the fireplace in Jack and Leo's big
cavelike room. The rain's angry fingers sounded muffled and
far away, but they were still there, biding their time.

A large piece of meat was barbecuing slowly over the
crackling flames and we were drinking sugary tea. Jack had
given us some old clothes to wear while ours dried by the
fireplace, along with my camera case. I looked over at my
camera sitting on the beam above the fire. I didn't know
how, but it wasn't wet at all. Maybe that old case was better
than it looked.

"OK, I'm done. You're going to have a scar," said Nathan,
finishing the stitches on Eric's face and covering them with a
clean white dressing.

"I don't mind—I like scars," said Eric, with a little less
enthusiasm than usual.

"You'll look cool!" said Sam, trying to cheer him up.

Nathan unpacked a kit of vials and a syringe. "Now I
need to give you the inoculation."

"You almost have a whole hospital down here," said
Madison, looking at the equipment in Nathan's medical kit.

"We need to: Things happen all the time and it would take too long to get into town. And the hospital staff don't really like to treat us, so we steal the stuff we need. Nathan is a trained doctor," Jack explained, taking a sip of his tea.

"Will it hurt?" asked Eric.

"It will sting a little. I'll give one to the dog first so you can see how simple it is."

"His name's Jellybean. Don't hurt him," said Sam defensively.

"OK, Jellybean, here we go." Jellybean looked up at Nathan with his big sad eyes, his ear all bandaged, and then winced as the needle went into his behind. He turned and barked at Nathan, who stepped quickly away.

"It's OK, boy," Sam said, stroking his side.

"I hate needles. I don't want any of you guys watching," croaked Eric, getting ready for his inoculation. He turned around and began to undo his pants.

"Uggh! Gross! I don't want to see your butt! Go in the other room," shouted Madison.

"Your arm will do just fine," Nathan said with a smile.

Eric looked embarrassed. "I was only kidding," he said, and immediately turned away as Nathan rolled up the sleeve of his sweatshirt. "Ow! That hurt!" moaned Eric.

"All done," said Nathan, quickly packing up his stuff and heading out into the corridor.

"How can you live here with all those rats?" Eric asked Jack.

"You get used to it. People get used to anything in the end."

"But you can die from the diseases they carry," Eric said, touching the bandage on his face.

"That's why we have the inoculations." Jack put his face in his hands and his voice got thick. "We do our best to stay alive through it all—the dirt, rain, rats—and then they just . . ." He started to sob to himself and then stopped.

It was hard to know what to do when a grown-up was upset. I looked at Butterfly and Sam and they looked back at me. Eric shrugged as if to say, *How am I supposed to know what to do?*

I went over to Jack and put my hand on his shoulder, but he quickly took his hands from his face and sat up, wiping his eyes. "I'm sorry, I don't want to involve you in this."

Something was wrong and I wanted to know what it was. I hated it when people did that. It was like when your friends say, "I've got a secret, do you want to hear it?" and then say, "No, I really shouldn't tell you." Why say it in the first place if you don't want them to know? Jack's tears were like a secret he wasn't sharing.

"Who's hungry?" called Jack as he began to carve the caramel-colored meat that had been roasting over the fire, filling the room with homey smells. We all eagerly raised our hands. Jack put meat on plastic plates and passed them around. We were quiet then, while we ate, enjoying the sweet-tasting meat and how it made us feel warm from the inside.

"What kind of meat is this?" asked Madison, licking her lips.

"It tastes good, right?" asked Jack. We all nodded. "That's all you need to know. All meat is the same when it's cooked."

Gradually our chewing slowed down as we began to

wonder what we had just eaten. I looked at Sam and the thought came into our minds at the same time. *Rat. We've just eaten roasted rat.* Sam nodded solemnly. We looked at Madison, who was happily chewing away. Sam looked at Eric and Eric looked at Butterfly. Then we all looked back at Madison, who was oblivious.

"What?" she said defensively.

"Nothing," I said, and she kept eating until the bone she had between her fingers was licked clean.

"Is there more?" she asked.

"Help yourself," offered Jack, and Madison got up and carved herself a little more barbecued rodent.

I took the folded pickle label out of my pocket. It was damp and tore a little as I opened it — but Herman's picture was still visible. "I know my dad was here, asking you questions for a story he wanted to write. You gave me that photo, remember?"

Jack nodded.

"But do you recognize this man? My dad wrote a story about him, too."

Jack's mind was elsewhere, like someone had put a spell on him and he couldn't bring himself back from that other place. He looked so sad. He hadn't looked like this before.

Butterfly, who was always kind of fidgety, had stood up and was walking around the room looking at things. All kinds of strange items decorated the place. It was a bit like a museum, with all these objects on little shelves or hanging from the compacted mud, stone, and used-car walls. There were tops of Russian dolls; an elephant ashtray; a ceramic hand unfolded and reaching up, a couple of the fingers carefully glued back on; there was a colorful puzzle cube; a bright red propeller; a bicycle wheel with colored pieces of paper stuck between the spokes. They must have all been things they'd found and really liked.

Jack finally looked at the label. "That's Herman," he said. "He was with us for a while. He was a rich guy but he lost it all—his house, his business. He said the people who bought his company cheated him. He said they ruined his products somehow and then bought the business cheap. All he talked about at first was how he was going to get his house back. He was really mad about that for a while. Then he realized there are worse things, much worse . . . and he wanted to do something about it. It was Herman who introduced your dad to us after he'd written a story about him. Your dad came here and started investigating, trying to find out why people were disappearing. Herman went to the Palace, just before your dad. But Herman came back—most don't. He was lucky he only lost his eye."

"What's the Palace?" I asked.

Butterfly was sitting on Leo's bed. Where *was* Leo? I wondered. She picked up Leo's book from the floor, the one he had read aloud to me. "*Frankenstein.* I like this story," said Butterfly. "Is it OK if I borrow this?"

Jack rose suddenly from where he was sitting, strode over to Leo's corner, and snatched the book violently from Butterfly's hand. "No, you can't!" he shouted. Butterfly was so taken aback that she lost her balance and fell backward onto the mattress. "I told you kids not to come back here!

I want you to go now!" He pulled our clothes roughly from the line they were hanging on and shoved them into Sam's arms.

"OK, take it easy. Take it easy," said Sam, the way I'd seen him talk to bigger guys from town who wanted to fight him. Jelly started barking.

"Don't tell me to take it easy! You have no idea how dangerous it is here. Leo's gone. He hasn't been home for days. They've taken him!"

"But we want to help!" I said. "Don't tell us it's dangerous, because we're already involved. We're already in danger and we can't stop now! Herman knew what was going on and he wanted my dad to write about it. We saw Herman's body, and since then his ghost has been trying to tell us stuff. He wants us to tell the truth about how he died, but not just that, he wants us to tell the whole story—whatever that is. We don't care how bad it is; we have to know, for Herman's sake. You see, he can't rest until we find out the truth."

There was a silence as Jack stared at me, his face a mixture of emotions, as if he didn't know what to think. Then finally he said wearily, "Herman is just one of many. Come with me." Without waiting, he left the room and led us down a long underground corridor. As we passed the dark burrows, angry, frightened eyes flickered like fireflies, watching us from within. Jack stopped in front of a little cave and pulled out a skinny, frightened-looking man.

"Show them your shoulder!" Jack commanded.

The man obliged, rolling up the sleeve of his torn sweater. There on the top of his arm was what looked like a burn. It was lumpy and round, and there were red raised parts and indentations. "The ones who come back, *if* they come back, have this mark."

"Thanks, Tom," Jack said, helping the man roll his sleeve back down.

"Wait!" I said. "I need to get my camera."

I ran back down the corridor, grabbed my camera from Jack's mantelpiece, loaded the film, and ran back to where the others were waiting. "Can I?" I asked Tom carefully. He rolled his sleeve back up and I got ready to take the shot. Tom gave me his best photo face, despite his bad health, and proudly showed his burn mark to the camera.

We followed Jack farther down the corridor until he stopped outside another cave entrance. "Is Grace inside?" he called, and after a moment of shuffling, a woman who would have been pretty if she didn't look so frightened and so tired came forward. "Show them the mark, please, Grace. Grace only found her way back to us this week. Her mark is more recent."

Grace looked down shyly as she lifted her thin, faded T-shirt, and there on her shoulder was the same circular burning. My camera flashed brightly, lighting up Grace's arm and the muddy tunnel we were standing in as it recorded the image.

Butterfly frowned. "I'm sorry, could you show us again?"

Grace nodded slowly.

"Bea, where's the ring?" Butterfly asked.

I'd forgotten about the ring. I felt for the shape in my jeans pocket and pulled it out. Butterfly took it from me.

"We need more light," she said. Jack pulled the oil lamp from its place in the wall. Butterfly held the light near Grace's arm and brought the ring up to meet it. Then she turned the ring upside down, pressed it gently onto the shape on Grace's arm, and it fit, exactly, like a puzzle.

We all looked at each other. "Why would somebody do that?" asked Madison.

"We don't know—we only know they don't remember anything about how they got the mark or the scar—they all have scars, too," Jack answered. Grace lifted her T-shirt and showed us a long, neat scar running along her stomach to the right of her belly button. I took another photo.

"Thanks, Grace," said Jack kindly, and Grace turned slowly, stepping back into the darkness of her room.

I moved my camera a little to the side and looked at Jack through the viewfinder. Jack was looking away into the distance, and his head was hanging down with what seemed like the weight of worry and sorrow. It was as though a light had gone out inside him. I knew he was thinking about Leo, about where Leo was and whether he would be coming back. I took a picture of Jack's unhappiness.

"How could our ring have done this when we've had it way over a week?" said Butterfly.

"Maybe ours isn't the only ring like this," I said.

"But what about that *Darling Agnes* stuff?" Butterfly was shaking her head. It didn't make any sense. Our ring was obviously a special ring, a gift from John Elbow to Agnes, not a ring for branding marks on poor homeless people.

"Did Herman have this mark on his shoulder?" Sam asked Jack.

"Yes, he had the mark and he lost an eye," replied Jack. "He said he'd been to the Palace and that it was worth losing his eye because he had the 'proof'; and that even though Josef Klednik was dead, he was sure that somebody would find it. Then he went back to his house, even though they'd taken that, too. After that, he was killed."

"So this ring is 'proof,'" said Butterfly. Sam nodded to himself, like it was exactly as he'd suspected.

"Proof of what?" asked Eric.

"Of the nasty thing somebody was doing with that nasty ring!" Madison shrieked.

"You need to get out of here now and please don't come back. If you want to stay alive, please never, ever come back," Jack said, half pleading with us and half angry.

As we stood at the door aboveground, the one I'd left through after my first visit, I wondered if I would ever see Jack or Leo again. I hugged Jack and he hugged me back for just a second, and then put his hands on my shoulders and pushed me away before lifting the big metal door for us to leave.

Sam drove as fast as he could to get Bertha's car back in time. We knew we had to get it home and clean all the mud off it before she got back from work. Shivering slightly under damp clothes, our stomachs tried to bargain with the uneasy meal we'd eaten. We hardly spoke, letting the click and drag of the windshield wipers and the *swoosh* of deep water on the roads do most of the talking. We all had questions going back and forth in our minds, though. There was one thing we all knew for certain now, and that was that Herman's death was part of something else, something bigger and much more sinister.

CHAPTER 33

It was the day of the meeting at the secret club, the one that Mr. Jeeks and Madison's dad were members of. We'd decided that somehow we had to get in there that night because we were sure we'd find out what connected Jeeks, Smytheson, Herman, and the palace ring. But we'd have to wait until the afternoon to get together, because Sam had to work at the arcade and Butterfly was Nelson-sitting. Eric, in the meantime, was hard at work on his invention—which he refused to talk to anybody about.

Sam had spent the last couple of nights at Madison's house in the garage. He figured it was easier than trying to stop Jellybean from making Bertha sneeze. I wondered how long it would take Madison to sneak into the garage after the housekeeper was asleep, offering him cookies before climbing into his sleeping bag. Madison seemed very grown-up sometimes; she knew how to act around boys—I think it's what she and her school friends spent most of their time talking about, after all—that and shopping.

I slept right through till ten o'clock, but I lay in bed for another hour. My body didn't want to go anywhere, it just wanted to lie still, still as a stone, wrapped up in the feather quilt. My body was so motionless I could hear my breathing and my heart beating. It scared me how that beat was what was keeping me alive. What if it stopped? What would happen to all my thoughts and my feelings? What would happen to my me-ness? Would I become a lonely ghost like Herman, trying to put right the things that had gone wrong in my life? Or would I just go out forever, a little light switched off for good? Surely it couldn't be like that? Otherwise what were all these thoughts and feelings for? There had to be more to it than that.

I watched the rain trickle rapidly down the skylight in mercury streaks, lightning forks of furious water that never stopped coming. I wished I'd remembered to lower the blind, but I was too tired to lift myself out of bed now. I reached for the large soft pillow and let it drop over my face. *Just stop! I can't take it anymore! Please, rain, just stop!* I thought.

I opened my eyes into the pillow and saw black. Just black. Then pictures started to swirl in front of me. There was Herman's body, floating in that dark green pool, his mouth wide open, one pale white-blue eye, the other a jagged hole, letting in water just like his gaping mouth; then I saw the ring, and Tom and Grace being burned by it, the long pink scars on their bodies; then those massive beady black eyes of the hungry rat looking into mine; Leo reading to me; Jack hugging me; Sam kissing me and the way it made my stomach wheel and spin; and then I saw myself, sinking slowly into mossy green water, slowly descending and drifting, my clothes swaying with the currents like seaweed, my skin so pale I was almost transparent, my eyes closed, my mouth open like Herman's, my arms lifting above me, my loose white fingers letting the water play through them, making them gently curl and dance. I threw the pillow to the floor and quickly breathed in, a long, deep breath, sucking in air, as if I'd been pushed up and out of the sea by a wave for one last chance of life.

I threw my tired legs out of bed and dragged myself down to the darkroom. In case there was somebody waiting for me inside, I peered around the door slowly before switching on the ruby light. I took out the film of Jack, Grace, Tom, and the corridors of Garbage City and made up a contact sheet, then developed the prints I liked best.

Unlike the pictures of Herman, which were still hanging there like strange, stark laundry, blank pages empty of information, these images appeared quickly and easily, coming into being on the paper almost immediately. There was Tom, with his proud photo face, holding his shoulder forward so you could see his branding; then a close-up of his mark; then a scared-looking Grace; close-ups of her mark and scar; the picture of Jack looking away, heavy with sadness; and shots of the dirt-sculpted corridors, the compacted garbage, Jack's room; and a couple of shots of the exterior of the dump itself, that giant heaving sea of human waste.

I'd watched how my dad took photos. He took pictures so that they told the story in their own right. He used to say, "Let the camera do the talking." I hung the pictures to dry next to the blank sheets that should have told the sad story of Herman's death—or at least part of it.

Brushing my teeth, I looked at myself in the bathroom

mirror. I looked terrible. Not like a kid should look. The little buzzing fluorescent light over the mirror made the bones in my face stand out and exaggerated the shadows under my eyes. Was I normal? I already knew it wasn't healthy to be in Elbow. I knew that it could do things to people's bodies and, more important, to their minds. I knew it was dangerous to want to know things that people didn't want you to know. But was it normal to think about dying? To have nightmares about drowning? Weren't kids supposed to do fun things and think fun things, like what they're going to get for their birthday, what movie they're going to see over the weekend, who their new best friend is, normal stuff like that?

It was about two thirty in the afternoon. Madison had asked to meet me at the mall, to go shopping with her. I can't say it was exactly what I had in mind. I only went to the mall when I needed new socks, and even then I was in and out in a few minutes. I didn't like shopping. I didn't like the way the shop assistants looked at you and how they tried to force you to try on stuff you hated and then told you that you looked "cute." Like looking cute was something good. I didn't want to look cute (although I did like the way Sam said I was cute in the photo my dad had given Jack). I liked to blend in so I could watch other people. If people didn't notice you, you could notice them more. Other times I liked to look different, even odd. I felt odd inside sometimes, so why shouldn't I look it on the outside?

I pulled on my raincoat, then took a frozen bagel out of the freezer and put it in my pocket, hoping it would thaw on the way. Bertha had stopped making me pancakes since

I confessed to stealing the locket that I didn't really steal. I hardly saw Bertha anymore, and when I did, she was watching TV. I wondered whether it wouldn't be more fun to run away to an orphanage. *I'd have company*, I thought, *but I guess I wouldn't have my own room.* And at least at home I got to use dad's darkroom. Also, there was something kind of nice about having all my parents' old stuff around, like they hadn't really left, like we were just a regular kind of family, really, just on hold for a little while. Maybe Mom would come home from St. Agnes's soon. She'd unpack her things and say, "Who's helping with the dinner?" And in the mornings she'd ask me to get her an apple and I'd get into bed with her and she'd make a chair out of her legs and I'd rest my legs over hers under the quilt while she laughed and munched on her apple. And then we'd discover that my dad hadn't really died at all, that they had mistaken somebody else for him, some poor drunk guy who'd fallen asleep in the cold, but not my dad.

I was on my way to the mall, kicking away the deep puddles of rainwater as I went, when I saw the warm yellow light from the thrift store reflected on the watery sidewalk.

The old bell on the door rang as I pushed it open. "Hey, Pete!"

"Look who the wind blew in!" said Pete, throwing a smile over his shoulder at me as he arranged a handful of books on a shelf. "What happened with the photo competition?"

I shrugged. "Nothing." Pete stopped what he was doing and looked over his shoulder at me again. "I'm working on something else now."

"That's good. Got to keep growing, man."

As Pete continued to arrange books on the high shelf, I watched his back and wondered if I could trust him. Some adults you could trust but some you couldn't. It was hard to know which were which. Sometimes the ones you think you can trust the most are the ones who let you down. There's no way of knowing for sure. But Pete talked about homeless people a lot, about how some couldn't afford the payments on their places anymore, either through losing their jobs or because they got sick; especially the crazy kind of sick. Sometimes both things happened—like with Herman. "I've taken some photos of people who have nowhere to live," I said at last.

Pete stopped what he was doing and got down off his ladder. He looked sort of impressed and sad at the same time. "People in the shelter?"

"Kind of. They've made their own shelter," I said.

Pete narrowed his eyes at me and his expression changed; it was like he knew I'd been to Garbage City, a place he'd heard stories about but had never been to, and at the same time he wasn't sure. No way would a kid go to a place like that—would they?

Then he said, "I don't need to tell you to be careful, because you're an intelligent girl, right?"

I nodded slowly. "It's true, the stuff you always say, there is some really bad stuff out there. But I'm going to get to the bottom of it, I'm going to find out what's really going on—I'm going to take photos of it all and when people see the photos, they'll change things!"

Pete smiled and looked at me with his sparkly hazel eyes. He scratched at his messy head of wild, curly hair and said, "I saw some of your dad's articles—he did good work. But you know, sometimes we have to understand that there are things we can't change." Pete said this with a weary but wise tone to his voice. After all, he had been working here for years and things hadn't gotten better; if anything, they'd gotten worse.

"But how do we know if we don't try? If nobody tries, nothing will ever change."

Even though I liked Pete, I felt like I was about to get into a fight with him—I could feel it. I could feel the hairs on the back of my neck and around my scalp standing up. I had that same feeling when I questioned what the teachers said at school.

Maybe I *was* like my dad. He thought the truth was important, and so did I. The truth was something you couldn't just give up on. If you gave up on truth, you might as well give up on life. That's how I saw it, anyway. Maybe as you get older the truth becomes less important, or maybe it just becomes more scary.

Adults start to look uncomfortable when you ask certain questions; they sort of squirm and fidget like they don't want to be there, and can't look you in the eye. I've noticed that about grown-ups. Sometimes you'll ask a question and they'll say, "That's just the way it is!" or "Haven't you got home-work to do?" or "Curiosity killed the cat." Or they'll change the subject or pretend not to hear you. Chances are, if they say or do those things, you've just hit on something really important. That's the question to keep asking.

Pete was about to persuade me that while taking photos was a good idea, to raise awareness of "The Cause," I shouldn't hope to achieve too much with them. At that moment Madison streaked by outside, on her way to the mall, in a brand-new pale blue raincoat with silver stars all over it. I pulled the door open, making the bell ring loudly. "Madison!" I yelled, making her jump.

"What are you doing in there?" she said, wrinkling up her nose.

"Come inside, we can go to the mall later."

Madison stepped in reluctantly, putting her silver booties carefully down onto the dirty brown carpet.

"This is Pete," I said. Pete was back to stacking books and didn't turn around, but raised a hand to say hi.

"Hi," said Madison, not impressed. "It stinks in here," she whispered.

"He who smelt it dealt it," said Pete loudly. Madison looked embarrassed, not realizing he had heard her.

"He who said the rhyme did the crime!" I chanted back. "It's the clothes," I explained to Madison, pulling a blue-and-orange striped T-shirt off one of the racks and waving it under her nose. "They smell a bit sometimes, but they're OK once you wash them."

I put the shirt back on the rack and headed over to the shoe corner. "There are lots of cool shoes, come and look." I indicated the racks of multicolored secondhand shoes all competing for space, all different shapes and sizes, like small exotic animals in a strange zoo.

I could see the idea of trying on used shoes was almost

sickening to Madison, because her face was all twisted up.

"Here—try these green ones!" I said, picking up a pair of square-toed, sparkly emerald shoes by the heels and offering them to Madison.

"No, it's OK, you try them. I'll just sit here." She moved some clothes from a faded blue beanbag and sat down slowly on the soft shape.

After she'd gotten used to the smell, though, she clearly began to feel right at home in the small but select shoe department of the thrift store.

"OMG! You have to try these!" Madison screeched as she handed me a pair of red strappy shoes with platform soles. My socks were too lumpy to fit inside, so I started to take one off. I was shocked by how far the green mold had spread between my toes, and quickly put my sock back on, hoping that Madison hadn't seen. To my surprise she said, "Don't worry, I've heard that happens to everyone who stays here over the summer," and I was even more taken aback when she pulled off her pristine white socks to reveal her own moldy feet. "Look, I even have a webbed toe," she said as she flexed her little toe, letting the webbing spread out like a baby wing. That made me feel a whole lot better about my own moldy feet.

"Maybe we'll grow fins and gills before September—I've always thought it must be really peaceful being a fish!" Madison nudged me as I said this, smiling conspiratorially before putting her sock back on.

"You don't want to see my feet!" came Pete's voice from up the ladder. "My girlfriend calls me Merman!" Madison and I looked at each other and I'm not sure what was so funny, exactly, but the thought of Pete's naked, flippery feet was so ridiculous that we burst out laughing and found it hard to stop.

Still giggling, I tried on the red strappy shoes and suddenly felt completely different—incredibly tall and glamorous. I was a new person in those shoes. And for a second Madison's shoe collection made complete sense to me. But because I was giggling and because the red shoes were way too big for me, I suddenly wobbled uncontrollably and, reaching out to one of the shelves, brought the shelf and all its contents crashing to the floor. This made Madison laugh even more. We lay there on the floor, giggling helplessly under a heap of old clothes and books.

When the bell rang and the door opened, something in me knew to be quiet. I held my hand over Madison's mouth to stop her from laughing, just as the tall man in the wide-brimmed hat, the shadowy man who made my skin freeze, crept up to the counter to pay for a book. "It's him! Smytheson, the surgeon!" I whispered to Madison as we watched him through a coat that had become a tent.

"I'm much obliged to you for calling me," he said with a hushed voice that exuded power. I said the word *exuded* to myself a couple of times—I'd read it in a book and I liked the sound of it. It was a word that sounded like it meant "to give off a smell" or smoke or something.

"No problemo, Mr. Smytheson, anything else you're looking for, just let me know," said Pete in his usual way, like everybody was his friend.

Then, as the surgeon held the book in his right hand and turned to leave, that's when I saw it. He was wearing the castle ring. The exact same ring that we'd found in Herman's intestines. The ring that Mr. Jeeks had wanted so badly. The ring that somebody had been using to burn onto people's skin—the people who were taken from Garbage City.

"Madison!" I whispered. "Look!"

I saw her eyes scan the dark figure in the hat and finally alight on the hand holding the book and then on the ring.

"Oh my God!"

Then he was gone. We just caught the sound of Smytheson's menacing whistle as the bell rang and the door clicked behind him.

We waited a couple more seconds and then threw off the coat.

"Did you see it?" asked Madison.

"You mean the ring?" I nodded.

"Huh?" said Pete.

"Nothing. Pete? What book did that man buy?"

"It's a kind of dictionary of pictures and signs—symbols, I suppose. It's called *Symbology of the Neo Gothic.*" It must have been weird for Pete when he looked up from the ledger he was filling in, because Madison and I had evaporated. We'd slipped quickly out of the thrift store and up the watery street after the surgeon in his wide-brimmed hat.

"How could he have the ring when I have the ring?" I said to Madison as we watched the shady figure stalk up the sidewalk, raindrops bouncing off him like bullets.

I pulled the ring from my jeans and rotated it between my fingers so it caught the light from the stores.

"There must be at least two rings," she mused. "Maybe one of them is a copy."

"Come on!" I said, grabbing Madison's arm. "Don't you want to know where he's going?"

"Not really—he doesn't seem like a very nice person."

"Exactly. I'll bet he's the one who's been making those nasty burns on people's arms. Like we thought back in Garbage City, there *has* to be another ring, of course, because Grace's mark was made *after* we found our ring!"

Madison was breathless, trying to keep up with me. "But why would he do that?"

I walked as quickly as I could, so as not to lose sight of the surgeon. "I don't know. Maybe so he would remember them. Something like that."

We followed Dr. Smytheson right across Elbow, up the steep streets into the old part of town. When he turned suddenly, looking behind him, we hid in the large stone doorways and disappeared into the shadows of the watery darkness. Finally he stopped. We saw the half-circle brim of the surgeon's hat glisten under a streetlight. Then he took another look behind him before stepping into a large ornate building. That building was the Grand Hotel.

"He's going to the secret meeting. We have to get in there!" said Madison as we watched from a dripping doorway on the other side of the street. We waited until the surgeon had stepped inside the imposing building and then we crept quietly across the road and up the large stone steps to the entrance. Just inside the glass doors was a sign that said: MONTHLY MEETING OF THE RADIANT BROTHERHOOD.

We peered inside and saw the dark figure of the surgeon hand the book to the receptionist and exchange a few words. Then he turned and raised his hand. "Until this evening, then," he boomed and began to head back in our direction.

"Quick!" I hissed, pushing Madison out of the way.

We stumbled down the steps as fast as we could and hid in the shadow of a gray stone pillar. We held our breath as the surgeon swished past.

"There's no way we'll get in there by ourselves. We need a grown-up to go in for us," I said.

"But who?" Madison said helplessly.

CHAPTER 34

We went back to Madison's house to wait for the others as we'd arranged, and sat on Madison's bed sipping some kind of tea, which I didn't much like the taste of. It was kind of smoky, like you'd just breathed in a bit of bonfire. "It's called Lapsang Souchong. Daddy says it's an acquired taste. This is the real kind. He gets it sent over from China."

"It's OK," I shrugged, not wanting to be rude. The teacup was fiddly to hold and covered in roses. I wondered if the gold on the edge of the cup was real. I wanted to say the tea was bitter and stinky and could we please have some hot chocolate, but instead I forced myself to keep sipping.

The rainy fingers began tapping a little more loudly on the window, whipping the glass with little insistent flicks, just in case we'd forgotten about the watery presence outside. Then the weather turned nasty. The fierce rain joined forces with the black clouds, conjuring an electrical storm that rumbled, ripped, and cracked across the sky with flashes of burning white, making the whole house shake.

"I hate thunderstorms." Madison's voice trembled.

I rubbed my arms to comfort myself. "Me, too."

Then came a big crash of thunder, which sounded like the roof had fallen in, and at the same time the other Convicts tumbled into Madison's room. Jellybean bolted straight into Madison's closet and hid among the shoes, covering his ears with his paws. I don't know who screamed first, but we all did, including Eric, who was a little embarrassed once we'd all stopped.

"You scared us!" I yelled at the others.

"You scared *us*!" protested Butterfly.

Sam—who was still wearing his raincoat—picked up my teacup, sniffed it, made a face that said he wasn't impressed, and put the cup down again. "So what's the story, you guys?" he asked in his usual laid-back way, his thumbs in his pockets.

Madison and I told them how Smytheson had come into the thrift shop, and how we'd seen the ring on his finger after he'd bought that book, and how we'd followed him through the rainy streets of Elbow. (We only left out the part about trying on the crazy secondhand shoes, I guess because it seemed so silly and girlish compared to everything else that had happened.)

"We should get going right away!" Butterfly's eyes were glistening and urgent.

"Yeah, right away!" agreed Nelson, ready for action.

"Anyway . . . I told you, it was just like our ring—exactly the same—and we saw him go into the Grand Hotel," I explained to Butterfly, Sam, and Eric. "Tell them, Madison!"

"It's true. We followed him, just like Bea said, and in the lobby of the hotel there was a sign for a meeting of some 'brotherhood.'"

"That proves he's one of the cannibals!" Eric punched one of his hands with the other.

"Well, he might be the one branding those poor people in Garbage City, but I still don't get it," frowned Butterfly. "Our ring was a gift, kind of like a love letter."

"Maybe, but like we said, who's to say there aren't more rings? What if they all wear them, to show they're in the club?" said Sam.

"Yeah, the cannibals need to recognize each other so they don't get eaten!" Eric joked.

"Eric." Butterfly was losing her patience. "This is serious."

"We just need to ask a grown-up to help us get inside the Grand Hotel," I said, trying hard to think which grown-up that might be. "Pete might do it," I suggested, but I knew as soon as I had spoken that Pete would be at home eating dinner with his girlfriend, and I could imagine her face as she opened the apartment door to the six of us. The others had blank expressions and it was clear they didn't have any ideas.

"Mitzy might do it," offered Butterfly.

"Women aren't allowed," said Madison.

We all fell quiet, deep in thought for a moment.

"DW told me he used to be the night porter at the hotel," Sam said, like it was no big deal.

"Why didn't you say so?" I hit Sam's shoulder and felt the warmth of him through the wet nylon of his raincoat. He looked at me in a weird way, a bit like the way he had the night he'd kissed me.

"Oh, a fire truck! Is that for me?" Nelson chirped, reaching for the toy lying on Madison's nightstand. For a few seconds he felt the cold metal of the truck between his fingers and noticed how the paint was peeling to reveal the silver-gray underneath.

"Don't touch that!" Madison said sharply, rushing over to him and prying the toy from his hand.

"I never get to do anything I want. I hate being seven!" Nelson exclaimed.

"Give the kid a break," Eric said, rolling his eyes. "What do you want a toy fire truck for anyway, Madison?"

"You can't just go taking stuff that doesn't belong to you, Nelson, OK?" Butterfly tried to explain.

With the saddest expression any of us had seen so far, Nelson took himself to sit in the closet with Jellybean. For a moment, Madison looked at Nelson, sitting cross-legged with his face in his hands, and then at the rows of shoes surrounding him, like invisible people resting, their feet neatly pulled together so they would all fit in. She picked up the fire truck and went and sat down next to Nelson. "I'm sorry I snapped at you," she said quietly.

"That's OK." Nelson shrugged.

"I . . . it's just that, that fire truck used to belong to my brother . . . but he died."

We understood a whole lot more about Madison that night, when we learned about the brother she'd once had. We realized that bad and sad things happen to everyone, even perfect, popular Madison. It made me think about other people who I didn't really like and it made me wonder what had made them the way they were; what kinds of things had happened to them; who *they* might have lost and what things *they* might be hiding in a box under the bed.

CHAPTER 35

It must have been about six in the evening by the time we got to DW's store, which was dense with sweet-smelling cigarette smoke. The gray mist drifted and curled its way around the yellow lightbulbs like the hair of a ghostly maiden, before gathering and sinking down slowly toward the racks of colorful records. As soon as we opened the door and walked inside, Jellybean sneezed.

Nelson laughed. "*Aaaahhtishu!* Do that again, Jelly! Do it again!" he said, tapping him on the nose.

"Leave the poor dog alone, Nelson," Butterfly chided.

DW raised his hand from behind the counter in a kind of laid-back wave. "Welcome!" he said, like he was expecting us.

"This is DW, everybody," said Sam, standing behind him and patting DW affectionately on the back. DW nodded gently at us, but his eyes narrowed with a little suspicion when he looked at Sam and me.

"I love the record you gave me, I've been playing it a lot. It makes me sad, though," I said.

"Sometimes it good to be sad — so you can feel happiness when it come! Y'understan'?" DW said, before taking a puff of his squashed-up cigarette.

Eric had found the main record deck, and the mellow tune that was playing screeched to an abrupt stop. This had a visible effect on DW, who made a face like somebody had stabbed him. "Move away from the turntable!" he stated. Then he lifted himself out of his comfortable seat and pushed Eric out of the way. "My record player, she is like a lady. She hate to be rushed and she hate it when you mess her about."

Sam was trying to suppress a smile because he knew DW compared every object to a woman.

"Sorry," said Eric sheepishly.

"Very slow and careful," said DW, taking the record Eric was holding. "You like Jimi?"

Eric nodded as DW laid the record slowly and carefully on the black rubber deck and lowered the needle.

"Eric, you really like Jimi Hendrix?" said Sam, impressed. "I can play this song on my guitar."

". . . and so castles made of sand, fall in the sea, eventually," sang the man on the record, as if he were in the store with us, and Eric and Sam moved their heads together to the rhythm of the music.

"I like this song," said Madison, and Sam smiled at her.

"Me, too," said Butterfly with a serene expression on her face.

"I want to choose one!" said Nelson.

"OK, but wait until this song done," said DW, winking at Nelson. Nelson smiled and ran down one of the aisles, pulling out record sleeves that had pictures and colors that he liked and making a pile of them.

"Are you always the one who take care of your little brother?" DW asked Butterfly. She nodded with a resigned expression. "Let me ask you this: How you ever gonna enjoy bein' a child yourself?"

Butterfly shrugged. "My mom works and she's studying to be a lawyer."

"Me just wanted to ask," said DW, but I could see from Butterfly's face and the way she bit her lower lip that he'd planted a seed in her thoughts and that seed was beginning to grow.

"I love my brother," said Butterfly, looking over at Nelson, and then at Madison in case she had upset her, but Madison smiled as if to say, *It's OK.* "It's just that I don't like it when I have to scold him and sometimes I just want to do my own thing, you know?" But DW was already walking over to Nelson at the other end of the shop, and Butterfly looked a little embarrassed that she'd spoken her thoughts out loud.

DW put his hand on Nelson's head and Nelson looked up at him with one of his biggest and best smiles. Then DW took a record off the top of Nelson's pile and headed back over toward his counter. Nelson's face became serious again as he began to rearrange the order of his record choices. In the corner of the shop, Jellybean looked up drowsily for a second and then rolled onto his side, stretching his legs right out in front of him before closing his eyes and going back to sleep.

Butterfly nudged me. "Who's going to ask him?" Madison's face questioned me, too.

I looked over at Sam, who was flicking through records, but it was as if he knew I was looking at him because he waited a moment and then, without looking up, said, "DW, we need your help. Remember you told me you worked at the hotel in town for a while? Well, we need to get in there tonight. We need somebody who knows their way around."

DW watched the record spin for a few seconds. He put the Hendrix record gently back into its cover before his brown fingers reached for Nelson's album choice. He allowed the black disc to drop from the crisp white protective sleeve into his palm and carefully lowered it onto the spinning deck. Very slowly, he lowered the needle onto the vinyl, just like my mom used to.

"That's my song! That's my song!" said Nelson, hopping up and down at the far end of the store. I looked down at Jellybean, whose legs were jerking in his sleep.

DW looked at us all in turn. "Me told you before to stay off the street, it not safe, y'understan'?" he said, raising his voice, his eyes filling with fire suddenly.

There was a long pause. Sam looked at me and I looked at Butterfly, who looked at Eric, who looked at Madison, who looked back at Sam, who looked back at me.

"How about you tell me the reason why you want to go?" DW said, calmer again.

"Well, there's a meeting. A secret meeting. And one of the people who's at the meeting might have something to do with a story my dad was investigating." I spoke carefully but truthfully.

"Wha' kin'a story?" DW's expression changed to one that said, *Come on, give it to me straight.*

"Well . . . ," I started, but Butterfly took over.

"We can't talk about it right now, because it's confidential, but it concerns the mysterious death of a well-known Elbow businessman and also the disappearance of certain members of an . . . um . . . underground community." We all looked at Butterfly, impressed.

But DW wasn't impressed, and his face said so. His eyes were filled with weariness, and I imagined it was because he knew that people had been going missing for a long time. The situation was real and scary and a few well-chosen, clever words were not going to solve the problem or do you any favors if the people responsible came looking for you.

"What we meant to say was, we need your help getting inside but we . . . well . . . we also kind of need someone to watch out for us," said Sam, and DW's expression changed instantly.

"Why you never say it before, man?" he said, smiling a mischievous smile.

DW opened a metal locker in the back room of his record store. He pulled out a dark blue suit and tie that he kept for special occasions. He held it up to the light and patted it gently, making tiny flecks of silver dust rise and dance in the air. We waited a few moments while DW got changed in the bathroom and reemerged in his suit, tie, and porkpie hat. "Tell me if me look good?" he said, giving us a twirl.

"Now you just need this," Madison said as she attached the little gold pin from her father's secret suitcase to DW's tie. "You should probably try not to talk to any of them, but if they insist, this will make them think you're one of them."

DW readjusted his tie and buttoned up his jacket. "C'mon—what you waiting for?" Then he led us out of the record store, turning off the light and switching the sign on the door to CLOSED before locking it behind us.

CHAPTER 36

We watched from across the street as DW walked up the stone steps to the Grand Hotel. Lots of men were arriving at the same time, and they nodded to each other in a knowing way or shook hands before going inside.

Once DW was inside and the uniformed man at the desk had taken his coat, he came back out to the entrance and winked at us. We waited under the old-fashioned awning of a storefront that sold cigars, pipes, and tobacco. "They don't *look* like cannibals," said Eric.

"You can never tell from just looking at somebody," replied Sam.

"DW said I can play in his store whenever I want to," said Nelson, tugging at Butterfly's raincoat.

"It's Jeeks!" hissed Eric suddenly.

And there they were, Dr. Smytheson and Mr. Jeeks, heading up the street toward us. They came quickly into focus: Mr. Jeeks's pale waxy face, pink rodentlike eyes, and pointy features; and Smytheson, taller, slightly stooped, his wide-brimmed hat masking his black unblinking eyes. "Can't you walk any faster?" spat the surgeon, making Jeeks cower slightly.

Butterfly lowered her brand-new navy umbrella in front of

us just in time, and they *whoosh*ed past. We held our breath as we saw their shadows pass across the taut material, but the blur of conversation was quickly drowned by rain as they crossed the street. Butterfly raised the umbrella again and we saw them both disappear inside the hotel.

"Come on, let's go," Eric said as he stepped into the road.

"No—we have to wait for DW," I said, yanking him back into the doorway.

"Jeeks is so horrible, he better not be friends with my dad," said Madison.

"Yeah, you might want to ask your dad, you know, about some of the company he keeps." Sam looked right at Madison when he said that, like he was accusing her of something, and she looked uncomfortable.

Once the men in coats and hats had stopped arriving, DW appeared at the hotel entrance. He tipped his hat at the uniformed man at the door, lit a cigarette, and let the smoke rise in the damp air. Then DW whispered something to the doorman, who nodded and patted DW on the shoulder. The doorman traveled quickly across the large tiled hall to speak to the receptionist, and they left the room together immediately.

DW looked over at us, throwing his cigarette into the fast-flowing gutter. The water carried it away like a boat heading for rapids. He put his fingers in his mouth and blew a high-pitched whistle. "C'mon!" he whispered loudly, looking back over his shoulder to see if the coast was still clear.

We rushed across the road to where DW was standing and through the entrance door. "Hurry!" said DW. "We're going to the gallery, we can see the Grand Hall from there.

Me have the key!" His eyes twinkled as he jangled a large bunch of keys.

"What did you tell the doorman?" I asked.

"He tell the receptionist boss askin' for him." DW winked at me. "He an old frien'."

DW led us through an unused coatroom and unlocked a carved wooden door that seemed like it was part of the wall. Butterfly, Nelson, and Jellybean went first, and Madison, Sam, and I followed. I just saw the receptionist heading back to his post as DW closed the door behind us. Suddenly we were standing at the entrance of a pitch-black corridor. I could smell mold and hear the slow drip of heavy raindrops making a small pool somewhere in the distance.

"Have you got a flashlight, Eric?" asked Sam.

"Of course," said Eric matter-of-factly.

"Do you think you'll be switching it on sometime soon?" said Madison.

There was a rustling sound as Eric rummaged through his backpack, and a *click* as the yellow beam made a circle on the ceiling. Then Eric aimed the flashlight forward, the light flooded the carved walls of the narrow stone corridor ahead of us, and DW led the way.

"OOOHHhwah!" yelled Nelson, making the tunnel vibrate with the echo of his voice. Jellybean barked and his bark echoed, too.

"Do you want us get in trouble, Nelson?" DW asked, and Nelson shook his head.

"No. I just like echoes. I like the way my words bounce back. I can catch them in my mouth—watch!"

"Ooohhw—" Nelson started again, opening his mouth wide as he waited to collect the sound. DW put his hand over Nelson's mouth. "Now is not the time to play. Do you want them to catch us?"

Nelson shook his head.

"Then you must be very, very quiet," said DW, releasing his hand.

"Can I still play with the records in your store?" whispered Nelson, so quietly that DW had to bend down to hear him.

"Of course! Me always keep me promise!" he said, and Nelson smiled and took DW's hand.

"Which way now?" asked Sam as we came to two corridors going in opposite directions.

DW wasn't sure. He scratched his head. "Let me think now. Yes, me remember—this way!" he said, pointing to the right. "No. Wait! It the other way!"

Eric's flashlight fizzled, blinked its yellow eye off, and then opened it again slowly. When it buzzed shut completely, Eric tapped it hard to try to make it work again. "I think it's the batteries. Sorry."

"I can't see a thing! How are we supposed to get there now?" whined Madison.

"Wait! Quiet!" said Butterfly. "I can hear voices."

"Me, too!" said Nelson.

The sound of men's voices made a distant hum, and above it rose the faint sound of one man's voice giving a speech. "Brothers!" he announced, and then we lost his words again. Then there was loud applause.

"It must be this way," Sam said. "Grab on to each other's clothes. Jelly will lead the way. Go, boy, go on — follow the noise." Jellybean let out a little breathy *woof* to say he understood, and Sam held on to his fur as he began walking toward the voices. DW held on to Sam's jacket, I held on to DW, and Madison, Eric, Nelson, and Butterfly followed in that order, all holding on to each other's raincoats as we walked slowly down the long, gloomy tunnel. I strained to see if I could make my eyes focus on some shaft of light, a little beam shooting through a hole in the stone, something, anything — but there was nothing. It was so dark I couldn't tell if my eyes were open or closed. Was this what it was like to have no eyes? I closed my eyes tight and hoped it would be over soon.

"Ow! Watch where you're walking!" Madison hissed at Eric, who had stepped on her heels. "Do you have to be so clumsy?"

"Sorry," said Eric. "I've got big feet."

"He didn't do it on purpose!" Butterfly spoke into the darkness where she imagined Madison to be. Then she wondered aloud, "What was that? I just felt something drop on my hair."

"Probably just some dust." I hoped.

Then Madison let out a muffled yell: "Ugghh! I touched it!"

"What was it?" asked Eric.

"How am I supposed to know? I can't see a thing," snapped Madison.

"Maybe the ceiling's loose," came Sam's voice from up ahead.

"Nope. I don't think so. The thing that dropped on my head—it moved," said Butterfly.

"Get it off me! Get it off!" shouted Nelson as he tried to flick whatever was falling from the ceiling off his body.

"Everybody, quiet!" whispered Sam. "There's a roomful of men on just the other side of this tunnel. We don't want them to know we're here, remember?"

"It's OK, Nelson. . . . Ugghhhh! I think it's a roach!" squeaked Butterfly.

"I want to go home!" pleaded Nelson.

Then one of those fat beetles fell on me. I touched its hard, shiny body and feelers and its squirming legs, which had been trying to run through the air as it dropped.

"They're definitely roaches!" said Sam as quietly as he could while trying to squash one hard under his heel. "They don't squish easy." Then came the familiar sound of Jelly crunching, slurping, and licking.

"Uuuughhh!" said Madison, sounding like she was going to throw up.

"Put your hoods up, or your rain hats on!" suggested Eric, so we did, and the roaches continued to drop one by one with a *click, click, click* onto our raincoats like hard, crispy raindrops, and the strange thing was that it felt kind of normal—normal for us, by now, anyway.

Sam walked ahead, squashing as many cockroaches as he could under his feet. "They must be trying to escape the wet weather," said Eric softly, as if making a mental note to himself.

We stumbled into the end of the corridor and felt the outline of some stone steps spiraling upward. "What the—?"

said DW, squinting into the darkness. "It look like the stair be moving!"

"That's because they *are* moving," said Sam.

As we began to climb the small twisting steps, the roaches formed a current of what I imagined to be a red-brown sea against us. Using our hands on the steps to steady ourselves, we felt the bugs crawl over them.

"Just try not to look too close, Nelson," said Butterfly, pulling him onto her back so he didn't have to touch them. Finally, at the top of the bug-infested staircase, we arrived at another wood-carved wall and DW felt along the ornate shapes for the secret door.

DW's fingers fumbled for the right key. Butterfly's expression was just visible in the half-shadows and I saw her notice how DW's hands were shaking. "We gotta be quick, me got to get the key back before receptionist find out."

DW's key tried to find the lock but missed. The keys fell to the ground with a loud *clash* and we could hear the sudden hush in the Grand Hall on the other side of the wall. Had they heard us?

Jellybean's eyebrows twitched as he watched a large, shiny, aubergine cockroach scuttle over the keys. I don't think he was impressed with the flavor of the beetle he'd just eaten, because he waited until the roach had scuttled away and then picked the keys up, very gently, with his teeth.

"Thank you, Jellybean," said DW as he selected the right key again, placed it in the lock, and turned. The latch clicked and the door moaned open as the voices of the men gathered in the hall below suddenly grew louder.

Sam lay flat on his stomach, slid across the polished wood flooring of the balcony, swept a couple of stray roaches out of the way, and signaled for us to follow. DW shook his head and pointed to the solid top step with an expression that said he was staying right there, even if it meant putting up with a few more roaches, because the last thing he was going to do was lay down on his stomach and slide like a snake. Madison wasn't too impressed with lying on her stomach, either, but I could tell she was relieved to be away from most of the bugs—and after all, when you've shared a stinking bath with giant rats, everything else is really kind of pleasant in comparison. Jellybean lay down next to Nelson and put one paw over his nose, and Nelson seemed to understand that this was a time to be really quiet.

So there we were, lying side by side in this gallery, peering through the ornate wooden balcony, and underneath was a hall full of men in costume, like they were at a private costume party, except they were all dressed the same and there were no women.

They were all lined up facing a kind of altar, and there were candles dancing jerkily in the drafty hall. The men were humming together, making a weird hypnotic kind of sound.

"What's going on?" whispered Sam.

"It's like they're praying," said Eric.

"Shhh!" Butterfly blew the sound at them like a gentle wind. Nelson had propped himself up on his elbows like he was watching TV, but Butterfly quickly pushed him, and his elbows slipped easily, making him flat again.

Standing at the very top of the room, in front of the altar, was the surgeon, Dr. Smytheson, wearing a big hat that was kind of like a bishop's, only red-and-black instead of gold, and on it was the symbol of the sunshine-eye inside a triangle, just like the one we'd seen on Madison's dad's stuff.

"Do you think he's the boss?" I asked.

"It looks that way," whispered Butterfly.

Smytheson rang a little bell. The men in the red robes broke away from the formal lines they were standing in and began chatting among themselves. Taking his hat off, the surgeon stepped down into the main hall toward a group of men talking under a large picture. The picture had an elaborate gold frame and showed a man holding up a glowing ice-cream cone in one hand and a globe in the other.

"That picture," I said in a hushed voice. "Over there, with the gold frame—where have I seen that man before?" I asked.

"That's John Elbow," said Butterfly.

"That's right—like the statue in town."

"Look!" squeaked Madison. "That looks like the guy who delivered the guts to Jeeks at Eric's house." She was right; it was the same stocky bald guy we'd seen handing over the yellow bag that Jellybean stole. Here he was now, dressed in one of those weird robes.

"I don't believe it," said Sam. "Take a look over there—those two guys in the corner!" Standing near a kind of ornamental fountain, the kind you find in churches, were a blond man and a red-haired man who also looked familiar. "The cops," said Sam. "The ones who came to your house and ripped up the report."

At that moment Sam and I looked over at DW, who registered our expressions. He shook his head, and his eyes filled with a strange sadness that seemed to say that his suspicions had been confirmed.

"They're all in on it. They all know each other." I tasted the words as I spoke them, and they were as bitter and sharp as blood.

We watched a man walk toward the surgeon, also in robes and a hat, this time a kind of floppy red-and-black hat with a big tassel hanging to one side. He reached out to take the surgeon's hat, and as he turned, we saw his face. "There he is, there's Jeeks," I whispered, and as I did, the surgeon aimed a sudden, fierce look right in our direction. We lay as flat as we could. It was hard to breathe, lying flat on that wooden floor. I could see my breath make a cloudy condensation mark on the polish around my face.

"Did he see us?" I was face-to-face with Butterfly.

"I don't know," she said, her big dark eyes moist with fear. "I hope not."

We knew we hadn't been seen when Dr. Smytheson began speaking to all the men again. "Brothers, as you know, this is a very special night. It's not just our monthly joining together: We're here to celebrate the anniversary of the Radiant Brotherhood, and the man who brought this ancient society to Elbow: Maximillian Horatio Feverspeare! To Maximillian!" His voice bellowed as he raised a jewel-encrusted goblet.

"To Maximillian!" sang the men in their deep voices before breaking into a loud cheer. They raised their silver goblets, downed a mouthful of bloodred wine, then raised the cups again. "Hooraaaah!"

"Who is Maximillian Horatio Feverspeare?" whispered Sam.

"The guy must be one of the Feverspeare family, you know, like the library's named after—maybe he was related to Agnes?" suggested Butterfly.

"These kinds of secret societies are really, really old. I read about them," said Eric. "Do you think that's blood they're drinking? Where's the person they sacrificed for it?" he continued, anticipating the gory act we imagined could still be about to happen.

"Behind the curtains?" said Madison weakly.

Crouched down in the doorway, DW waved at us and tapped his watch. His forehead was wrinkled up with worry and his face was twitchy.

The robed men had divided into small groups and were chatting and drinking like they were at a regular party, and Dr. Smytheson and Mr. Jeeks had disappeared. My eyes moved quickly around each group in the hall to see where they were. "Where did they go?" I whispered.

"He's coming this way," said Eric, a little too loudly, as Smytheson made his way toward a group of men standing right underneath us.

"Shhhh," hissed Madison.

Smytheson and Jeeks were surrounded by a circle of robed men and they were all standing right under our balcony.

"I've never seen him—how shall we say?—in the flesh, but I'm hoping to persuade old Jeeksy here. He's a bit of a dog in the manger—likes to keep him all to himself, don't you, Jeeksy, old boy!"

"It must be quite something working for him, there's never been *anyone* like him," said a plump man with rosy cheeks, taking another greedy gulp of his wine.

"He's been very . . . generous over the years. He's taken care of my family—but we have worked hard in return." Jeeks stuttered slightly as he spoke.

"Of course there isn't anyone like him! There's nobody like him in the entire world! He's a genius! A veritable da Vinci—a brilliant scientist and a true artist! There'll never be another Max Horatio Feverspeare!"

"Hear! Hear!" sang the men in the circle, raising their cups again.

I could just make out their heads and the tops of their faces as I pushed my nose through a gap in the balcony and peered down. They moved a little as they talked, coming a bit more into view, and then going again, under the wooden ceiling. Jeeks looked uncomfortable with the way the surgeon was talking.

"As you know," continued Smytheson, "Jeeksy has been his personal secretary for many years now—how I envy him!" he said, hitting Jeeks hard on the shoulder. When the surgeon raised his hand to speak again, Jeeks flinched. "I'd just like to ask the Great Man some questions. Instead I have to satisfy myself with collecting memorabilia. I have letters from his sister, Agnes, I have a family portrait, and, of course, this . . ."

He raised his right hand and flashed the palace ring for

the other men to see. There were a few sounds and nods of admiration as the ring caught the lights of the chandelier.

"Did you see it?" whispered Butterfly.

". . . I only have John's ring, which I bought from a dealer," Smytheson was saying. "I would have loved Agnes's. I think of hers as the original—maybe because she actually got to wear it. Heaven only knows where it is now . . . we lost track of it after that irritating . . . er . . . pickle man, Henderson, stole it. Swallowed it, would you believe!"

"So that's why there are two rings. One for John and one for Agnes. They *were* engagement rings," said Butterfly under her breath. Agnes's ring suddenly felt bulky in my jeans pocket, its sharp edges pressing into my leg as I lay on the wooden floor.

As Smytheson spoke, Jeeks squirmed and contempt began to grow in his eyes. He got more and more red in the face, as though he wanted to say something but was holding it in— and had been for a very long time.

Smytheson sighed. "Unfortunately we haven't been able to locate Agnes's ring since then. It could be, shall we say, very awkward for all concerned if it should fall into the wrong hands," he said, darting an accusing look at Jeeks.

Finally Jeeks's redness exploded into a sentence. "It wouldn't be a problem, my dear Smytheson, if you didn't insist on playing medical school pranks!" he spat.

"A bit of viscera is good for the constitution—besides, it was high time *you* got your hands dirty," Smytheson shot back, to which a weasely-faced man said, "Touché!"

Sam slid along the floor and squeezed himself in between me and Madison. "Did you hear? He said the ring belonged to that Feverspeare guy. That's who Herman stole it from."

"Maximillian Horatio Feverspeare," Madison repeated.

"Agnes Feverspeare's brother," added Butterfly. "Do you remember that bit in her book—and the note that said she was scared of someone named Max? Do you think she was scared of her own brother?"

I thought for a moment and then nodded slowly. But I still didn't get it. "What do the Feverspeares—two people from, like, two hundred years ago or something—have to do with Jeeks and Smytheson and Herman and the people from Garbage City?" I was confused.

Then I remembered what my dad had said once about stories, about things slowly falling into place, one piece at a time, like a jigsaw puzzle. "You never have all the pieces at once and sometimes you can't see the whole picture until you put the final piece down," he would say to me.

"What *I* don't understand," said Eric, trying his best to be quiet, "is how Jeeks can still be working for somebody who started the Radiant Brotherhood, like, two hundred years ago."

"What have you gotten us into, Bea?" said Madison weakly.

"It wasn't me!" I opened my mouth wide at being wrongly accused. "It was Sam! I wanted to get out of Elbow, remember? It was Sam who took me to Herman's body!"

"You didn't have to come." Sam looked at me, his eyebrows raised, his blue eyes sparkling. He was so close to me, our noses were almost touching. My stomach did a somersault. I looked away to catch, for the first time, the look in Madison's eyes, the look that said that somehow I had broken an unspoken promise.

Smytheson spoke again. "Luckily Jeeksy has it all under control, don't you, old boy? He's just a hairbreadth away from finding the children who are responsible."

We froze, and tried not to breathe in case we made a sound. Butterfly, Sam, and the others looked at me with terror in their eyes while DW wiped the sweat from his face and tapped even more deliberately on his watch.

"Children?" asked a man with a thin mustache and pale beady eyes.

"A harmless game," came Jeeks's nasal voice. "I intend to return the ring to Max before he realizes it's missing."

DW was signaling to us that it was really time to leave now, but Sam waved back for him to wait. Nelson, nestling against Jelly's wet coat, was starting to get a tickly nose. "*Ker-kerchhhhew!*" he sneezed, scrunching up his little face. He smiled one of his big wide smiles, and then realized what he'd done. We lay there for a split second, hoping the surgeon and Jeeks hadn't noticed. Slowly, Sam and me peered over the balcony.

All the men below were looking right up at us.

"Let's go!" ordered Sam, and we pulled ourselves as quickly as we could along the floor back to the entrance of the corridor. But it was too late.

"It's them!" shouted Smytheson, pointing up at us as our

bodies bumped into each other trying get out through the gallery's door. "Don't let them get away this time!" he boomed.

We stumbled down the stone stairs into the tunnel, slippery with roaches. DW stopped suddenly ahead of us. "You can't go out the entrance," he said, finding it hard to catch his breath. "They'll be waiting."

"Where does the other tunnel go?" Sam's voice echoed off the walls as we stood for a moment in the darkness.

"Don't know," said DW helplessly. "I'll go out the front. If they stop me, I say me not see you."

"Thanks, DW," said Sam.

We heard DW's feet make the roaches crunch as he walked back down the stone corridor. The crunching faded the farther down the tunnel he went.

"Will he be OK?" asked Butterfly.

"Sure he will. Come on!" said Sam, leading the way past the corridor we had come in through.

"Where does this go?" asked Eric.

"I don't know," said Sam. "I guess we'll find out."

The feeling of the ground changed suddenly under our shoes, like we were walking on hard sand, not stone anymore, and it smelled damp and a bit like rotting fish.

"Shhhh! Did you hear that?" said Madison. We stopped and listened.

"This way! Hurry, Jeeks!" came the distant echo of the surgeon's voice, and then the sound of two far-off sets of footsteps. We saw the beam of a flashlight fan around part of the tunnel wall.

"They're coming, we have to move faster," whispered Eric. We held on to each other, with Jelly leading the way, and tried to speed up, which was hard in the pitch-black. The *drip-drip* of gloopy raindrops was getting louder.

"I don't like it here! I want to go home!" whined Nelson. "I'm sorry I sneezed. Can we go back now?"

"No, Nelson! There are some bad men after us," said Butterfly.

"Is it my fault?" said Nelson.

Butterfly didn't say anything for a second, and then she answered softly, "No, it's not your fault."

"Remember when we played pirates?" I could just make out the line of Nelson's head.

"Yes," said Nelson sadly.

"Well, we're pirates now and some bad pirates are after us, so we're running away, OK? But it's just a game, and we're having fun — right, everyone? *Right, everyone?!*" I whispered as loud as I could.

"That's right," said Madison quietly.

"We're having fun!" said Eric more enthusiastically.

"Look, there's a light," said Butterfly.

"Go on, boy!" said Sam, and Jelly ran ahead. When we caught up with Jelly, he was drinking from a dark green pool that was completely coated with thick green slime.

"That's where the smell was coming from," I said, indicating the stagnant pool. Madison held her hand over her mouth. Next to the pool were clusters of long, thin white mushrooms, a miniature forest growing silently in the darkness. I picked one up by its thin stalk as if I were picking a dandelion. It had bluish folds underneath its hat, like a delicate book opening up its pages all the way around.

"Can you believe this place?" Eric's voice was full of wonder as he took in the cathedral-like space carved out of gray-black rock. There was a big old electric light burning on the wall and it shone up into parts of the cave, making it glint like a dull jewel. Leading away from the pool was a streak of bright green water littered with the dead bodies of pale white fish. Jelly gave their swollen corpses a disinterested sniff—even he wouldn't eat fish *that* rotten.

"We've got to keep going!" urged Sam, looking down the corridor we had just come from. "They can't be far behind."

It was getting darker again as we ran along the black earth and stone, and Jelly's sharp barks bounced around the walls up ahead.

"There's no use running!" shouted Jeeks.

"We just want to talk to you! . . . *talk to yooou!*" Smytheson's words almost sounded soothing as they echoed around the tunnel after us. Maybe he *did* just want to talk to us. Then I remembered the sign of his ring burned into the flesh of the people who lived in Garbage City.

Panic gripped at my throat and my heart pounded in my chest. *Where are we going? I can't see anything! They're going to get us!* I couldn't keep the scary thoughts out.

"Keep going, that's it! You're doing great!" I managed to say to Nelson, who was running alongside me.

"I think they're going to catch us." Butterfly's voice broke up a little as she ran.

"They can't catch me!" sang Nelson happily.

The green streak of water had gradually grown and was snaking itself into a small stream. As we ran alongside it, the ground got narrower and narrower and the stream took over. Before long the stream had become a river.

"At least we know how the fish got in," Eric called back to us as we shifted into single file.

"You might as well stop running. There's no way out!" Smytheson's voice shot out of the shadows behind us.

"We just want the ring back. Give us the ring and you can go home!" Jeeks's thinner voice joined Smytheson's.

"Maybe we should just give them the ring," Madison said.

"Are you crazy?" Sam yelled back at her. "We've got to keep going!"

The syrupy river was heaving and moaning with the weight of its icy blue-black water, and it lapped at the sides of the tunnel and at our feet. The footsteps got faster behind us. They were catching up with us now, the surgeon and Jeeks.

"In here!" Sam shouted suddenly, finding another corridor leading off to the left. "This way!"

"Come on, Nelson!" shouted Butterfly back at her brother.

Nelson had lagged behind; he had shorter legs and couldn't run as fast as the rest of us. The rest of us were almost all the way down the new tunnel when Nelson turned the corner too sharply and skidded.

"Hhheeeelllp!" cried Nelson as he fell into the freezing river.

"Where are you, Nelson?" I called for him.

"I'm here! Heeellllpp! I c-c-can't swim!"

I kneeled down on the ground and waved my arms around blindly, straining to see Nelson's shape in the water.

"Hold out your hand, Nelson!" I told him.

"What's happening?" yelled Butterfly from way down the corridor.

"It's OK," I said, grabbing Nelson by the hood of his raincoat. "I've got him!" I called back to Butterfly as I lay down on my stomach, my face almost touching the jagged waves of the subzero river. I plunged my hands into the water, my hands burning with cold, and reached under Nelson's arms, pulling him up. No sooner was he out than he got up and ran down the tunnel toward the others, his clothes making a sloshing sound as he went.

"I'm not going to let the bad pirates get me!" His voice echoed behind him. "I'm not going to let the bad pirates get me!"

That's when I felt sick. I must have had one of my fainting attacks because all I remember after that was being so cold I couldn't breathe. I had fallen into the lonely blue-black of the freezing underground river. Its arms were happy to embrace me and take me deep into that watery place where its currents played with my floating hair and prodded my unconscious body like evil mermaid's fingers. I think I heard the nasty river laugh at having swallowed me up. And when I was underneath, in the murky vaults, I saw Herman. He smiled at me with his kind face and held out his hand to me the way my grandpa had when he was alive, like we were about to go on a lovely long walk together, to a beautiful but secret place few people were allowed to visit.

CHAPTER 37

It was not until much later that I found out what had happened, about how the others didn't know that I was lost, that I had been taken by the night-water. They also had to fill me in about how Jellybean had bolted back down the tunnel to save me, jumping into the river and diving under the inky indigo waves until he found me and pulled me up by the nape of my raincoat, as if I were one of his puppies.

Unfortunately, Smytheson and Jeeks were waiting on that shadowy bank. They lifted me out, blue-lipped and pale as a ghost, and took me away. Jelly followed their car all the way out of town; he must have run faster and farther than ever before, and I still don't know how he did it.

My eyes felt sticky and bruised when I woke up, and my head was throbbing. I was lying in a big bed with bright white sheets. On the pillows (near where I had dribbled in my half-sleep) were embroidered initials that kept coming in and out of focus. The initials were *MHF*. Where had I seen those initials before? They seemed so familiar. The large black ornate letters were intertwined so as to make up their own strange shape. *I must be in St. Agnes's*, I thought, *because* of the white bedsheets and the high white walls. *The rainy fingers must have reached all the way inside me after all, just like I'd always feared they would. They reached inside my mind and now I'm finally here, in St. Agnes's. I wonder where Mom is?*

"I really want to go home now," came Nelson's sad little voice from a bed not far from mine.

"Nelson? Is that you? I thought you ran away. . . ." I tried to lift my sore head and focus my fuzzy eyes in his direction.

"I did, but the bad pirates were waiting. This game isn't fun anymore, Bea."

"I know. This is a tough game—but we're doing OK. I think you've already scored about four hundred and thirty-two points!" I managed to say before the deep, dozy feeling took hold of me again, my face sank into those white pillows, and I was pulled back toward the heavy sleep I'd just woken from.

I didn't know if I was asleep or dreaming when a yellow light shone into my eyes and the figures of Jeeks and Smytheson leaned in to look at me. They were both wearing white coats, so even Jeeks looked like a doctor, and their heads seemed so big and their faces so funny that I wanted to laugh. "You are terrible pirates!" I said, my tongue feeling too fat for my mouth. "You may as well give up right now because we're going to win!" I rolled my head to the side to see Nelson's face poking out from under his quilt. He was smiling and his big dark eyes were twinkling with mischief.

"What did she say?" Smytheson said impatiently.

"Something about pirates—she must be seeing things," murmured Jeeks.

"We'll have to test it, see if it's beating properly before we operate," the surgeon said seriously.

"What could possibly be wrong with it? She's a kid," said Jeeks.

"We need to be sure," said Smytheson.

I reached for the strange necklace Butterfly's grandma had given me and I felt the soft feathers, cold wire, and shell-like heart, sitting not on my chest but between my shoulder blades; but I still wasn't sure if I was imagining it.

"He wants to meet her first. He wants to see her for himself, to be sure she's right," said Jeeks.

"What about the boy?" snapped Smytheson.

"We'll throw him back in the sea—let him get a little bigger," quipped Jeeks.

"I'm not a fish!" protested Nelson to himself, from under the quilt. "I'm a pirate!"

When I lifted my heavy lids again, Jeeks and Smytheson were gone, and Nelson was curled up beside me, asleep.

I fell back into a deep slumber myself and dreamed of Sam, Butterfly, Madison, and Eric. I dreamed I heard Sam's voice saying he'd never stop until he'd found me. I dreamed of them asking DW and Elenor for help and about Jellybean finding Sam, the way he always does, no matter where he is, and leading him and the other Convicts all the way to whatever strange place Nelson and I were being held prisoner in. I dreamed of them rescuing us, and about the warm, bright sunshine that followed them in, flooding the room with golden light as we laughed and hugged.

The distant sound of Jelly's barking made the dream

seem even more real, and the funny thing was, I could still hear him when I half opened my right eye. Nelson was trying to wake me up by tugging on the sleeve of my white nightgown.

"What is it, Nelson?" I said, slurring the words drowsily.

"I can hear Jellybean," he whispered.

It took me a few seconds to register what he'd said, and then I heard Jelly yowl loudly.

"He's really here! He really came!" I was so glad to hear the real Jelly that tears sprang from my swollen eyes, making them sting, but I wiped them on my pillow so that Nelson wouldn't notice and get upset.

Jelly's bark was so insistent. With each sharp sound he said, "Get up! Get up now! I'm not going to stop until you get up!"

I flopped my droopy legs onto the floor and slowly pushed myself up, and all the while Jelly kept barking: "You're in danger! You have to get out!"

"Nelson? I think now's our chance to beat the bad pirates . . . ," I said as clearly and cheerfully as I could, dragging my sleepy body slowly across the room. I gripped a chair and shuffled with it toward the strips of rain-light rippling on the polished floor. "Maybe we can get out through the window."

"How many points would we get for that?" asked Nelson, sitting up.

As I raised the blinds and looked out through the window, panic gripped me. We weren't in St. Agnes's at all. I didn't know where we were, but I knew the view from St.

Agnes's, and this wasn't it. All I could see for miles and miles were high, thick, blue-green pine trees reaching into the gloomy sky. I could see and hear the rainy fingers flicking and tapping at the window — the rainy fingers that told me we must still be in Elbow, I just didn't know exactly where. My mind wanted desperately to run but my body still wanted to sleep. I wondered what they'd drugged me with. I tried to make my legs move fast, but they refused. I shuffled slowly to the door and tried to open it. Locked! I dragged my reluctant feet back to the window, while Jelly's warning barks got louder still. Where was Sam? Where were the others? My mind called out to them, but it was no use, we were alone. Trapped.

Whatever happens, I thought, *I can't let Nelson see how scared I am.* I tried as hard as I could to make my limp lips smile at him, and for a second, when he smiled back with his big happy face, I felt almost safe.

I pulled open the window and let the howl of the wind and the angry spitting tongues of the rain inside and onto my face. Nelson peered out, too, squinting to see through the downpour. There was a ledge and then a smaller roof below the window. I tried to lift myself out, but my arms and legs were numb and wobbly.

"I think it's too far down!" I heard Nelson say.

I leaned out the window and pressed my face as far out into the rain as I could, and then I yelled with all of my strength: "JELLY, FIND SAM! GO FIND SAM!" Then I collapsed onto the floor, drenched with a mixture of rain and sweat.

*   *   *

I was still lying on the floor when the door opened and a pair of brown stockinged legs in black squeaky shoes came in and walked straight up to me.

"So they finally found one! You must be a pretty spunky little girl for him to think you're good enough," said the gravelly voice. When I sat up I saw a very tanned woman dressed in a nurse's uniform. *This is odd,* I thought. *Nobody is tan in Elbow in the summer unless they've come back from a vacation.* She was incredibly wrinkly, but not in a nice way, like Butterfly's grandmother, where all the lines looked like they were there for a reason and made her look even more beautiful. This lady's wrinkles were different. They looked like angry scribbles. She wore bright red lipstick that made it seem like her mouth was starting to bleed into her face.

Nelson gripped my hand. "Bea? Is this really a game?"

I bent down and whispered in Nelson's ear. "She's the evil pirate queen—if we get past her, we score double what we already have!"

That seemed to make Nelson happy. "How many points would we have then?"

"Let me see . . . That would add up to eight hundred and ninety-two."

Nelson's eyes sparkled with excitement and he looked up at the lady with a determined expression followed by a kind of knowing nod.

"Get a move on—you're to come with me," said the nurse. Her mouth turned downward when she spoke and two deep lines appeared in the dark brown papery surface of her face. "You'll need to be decontaminated one more time."

"It's my turn first, Nelson! You wait here," I said playfully.

The nurse bundled me into a bathroom with a large shower in one corner. She clicked her spidery fingers and pointed to a hook with a towel and clean pj's hanging from it.

"You're to shower and get changed. Can I trust you to shower properly? I don't have *time* to babysit." She stood there with her arms folded, staring at me. I nodded nervously, hoping really hard she wouldn't detect my special necklace. "Good. When you're done, I'll administer your decontamination." And with that she swept out of the room.

When the nurse came back she squirted me—on top of my clean pj's—with a white powder that made me sneeze. "You can never be too careful with germs," she proclaimed as her rubbery soles squeaked away again. "Come on now, we don't have all day." I followed her out of the room and down a long white corridor, feeling a little comfort from the necklace, still hidden and close to my heart.

"Where am I? Where's Bertha?!" I wanted to be angry, but my voice came out thin and feeble. I hurried behind the nurse, hoping she would fill me in on what had happened and why I was locked up, but she didn't say a word. We walked down one spotless white corridor after another, each one with an enclosed curling staircase at the end of it. The staircases and corridors seemed to spiral endlessly downward.

Finally the nurse turned to me, holding open a large

brown door. "The Master will see you on your own. Just follow the corridor and then take the elevator on your right."

I wanted to cry. I felt so alone and I felt scared. Why was I here? Why didn't anybody care about me? I thought about Sam and the others. Jelly *always* knew how to find Sam; it was his special talent. I just knew they'd come for me. I thought, *Sam won't let me down. I bet Jelly's already led them all the way here and they're outside with the police right now.* I held on to that thought like a warm light and it made me feel a whole lot better.

As I started to walk down the corridor, I noticed pictures—photographs—all around me.

Hundreds and hundreds of photographs lined the corridor like wallpaper. There were shots of families, all smiling, some with only a dad or only a mom, some with lots of brothers and sisters and some with pets included. *Whoever lives here must have a lot of friends,* I thought as I walked along, taking in all the different faces. *Or maybe the person who lives here is a photographer.*

The photographs continued as I walked along first one, then another seemingly endless corridor. When I came to an elevator, I pressed the button and got inside. As it traveled deep into the ground, it pulled at my stomach and my ears popped. *How much lower could this building go?* I thought. *I must be underground by now—deep, deep, deep underground.*

The doors slid apart with a single electric note sung into the air and then closed again behind me. I was in a room that felt like it was in a giant old museum. It had dark wooden floors and high ceilings and it smelled about as clean as a room could smell. Even my slippers squeaked on the polished floor. There was nothing in that room except for a massive old-fashioned sepia photograph on the towering wall, a picture of a handsome man wearing a monocle and holding a cigarette in a special holder. He was wearing a fancy three-piece suit and a top hat, the kind of outfit that rich people wore around the time of Abraham Lincoln. Music played while I looked at the photo, and the more I looked at it, the more alive it seemed. The man had very intense eyes, like a powerful magician who could hypnotize you and make you do whatever he wanted. He seemed to be staring right at me. Right through me.

There was a buzz and the nurse's shrill voice came through a speaker. "Put your mask on now!" I didn't know what she meant. "Around your neck!" I looked down and saw a paper mask like surgeons wear, so I pulled it over my nose and mouth. Then the photograph split into two and revealed a large wooden staircase heading yet farther into the ground. My feet made a *squeak-squeak* on the steps as I went farther down and farther still. The air seemed to get colder and colder, until I could see my breath form a thick mist. Feeling as faint as a fading ghost, I finally came to a dimly lit, cavelike room, and the nurse's electronic voice told me to take off my shoes and stand in the footbath. Although I was shivering, I did as I was told, and again my feet were sprayed with strong-smelling disinfectant. What kind of place was this? An underground hospital? And who was "he"—who was "The Master"?

A metal door opened to reveal another room, and at the

very end of that room was something that looked like a large, low cavern. Icy smoke was coming from the cavelike room, drifting out and along the floor toward me in thick clouds, and I could hear a faint mechanical whir and a slow sucking sound followed by a long hiss. As I got closer, I could see that the whole of that room was a block of ice, and inside the ice were red shapes, like bloody flowers caught in a frost. Then my eyes found the outline of something or someone around them. There was a figure, suspended in a pale liquid. It was the palest, skinniest figure you have ever seen. He, she, or it was so transparent that you could just make out the outline of skin and the silvery bones that made a delicate cage around the heart, lungs, liver, and stomach. The organs seemed to blossom with blood.

I was just thinking to myself how sad the eyes on that face looked . . . when it spoke. Although the creature barely opened its mouth, the sound was transmitted through speakers near where I was standing.

"You have found me"—*suuuuuck, hisssss!*—"Or, rather, I have found you," came a frail, whispered man's voice. And then he said, "I apologize for my strange appearance"—*suuuuuck, hissss!*—"skin is the most difficult organ to transplant. I seem to react terribly to other people's skin. . . ."

His eyes looked at me through the ice. They were veined with pink and blue, and so watery he looked like he was crying. The tears trickled down his face and mixed with the fluid he was suspended in, like paint in water. There were tubes coming from his nose and different parts of his body — probably feeding him, keeping him alive. It was hard to tell if he was human or not — and if he was, how old he was. All he was wearing was a loose pair of pants, a bit like the kind you see Jesus wearing in paintings.

I wanted to cry just watching him — he looked so painfully lonely. He was down here in the deepest part of the ground, with a big house somewhere up above, but he was trapped and he was alone.

"How do you like" — *suuuuuck, hisssss!* — "my photographs?" his weak voice crackled. It was barely there and yet there was still something menacing in it. I remembered those piercing eyes on the sepia portrait outside, and I was scared. "I was handsome once, was I not?" He seemed to say this to himself, and then he spoke to me. "The people of Elbow sent me those photographs — so kind, so kind . . ." *Suuuuuck, hisssss!*

And then I realized. The photographs I had seen lining the walls of those two corridors were photo-competition entries. Photos from the "Win a Trip to Florida" competition. For a moment I thought, *Maybe I'm here because I've won the competition.* But that would have been impossible, because I didn't send in any pictures. If I had managed to take any of my own, pictures of Mitzy, Pete, and DW would be looking down from those walls, too. Something inside told me that nobody had won that competition — that the competition hadn't been a competition at all.

"I like to keep people around me. The people of Elbow seem so . . . alive," continued the voice.

I touched the heart made of bone and wire that Butterfly's

grandmother had given me. "Well, you won't be keeping *me*. My friends and Bertha will be here soon." I made my voice as bold as I could, but inside I was afraid. The only sound that was returned was the slow suck and hiss of air from one of the machines. All around the man, different machines were ticking, whirring, and clicking, and pale liquids were traveling to and fro in long, thin plastic tubes. Little green and red lights flashed and beeped around me.

"It's true what they say, you have her spirit," he wheezed from inside his ice chamber.

"What do you mean?" My stomach sank the way it did when I knew something awful was about to happen. I felt sick.

"*Suuuuuck, hisssss. Suuuuuck, hisssss,*" came his reply.

As I waited for the man in the ice to speak again, I looked at his face and a strange feeling came over me. The closer I looked, the more I was certain that his eyes were two different colors. One of the eyeballs was bright blue and looked at me differently, kind of affectionately. It was a very familiar eye. The other eye was brown, a kind of deep brown that was almost chili-pepper red. That eye seemed familiar, too.

Because the man's skull was skinless and almost transparent, both eyeballs were visible and seemed to have a life of their own. The more I looked, the more certain I became. My heart began to beat fast in my chest and suddenly there was no doubt in my mind that the red-brown eye was Herman's . . . and the other, the blue eye, was my dad's.

I thought back to Herman's body in that green water, that dirty water, lapping in and out of his empty eye socket. Did this demon-man take my dad's eye before he died, too? Did this man kill my father? Is that how he really died?

My heart thumped faster and faster and my mind began to race. Everything was beginning to fit into place. I traced the sketchy shape of the iceman's body downward with my eyes and found his right arm. Thin blue veins shone through the pale flesh, red arteries glowed from beneath, and twisting its way across them both was a red-and-green snake tattoo. I thought back to my time with Leo in the dump and knew right away that the iceman's right arm was Leo's.

Who did the other organs belong to? *What* was this man? He was like some kind of Frankenstein's monster. The scars of the people in Garbage City flashed into my mind. My face was suddenly hot and my eyes burned as I fought back tears. My heart pumped so fast I could feel its rhythm in every part of my body. "What . . . kind of thing are you?" My lips were trembling as the words fell limply out. I was fixed to the spot, in a kind of trance. This had to be a bad dream.

"I'm sorry, how terribly rude. Allow me to introduce myself. I'm Maximillian Horatio Feverspeare."

"But how . . . how can you be? He was alive hundreds of years ago," I stuttered.

"So he was . . . and *is*. Anything is possible, my dear, if the desire is there" — *suuuuuck, hisssss!* — "Anything." I could have sworn I saw a smile flicker across his thin lips (or were they somebody else's?). His brain, which seemed to glow at the top of his skeletal body like a fat pink crown, pulsated with life.

It was then, at last, that my finger started up. The pinkie finger on my left hand began its familiar fizzing and twitching. It was being drawn toward a gray door on my right. I wondered if the iceman could see it move. I put my arm behind my back but my finger kept spazzing. *What have you got to lose?* Sam's voice came into my head. He was always daring me to do stuff, testing me. He liked the excitement of unknown things and he didn't care where they led him. This summer his excitement and my curiosity had led me here. *My finger hasn't let me down so far,* I thought as I pressed the handle of the door.

"No! Don't go in there! *(suuuuuck, hisssss!)* It isn't time yet!" the iceman shouted at me.

But I'd already flung the door open, and as the freezing steam dispersed I could see another figure encased in ice, but this time the ice was slowly being thawed. "It isn't time yet," he said again. "They are preparing her body."

The figure of the woman was clothed in a lace dress that looked like it was made of hundreds of tiny snowflakes. Her skin was a pale lilac color and her long hair was a swirling sea of strawberry blonde around her small, pretty face. Her eyes were closed, just as during a gentle sleep, and her hands were crossed lightly across her heart.

I shuddered.

"She has been perfectly preserved *(suuuuuck, hisssss!)* and in a few short hours she will be reborn *(suuuuuck, hisssss!)*. It has taken a long time to perfect the procedure *(suuuuuck, hisssss!)*, but the time has finally come *(suuuuuck, hisssss!)*. We will be reunited at last."

"Who is she?" I whispered, although in my heart I think I already knew.

"My sister, of course! Agnes. Sweet (*suuuuuck, hisssss!*), innocent Agnes."

Just then the door I had come in through pulled apart with an electronic drone, and Jeeks and the surgeon entered. The surgeon fell to his knees in front of the iceman.

"It—it is my great honor, sir, to meet you after all this time."

"You're just here for the operation, Smytheson," Jeeks reminded him.

"Will she do, sir?" Jeeks made his voice humble for the iceman.

"She'll do very well (*suuuuuck, hisssss!*)." He turned to me. "I look forward to our next meeting, though perhaps you will not remember it so well yourself."

I stared at them in terror and suddenly my legs filled with what felt like electricity—they unfroze and I tried to make a run for the door.

Smytheson and Jeeks came toward me and each of them grabbed one of my arms. I looked at Agnes's defrosting face and then at her brother Max's, where my father's blue eye and Herman's brown eye looked back at me, before a piece of white cloth was put over my nose and mouth, and a strong smell overpowered me. I was pulled quickly toward a deep, dark tunnel of sleep, and slumped to the ground.

CHAPTER 38

Back in the white bedroom, my eyes were heavier than ever and wouldn't focus, but I knew I had to get us out of there. The iceman, Jeeks, and Smytheson were planning something too terrible to imagine. Somehow they were about to try and use me to bring Agnes back to life. My mind struggled with my body, which was sluggish and just wanted to sleep.

"You've been napping again, Bea. How will we ever win the game if you keep napping?" asked Nelson wearily.

"Pirates are always taking long naps—especially when they've had too much rum! Yo ho ho!" I did my best pirate laugh, pretended to take a long swig out of a big cask, and then burped loudly. Nelson's eyes widened as he watched, impressed at how piratelike I was. But he was right: I had to beat that sleepy feeling if we were going to get out of here alive.

I pushed myself up and lifted my legs out of bed. As I sat there, I could hear somebody singing softly in the next room.

"We're going to get off this ship once and for all!" I mustered up the strength to say to Nelson.

"And get all the points and win the game!" added Nelson.

"Exactly! You ready?"

Nelson nodded eagerly.

I dragged myself to the wall and noticed a door. To my surprise it opened quietly and easily into the next room. The suntanned nurse was singing to herself as she flitted in and out of a large closet, piling clean white sheets onto a table. When she was back inside the closet, I seized my chance, and with all the energy I could summon I stepped swiftly but quietly toward the door.

"Now!" I whispered urgently, and Nelson and I pushed as hard as we could on the closet door. We turned the key and, hearing the nurse begin to shout, we shot out of the room.

"We got the pirate queen! That's got to be lots of points!" Nelson said with renewed excitement as we ran.

We hurried down another long corridor lined with old pictures of serious-looking people with swollen gray-green faces trapped in fancy gold frames, and they all seemed to be watching us with their cold eyes. I needed to find the way out — any way out. I came to a door, and through that door I could see another door with a silver handle. I ran over and pulled the handle to open it, and was hit by a wall of cold air that astounded me.

It seemed to be a giant freezer, like the one at home, except this one was a whole room unto itself, and instead of TV dinners it was filled with what looked like human organs — hearts, livers, even lungs. They all hung there in the ice, as though they had been flying through the air and a spell had stopped them there. Each one was in a transparent bag attached to a tiny tube leading from the organ to a large machine at the back of the room, which beeped as a green light flashed.

Nelson stared for a second.

"These bad pirates, they eat all kinds of stuff," I said, tutting the way Bertha always did, and pushed Nelson in the opposite direction.

We ran again and came to another door, which I hoped would be the way out. Instead we found ourselves in another giant walk-in freezer, this time filled with eyeballs. A hundred eyeballs, all suspended, all unblinking, all focused on us. Each one frozen until the time came to see again—and what would they see then? The white walls of Max's ice prison.

"Do they eat eyeballs, too?" asked Nelson.

I nodded. "I've heard they can be pretty tasty, barbecued with a few fries on the side."

My skin was clammy and sweat was trickling down my face. One of these doors had to lead out of here.

I pushed Nelson in a different direction, and we ran back down the corridor with the gold-framed pictures. When we came to the room we'd been sleeping in, we slowed down, just in case anyone was there, then, seeing it was clear, sped up again. By now the feeling in my hands and feet was starting to come back. At the end of another long corridor, we turned a corner and came to a spiral staircase, and at the bottom was a big hall. There were a few people—servants, maybe—moving back and forth beneath us. I signaled for Nelson to wait, and kept looking around to check that nobody was coming from the corridor.

When a couple of maids turned a corner, leaving the way clear, we sprinted as fast as we could down the spiraling side stairs, through a stone corridor, and out one of the house's side entrances. Down the gray stone steps we ran, out into the pine forest and under the shelter of the dark, heavy storm. "Where have you been?" the watery fingers seemed to say, tapping on my skull as we ran and ran, into the trees, into the night, into the rain.

"You're doing great, Nelson!" I said, trying to catch my breath.

"Is this the right way?" asked Nelson.

I had no idea; the forest was thick with spiky branches and black rain.

"Sure, this is the way!" I yelled back.

Then the flashlights appeared in the distance, coming from two directions, shooting beams of yellow into the misty air. And there were shouts.

"Don't let them get away!"

"This way!"

"I see them!"

I looked around and saw the lights closing in. Faces were appearing through the darkness.

"Which way now?" Nelson's voice was breathless as the sound of boots on the wet forest floor came closer. I pointed in the direction we were running, away from the two groups of searchlights. *That's got to be the way out,* I thought.

At that moment a shadow loomed over me, then grabbed my shoulders. Struggling, I fell to the ground. Nelson was still in front of me, running away from the pirates as if his life, and those hundreds of points he was going to win, depended on it. "Keep running, Nelson! Don't stop! Find the others!" I yelled after him as I watched him zigzag away, farther and farther into the depths of the forest. As my eyes squinted in the beam of the flashlight that was flooding the forest around me, I just kept thinking, *He got away. Nelson got away.* And very faintly, in the distance, I could have sworn I heard Sam's distant whistle and Jellybean's bark.

It was as I was being carried back, horizontally, through the sweet-smelling nighttime forest, with fat droplets of rain hitting my face, that I lifted my head and caught a glimpse of the Palace for the first time.

"Where are we?" I said feebly. I was tied to a kind of stretcher, and Jeeks and a man I didn't recognize were each holding an end, moving me bumpily back to the house.

"Did you really think you could escape?" A raindrop trickled down Jeeks's nose and hung there for a moment before falling into my eye. "Nobody escapes Mr. Feverspeare," he said wearily. I felt tired and so heavy, and didn't want to fight or run away anymore. I just wanted to go back to sleep.

Then the other man, the one in front, spoke. "You shouldn't have started poking your nose into matters that didn't concern you. Things are kept quiet for a reason. Mr. Feverspeare is a very powerful man and he doesn't want the whole world knowing his business."

As we got to the iron gates of the vast building, the gold letters *MHF* shone in the beam of Mr. Jeeks's flashlight. *MHF.* I said the letters to myself and remembered the initials we'd found on Herman's pickle jar, on the glass in Mitzy's

Diner, and on the side of the Bert's Big Cheesies bag. MHF Inc. was the company that had bought up Herman's Pickles and all kinds of other stuff, too. Just like DW had said. He was the man who owned all the names of all the companies, he owned all the letters in all the names; he was the man who owned the alphabet.

Maximillian Horatio Feverspeare, the man in the ice, secretly and silently owned and controlled all of Elbow.

The man holding the front of the stretcher stopped to wipe the rain from his face and readjust his grip. Jeeks spoke solemnly. "This is Mount Abora. You're a very lucky girl — only a few people get to see the Palace from the outside." I looked up again and, as he spoke, the golden lights of the Palace appeared through the green-black of the forest. It was then that I remembered being right here, in my dad's car, watching the Palace with him through the pine trees, nearly three years earlier.

It was the kind of building that took your breath away. High on the mountainside, maybe even carved from the rock itself and concealed by the dense forest that encircled it, the castle loomed silently, like an invisible shadow, over the twinkling lights of Elbow.

It was the kind of place that could swallow you up the minute you set foot on the stone steps. You could get lost on that doorstep and then disappear inside forever.

The long branches of distant trees stretched across the moon like the hair of a night witch, and the gloomy splendor of the building was bathed in cold blue light. The thought that came into my mind was that this was the kind of place where Dracula would live, and that was just what I'd thought the first time I saw it with my father, the first time I saw him truly frightened.

There were ugly demonlike stone creatures hanging off the roof, like you see on old churches. In the rain-light, they looked like they were just biding their time before flying at you with a piercing cry.

And yet, strangely, the place wasn't spooky at all, just neglected. It had grown sooty over the years, and mold and moss had crept across it the way they did on gravestones. One day, a long time ago, it must have looked like a fairy-tale castle, somebody's dream palace, conjured from picture books and old photographs and black-and-white movies. But now it was a place of broken dreams, of dreams gone bad, of rotten hope and lost love.

Finally I registered the shape of the Palace, and saw that it was the same shape as the castle ring we had rescued from Herman's guts. *That's why he wanted somebody to find that ring*, I thought. *It's all here, the story Herman wanted us to tell.* As I was lifted inside, I understood why Herman had been so scared, because I felt that same fear deep in my own guts as I realized I was about to share his fate.

CHAPTER 39

I was placed on a long table with metal bands around my wrists and ankles. It would have felt cold, except my skin was numb. A large lamp was pulled over me, and I squinted to see through the powerful blast of light. I tried to imagine it was the Florida sunshine and that I was in our bug-shaped car with Mom and Dad. But the light wasn't warm and there were no rainbow-colored jewels on my eyelashes. I could hear the *suuuuckk* and *hisssss* of Max's breathing machine. He was waiting for me to die. He'd been waiting for this moment for years and years.

Then came a slow mournful whistle and the clatter of metal instruments on a steel table as the surgeon prepared. Lying next to me was Agnes, a little pinker now, with rosy cheeks and dewy hair, her eyes still closed.

"You'll see, Mr. Feverspeare. With her new heart she'll be back to her old self. It'll be as though she never left," said Smytheson cheerfully. *Suuuuckk, hissssss!* went Max's machine. Then a small mask was placed over my nose and mouth, and I breathed in thick, chemical air as I watched Agnes's moist eyelashes drift out of focus. I was on the brink of unconsciousness when something sharp and icy touched my chest.

I don't know if it was the shouts that woke me, or the feeling of fire burning my chest, but my eyes were open and I was alive. Smytheson was holding his hand and hopping around the room, shouting and yelling. Max's machine was beeping twice as fast. Mr. Jeeks was waving his hands through the air as if they had caught fire.

"Take the necklace off (*suuuuuck, hissss!*)," ordered Max from his room of ice.

"We can't, sir! It's burning hot!" yelled Jeeks.

I peered down toward my chest and saw my bone-heart aglow with amber light. The light warmed my face for a few moments and then gradually faded like a dying ember in a fire.

A warning siren screamed suddenly and a large light on the wall flashed an urgent red, lighting up the whole room and making it throb with life.

"Intruders!" shrieked Jeeks. "We'll have to stop the procedure!"

"No, continue with the operation!" ordered Max.

I didn't know this until they burst into the underground room where I was lying, but the red light meant that Jelly and Nelson had led Sam, Eric, Madison, and Butterfly to the Palace.

"We tried to stop them!" said one of three embarrassed-looking men dressed in gray uniforms as my friends pushed their way in.

"Bea!" shouted Sam. "Are you OK?!"

I smiled weakly but no words came out. The guards were trying to hold the others at the door, but Jelly pushed his way underneath them and leaped onto me and licked my face. I was so happy to see him I wanted to cry. "You did it, Nelson. You did it, Jelly!" I whispered.

"Get those kids out of here, we've got an operation to perform," said Smytheson, unimpressed.

"There'll be no more operating here!" proclaimed Eric, who pulled out what looked like the arm of a vacuum cleaner and aimed it at Jeeks. As soon as he'd pulled it out, he looked uncertain, not sure his invention was going to work.

"What are you going to do with that? Give us a spring cleaning?" Smytheson started laughing and picked up a sharp instrument, ready to continue with the heart transplant. The guards pushed the others out and the heavy electronic door began to slide shut.

But just when they had almost disappeared from sight, Madison bit one of the guards on the arm. He yelled in pain and let go. Nelson quickly slipped through the door and pressed the button on the inside, which opened it again.

"Good work, Nelson!" said Butterfly. Then Madison stomped hard on the other guard's toe and right afterward looked like she wanted to apologize for being so impolite. Butterfly kicked them both in the knees for good measure.

The heavy door shut, leaving the guards outside. "I'm beginning to tire of your little games . . . ," said the surgeon. Eric turned and aimed his silver vacuum cleaner at him. Out shot a little red apple, hitting him hard in the chest.

Smytheson looked confused for a moment and then began to pace toward him, looking very angry.

"Eric? Did you seriously load it with apples?" said Sam, fearing that we'd lost our chance.

"From the trial phase," Eric muttered distractedly. "Forgot I put that in there." Eric adjusted something on the space-age-style weapon he was wearing like a backpack, and aimed the tube again. This time a giant blast of fire roared from it like a blowtorch, making Smytheson and Jeeks cower in the corner.

"Untie our friend!" demanded Sam. The surgeon hesitated. "Now!" Sam yelled, and the surgeon pressed a button on the metal bed, making the cuffs around my wrists and ankles unclick. Eric aimed another blast of orange fire in their direction while Jellybean barked at them, showing his fangs.

"Not my face! Don't burn my face!" whined Smytheson.

Madison and Butterfly helped me up from the bed. "Your grandma's necklace—it worked!" I said.

"Sure it did," said Butterfly as her whole face lit up with a smile.

While Eric kept his vacuum cleaner aimed at Smytheson and Jeeks, Sam took some tough blue rope from his backpack. "Back-to-back!" ordered Sam, and the two men shuffled reluctantly together. Sam quickly wrapped the rope around their bodies and their wrists and pulled tightly.

"I didn't think it would work," said Eric.

"Sure it did!" said Butterfly again, beaming.

"It's the first thing I've made that's worked!" Eric said

proudly. Just then the tube of his blazing vacuum cleaner belched, like a person who'd eaten a spicy meal. Eric looked down the end with a confused expression, and a spurt of soot hit him in the face.

Suuuuckk, hisssssss! went Max's machine in the background. With all the excitement, the others hadn't noticed Max or the ancient, thawing body of his sister lying next to me. "A nice (*suuuuckk, hisssssss!*) show," he said suddenly, his voice echoing around the chamber. "But I have guards all over the Palace and I practically own the police (*suuuuckk, hisssssss!*), so better luck next time!"

His presence was like a ghost they all felt but weren't sure they wanted to see. They turned their heads slowly toward him.

"Meet Maximillian Horatio Feverspeare," I said. "Also, meet Leo's arm, my dad's right eye, and Herman's left eye. I'd introduce you to the other parts of him, but I'm not sure who they belong to."

The others just stared, as if they, too, were frozen and unable to move.

"The MHF guy," said Sam.

"He must be, like, two hundred years old," said Butterfly, her eyes unblinking.

"Two hundred and nine (*suuuuckk, hisssssss!*), to be precise."

"Is he a monster?" asked Nelson.

"Yes," said Madison. "A real monster—somebody who has done terrible, terrible things to people."

"Is that . . ." Butterfly pointed at the dripping body

of Agnes, which by now was starting to smell of strange chemicals.

"Agnes, his sister." I nodded. "He wanted to put my heart into her to bring her back to life!" I touched my chest gratefully for a moment.

"Dr. Smytheson (*suuuuckk, hisssssss!*), you must put her back in the ice and attach her to the machine or she will die (*suuuuckk, hisssssss!*). There isn't much time!"

"Believe me, I wanted the operation as much as you — it's taken me a lifetime to perfect. But, as you can see, Mr. Feverspeare, my hands are tied!" The surgeon's sharp voice cut through the air. Jeeks fixed his pink eyes on Sam, but Sam ignored him.

"Actually," Sam said, turning back to Max, "we met up with Elenor Bailey, who I think you know."

"That meddling journalist (*suuuuckk, hisssssss*)?"

"She was a little frightened at first, but then she was very wiling to help. Turns out she knows some people in the FBI." Sam smiled, and for a while there was nothing to be heard but the slow suck and hiss and little beeps of Max's machine.

"What did the girl mean, Jeeks (*suuuuckk, hisssssss!*), by giving names to my eyes and my arm?"

Jeeks squirmed and his eyes shifted from side to side. His face filled with shame and then contempt. "How could I have listened to you, Smytheson? Everything was just fine before you came along with your greedy plans! Mr. Feverspeare already owned the whole of Elbow — I saw to that — I collected all of the profitable companies . . ."

"You ruined those companies by polluting their products so they were forced to sell out for almost nothing!" Smytheson shot back.

"But we didn't need to take their homes!" Guilt was creeping up on Jeeks a little more at a time and his voice was beginning to crack as though he was realizing all that he'd done.

"No, we didn't, but they were an added bonus—a little nest egg—along with the rest of the money. And you're forgetting one small fact, Jeeks: Mr. Feverspeare here needed to live and live and live—we couldn't find body parts fast enough!" he yelled.

"I've paid you handsomely for legitimate donors all these years." Max's voice crackled slightly, like an old record.

"Oh, come now, Mr. Feverspeare, did you really think there were that many people willing to give up their body parts? You must have realized . . ." The surgeon smirked as he spoke.

Nelson tugged at his sister's raincoat. "What does leg-git-imut mean?"

"It means right and honest and within the law," whispered Butterfly, thinking as she spoke.

"And let's not forget," continued Smytheson, "how you were prepared to take a child's heart for your sister!"

"You were the ones who persuaded me. You said only hers would do!" Max grew angry and needed to draw an extra-long breath through his machine.

"We found these," said Sam, pulling a piece of paper from

Eric's backpack. "It proves that you were in business together." Sam waved the papers in the air for Max to see. "Your names are written right here: *Jeeks and Smytheson Property Co.*"

"What garbage are you talking now?" spat the surgeon.

"Garbage. Exactly," said Sam calmly. "We already know you kept the money Max gave you to buy organs to keep him alive, and how you took them from people you didn't think anybody would notice. People you thought were garbage. Then, using the organ money, you bought up homes people couldn't afford anymore, people like Herman Henderson, and sold them to make even more money." We all watched Sam as he spoke; he told it exactly like it was and we felt proud that he was our friend.

"All you've got are a few pieces of paper. They prove nothing," the surgeon growled.

"Actually, we know the people you've been stealing from," I said. "They're our friends. Herman may be dead, but the others are alive. I have photos of the marks you left on them! We know you used John Elbow's ring to brand them!"

The surgeon laughed a nasty, arrogant laugh. "Who's going to believe a bunch of young criminals? The police are already well acquainted with your brother," he sneered, staring at Sam. "He's the one they want. He's the one who murdered Herman."

Sam's face twitched and his jaw clenched. He was beginning to lose it.

"That's not true, actually," said Madison, still being as polite as she could. "Sam's brother broke into your house and stole your money. We caught him trying to stash it in the tree house we use as a hideout when we were trying to figure out where you'd taken Bea. Jed told us all about you guys. He said it wasn't fair that you were getting all the money while he was going to take the blame for Herman. But we persuaded him to take the cash to the police." Madison smiled sweetly, as though she'd just finished reading a book report out loud in front of class.

"I'm sure the FBI will be more interested in the men who made him do it in the first place—meaning you guys," said Butterfly, making a "so there" kind of expression.

"Why did you have to burn that ring onto people's skin?" I asked, shaking my head in disbelief.

"So that I knew which ones had been used, of course. No point in going to the trouble of opening somebody up if you've already taken what they've got to offer," said Smytheson in his smooth tones.

"But why use the ring?" I asked again.

"He liked the feeling that he was working for Max and wanted to leave the sign of the Palace stamped all over everybody." Jeeks shot the words angrily at the surgeon.

Gradually the room began to fill with soft sobs, which grew louder and louder. It was the sound of Max weeping. It would have sounded funny if it weren't so loaded with centuries of pain and suffering. Crying made my father's and Herman's eyes red, and the tears made the liquid he was suspended in turn milky. He wouldn't stop wailing. There were so many tears that they began to escape and, frozen in their frosty tracks, became icicles of sorrow.

We all looked at each other, not knowing quite what to say or do.

"Please don't cry. It can't be all that bad," said Nelson, kneeling in front of the giant ice chamber.

"It's worse. I've become the evil man I always believed I was. How did I let that happen? I just (*suuuuckk, hisssssss!*)... I just wanted to bring Agnes back. Is that so bad? I built all this for her. I just wanted her to see the beautiful palace I made for her."

Madison's raspberry-colored rain boots squeaked as she moved forward. She looked intensely at Agnes's lilac-blue face for a moment, and touched her damp hair. "Bea," she whispered, signaling for me to come over. I hesitated for a second, but seeing the new gentleness in Madison's eyes, walked over to join her at Agnes's body. "Butterfly's grandma said you were sensitive or something. Maybe you could do something." We both looked over at the pathetic figure of Max, suspended in his frozen grave. "Sometimes you can love people too much and that love can turn bad." Madison spoke from the heart.

I lifted my left hand and placed it on Agnes's. This time I felt not only my pinkie finger but my whole hand vibrate slightly; and then what felt like a gust of wind blowing right through me, the same way Herman's ghost once did. Only this time it wasn't so bad because I knew what to expect.

Suddenly the room turned even colder, and what felt like an icy tornado screeched around the room. "*Killed my love . . . you killed John . . . you killed him . . . you killed him!*" howled the woman's voice.

"Please forgive me, Agnes. Please forgive me. I know what I did was wrong. I did it because I was selfish. I didn't want him to marry you. I didn't want him to take you away from me. You were all I had. I did it because I loved you." Max's voice struggled with tears and the limits of his breathing machine. Then the circling wind stopped, and Agnes's image flitted across the shiny glass of Max's prison.

"Agnes?!" shouted Max, suddenly filled with surprise and joy.

Her shimmering image came again and settled for a few moments. But this time her silvery features started to shudder and stretch, her piercing cry tore through the room, and her white eyes were aflame with rage. The windows of Max's ice coffin began to shake, gently at first and then more and more, until it looked as though the glass was going to shatter into a million pieces. It was only then that Agnes's face became still again. Her eyes softened, flooding with sorrow as she seemed to notice her brother's helplessness and his regret. Finally her face became beautiful, and glowed with something like love. "I don't want to hate you anymore, Max. I feel so tired . . . I forgive you, Max." Her voice fluttered around us like a sweet summer breeze. She smiled at Max again for a brief moment and then was gone. There was silence in the room, and then a long, heavy sigh from Max's machine.

"I'm deeply sorry *(suuuuckk, hisssssssss!)* for the suffering I have caused. I will speak to the officers when they arrive, and then I would very much"—his mechanical breaths seemed to turn into large yawns and his words came more and more slowly—"like you to . . . to let me join my sister . . . by switching off this . . . tired contraption."

The sounds from the machine seemed to speed up slightly and become more insistent. *You can't do that! You can't do that!* the machine seemed to beep and buzz. But it might have been my imagination.

CHAPTER 40

When the FBI men tore open the heavy metal door, their shouts breaking the strange, sad atmosphere, Max had already gone to sleep. Eric had agreed to be the one to turn off his machine, and we had all listened to his breathing slow to a stop.

We knew those men would never understand what had really taken place in there. They would probably discuss the gory details over beer and burgers in the weeks to come: "The guy kept himself alive for over a century using other people's body parts. His castle was full of freezers packed with eyeballs and stuff—I'm serious! And he kept his dead sister in the room next door!"

Then his friend would say, "What a sicko!" and they'd both laugh and take a swig of their drinks.

Jeeks and Smytheson were handcuffed and bundled down the corridors and into a police van where they sat guarded by two German shepherds. Jeeks had a sullen expression on his face as he sat there. He looked gray and deflated and shameful. But Smytheson had a cold hard look in those black unblinking eyes of his, a look that said he'd play along for now but that, one way or another, he'd be back.

Sam unzipped his backpack. He pulled out my cracked leather camera case and handed it to me without saying a word. "Thanks," I said, feeling the weight of my dad's old camera in my hands. I looked at the silent figure of Max and the weeping body of his sister but wondered if it was right to take pictures of the dead. After all, that's how all this had started.

This time, somehow, it felt different. It was part of the story, part of Herman's story. I attached the big rectangular flash, took off the lens cap, and framed Agnes's face with the viewfinder. The light of the photo lit up the room like a muted firecracker. Next I took a shot of Max, or the thing that Max had become. The flash bleached the thin and sorry shape of Max's ice-monster like silent lightning.

"No photos!" shouted a man from the FBI. But it was too late. Sam quickly bundled the camera into his backpack, and the pictures I needed to tell Herman's story were safely inside.

We were wrapped in silver sheets and led out of the room. As we headed down the white corridor, Sam put his arm around me.

"I'm glad you're not dead," he said.

"Thanks so much!" I said, shoving him, but then I could see how much he meant it. "Seriously, thanks for coming to get me."

"No problem," he said. "Who else could I watch cartoons with?"

I shoved him again and he laughed, pushing me back.

"Ow!" I moaned. "Take it easy!" My ribs ached. In fact, I ached all over, as if I had bruises on the inside.

"Sorry," said Sam. He bit his lower lip and looked at the floor for a second. Then he reached out and held my hand under the shiny silver blanket so nobody else could see. We walked down the whole corridor like that, Sam's warm hand in mine, and it felt good.

All along the corridors were the competition photos people had sent Max, and suddenly they looked different to me. Before, the people in the photos had looked kind of sad and lonely, but now I realized there was something happy about them after all. They didn't look happy in the way people in toothpaste commercials did. They looked happy in a less obvious, more real way. Their faces seemed to say that although life could be sad and difficult sometimes, just having each other made things better. I could see why Max wanted those photos.

Nelson was the last to leave the underground room. He couldn't take his eyes off the frozen figure of Max. He stood there like an explorer in awe of the prehistoric creature he'd just discovered. Nelson's head was tilted and his eyes were filled with a mixture of sadness and curiosity. "When will he wake up?" he asked.

"He's not going to wake up again, Nelson," said Butterfly, walking back toward her little brother and taking him by the hand.

Nelson's legs began to walk as his sister led him away, but his head was still turned toward Max.

"He's gone to heaven," said Butterfly.

"I thought only good people get to go to heaven," said Nelson.

"Well, the way I see it, everybody goes to heaven, because God forgives everybody, no matter what they do. Especially if they're sorry."

Nelson took this in, seemed satisfied, and skipped along the corridor behind us.

Bertha was waiting with Eric's mom and Butterfly and Nelson's mom in the cathedral-like entrance hall. They all had their arms folded and the life had been washed out of their faces by worry.

I thought Bertha was going to be really mad, but when she saw me she opened her arms as wide as they would go and waited for me to throw myself into them. Then she wrapped her arms around me and I let myself get lost in the folds of her big warm body. "Don't you ever do that to me again," she sobbed, her brow all wrinkled up and her eyes glistening.

Madison's housekeeper waited stiffly for her to say her good-byes and then trotted neatly behind her, opened the door of her parents' limousine before getting into the driver's seat, and then drove off to take her home.

Eric let his mom hug him but grimaced at us, embarrassed, behind her back. "So that's where my vacuum cleaner went!" she said, noticing the charred device at his feet.

"He saved our lives, Mrs. Schnitzler," said Sam, squeezing Eric's shoulder. "And you definitely passed your initiation," he finished quietly, so only Eric could hear. Eric tried to stifle a proud smile.

Butterfly and Nelson's mom looked sternly at her kids until Nelson gave her one of his beautiful smiles and, pulling her to her knees, hugged her so tightly she almost lost her breath.

"I won the pirate game, Mom! I got more points than everybody put together—Bea said so! Isn't that true, Bea?!"

"You bet!" I replied. "You got one thousand three hundred and forty-four points. Nobody's ever gotten that many points before!"

"See? What did I tell you!" he said, turning back to his mom.

"I'm sure you're the best pirate ever," she said, covering his cheeks with two big kisses, which were immediately wiped away by a blushing Nelson.

Butterfly walked up to her mom slowly, her eyes downcast, expecting to be scolded, but her mom pulled her in, squashing Nelson between them. "We'll talk about this later," she said softly.

Sam was the only one with nobody waiting for him. He bent down and messed up Jellybean's fur. Jellybean wagged his tail happily and twisted himself around so he could lick Sam's hand. "Time to go home, boy," he said, stroking Jelly's soft, shaggy ears.

CHAPTER 41

Bertha stayed home from work for two whole days. She made me stay in bed and prepared proper home-cooked meals. She made a Caribbean stew her mother used to cook for her, which was really spicy, and chicken with rice and peas; and we even had fried plantain, which is like a big banana but not as sweet.

The first day after the nightmare at the Palace, an FBI detective came to the house. He had a kind, weathered face and spoke softly. It was his job to go to all of our houses in turn, to get our version of what had happened.

I asked him if, even though it might sound crazy, there was any way he could put Herman's eye back so he could be buried with it. He told me that Herman hadn't been buried, with or without his eye, because his murder hadn't been solved until now, but that he was certain Herman would have liked to have been buried with both his eyes and he would see what he could do.

"What made Smytheson take Herman's eye and my dad's eye and give them both to Max?" I asked.

The detective looked at me for what seemed like forever before saying, "Elenor thinks it was — what was the word?

Symbolic. Your father and Herman were both men the surgeon thought of as people who 'saw' too much. He thought they were nosy—or, rather, 'eyesy'—is that a word? I guess it was a punishment and a kind of nasty joke that only Smytheson understood."

I asked that FBI detective for one more favor, which is how I know he gave Herman his eye back. The next day, while Bertha was out at the supermarket, the detective brought me a small padded freezer bag. Inside was a shiny silver box. He looked deep into my eyes as he handed me the box, which was a bit bigger than the size of my palm, and his eyes turned red and moist and I thought he was going to cry. "Take care now," he said in his deep, warm voice, before stepping outside and disappearing into the rain.

I put the silver box into the freezer compartment at the top of the refrigerator, next to a stack of frozen TV dinners, and made sure it was comfortable there, in the fluffy nest of white frost.

They let Mom join us for dinner that second night and it was so nice to have her home, even if it was only for a couple of hours. I don't think she knew where she was, but at one point, halfway through the meal, her eyes drifted toward mine and it seemed like, for a split second, she recognized me and smiled.

"Now you go right back to bed, young lady," Bertha said to me later that evening, as she did up the zipper on my mom's raincoat, ready for the drive back to St. Agnes's.

"OK," I mumbled. I heard the *thuck* of the door closing behind her and my mother, and waited a second, then ran downstairs to the darkroom. Bertha kept telling me I needed to rest before school started again, but there was only a week or so left and I was desperate to develop the photos of Max and Agnes.

I swished the pictures around in their trays, under the glow of the ruby light, listening to the rainy fingers tap out their rhythm on the trash cans in the alleyway outside. After a few seconds, Agnes's deathly beauty blossomed onto the watery sheet. I moved the image along to the next tray and watched the ghostly figure of Max appear on another sheet. After rinsing the prints, I let the water drip from the photos a little and then hung them up to dry properly, next to the photos of Jack and Grace and the other people from Garbage City.

The whole story was here, hanging from twine in my dad's darkroom. It was as if my dad were there with me. I thought of how proud he would be. And then the strangest thing happened: Hanging from the line above the little black window were the blank sheets that had once held images of Herman's dead body. As mysteriously as those pictures had evaporated, they returned now, in front of my eyes. Shadows gathered quickly on those blank pages, and there was poor Herman's body, floating in that grimy water, the way me and Sam had found it when all this had started.

Then came a sudden sound like a kettle hissing steam and, out of nowhere, the castle ring dropped from the air and onto the counter, smoking slightly and spinning, quickly at first and then slowing to a stop.

"Herman?" I called. "Herman, is that you?" But there was

no reply. I'd lost the ring in Max's Palace. They must have taken it from me after they'd kidnapped me and knocked me out, to be "decontaminated." And now, out of thin air, it was here. I guessed it was Herman's way of saying thank you.

"You're welcome," I said into the warm dark air, knowing that he would be leaving now. We had found the men who caused his death. We had uncovered the truth, his own and the story he wanted us to tell, and that meant he could rest now.

As I circled the ring between my fingers, I looked at the pictures hanging around the room. *I'm going to put those together for other people to see,* I thought. *I'm going to write the story that goes with the pictures. That way everybody will know what happened.* Well, everybody at school, anyway.

The others had already filled me in on how they got DW, Elenor, and even Jed to put together the evidence against Jeeks and Smytheson while I was a prisoner in Mount Abora, and how they planned my rescue. We'd pieced the whole business together and now I could write about it: about poor Herman, about how Jeeks and the surgeon exploited Max's power and his pride and his vulnerability; and how they would stop at nothing, stealing people's homes and even parts of their bodies so they could get rich. I'd write about how they came to an end because of Herman's bravery and determination; about how, although at first he wanted revenge, he became more concerned with getting justice for the people being stolen from Garbage City; and how, despite losing an eye, he managed to escape with the ring that held all the clues.

I looked at the dull golden ring, the red darkroom light

becoming a setting sun against the miniature turrets of the castle. I realized that I still didn't know why Max had built Mount Abora in the shape of a ring that another man gave his sister. Or what terrible thing had happened to John Elbow and Agnes Feverspeare. Just when you think you've answered all the questions, another one always seems to come up. I think that was something else my dad used to say.

Later, when Bertha was asleep, I crept back into the darkroom and laid out the photos, starting with the one of Herman's body and ending with the photo of Max's body, and then began writing, just the way it happened, in the order that it happened. I'd have to figure out the final questions later. For the first time it seemed like the dark music of the rain was urging me on, helping me to remember all the storm-soaked parts of the nasty story. It was three in the morning when I finished and tiptoed up the creaky stairs to bed.

CHAPTER 42

Elenor Bailey was expecting us. She was standing on the porch, wearing a coat that was so big she looked lost inside it, and her electric white hair was blowing in the rainy air. As we splashed through the mud, I missed seeing Nelson's red galoshes jumping in and out of puddles. Butterfly had convinced her mom that she couldn't babysit her brother *all* the time, and her mom had agreed to hire a lady to help. Nelson was happy about that because the lady had a boy his age and now they got to play together.

"Hi, kids!" croaked Elenor, waving at us as we got closer. The others marched right in—they'd been here before, while I was trapped at the Palace. "Good to see you, Bea," she said, putting a hot little hand on my back to welcome me inside.

Madison, Butterfly, Eric, and Sam looked totally at home in Elenor's chaotic but cozy parlor, with its piles of books and crooked photographs. Butterfly was sitting cross-legged in a saggy armchair, stroking Elenor's fat calico cat, which was curled up in her lap, purring happily. Every so often Jelly would come over for a sniff and Butterfly would push him gently away.

Elenor brought in a tray of tea with a teapot that was wearing a kind of stripy knitted hat. "You kids have been very brave." She narrowed her intense green eyes and smiled. "Very brave indeed."

"May I?" Madison pointed at the teapot. Elenor nodded and Madison poured us each a cup of tea, then sat down after passing them around. "You said you'd tell us about Agnes," she prompted, crossing her legs, balancing the saucer on her knee, and lifting the teacup elegantly to her lips.

"We found a lot of letters when Jed took us to Smytheson's house—we've got some that John and Agnes wrote to each other. It's all lovey-dovey stuff," said Eric, taking a pile of yellowed envelopes out of his backpack and handing them to Elenor with a look of distaste.

"Thank you," said Elenor.

"Hey! I haven't seen those yet!" I said, annoyed.

"You can come and read them anytime—but I will be giving them to the library. They have a small collection of documents relating to the history of Elbow. I already gave them my copy of Agnes's book—I think I even wrote some notes in it once. They'll be most grateful to have these letters as part of the collection."

"I guess they'll be wanting this, too," I said, taking the palace ring reluctantly from my jeans. I paused for a minute to feel the weight of it in my hand for the last time, and then passed it to Elenor.

"Thank you. This ring has been on a long journey. A bit like all of you," she said, looking at each of us in turn. Jelly let out a *woof* that caused the cat to look up and rearrange herself on Butterfly's lap. "Not forgetting you, Jellybean," she said.

"Come here, Jelly-belly," I said. "Jelly saved my life, didn't you, boy." Jelly licked my face enthusiastically.

"Elenor interviewed Max when she was young," said Sam.

"I did. I was twenty-three and a fiery young journalist, but he frightened me even then. It was his ambition more than anything." Elenor made herself comfortable and wrapped her bony hands around her hot cup of tea. "It was back in 1943. I was working for *The Elbow Herald*. I found out about him through my own research. I discovered he was one hundred and forty-three years old even then. He allowed me to talk to him, but warned me against trying to publish the article. The fact that he was still alive was a closely guarded secret, and his men, Mr. Jeeks's grandfather being one of them, would do anything to keep that secret. All these decades later, after Josef, Bea's dad, disappeared, I started doing a little digging again myself, but Jeeks made it quite clear what he'd do to me if I carried on. I'm ashamed to say, I was scared for my life. I had my suspicions about how they were keeping Max alive when I met him all those years ago, but I never imagined something quite so . . . terrible was going on. Who'd have thought he'd become his own Frankenstein's monster?" said Elenor, absorbing our story.

"But tell us about Agnes and John!" insisted Butterfly.

"Well, let me see. . . ." She took a big gulp of tea and linked her hands around the cup once more, for warmth. As she sat back in her chair under the low lamp, a long, wiry white hair glinted on her chin.

"Max adored his sister. He treated her more like his own daughter, even though she was only four years younger than him. They grew up with a cruel father and a timid, sickly mother, so it was always Max who took care of his sister. When they came to America, and Max set about designing and building the town of Elbow with John, he was unaware that his sister and his business partner were falling in love. John Elbow was fifty-three, an old man in those days, when he proposed to Agnes, who was twenty-seven. He designed two engagement rings, one for Agnes and one for himself, based on a drawing he had done. The drawing was of a beautiful palace, the home he intended to build for her as a wedding present. John wrote to Max of his plans."

At this point Eric got up and rifled through the letters he had handed to Elenor a moment earlier. "Here it is!" he said, pulling a lace-thin letter from an envelope and unfolding it to show us the ink drawing of Mount Abora. We craned our necks to see.

"It's so pretty," said Madison.

"But Max said *he* built it for his sister," I said, confused.

"I'm about to tell you about that," said Elenor sternly. "When Max received the letter from John, who was out of town, he was furious. Nobody was going to take his sister away from him — least of all his elderly business partner, who had begun to resemble Max's own father more than he cared to admit. He knew which train John would be returning to town on, bringing with him the unique engagement rings he had written about. Max was going to stop him, no matter what. So he planted explosives around the train track, timed to go off when John's train arrived."

Elenor paused and cast her eyes downward at her colorful fraying carpet. "There was one thing Max didn't count on, though, and that was the effect John's death would have on his sister. Agnes heard about the explosion and already knew in her heart that John was dead. They found the palace rings on John's body, and Max reluctantly let his sister keep them. They should have been happy symbols of a couple about to embark on a life together. Instead they became a reminder of John's death.

"Not long after, Agnes went into a decline, losing her grasp on reality. Max didn't know what to do with her, and began to deeply regret his actions. He built a hospital for his sister, St. Agnes's, and hired every doctor he could find. No matter how hard they tried to keep her incarcerated, though, Agnes frequently ran away to the railroad track where John was killed. Max would be called to try to persuade the wailing Agnes to return to the hospital."

"I think we heard her crying when we were there," said Madison.

"That wouldn't surprise me one bit," replied Elenor.

Butterfly's face lit up with realization. "And that must be why the trains stopped running!"

"So they say." Elenor nodded. "Every time a train came into Elbow after John Elbow's death, it would stop, for no reason, at the exact spot of the explosion. For years people had to get off the train and walk along the track for a few miles until they got to the platform. I guess the railroad company just sort of gave up after that."

Elenor paused, lost for a moment in her thoughts, then continued. "Max also began building the palace that would have been Agnes's home, the home that John created for her in his imagination. But Agnes stopped eating and began to waste away. The day Mount Abora was completed, he rushed over to the hospital to collect his sister, but it was too late. Her palace ring was still on her finger when she died."

Elenor pressed her hands onto the arms of her chair to lift herself up. "Now, that's enough about the past," she announced. "I've got something to show you." She padded out of the room. I looked at the others and they shrugged. Then came the sound of men laughing. The chuckling came nearer until, standing there, towering over Elenor, were Jack and Leo, whose right arm was in a cast.

"Leo!" I said, jumping to my feet. "I thought you were dead!" I gave him a hug and he hugged me back with his left arm. "Your arm! You got it back!"

"It's still a bit sore. They said it would take a while to heal."

"Who painted the snake?" I asked, noticing the colorful childlike tattoo illustration on Leo's cast.

"Dad," he said, looking tenderly at Jack. "As good as the real one underneath, right?"

Jack smiled at me. "I want to thank you, Bea—thank all of you—for taking a stand against those terrible men. I've never met such a courageous bunch of kids." He looked proudly at us and shook Sam's hand.

"It's so good to see you!" I said, throwing my arms around

his belly. He rested his big warm hand affectionately on my head. "Good to see you, too."

"Well, do you know what I think?" asked Elenor.

"What?" we asked.

"I think we need a couple of extra teacups!"

"Did me hear somebody say tea?" came DW's voice from the hallway.

"We're in here, Mr. Washburn!" called Elenor.

Elenor shuffled off to the kitchen to brew another pot of tea and we all sat in her shabby-chic parlor talking about our adventure. DW told the story of how he had gotten the others out of the Grand Hotel by starting a small fire in the dining hall.

"Me nearly set fire to me trousers!" DW exclaimed, and everyone laughed. But he shook his head and shuddered. "Never before did me see so many roaches, it was horrible . . . nasty!"

Elenor returned with the second pot of tea and cups for the three new guests. Sam looked up at her sheepishly as she refilled his cup. "I'm sorry we went to get Bea when you told us to stay here," he said.

Elenor frowned and shot a look back at him. "You should have waited for the FBI, Sam."

"But time was running out! And when Jellybean showed up, we knew he'd lead us to Bea. We had to make sure she was OK. Besides, we'd already given you all the evidence, and DW was guarding Jed, and . . ."

"What if we hadn't been able to tell the police where to find you?" Elenor challenged. "It took me a while to figure out what Eric's drawing was. I only went to Mount Abora once, and it was many, many years ago."

"Yeah, Eric's drawing did look kind of unusual," Sam said, looking mischievously at Eric.

"It was an almost perfect drawing of the ring!" Eric insisted.

"Anyway, it all over now and everythin' turn out fine!" said DW.

"Thanks for all your help, Elenor, DW," said Butterfly sincerely. We all nodded, realizing none of us had said it yet.

"No need," said Elenor, waving her bony hand but smiling.

"Anytime." DW nodded.

Sitting around the fire, its burning embers expertly prodded and stoked by DW, drinking tea with the Raintown Convicts and talking to Elenor, Leo, and Jack—well, it felt like being part of a weird, oddball kind of family. And it felt good, really good.

That night I went home and added the story of Agnes and John to my article. Then I put it in a special folder I'd bought at the mall on the way home. The others wanted to go to Mitzy's for cheeseburgers, but I said I wanted to finish my story. I closed the purple folder (I chose a purple one because purple is my lucky color) and felt the weight of it in my hands. Then I put it back down on the counter until it was time to take it into school.

Bertha had fallen asleep in front of the TV with an empty TV dinner tray on her chest. I walked up to the fridge and opened the freezer door, feeling the icy air on my face, and thought of Max. I reached for the silver box and, turning to check if Bertha was still asleep, opened it to see the precious jewel nestling inside.

"Night, Dad," I whispered softly to the silent eyeball with its frozen blue iris. "Sleep tight, don't let the bedbugs bite," I sang. Then I blew the eye a kiss, closed the metal box, and put it back in the freezer.

Bertha was snoring, so I nudged her gently. "You fell asleep," I said. Bertha gurgled something, opening her eyes a fraction, but the weight of her lids closed them quick enough and she went back to sleep.

CHAPTER 43

It was the day before the start of school. The Raintown Convicts had agreed to meet at the greenhouse in the horticultural gardens. Eric told us about the place. It's part of the big state park at the foot of the Pinehills, but it's got a roof, so he figured it would be a nice place to go in the rain. Kind of outdoors and indoors at the same time.

I was excited about handing in my photo-story at school, so on my way out of the house, I headed down to the darkroom. I just wanted to touch the report's cover and feel the weight of it in my hands again. But it wasn't there; it wasn't anywhere. It was gone. Maybe Bertha had moved it, tidying up. But I'd told her the darkroom was my private place, and she respected that by not going in there. Still, it must have been Bertha, because no one else had been in the house.

I zipped up my orange raincoat, hopped on my purple bike, and made deep squelchy tracks as I biked down the wide muddy path on my way to the state park. My hood covered one of my eyes and the other fought with the rain, but as I arrived I could just about make out the colorful blurs of the other Raintown Convicts waiting outside the giant glass greenhouse. The rain made everything look like a living watercolor.

Madison was a distant smudge of pink, Butterfly a haze of blue, Sam a faded red, and Eric a long yellow smear. Jellybean galloped over to greet me, heat rising from his pink tongue and dripping gray fur. "Hello, Jelly-belly. Good boy!" I patted his middle and he leaned into me, almost pushing me over as I breathed in his wet doggy smell.

"I told you this place was cool," said Eric as we looked up at the deep green leaves stretching like shiny umbrellas toward the domed glass roof. "My mom used to bring me here when I was little. I'd forgotten she used to do that. We'd come here for picnics when my dad was away. I used to pretend I was in the jungle. They even have carnivorous plants—plants that eat flies and stuff! I sometimes sneak in Sigmund. It's like taking him on vacation."

"How about here?" asked Butterfly, finding a spot under a giant palm tree. We agreed it was fine. Madison spread a checkered picnic blanket on the bark chippings and we sat down. She opened her picnic basket, which had its own waterproof jacket, and began handing out napkins and little plastic plates. We emptied the food we'd brought into the middle: Bert's Big Cheesies; damp banana-and-baloney sandwiches; half a leftover pizza; peanut butter and jelly bagels; a package of beef jerky; five cold cheese pancakes; a jar of Herman's Devil Tongue Relish; a can of pineapple chunks; and a carton of chocolate ice cream. Madison had brought a flask of hot chocolate, and she poured it out into five little plastic cups.

"Are you sad about your brother going to jail?" Butterfly asked Sam.

"No way. It's good to have a break from him pushing me around. Anyhow, he got a reduced sentence for cooperating with the police."

"And he didn't do it on purpose—manslaughter sounds bad, but it means Herman's death was actually an accident. It's true Jed got angry and pushed him around, but he didn't mean to kill him." As Butterfly spoke, Sam nodded, and seemed relieved that his brother was not as evil as he'd always feared.

"This tastes way better than barbecued rat!" Madison declared, chewing delicately on a piece of cold pizza.

"You had seconds!" said Sam, laughing when Madison blushed. "Anyway, I think that rat tasted pretty good."

"Me, too," said Eric. "I'm gonna get my mom to make roasted rat-and-banana sandwiches for my school lunch every day."

"Ugggh!" said Madison.

"Mmmm, *rloast rlat*!" said Eric, showing Madison the mush inside his mouth.

"You are disgusting, Eric Schnitzler!"

Realizing she had also revealed some pink squish as she spoke, Madison quickly swallowed her mouthful of pizza. She thought for a moment, and then pulled a small metal box from her bag. "I wanted to give you this, Bea. I'm sorry if I got you into trouble," she said, opening the box but holding the lid up so we couldn't see the other things inside. She pushed something cold into my hand. It was Bertha's locket. Madison looked away, embarrassed, and I could see she didn't want to talk about it.

"Thanks," I said, and put it in my jeans pocket.

As I was putting a spoonful of Herman's Devil Tongue Relish on my pancake, the others suddenly fell completely quiet. When I looked up, they were staring at me like they'd seen some kind of miracle. Then I realized what it was: The sun was shining on my face. Not a hot, shimmering Florida sun—more of a pale, moonlike sun, struggling through the last clouds of summer in Elbow.

"Listen," said Sam.

"What is it?" asked Madison.

"Shhhh!" Sam insisted.

"I can't hear anything," said Butterfly after a few seconds.

"Exactly," said Sam, triumphant.

Then I heard nothing, too. "The rain has stopped." I spoke the words gently. I didn't want my voice to make the weather change its mind and shake more rain from the sky.

"Look!" Butterfly pointed up at the domed glass roof. We watched the thick gray clouds pass over and the silvery sun aim its luminous rays down through any gaps it could find. The beams found all our faces and for a few seconds nobody spoke as we joined the plants in drinking up the liquid sunlight.

"Come on, let's go outside!" Sam stepped under the door to catch the last raindrops traveling down the greenhouse and out into the sweet air. "It's really stopped!" he said, holding his hands and his face up toward the sky.

"When are you going to tell Bea?" asked Butterfly.

"Tell me what?" I said, looking at my blue rubber boots against the bright green grass. Suddenly the world seemed to have come alive again, like it had been buried underwater, all its colors dampened, all life watered down, but now everything looked brand-new, newly painted, newborn.

Madison put a waterproof sheet down on the grass and we began our picnic over, this time outdoors.

"I feel like I can breathe again!" I said.

"Me, too," sighed Madison and Butterfly together.

"You better tell her now," said Eric.

"Tell me what?" I asked again. "Sam? What are they talking about?"

"You know how you wanted to go to Florida?" Sam began.

"Yeah," I answered.

"Well, now you can."

The others waited and I looked at each one of them in turn for an explanation, but their faces gave nothing away.

"I got you a good price," Sam said seriously.

"Elenor did most of the talking," added Madison.

Then Sam dropped a whole lot of damp dollars into my hands. "I asked for cash because I said you didn't have a bank account. There's five hundred dollars there and it's all yours." He pressed the bills into my palm, spreading them out a little. "They got a bit squashed in my pocket," he explained.

"Did you steal it?" I'd never seen that much money in real life.

"No, stupid! It's from this." He pulled a fat, folded newspaper out of Eric's backpack and held up the front page. "It's the lead story."

"Look." Butterfly pointed. "It has your name on it. That's got to be better than winning some photo competition."

"My story—how did—?" I began.

"Sorry. Hope you don't mind I borrowed it," said Sam, looking a little embarrassed.

There it was in big printed letters in front of me: my story.

Eric began to read. "'The Pickle King Mystery, by Bea Klednik.'" I felt my heart swell inside my chest, the heart that I nearly lost to Agnes Feverspeare. My eyes suddenly filled with tears, and I looked down so the others wouldn't see.

"What's the matter? We thought you'd be happy. You can afford to go to Florida now!" said Butterfly.

"She's just a little overwhelmed," said Madison, coming over and putting her arm around me. Butterfly did the same.

"I'm not good at hugging and stuff," said Eric.

"How do you know if you don't give it a try?" said Butterfly a little impatiently. Eric dragged himself over and put his wiry arms around me and Butterfly.

"Sam!" yelled Eric. "Come on, dude!"

So even Sam joined in the group hug, awkwardly at first, ruffling my hair like I was another stray dog, and then putting his arms around the outside of us all. Then Jelly himself squeezed his way between our legs and barked, thinking we were playing a new game and leaving him out.

"There's just one thing, you guys," I said, looking at the chaotic shape of our shoes on the squishy grass. "It's too late to go to Florida. School starts tomorrow."

Before we left the park, I counted out the damp dollar bills Sam had given me. I gave one hundred to each of the others and kept a hundred for myself. "I couldn't have written the story without you guys. You should all have your share of the money. Next summer we can all get out of town if we want."

Then Butterfly looked at us and smiled, a big, wide, innocent smile, the kind of smile we'd seen Nelson smile a hundred times over the summer. "We'll still be friends when we're back at school, right?"

There was a pause and Madison let out a little cough.

"Definitely!" said Eric, offering us a toothy grin.

"Definitely," said Sam casually.

"I'd like to be . . . ," said Madison.

"We'll always be friends now, right?" I hoped cheerfully, but I knew things were different at school. We all knew it. We had our own groups and those groups just didn't mix.

"Do you guys want to get a photo taken at the old station? It's on the way back," Butterfly asked cheerfully.

"Sure," said Madison.

The boys shrugged their shoulders and dragged along behind us.

In the old train station, there's this photo booth — it's pretty old and it only takes black-and-white pictures. It makes five little square portraits in a row, and is really cool because it makes you look like you're a star in an old movie.

We squashed ourselves inside the old photo booth and had to press our faces together to fit in. This made us laugh a whole lot. We made goofy faces just before the flash went off, once, twice . . . five times. Then we climbed out of the booth, still laughing, and waited for the photos to develop.

Finally there was a whirring sound and a blast of hot air, and the strip of photos dropped down in the cage. They were still damp and smelled of developing fluid. Madison and I reached for them at the same time.

"Let's see! I want to see!" Madison squeaked, getting to them first. She waved the paper to help it dry and to stop us from seeing. "I have to see first—if I look bad I'm going to tear them up!"

Sam crept up behind her and snatched the photos out of her hand.

"Heeey!" she screeched. Me and Butterfly looked at each other and then back at Madison, and we all smiled.

"Sorry, I know I'm annoying, but sometimes I can't help it," said Madison, noticing our look.

"That's OK," I said, "we like you that way."

Sam tore the strip into five along the white lines and handed everybody a little square to keep. The only face that came out each time was the face of the person sitting in the middle—the rest only got an eye inside the frame, or a chin. But you could tell we were having fun. I put my photo in the back pocket of my jeans and the others did the same, except for Sam, who slid his into his wallet. He must have been the only kid in our school with a wallet.

We walked along for a few moments, listening to the sound of our shoes on the wet sidewalk, watching the sun turn the puddles silver.

"See you at school," said Butterfly.

"Bye, guys," said Eric, heading off by her side.

"I'd better get home, too," Madison said, turning in the opposite direction.

"See you tomorrow," I sang, trying to hold on to the illusion.

"Yeah, see ya," said Sam, setting off on his own, head down, hands in his pockets, Jellybean skipping along by his side.

We all stopped for a minute and waved to each other before walking our separate ways along the glistening, silvery streets.

When I got home, I went up to my room and put my hundred dollars in an empty Devil Tongue Relish jar. I took another look at Herman's twinkly smile as I put the jar back on the shelf. Whatever happened during my first year at junior high, I knew I'd be able to get out of Elbow next summer and escape the rain, even if it was only for a day or two.

There was a postcard waiting for me on the kitchen counter downstairs. It showed a picture of a beach in Florida and it was addressed to me. The ink was all blotchy from the rain, but I could still read it. It said, Congratulations on your first article. X

At first I thought it was from Elenor Bailey, but then I realized that I recognized the handwriting. "That's weird," I said out loud. "It looks just like my dad's."

CHAPTER 44

There was a rainbow in the sky when I biked to school
the next morning. The early fall air was fresh and sweet to
breathe, and every time the sun shone out from behind a
stubborn cloud it warmed my face.

At school we were in a new building, a much bigger one.
A part of me wanted to go back to our old building, the one
I knew well, even though I was twice the size of some of the
kids there.

The principal and some of the other teachers gave a speech
in assembly about how we were in junior high school now,
and that meant they expected more from us. Not just in the
standard of our schoolwork but also in how we behaved. We
weren't little kids anymore, we were on our way to becoming young adults, and that meant being kind to each other
and treating people with respect. It meant thinking for ourselves and being responsible. I looked around for Butterfly,
Madison, Eric, and Sam, but there were so many faces in the
auditorium that I couldn't find them.

Later, at lunch, I sat next to a girl I didn't know in the cafeteria. She seemed nice until her friends came to get her. Then
they all looked down their noses at me as if to say, *Just because*

she couldn't find us, don't think she's going to be your *friend.* And they all walked off together, flicking their hair and sticking out their chests. Across the cafeteria, I saw Madison join them. She looked over at me for a second or two and half-smiled, until another girl at the table won her attention.

Sam was sitting on a table with his feet on a chair, listening to music on his headphones. His two friends were throwing a carton of orange juice at each other, making it spray out onto the kids around them. I watched Sam for a moment, to see if he would notice me. He lifted his hand to say hi, and I smiled back at him. Then his friend punched him in the shoulder.

Eric and Butterfly were on opposite sides of the cafeteria, but I saw them catch each other's eye. Butterfly held Eric's gaze for a little too long. He looked away, embarrassed, and went back to the serious conversation he and his friends were having, probably about meteors.

Then something strange happened. We all looked up at the same time and it was as though everybody else in the cafeteria froze except us, and there was an unspoken understanding between us. We'd experienced something amazing, something we'd never forget. We'd been thrown together and had become friends. But now things were different. Things were back to normal. *Normal* meant kids had to stick to their own cliques and act in a way that wasn't really who they were. But that's just the way things are.

Bertha was still at work when I got home. I was glad to let my schoolbag drop to the hallway floor. It was a lot heavier than I was used to. I had more books now, because I had a lot of new subjects. *Homework can wait till after dinner,* I thought as I opened the freezer door. My eyes flicked up and down the choices: lasagna, beef stew, fisherman's pie . . . I read them again, hoping they'd sound a little tastier if I said the words differently in my head.

It was around then that I sensed something was up. There was something odd about the freezer compartment, something different, but I wasn't sure what. For a second I thought Herman's ghost might be back, with a new taste for TV dinners.

I reached to the back of the freezer and pulled out my secret silver box. I wiped my hands on my jeans and opened the lid. My stomach felt hollow inside, and it wasn't because I was hungry. Then my heart started beating. I could even feel it beating in my fingertips as they stuck to the sides of the ice-crusted container.

Inside the box was a little circle of frost where my dad's eyeball had been, but no eyeball. The eyeball was missing. Maybe Bertha had decided a human eyeball wasn't the kind of thing she wanted in her refrigerator. Maybe it had already found its way to the dump and was lost somewhere in that stinky Garbage City soup. Maybe it had already made a nice evening snack for a hungry giant rat. But something told me that wasn't true.

Somebody had come looking for that eyeball.

Somebody who knew where to find it.

ACKNOWLEDGMENTS

Thank you to:

Piers Bearne for remembering his beautiful wonder and for sharing the big adventure with me;

Henrietta Promitzer for a lifetime of stories, and for the magic key;

Kurt Promitzer for being my favorite character from the very best kind of book;

Benjamin Promitzer for being my Nelson;

Meg Davis for sharing and supporting my strange visions right from the start;

Sophie Gorrell Barnes for believing in Bea and persuading others to;

Imogen, Barry, Rachel, and everyone at Chicken House for finding Bea and her friends and letting them loose in the world;

Mrs. Williamson for the beautiful book of fairy tales she bought me for my birthday;

Judith Ramm for telling me how my writing made her cry and for making great works of literature even greater for her teaching of them;

Eva Fox for her inspiring teaching and her kind heart;

Emma Thompson and Alan Rickman for kind letters and cards when I needed them most;

Lucy Darwin for all her generosity and support;

Amanda Hill for celebrating me when it all seemed like madness;

Gail Barrie for her wisdom, courage, and luminosity;

Silas Parker for his brilliant line: *I may only be seven but I'm still a boy!*;

Lulu for having the softest ears, the kindest eyes, and the waggiest tail in the world;

And thanks to all the story-makers who made me feel understood and loved as a kid, and who reminded me that magic is real.